THE
CURE

THE
CURE

ATHOL
DICKSON

BETHANY HOUSE PUBLISHERS
Minneapolis, Minnesota

Published by Bethany House Publishers
11400 Hampshire Avenue South
Bloomington, Minnesota 55438

Bethany House Publishers is a division of
Baker Publishing Group, Grand Rapids, Michigan.

Printed in the United States of America

ISBN-13:   978-0-7642-0163-9
ISBN-10:   0-7642-0163-8

Library of Congress Cataloging-in-Publication Data

Dickson, Athol, 1955-
    The cure / Athol Dickson.
        p.   cm.
    ISBN-13:   978-0-7642-0163-9 (alk. paper)
    ISBN-10:   0-7642-0163-8 (alk. paper)
    1. Maine—Fiction. I. Title.

PS3554.I3264C87   2007
813'.54—dc22   2007009712

FOR GREG WILLIAMS

———⟩◦⟨———

THE
CURE

❦

What a wretched man I am!
Who will rescue me from this body of death?

—Book of Romans

I

Riley Keep returned to the scene of his disgrace in the back of a northbound pickup truck with New Brunswick plates. It was late October or maybe early November; all Riley knew for sure was that the leaves were mostly down, it was already wicked cold, and his old friend Brice was shivering so badly it took a while to get him over the tailgate. The Canadian behind the wheel spun his tires getting back onto Route 1, spraying them with gravel. Riley figured the man was mad because he and Brice had moved so slowly, or maybe because of what they were.

With Brice clutching his arm, Riley took the old shortcut through the alder grove behind the Whitfield place, one scarecrow leading another. They passed beneath a naked oak and emerged from the woods, crossing the railroad tracks and stumbling down the gravel bed to reach the turn in Ellis Street where the harbor could be seen at the bottom of the hill. Although Riley's weak eyes would not focus on the details, he imagined Dublin, Maine, below them just as he remembered: James Neck away off to the west and McCleary Point with its lighthouse down east, the two rocky points nearly meeting in the distance like Atlas' granite arms around the world. Riley blinked at a large slate gray smudge below and knew it for the old harbor, adorned with lobster boats and unused mooring balls, which had been abandoned by last season's fancy yachts already gone south to Florida or put up on the hard for the coming bitter winter. Out among the workboats and empty moorings Riley thought he saw some fuzzy shapes that might be lobstermen's floats, short wooden docks unconnected to the shore, bearing piles of traps and brightly colored buoys. For the first time in a while Riley wished he had not lost his glasses. After being so long gone it would have been nice to see his home more clearly.

Riley strained to use his imagination, or his memory; it was hard to tell the difference. He remembered Main Street running down to intersect with Water Street at the center of Dublin. Five blocks wide and three blocks deep, the red brick mercantile buildings and white clapboard storefronts lined the roads downtown. On Ellis and Thompson and a few other winding streets higher up stood many antique houses clad in pale gray shingles or white siding, with front doors painted glossy black or bright red, windows divided into hand-made rippled panes, and roofs of green and black Vermont slate or mossy cedar shakes pitched steep to shed the snow, picture-postcard houses down around the harbor and up among the spruce and pines and winter-stripped birches of the surrounding hills, ancient houses looking down on Dublin just like Riley, still looking down from where they had been fashioned for rich builders of wooden whalers, clipper ships, and schooners, for merchant mariners and privateers, back in olden times when Dublin was the center of the shipwright world.

With the burden of his old friend heavy on him, Riley Keep descended slowly toward downtown along the bricks of Ellis Street. He had to find Brice someplace warm to sleep. He had to get himself a drink.

They had arrived at quitting time. Many working folk of Dublin passed them, heading uphill toward their homes. With Brice's arm around his shoulder Riley peered at the oncoming pedestrians closely, hoping to make eye contact, hoping he could hit some of them up for a buck or two. As usual, not one looked his way. He might have been invisible.

Riley was at peace with this, but it had not always been so. Before leaving Dublin he had assumed most solid citizens ignored him because of his matted hair and filthy clothing. He used to take this personally, railing at the callousness of so-called decent people who judged a man so harshly for a little dirt. But three years on the streets had taught him there were some who simply feared they might become like him one day, disappearing into the weakness of their flesh, faded creatures without substance, ghosts, specters of the people they once were. Riley knew this fear was reasonable, so he did not blame the ones who looked away as he bore the skeletal burden of his old friend to the edge of downtown Dublin.

The hillside back behind them slowly donned a veil of shadows. Riley Keep began to worry. It was slow going with Brice so feeble and Riley loathe to make him hurry. But as the Maine evening crept down with its icy claws extended like a heartless predator, Riley was reminded that the cold killed homeless people every winter night in northern cities. Alcohol and hypothermia conspired together, liars both of them, whispering there was no harm in sleeping right there where you were, and the next morning someone came and carried you away, stiff from the cold or the rigor mortis as the case may be, but stiff as a board one way or another. Those who could maintain a thought from day to day headed south in early autumn, or else stayed down in warmer states full time, but Riley Keep had done the opposite; he had braved the deadly cold to bring Brice home to Dublin.

The idea had come to him below a highway overpass in Florida. Brice was flat on his back, delirious and making threats. Riley was pleading with his friend to swallow some warm Gatorade. Brice had belched a curse or two and swung a bony fist at Riley in slow motion. He could not sit up, much less stand, so there was no real danger of violence. But there was danger, nonetheless. Even in Brice's appalling infirmity Riley knew the urge enticed his friend the cruel way a shimmering mirage might lure a thirsty pilgrim deep into the desert. Riley knew this because the same urge beckoned to him just as cruelly.

It had been a time for drastic measures. That much was clear after listening to Brice's diagnosis at the free clinic. With the nurse's disillusioned eyes on Riley the way policemen stare at murderers, he had promised they would sober up together. After that, whenever Riley panhandled enough change to buy a meal for Brice and a little something for himself, he always hid the bottle, cutting off his old friend. Drinking alone, Riley hated his own weakness. He hated the disloyal lies he had to tell to sneak a drink for himself, and he hated drinking while his old friend died of drink. Something had to change. So, batting Brice's wandering fist away below the overpass, Riley Keep had tried to make a plan. For an hour or two his mind had wandered as it usually did, roaming back into his history, losing track of reason in the pain of long-lost possibilities. Then he suddenly remembered a strange story they had often heard, rumors in so many places—shelters, alleys, jails, bars—crazy drunken stories of a place that rid a person of disease and pain and scars and habit. Some said you must sleep beneath a certain tree in this place; others said you only had to drink the water. Some maintained this magical release would only work for men; others said it worked for women too. All you had to do was find the place where miracles were happening. No one knew its name, but everybody knew someone who did, and mostly they believed it was back east.

Another flash of intuition had come below the overpass. It was a little later, with Brice asleep at last and Riley watching as the grackles swooped into the shadows higher up where the embankment rose to meet the bottom of the bridge. Riley saw one bird glide below a sweating concrete beam where *Dublin* had been painted in lovely cursive script, the letters three feet tall and Day-Glo orange. There was no explanation, no hint of a reason, just *Dublin* up there on the beam. Riley and Brice had been seeing the word everywhere. It had become a kind of fetish for the homeless, the way people used to draw that little cartoon fella above the words *Kilroy was here*. Painted on boxcar sides, scratched into the Formica in toilet stalls, carved into the wood of roadside picnic tables, *Dublin* had been popping up wherever homeless people passed. Was it a reference to the city in Ireland, or to Riley's hometown up in Maine? Probably there were ten other Dublins here and there around the world. It meant nothing to Riley until that moment when, for no particular reason, suddenly he wondered if the name might be connected to the rumors of a place where miracles were happening.

In the instant this idea occurred to him, Riley knew it for the truth—it must be true, or his old friend would surely die—and by this incoherent logic Riley also knew what must be done.

The trip had taken four weeks and a day. With Brice barely able to walk at first, Riley often carried him piggyback along the highway shoulder, although Riley himself was not in the best of health and could not manage such a burden long. They hitched most of their rides from truckers so hungry for company they would put up with the stench of men who had not bathed in months. One fella took them all the way from Pooler, Georgia, to Richmond, Virginia, popping small black pills and talking nonstop about nothing the whole way. Somehow Riley usually managed to beg food for his friend and find a warm place for him to sleep, even if he himself went hungry and remained awake and shivering—and sober, which was worse.

Now they had come home, shuffling down the hill to Dublin, two favorite sons disguised inside the wasted forms of strangers twice their age. As Riley Keep hobbled along it occurred to him that three years on the streets felt longer than most lifetimes, long enough to lose your memories. He was not sure if the storefront mission in his head was an image from this place or from some other little town along the way, or a fantasy he had invented. He only knew the cold was coming fast and if they did not find shelter soon he would break the display window glass at one of the small stores they were passing and leave Brice lying on the pavement to wait for the police to come. A night in jail would be far better than a night out in the weather.

Then they turned a corner with the vicious winter creeping at their heels, and the homeless shelter was right there.

Brice had given out, so Riley mostly carried him inside, taking all of his friend's weight except what little Brice could manage with a pair of legs wasted down to skin and bone. The first thing Riley saw was an image of himself in a full-length mirror just inside the door. Riley never looked in mirrors, never had the opportunity except in public washrooms, and who used public washrooms when there was an alley handy? So when he saw himself by accident, it gave him quite a start.

The man in the mirror was not just older than his memories; he was older than his years. He was filthy—deeply, pressed down into pores and wrinkles filthy—and wearing clothes so soiled that even Riley could not have said what color they once were. His whiskey-colored hair was wild and bushy, hanging clear down past his shoulders and clumped together here and there, with an alder twig above one ear. The long gray streaks in his beard especially surprised him. There had been no gray the last time Riley saw his own reflection. This stranger in the mirror stood with back bowed and shoulders bent by the burden of his old friend Brice, and the added weight of something even heavier. He could not meet his own eyes. The very thought of meeting them was frightening. Like the people on the street outside, he did not care to see a ghost.

"What do you think?" asked a small old woman who had somehow come up very close unnoticed. She stood with both hands on her hips, staring directly at him without a hint of subtlety, her manly jaw set square and stubborn.

Riley said, "I think I need a shower."

"We agree," she said. "Come on."

Still with Brice's arm around his shoulder, Riley followed the old woman through a small front room with exposed bricks on each side, past a couple of men sitting in orange plastic chairs around a chipped wood-grain coffee table, then on back down a narrow hall, the old woman pointing left and right, speaking in short energetic bursts as they moved deep into the building. "That was the waiting room back there. This is my office. You bring anything to drink in here and you're out forever. No second chance on that. Men's bunk room. You get the last two bunks tonight. Lucky. Probably be some others on the floor. Women's bunk room. Stay out of there. Meeting room, which is also where we eat." In that room Riley saw more men and a couple of women, all of them watching television. He was surprised. It seemed like a lot of homeless people for a town the size of Dublin. The little woman said, "You need to be here by nine at night, when I give a little talk. Miss that, and you're out. Don't bring drugs in, either. Same thing: no second chance on that. Kitchen back there. Stay out unless you're on duty. Clothes pantry. Laundry room. Women's locker room and bathroom. Stay out of there. Men's locker room. Don't steal anything or you're out forever. Men's bathroom. Got a shower stall back there. Soap and clean towels on the shelf. Keep the soap box and put your soap back in it. Don't use anybody else's. Drop your clothes on the floor there. I'll bring you something else to wear. See me when you're clean. You guys stink."

"Uh . . ." Riley cleared his throat. "Where's Jerry?"

Jerry was the guy who ran the place when Riley was last here. He had never seen this bossy little woman before. At the mention of Jerry's name she turned to look up at him, suddenly interested. He tried to return her stare, tried to look straight down into the rigid toughness of her square and wrinkled face, but there was something in the woman that pushed back at him fiercely, something he could no more have stood against than he could stand against the unremitting urge that ruled his life. "Jerry's gone," she said. "You've been here before?"

"A long time ago."

"What's your name?"

He did what he could to resist the accusation in her hard unblinking eyes. He did not offer more than necessary, saying only "Livingston." Brice had given that name to him a long time ago, renaming him as was right and proper for a man who had left everything to descend into the asphalt jungle, calling him after the old missionary who got lost and found in Darkest Africa.

The woman searched his face, and something changed in hers.

17

For the first time Riley saw emotion there. She stared at him as if the weight of every soul that suffers had just settled onto her. "I know who you are," she said.

Riley shook his head. "You weren't here."

Her mournful stare held him in place a moment longer. "No. I wasn't."

Riley marveled that a woman used to seeing men in his condition would display so much sorrow. Strangely ashamed, he dropped his eyes to his filthy shoes until the old woman walked away; then looking up to watch her go, it seemed to Riley that the burden bowing down his shoulders also pressed on hers.

He helped Brice into the locker room and bent to ease him onto a hard wooden bench. His old friend groaned as he lay down on his back; then Brice clasped his hands together at his hollow chest like a corpse in a coffin, closed his eyes against the stark fluorescent light and right away began to snore.

Riley stripped down for his shower and stood naked in the center of the room, feeling the cold air on his body. It had been months since he was naked. The absence of the pressure of his clothes felt strange, the way the empty space in his mouth felt during the first few days after losing a tooth. He had lost too many teeth. Thinking of that, he looked in the mirror over the sink. The beat-down man he saw there cocked his head up toward the light and bared his teeth and let him count the empty spaces. There were now five, three of them in front, which was why he seldom smiled. Riley did not want to show his empty places.

He noticed the darkness of his forearms, face and neck—everywhere he stuck out from his clothes. Some of that was from the sun; most of it was dirt. He turned away from the reflection of himself and stepped into the shower and twisted the knob. The water was freezing. He jumped back out and stood trembling just beyond the plastic curtain. He had forgotten that you waited for the water to get hot. When it started to steam, he stepped back in. Now the water felt good. He bowed his head beneath it, letting it weave its way through his matted hair. He saw dark brown rivulets running from his feet down to the drain, carrying the filth of him into the sewers. He thought of the pile of reeking clothes out on the floor and remembered something without warning, maybe it was something from a Roman play.

"Bad conduct soils the finest ornament more than filth."

Was that Plautus? He could not remember. He seemed to recall it had some influence on Shakespeare, but maybe that was wrong. Maybe it was Proverbs. Such unwelcome fragments surfaced to plague Riley Keep at times, disconnected from their context, the flotsam of another life. It was all but impossible to tell from whence they came. He had been so many things in other lives. Minister. Missionary. Educator of New England's finest young men and women at Bowditch, that little college with the far-flung reputation on the eastern edge of Dublin. Failed protector of an entire people. Weakling of a husband. Incompetent father. Drunkard. Friend as best he could. Riley shook his head, flinging water from his shaggy hair like a dog. He rubbed himself roughly in the luxuriously warm flow. He had forgotten to bring soap into the shower stall and did not want to step out to the chill of the bathroom to get it. He did his best with nothing but his hands. When the hot water started to fade he shut it off and used the threadbare towel, leaving streaks of brown on the white cotton. It was a poor imitation of a proper shower, but still he was much cleaner than before.

Outside in the bathroom Riley looked at Brice, still lying on the bench. He smiled to hear his friend's contented snores. He felt something swell within his chest, and quickly looked away. He did not like to think of losing Brice.

Someone had left a pile of folded clothes on the bench at Brice's feet: a pair of olive-colored work pants, underwear, a plaid flannel shirt, and a pair of white crew socks, all secondhand but clean at least. Only Riley's shoes and a few black bits of soil lay on the floor where his other clothes had been. He dressed and stepped up to the mirror again to run his fingers through his hair and beard, making a token effort to separate the tangled strands that grew out of him. By accident, Riley caught his own eye in the mirror. Startled, he looked away.

2

Brice sat as still as he could on a hard plastic chair, watching a housefly buzz furiously against the inside of the shelter's storefront window, hurling itself against the glass again and again in its eagerness to soar into the crisp November morning. His rusty hair and beard smelled like soap, he had slept as well as possible on the unfamiliar softness of the bunk bed's mattress, he had a little oatmeal in his concave belly, and he had special dispensation from the woman in charge, who had decided to let him remain indoors all day instead of running him off to look for work as she had run off Riley and the others. Brice knew he should be a contented man. Yet although he was much better now, his bowels were still not right. An unrelenting pressure lingered, and he could not help but see much of the housefly in himself, restless and dissatisfied, ceaselessly casting himself against an invisible barrier with impatience to be gone.

He concentrated on sitting as still as the persistent urge allowed. He tried to think of something else: philosophy, perhaps. A philosophic plumber, that was what Riley used to call him. He remembered a conversation they once had about water, about how it never really went away. It flowed hot and cold through the pipes that he installed, and down into the drain or toilet, and so on through the sanitary system, cleansed of its impurities to eventually emerge in nature, where it flowed into the sea and evaporated up into the atmosphere and soared back over land to fall again as rain and gather into streams and reservoirs and so back into the pipes that he installed, and on and on it went forever, yet not one single molecule was lost.

Brice wished it could have been that way for him.

He wished his life could be an unending cycle where the problem was the cure—drinking to resolve the difficulties caused by drink—but if his failing body taught him anything it was that no philosophy could make it so. He could only hurl himself against these invisible barriers so many times before the final part of him was lost.

He remembered Riley trying to tell him this a long time ago, Riley preaching in his cups about the linear nature of history and time. He remembered they were someplace warm; he remembered firelight from the fractured pieces of a shipping pallet burning in a metal trash can. Was it Tampa? Sarasota? Oh, the fine debates he and Riley had enjoyed down in the tropics! How pleasant it had been to annoy his friend with stubborn disagreement.

Alone now in a hard plastic chair, watching the housefly hurl itself against the window, Brice smiled to think of Riley springing up with eagerness to explain Almighty God to half a dozen fellow drunks around a trash can, as if they had not heard it all before. He remembered Riley shouting "The Bible says, 'Blessed are the meek, for they will inherit the earth!' Well now, think about that. Aren't *we* the meek? Why of *course* we are!" Riley laughing and shouting and dancing around in front of them, Riley harking back to his seminary days, pointing a finger toward the heavens and shouting, "We *are* the meek! I've studied it! I've been *trained* and or*dain*ed! I know what I'm talking about! We're not suffering here for nothing, fellas! This whole earth is *ours!*"

No one knew the gospel like the homeless.

An education in it was the price of admission to most shelters, this one included. But Brice remembered Riley preaching anyway, belly filled with some kind of spirit although it was unlikely to be holy, inflicting the old arguments upon them when he knew very well they would sleep beneath the stars that night and gain no benefit from listening. Still, Brice could not recall anyone complaining about Riley's preaching. Maybe that was because he preached so well, or maybe it was because Riley so clearly needed to get those words out of himself. Riley still believed in everything in spite of everything. Watching the housefly, Brice wondered if the irony of belief in spite of their condition was Riley's own invisible barrier. Perhaps he should not have egged Riley on. Thinking of it now he felt a twinge of guilt. But misery loved company of course. Wasn't that the reason he and Riley set out on the road together in the first place?

Brice found a slight comfort in his friend's surviving faith. At least someone had salvaged something from the endless cycle that contained them. Occasionally that slight comfort tempted him to wonder if Riley might be right: maybe there was a linear quality to life after all, a reason or a purpose. But inevitably the urge swelled up inside his chest and all philosophy was forgotten in the irresistible succession of difficulties that could only be cured by a generous application of their own cause, and with that self-fulfilling double curse Brice knew Riley was mistaken; he might be near the end, but it was a circular life that got him there.

Brice shifted his position and winced at the spike of pain in his lower back. Earlier in the morning the old woman had told him he was lucky to be alive and lucky to have a friend like Riley, as if that was new information. Brice was well aware Riley had saved his life and well aware he had been saved at no small cost to Riley. Brice was not a fool; he did not believe for a second Riley had actually stopped drinking, but his friend had not taken a drink in front of him for almost a month now, and how Brice loved him for that sacrifice. Only another drunk could appreciate the gravity of it. Brice could not imagine feeling anything but guilt if any other person offered such a gift on his behalf, but with Riley it seemed normal. He watched the housefly hurl itself against the glass again and thought back to that torturous time below the bridge. He remembered very little, just scraps of conversation and snapshot images of Riley holding something liquid to his lips, Riley wiping his forehead with a rag, Riley cleaning excrement from him, Riley with encouraging words, Riley begging him to live as if his life really mattered. Throughout that time Brice did not remember once awaking without Riley there.

Then had come the day when Brice realized he might live. He awoke and remained awake, unbeknownst to Riley, who was nearby cooking something on an open fire, and Brice had watched his friend and thought of what it meant to travel to the places he had been below that bridge and come back there alive, and he had said, "Dr. Livingston, I presume," their old joke given fresh new meaning; and his doctor Riley had been startled at the sound of his voice, and turned and seen his wide-open eyes, and smiled and spoken in his awful so-called English accent, saying only, "Hello, Mr. Stanley."

A few days after that had come the crazy, impossible idea to go home to Dublin. Riley had tried to explain it, had spoken in terms of miracles, and Brice had done his best to humor him. It was the least that he could do. He never thought the man would really take him, not until the morning when Riley packed up their few belongings and stooped to lift him on his back.

Oh, the pain! Every step his friend had taken jarred his insides like the twisting of a knife. Brice had done his best to bear it, but soon a moan had escaped him, and Riley laid him down again to rest. That became their pattern: a long rest, followed by a short burst of motion. It took a week just to get from Jacksonville to Georgia, but Brice began to find he could bear the pain a little longer so they went a little farther between rests, and it seemed perhaps a miracle might actually be possible. Sure enough, one day Brice found he could walk some without help, and Riley hailed it as a wonder beyond measure. Now, with perseverance and the passage of a month and the incredible sacrifices of his dear old friend, here Brice sat in a hard plastic chair watching a housefly at a homeless shelter in Dublin, Maine, which was indeed a kind of miracle when you thought about it.

THE CURE

How he wished it could go on and on in a straight line ending someplace unexpected and miraculous, yet of course life was what it was, and sooner or later he would have to drink to keep the cycle going, even if it killed him.

3

Hope dawdled in her old Pontiac outside the shelter, searching for a way to pretty up what must be said. Nothing decent came to mind. She tried speaking a few lines aloud. They made her sound like some other person, someone she did not want to be. She was thinking of leaving when Steve pulled his new truck into the space beside her and the die was cast.

Glancing over, Hope saw a deep gouge in the front fender of the truck. She thought about the insurance deductible for repairs to police department vehicles. It was fifteen hundred dollars, if she remembered right, so that was just great. Yet another conversation she didn't want to have. Sighing, she opened her car door.

"Hi ya, kid," called the chief of police, already out of the Ford Explorer and waiting on the sidewalk. He always called her "kid," probably because she looked younger than she was, maybe thirty instead of forty. It was not something she could take credit for, just the pure dumb luck of good Italian stock, a hint of olive in her clear complexion, huge clear eyes, a total lack of gray in her short black hair and her lanky, athletic build. Hope approached the chief, who stood with one hand in the pocket of his faded dungarees, jingling his coins as usual. The chief was a perpetual-motion machine, which probably explained why the big man in his sixties also didn't look his age.

Stepping over the granite curb, Hope made herself smile like a good little politician. "Looks like you got your fender kinda stove up there."

"Had to chase a fella through some brush yesterday."

"How old is that truck again? Three whole weeks?"

"Hey, sometimes ya gotta do what ya gotta do."

"Tell it to the council when the bill comes up."

Steve grinned. "That's what we got you for."

Hope did not return the smile. "Don't need the aggravation, Steve. Not on top of dealin' with all these people from away."

Her point made, she gave the chief a playful little punch in the arm in passing and headed down the sidewalk toward the shelter, where nearly a dozen unkempt strangers loitered by the door. She felt their eyes upon her as she approached, felt the cool assessment of their stares and took comfort from Steve's looming presence at her back. Just before she reached the door, one of the homeless men spoke. "'Scuse me, miss. You got any spare change?"

Hope started fishing in her purse, but Steve stepped between them. "It's against the law to panhandle, friend."

"Sez who?"

Steve pointed a finger back and forth between himself and Hope. "The mayor and police chief."

Panic flashed across the man's face. "I don't want no trouble."

"And I'd hate to hafta run ya out of town."

"Oh, I don't think it's come to that," said Hope, extending a dollar bill toward the raggedy man. He held both hands up, palms out, leaving Hope standing there with her gift in midair, unaccepted. "Go ahead and take it," Hope said, smiling. "It's okay this one time, I think. Right, Chief?"

"If ya say so," replied Steve.

Still the man refused to take her money. "I come a long way to get here, ma'am. Ain't about to take no chance on gettin' kicked out now."

"Where are you from?"

"Atlanta, ma'am."

She said, "What brings you to our town?" Asking it like he was a tourist, giving the man a little respect.

He glanced nervously at the chief of police. "I . . . uh, I need to get a little problem taken care of."

Hope did not need to ask him what his problem was. As the man's eyes shifted, she followed his gaze to see another group of ragged people gathered outside Sam Williams's printshop on the far side of the street, one of them in a wheelchair. The awning on the storefront above them had not yet been rolled up for the season. It cast a shadow on the top half of their bodies. Only the man in the wheelchair remained untouched by the darkness. Beyond them, beyond the glass, Hope saw the vague white smudge of Sam's face staring out from his shop. He must have seen her looking, because he moved closer to the glass. Their eyes met across the distance. He did not look happy. Sensing movement on her right, Hope turned to see two more disheveled strangers coming up the street, their shaggy appearance a strange contrast to the pristine New England townscape with its overhanging birches, red brick, white clapboard storefronts, and granite curbs. It suddenly occurred to Hope that standing right there she could count more homeless people than she'd seen in Dublin in all her years combined. As if speaking to herself, she asked, "What are all you people doin' here?"

The homeless man said nothing.

"Friend," said Steve. "We also got a law against loiterin'."

"Yes, sir. I'm moving on now. We all are. Right, boys?"

The others mumbled their assent and started shuffling across the sidewalk. Watching them go, seeing them merge with the other group across the street, Hope thought of old black-and-white photographs she had seen of the Great Depression, of stooped men wearing threadbare suits in soup-kitchen lines, children using bits of garbage as playthings, women staring out of tenement windows with stark surrender in their eyes. Hope suddenly wished the man had taken her dollar bill. She wished she had offered more. She also wished the filthy men were not in her town, and she hated that and felt again that she was turning into someone other than herself.

She closed her eyes, and opened them, and went into the shelter.

In the front room Hope saw four more ragged people she had never met. They sat in mismatched plastic chairs playing cards on a little table.

"Where's Willa?" asked Steve, behind her.

Only one of them bothered to look up from the game. "Who?"

"Woman runs this place."

"Back there somewheres prob'ly." The cardplayer waved a grimy hand toward the rear of the building and refocused on his cards.

They passed down the narrow hall and found Willa Newdale in the kitchen, standing on her toes beside a wire shelving unit with a stack of dishes in her hands. Hope thought she looked kind of masculine with her stiff gray hair cut very short and her usual starched khakis and her long-sleeved white shirt with the tail hanging out and the collar buttoned down. The old woman glanced over at them when they entered. "Steven," she said without moving. "Hope."

"Hey there. Need a hand?" asked the chief.

The woman laughed. "Actually, I do. I got hooked on something here, and I can't put these plates down to get unhooked."

Hope looked more closely and realized Willa was stuck in place with her necklace somehow caught up in the metal shelving. "Hang on," said Hope. "I'll get it."

"No!" The woman nearly shouted the word. "Steve, you do it. These plates need to go way up on the top."

Hope watched curiously as the chief walked around the steel worktable to take the dishes. He placed them up on the top shelf while Willa freed the necklace, which she quickly dropped inside her shirt.

Hope said, "I could've done that for you, Willa."

"I know it, sweetheart. Just thought it'd be easier for Steve. What are you guys doing here, anyway?"

"You forget we were coming?"

Willa turned to look at her, confusion in her tanned and wrinkled face. "Guess I did. Tell me why again?"

"We wanna talk about these alkies comin' to town," said the chief.

"Alkies?"

"The homeless people, Willa," said Hope.

"Oh, I know what he means, dear. Let's go to my office."

The old woman led them down the hall, moving fast. She turned into a small room with a single bookshelf and a desk piled high with clutter. She sat behind the desk. The chief of police stood in the corner and crossed his arms, leaving the one remaining chair for Hope. No one said anything at first. Hope stared at the strange string of shells and wooden beads around Willa Newdale's neck and wondered what hung out of sight beneath the woman's shirt. Willa broke the silence. "Don't suppose you guys want to donate to the mission?"

"Tried to at the door," said Hope. "Couldn't get a taker."

"Well then."

"Willa," said the chief. "What we gonna do with all these alkies?"

"Feed 'em. Bathe 'em. Save their souls, if possible. And you shouldn't call 'em alkies, Steven."

"Homeless people," said Hope.

"That's better."

The chief said, "I remember when we called 'em bums."

"Times change," said Willa.

"People don't."

"Steve," warned Hope.

The police chief shrugged. "I'm just sayin' . . ."

Hope turned to look across the desk at the old woman, meeting her remarkably dark eyes. "Here's the thing. There's just too many of them. Must be thirty or forty now, and it seems like more come every week. They're sleepin' in the park by the landing, loiterin' all over town, scaring everybody's customers away. All the downtown business owners are worried."

"Poor dears."

"Well, yeah, actually. They're gonna be poor. We're all gonna be poor if we can't figure out some way to get these people off the streets."

"Can't help you there. I'm already takin' in as many as I can."

"I can see that. We're just hopin' you can help us figure out why they're here." Hope paused, hating to go on. But she had a job to do, responsibilities to meet. She took a deep breath. "Maybe then we can find a way to make them leave."

Willa stared at her in silence. Hope felt herself shrink beneath the awful weight of the old woman's gaze, knowing she of all people shouldn't be saying things like this. Hope thought about equivocation. She thought of saying "That's not what I meant" or "We can reach some kind of compromise." It was a word that she had learned too well these last two years—*compromise*, a word she had not thought through nearly hard enough before she ran for office.

Just as she opened her mouth to make excuses a loud voice broke the silence, echoing down the hall outside the office. Someone shouted something, then shouted again.

"'Scuse me for a minute," said Willa, rising from behind the desk and hurrying away with remarkable agility for a woman her age.

Hope turned to look at Steve, raising her eyebrows. He shrugged, hands deep in the front pockets of his trousers, jingling his keys and change. The shouting down the hall continued, although now Hope also heard Willa's voice. It sounded like the old woman was trying to calm the person without much success.

"Should we see if she needs help?" asked Hope.

"Naw. She'll holler if she wants us."

The shouts grew louder.

"I don't know, Steve."

"Willa don't take to interference in her business."

Hope sat still, listening to the commotion. Echoes off the plaster walls robbed the shouts of meaning. She strained to hear, hoping to make sense of it. Steve's jingling keys annoyed her. She wished the man would just be still, or else go to see if he could help, anything but stand there all a-fidget like he was. Between her lingering guilt about her mission and the shouts and the *clink clink clink* from Steve's pockets, Hope suddenly had to *do* something. She stood quickly.

"I'm gonna go see."

Outside in the narrow hall she heard the chief's footsteps close behind. The two of them passed the kitchen and the bathrooms and approached seven or eight people crowded around an open door—a couple of the men she recognized from the card game in the front room and a few she had not seen before. One of them, younger than the others, wept quietly.

Joining the back of the little crowd, Hope stood on tiptoes and craned her head, but she could not see past the people. Someone in the room was talking. The rumble of a machine, a clothes dryer maybe, obscured the words. She thought she heard someone say, "I'm telling you the truth!" Another voice, probably Willa's, replied in a much lower tone. Hope could not make out those words. Then, very clearly, the man again: "Maybe he went outside to get it. How should I know?" The other voice replied, but still Hope could not understand. Then a little louder, "No!" A few more quiet words, a sense of urgency in them as if Willa or whoever wanted to persuade the man of something. Whatever the dispute, he was unconvinced. He shouted now, saying, "You tryin' ta say I *killed* him? That's plum foolish! I didn't give it to him!"

There was a loud metallic bang.

Suddenly Steve was past Hope, throwing his considerable bulk against the small crowd, pressing them aside to get into the room. Hope followed the chief instinctively, too intrigued by the unseen drama to consider that she might be moving toward some kind of danger.

At the front of the hallway crowd now, closest to the door, Hope smelled the unpleasant muskiness of a man on her left. Shifting to her right to get as much distance from him as possible, she caught a glimpse around Steve's broad back, enough to see he was indeed standing in a laundry room and the loud machine was a clothes dryer as she had suspected.

Steve said, "That fella drunk?"

Willa replied, "I'm afraid not."

At that, the stinking man beside Hope whispered, "It's murder."

The entire crowd began to murmur. Unable to restrain her curiosity, Hope pressed a palm against Steve's back. He glanced around, saw it was her and moved aside to give her space to squeeze into the little room.

In the harsh fluorescent light beyond Steve stood Willa and another man Hope had never seen before. The expression on the old woman's face shocked Hope. She would not have believed such heartbreak was possible for the fierce little defender of the broken people in the shelter. Willa's grief embarrassed Hope. It confused her. It made her want to take the woman in her arms. It made her want to look away. She shifted her eyes to the fourth person in the room, a skinny man slouched on the floor at everybody's feet. Propped against the vibrating clothes dryer, hands clasped around an empty plastic bottle in his lap, the man's head lay cocked toward his shoulder like a robin considering an earthworm. His long and untrimmed beard did nothing to conceal the beatific smile upon his face. Hope smelled the sickly death-room scents of rubbing alcohol and urine and felt the breath rush from her lungs at the sight of him, felt light flee from her eyes almost as it had from his. She reached out to support herself against the doorjamb, willing herself to stand, to remain upright until the dizziness had passed. After a moment, when she could see again, she refocused on the skinny man. Her second look did not alter the facts. He was indeed who he had seemed to be, yet he was not as she remembered. He was different in his death, and the mayor of Dublin Township fled before the awful fact of him. Turning away, she stumbled into the small crowd outside the room, gaining momentum, shoving rudely in her haste to escape. Once free of them she ran without restraint, down the hall, through the lobby and out the glass door to the street. She glanced wildly left and right, found her car, and continued her headlong flight in that direction. At the driver's door she grasped the handle, but it would not open. She yanked harder, again and again, before she realized it was locked. With a low cry of frustration she swung her purse around in front of her and searched for her keys. She had never locked her car before, never locked the front door of her home until all these homeless people started showing up in Dublin, a stream of them, a flood of them, a plague of them, coming from everywhere and nowhere for no apparent reason, bringing him, and with him death—death and Riley Keep as sure as death would follow life—and with Riley, another kind of dying she had hoped was gone forever.

4

About twenty others slept in the bunk room near as Riley Keep could tell, some on air mattresses on the floor. It was an awful lot of fellas for such a small room, an awful lot for such a small town, especially at that time of year, but the room still felt empty without Brice.

With all the competition on the streets Riley had not been able to bum so much as a dime all day. It was worse than anyplace he'd ever been, much worse than the big cities like Boston and New York. All the best corners and intersections were taken by dawn, some people sleeping out there in spite of the cold for fear they'd lose their spot. He had tried the park, the landing, the bus stop—pretty much everywhere—but Dublin was filling up with men and women just like him, everybody hungry for a miracle or, failing that, a handout.

It meant going to bed cold sober, which meant sleeping poorly, especially with a few of the others snoring like steam engines. It wasn't the noise; noise was nothing when you generally slept under bridges. It was the way the snores reminded him of Brice. Brice had always snored loudly enough to wake the dead, and Riley had gotten used to his particular sleeping sounds. He found their absence deafening.

Riley told himself to change the subject. Brice would want him to get some sleep, get up rested and get out there and get a drink.

Riley started counting to one hundred. It was a way he had to stop his mind from racing. Every time he got to a hundred he started over back at one, and after a while he started having trouble keeping count, and just as he began to drift away a fella somewhere in the bunk room started mumbling and then talking louder, and then he screamed to high heaven and kept on screaming until that old woman came to talk some sense to him.

Riley listened in the darkness as the woman told the fella to hang on, it was just the DTs and he would be okay. Riley figured it for a falsehood. He himself had seen some strange things sliding down the walls in times past. If he went much longer without a drink he'd be seeing them again. Ugly, terrifying things. The fella's screams made perfect sense to Riley.

Well. At least Brice was past it now. A week gone almost, and Riley figured if the God he used to serve had any mercy whatsoever, Brice was up there with him now, happy as a bug in mud. Riley tried to take some comfort in it. He figured underneath it all he was still a Christian. He figured he himself would be with Brice again one day. He tried to focus on that, to make it mean something, but what with the poor fella in the grip of alcohol withdrawal right beside him, and so many others sleeping outside in the cold to save a spot where they could beg for cash to buy a drink, somehow Riley could not conjure up much solace from the thought of heaven.

Lacing his fingers behind his head he stared dry-eyed at the bottom of the bunk above. He had decided long ago there was no value in the power of positive thinking. A lifetime of defeat could not be overcome by intangibles. Real change would take something outside him, something to come along and take control, just as death had taken Brice. Riley had no hope for that at all.

He knew where his hope lay.

Riley rose and pulled on trousers and a shirt and the old wool jacket that little woman found for him, and although it was still dark outside he left the shelter in pursuit of what would save him. His skinny legs flexed on their own occasionally when it had been this long between drinks. He moved them to walk and they did what he wanted, but also they quivered now and then and he had to stop until they settled down. Even in the cold he sweated. His stomach felt caved in upon itself, though the old woman had fed them all hot beef stew just ten hours ago. He was no longer thinking whiskey, or even beer or wine; he was thinking outside the box. In Washington, D.C., one time he and Brice had poured Sterno down their throats to stop the terrifying things from sliding down the walls. Mouthwash would do. Anything was better than those ugly, terrifying things. Even a bottle of rubbing alcohol. Even if it killed you. After they had carried Brice away someone said he did it on purpose. They said it because of the rubbing alcohol, but Riley knew better than that. You did what had to be done was all.

The horizon had begun to glow out on the Atlantic when he reached the little parking lot beside the wharf, what Mainers called the town landing. It was lit and busy, the lobstermen with foggy breath in coats and gloves and rubber boots, rowing out to their boats, unloading traps and whatnot from their pickup trucks or standing around drinking steaming cups of coffee and talking together. A couple of them saw him coming. He stepped into a pool of yellow light and they looked away. They could see what he was, even with a shower and clean clothes. Some things don't wash off.

Riley stood and watched the sun come up, dreaming ghostly waking dreams of wooden bars with padded stools and signs with Clydesdales hitched to huge beer wagons and rows of beautiful bottles on glass shelves and a cunnin' girl to pour. Dreaming of heaven, in other words, but willing to settle for a little mouthwash if need be. He watched the sun rise, and for some reason he got mad. Not because of Brice, exactly. It was more that he had not had a drink in maybe two whole days. A deadly serious situation. And there was God, pulling the sun out of his pocket like it was nothing. It made him mad to think how simple it would be for God to give him what he wanted, and how little he wanted compared to most people. The lobstermen, for example, who were constantly buying new pickup trucks and houses and clothing for their wives and children, and steaks and television sets and bowling balls and popcorn at the movies. And him, what did he ask? Nothing but a drink. It made him mad to think how stingy God could be, until he realized he had not asked for what he needed. Riley Keep had lost most memories, but he was pretty sure he had never asked the Lord for alcohol.

The clouds out on the ocean glowed golden now, with jewel-like pinks and royal purples, and rays of sunlight like a crown. Riley did not care. He turned and walked back up the hill, hoping for a dumpster behind a restaurant. Sometimes they threw out wine bottles with a little something left. Why not be optimistic? If you thought in terms of mouthwash, that was what you got. Why not think in terms of a nice Merlot or a Rioja or something along those lines? He was desperate enough to hope there was a power in positive thinking after all.

Passing a parked truck he saw a bumper sticker in the gathering light that said *Jesus Loves You.* He thought about that, and about Brice's last few moments on the floor in a homeless shelter laundry. He thought about what you did when you loved someone. You tried to make them happy, right? You tried to give them what they wanted, like those lobstermen buying popcorn for their kids. Riley put that together with the power of positive thinking, and the fact that he had never actually asked God for a drink, and thought, why not? What's he going to do, kill me? So he paused there by the bumper sticker and spoke out loud. "All right. In that case, give me something good to drink."

Nothing happened, of course.

Riley set out again, still thinking dumpsters, across the street and into a park area where the frost beneath his feet lay brittle on the grass. No snow yet, but he could sense it in the air, coming to make a lie out of that sunrise.

He blew into cupped hands as he walked. Why was he here? He should be in Miami. He *would* be in Miami except for Brice. As the urge rose ruthlessly within him, Riley had to fight to cling to Brice, the reason he had come, the thing that made this sacrifice worth-while. He had tried to save his friend. That should make some differ-ence. He had failed, but he had tried. If ever there had been an ounce of truth in what they taught him about God, that should make some difference.

Crossing the park, looking down as usual, searching for things people dropped—a dollar would buy a swallow—not looking ahead, Riley nearly walked into a tree. An ancient oak, he thought; it was hard to tell with the leaves down. He was a linguist and a missionary and an English teacher after all, not a botanist. He saw only giant roots writhing in the sod, smooth on top where people had stepped on them, and nestled among the gnarled roots a brown paper bag of familiar size and shape. Riley bent to pick it up and his legs gave a quiver and he stumbled, hitting his forehead on the tree trunk but ignoring that, reaching for the bag, lying beside it in the roots and lifting it, feeling the heft of it, the gravitational wallow of the liquid as it sloshed back and forth, and reminding himself it could be any-thing, yet swelled up to the edges of himself with hope.

Eagerly, he pulled the bottle from the sack. It was full, the seal unbroken, its contents golden like the sunrise but much more beau-tiful, a complete quart of the finest single-malt Scotch whiskey. He held it a few inches from his face, squinting without his long-lost eyeglasses, recognizing the label from when he was a college profes-sor with a wife and daughter, and his friend Brice was a plumber and they could both afford such things, and he pulled away the cap (it had a cork!) and thrust the bottle to his lips and took the Scotch into himself.

He sighed and closed his useless eyes. After the first swallow always came the best moment, when he felt the warmth go down and knew relief was on its way, not yet there, but coming, the antic-ipation better than reality would be. Some preferred the moment when the rosy feeling rose and anything was possible and you were a giant and all was well and would be well forever. But while that was indeed a fine thing, Riley Keep had always thought it second to the first anticipation because, of course, the promise in your mind surpassed the truth inside your body, and the solace of a bottle nearly full was lost to those who rushed headlong toward the emptiness to come.

Riley Keep lay among the ancient roots and drank again, less urgently this time, but still deeply. As the sunrise spread out on the Atlantic, he realized it was gorgeous. He thought of Homer's "rosy-fingered dawn." Ah, the irony, if only blind or drunk men truly saw the sunrise. Riley was proud of this cleverness, the professor returning, summoned from across the Styx by the warmth expanding in his caved-in belly. All was well in the fading rays and paler pinks and purples. He resolved to slow it down, the rising, to make it last as long as possible, and so began to sip instead of drinking as if bottomless. Time passed, time to savor, time for deep reflection. He considered the beauty of the scene below, the harbor in the virgin light, lobster boats alert and at attention, all pointing the same way, deep green spruce on the far hill across the water, the comic complaints of wheeling gulls, the perfectly proportioned church facing this little pocket park, its brick facade in exact conformance to the golden mean, the bell in its steeple ringing now, calling in the faithful. Riley's lacy rising breath reminded him of his wife in her white gown, walking toward him down the aisle of that very church, sunlight streaming through the stained glass, sunlight come a billion miles to dance upon his bride in that multicolored moment. He thought that memory might mean something. He thought there might be something in it of the reason he now lay among the ravenous teeth of a Maine winter, something of why he was not in Miami, a reason he could add to Brice, although the memory was frayed and hard to hold and very doubtful, as was the future and every other moment but the one he was living then and there, if one cared to call it living.

Riley took another careful sip, and ungrateful wretch that he was, not till then did it cross his mind that this was an answered prayer. He had asked for something good to drink, and look what he was holding. The finest kind, the absolute best Scotch in the world. He thought of something from the Bible, that most enduring work of literature, something about man's inability to imagine what God has in store. The exact words had long ago dissolved in spirits with a hundred thousand others, but he seemed to recall it applied to God's beneficent plans for those who love him, as opposed to the wrath awaiting those God hates. Why grant his request? Riley did not love God. Riley had once thought he did, had once even tried to serve him, had asked for many things in return, and receiving no answers had become sure God was not there, or not interested, and so stopped asking. You could no more love a god who did not answer than you could love a ghost. But if Riley did not love God, it was also true he did not hate God. He felt nothing except a little anger at the sunrise; he had no expectations whatsoever, and maybe that explained the Scotch. Riley tried to imagine what it must be like to be God, everybody always asking for something, pretending love when it came and angry when it didn't. Maybe God was glad to give a little Scotch to a fella who asked expecting nothing.

Riley remembered asking to be freed of his addiction, years ago right there in Dublin. He remembered asking that a thousand times to no effect. But never had it crossed his mind to ask for something good to drink, never but this once, and look at the result. Clearly, it had been a matter all along of asking for the proper miracle.

Riley Keep lifted the bottle to the risen sun, offering a toast. "Thanks," he said, and took another drink. His second prayer that morning, his second prayer in years. It did not seem enough and so he added, "Thanks a lot," and took another sip. Still, such casually expressed gratitude seemed insufficient. The Scotch was such a thoughtful gift, he should go and thank God properly. Looking around, Riley saw a hedge. He rose unsteadily and slipped the bottle into the branches, making sure it was completely hidden; and filled with happy feelings, knowing anything was possible, knowing he was a giant and all was well and would be well forever, Riley crossed the street and climbed the steps and went to church.

5

Sitting in the last row with her back to the wall as usual, she watched the man step into church and knew right off who he was. She looked a little closer and thought, oh, to wait so long and have it come to this. He walked in like he owned the joint, head up, full of himself, his condition obvious to her practiced eye: not sloppy drunk but in his cups for certain and trying hard to cover. He took a seat in a pew a few rows up. She said a little prayer inside her head, asking God to keep him out of trouble because if he caused a commotion they would look to her to handle things, and she must not be noticed.

Her prayer done, she opened her eyes in time to see Dylan enter with his new deckhand close behind. She was glad that was working out. Jim-Jim was a good old soul, and he deserved the job. Dylan glanced her way and smiled. She nodded. It was good to see the lobsterman here, good to see him bringing his new hand to the Lord's house, even if it did mean she would be out of part-time work. She looked down at the ugly old fingers clasped together in her lap, worn and scarred from labor at the shelter and out on Dylan's boat. She shivered. She stomped her feet a little, the wool of her long skirt scratchy against her unshaven legs. Why did they have to keep this church so cold? She knew for a fact the furnace was serviceable; she could smell it plain as day. All they had to do was turn it up, but every year was just the same: sitting there with freezing feet in spite of two pairs of socks and a sensible pair of Rockport shoes. One thing was certain: It would not be getting warmer for a while. Coming on time for long johns. Should have worn them today, in fact. Would've taken care of the scratchy wool against her legs. There was no other solution, really, since she had just the one winter skirt, and it made no sense to buy another—not when Sunday mornings were the only time all week for dressing fancy. Although she always wore her bone-and-palm-nut necklace with the wooden cross, she kept it underneath her blouse. She disliked jewelry for the most part, and makeup and hairdos and skirts and anything else that called attention. It wasn't just that she needed a low profile. When you wore old work clothes all week, dress clothes were pretentious—maybe not outright vanity, but unnatural for certain. She was probably not alone in this belief. Dylan did not wear a tie, for example. Neither did most of the other lobstermen, though a few of the women seemed to have a different pretty dress for every Sunday of the year. Willa Newdale would not bother with such nonsense. She did, however, believe in looking decent for the Lord's day, so here she was in one of her two skirts, with cold feet, itchy legs, and her back to the wall as usual.

Reverend Henry stepped up behind the podium and asked them all to stand. Willa noticed the drunk man wobble just a little on his way up to his feet. O Lord, she prayed again. Please don't. What if he passes out, or goes to chummin'? She tried not to imagine the contents of his stomach on the back of Emily Weatherspoon, who was standing just in front of him, tried not to think about the outrage, the disapproving stares as she went up to help him, which of course she would. She wished there was a way to get him out right now, before he drew attention to himself, and her. She should have seen this coming. There were just too many of them now, and more coming every day. Her fault, of course. She had to stop, that was all there was to it. She had to stop before it spread too far.

She thought about Steve and Hope, sitting in her office, wanting to talk about all these homeless people from away, and that fella dying in the laundry. What if his heart hadn't picked that moment to stop beating? What if they had gone on with their questions and asked her something direct, something she could not avoid, something she would have to answer, one way or another? Would she have lied to those good people? Hating the thought of that, she felt her breath come fast and shallow. She told herself to calm down. It would be all right, somehow. It had always been all right before.

But Willa Newdale knew it was too late already.

Behind the podium Henry called out a number, and everyone flipped through their hymnals, including Willa. Then the organ started playing and she stopped looking for the hymn. It was going to be "Take My Life and Let It Be," a good old song she remembered well from back before her troubles. She tried to sing, and thought about the words, and wanted them to be the truth. She wanted to be consecrated, had given nearly everything for that—her past, her career, her name—but still she stood there breathing way too fast and shallow, and no matter how many times she told herself it would be all right, the pounding of her heart was certain proof that giving nearly everything was not giving near enough.

The singing concluded; Henry made announcements and they passed the basket. She dropped her offering in and passed it on.

She had no moxie; it was just that simple. All these years, and still she could not make herself stand up and say "All right, you son of the devil, come and get me if you can." And if she could not do that, she ought to stop. Or else she ought to go. Because backing into it this way was worse than hiding. At least up to now she had been an honest coward. But if you did a frightening thing without thinking much about it, if you just let it happen, you were still a coward, and you were a liar too. Imagine if she did not come out of hiding exactly, but also did not stop; imagine if she did that and survived anyway. It wasn't likely, but just say things went that way. If all was well and she looked back later, would she have a right to pride? Of course not. That belonged to people who made their choice flat out, who stood for what was right and said "Here I am."

She saw Bill Hightower spot the drunk, her great disappointment. Her heart began to race again as the usher went to loiter in the aisle beside the poor man. From the stiffness in the old Pharisee's back, the way he held his shoulders, she could see he was getting angry. What was that fool of a drunk doing up there? Please, God, don't let him make Bill Hightower mad. You know how I dislike that man. You know I can't just sit here and let him disrespect that guy, and you know that's just what he will do, given half a chance. Please don't make me stand up here in front of everyone. You know I need to keep a low profile. You know I do, and you know why I do, so please . . .

The lanky usher bent down over the homeless man like a spider over a fly. Willa Newdale held her breath. She thought her heart would come out through her rib cage. But then Bill Hightower stood up straight again and she remembered to exhale. He was just doing his job as an usher was all, just passing the collection basket.

Nothing to be worried about in that.

6

The sour-looking usher by the door nearly blocked his way, but clean clothes and regular showers got Riley Keep inside. Besides, he had not yet reached the stage when his efforts at uprightness became stiffly transparent, when he held his head too high and forgot to bend his knees. No one here could possibly see him for what he was. Not yet. So, hiding the proof required to bar him from God's house, Riley approached with the fluidity and grace of an apparition.

The pews inside were mostly full, everybody dressed in Sunday best, some of the ladies even wearing hats. They had always been a conservative bunch, these Dublin Congregationalists, and yet a fertile field for abolition and suffrage. Riley believed that was why his wife had loved them so. She got to wear nice things, the rules were clear, and all was clean and orderly, although the mind was unconstrained. Being an obvious exception to all this, Riley's confidence abandoned him in the face of it. Instead of marching boldly along the aisle as planned—the prodigal returning—he took a seat at the first open pew a few rows up, hoping his entry had been barely noticed.

The organist held forth with a hymn as familiar as the seasons and just as old. A hundred voices joined, albeit faintly. The sun shone through the old stained glass, and Riley's gratitude to God evaporated in the subtle scent of heating oil and a sudden burning realization that his ex-wife and daughter might be here.

Three years drunk out on the streets was long enough to build a little universe. In rare moments of sobriety, as he huddled under bridges or falsely pledged to work for food at busy intersections, Riley had often thought of his wife and daughter, refashioning them into something he could bear, reducing them into an image cobbled together in haphazard fashion, pliable in faulty memory and comfortably unconnected to the facts. Although he had not come to church expecting a challenge to the petty way he had installed them in his visceral world, the familiar lofty space, the firmness of the pew, the smells and sounds and dimly recognized people in this place conspired to face him squarely with the fact that somewhere his ex-wife and child remained in total independence of his fantasies. Nothing of consequence outside of Riley Keep had truly changed despite his efforts to deny it. His family might actually be here, in the flesh. They were certainly somewhere, not just inside his head but out beyond him somewhere, seeing real things and breathing true air, possibly just a few pews up ahead of him right now, singing ancient hymns. This was obvious of course, yet to know it in a rush after forgetting for so long—to unwittingly come so close to the truth of his living family after years of fantasy—was terrifying. Riley Keep had entered sacred space with grand plans of thanking God for gaining whiskey, only to receive the crushing weight of vast forgotten loss.

Of course Riley knew the way to bear that burden, and as if in miraculous endorsement of his method an offering basket was passed to him. He stared at the contents. One-dollar bills, and tens and twenties, and small white envelopes with the name of the church preprinted on the outside. He knew the envelopes contained the real money, perhaps as much as a hundred dollars each. He lifted one. To hold so much was a heady business, enough to drive away all thought of his ex-family's exterior existence. Here were paper metaphors for many bottles of his method. Enough excellent corked Scotch to last a week. Enough to send his flesh-and-blood losses back into his head where they belonged, so everyone could be more comfortable.

Riley dipped his hand into the basket, slipping spread fingers through the bills and envelopes, sifting them like a pirate through his treasure. Should he limit this to just a little? Or, being near the door, should he run away with everything? It did not cross his mind to simply pass the basket until the watchful usher stepped too close. With the tall man looming at his elbow Riley had no choice. He passed the basket on.

As the money it contained was borne away and the promise of good whiskey became merely hypothetical, Riley Keep emerged briefly from the power that had nearly driven him to steal these people's tithes. He remembered where he was and why he had come. He remembered who he had once been. A minister of God. He sat empty-handed as a man stood up to preach. Ignoring his words, Riley thought of sunrises on the Atlantic and the harbor at the center of his hometown and bridal gowns and belated christenings in this very space where he was sitting, and he thought about the fact that he could go from mourning for his friend and longing for his wife and child to lusting for good whiskey in the time it took to sing a hymn. What kind of man could do a thing like that? It was an old question with an answer he knew well. The answer was the reason people would not meet his eyes, the reason sunrises made him angry, the reason he had stayed away from Dublin all this time. The real question, the one he could not answer, was why he had returned.

He thought about his answered prayer, that excellent bottle of Scotch.

He thought about the message on a lobsterman's bumper.

Jesus Loves You.

If that were true it would have been a kinder thing to leave him with no conscience, no remorse, no empathy at all. Yet here he sat in Dublin, having braved the deadly cold for the sake of someone else, to no avail. When would he learn his sacrifices were unacceptable? Why could he not simply be a drunk, a thief, a loathsome man who had abandoned wife and child for alcohol? Why could he not settle for the numbing anesthesia of all that? If he could not care about himself, why must he care for anything at all?

And yet, God help him, care he did.

The fella finished preaching, and someone passed the Communion platter to Riley Keep. The tray held many tiny glasses shaped like thimbles, little glasses filled with grape juice around the outside of the tray and red wine in the center. His eyes welled at the thought of Brice, who was beyond all this. He thought of his wife and daughter, possibly right here in this meetinghouse, a few rows up, facing forward and well beyond the sight of such a man as he, who had liquid eyes of such weak vision. They might be holding little thimbles full of wine like these, contemplating lofty matters, preparing to commit to something greater than themselves. And knowing that— even knowing that—still he dreamed of something good to drink. How he hated himself! How he longed to dream of other things, or failing that, to dream of nothing! But he had prayed that prayer a thousand times without results, except to learn that no one gets to choose his dreams. Riley thought about his wife's and daughter's minds on lofty matters and knew he could not join them, but against his will they had one thing in common. Right here in his hands, like them he held a thing much greater than himself.

Riley took a thimbleful of wine and drank it without pause. Then he took another, and drank it too. He took a third, a fourth, a fifth . . . He would have drunk it all had not the outraged usher in the aisle seized the platter and his feeble upper arm and pulled him to his feet and pushed him through the doors and on across the vestibule, and out the building and down the steps to shove him sprawling to the sidewalk. Riley rose without a pause and charged across the street into the little park where the answer to his first prayer in many years lay waiting for him in the bushes. He searched the hedge, and after one long frantic moment when he thought it had been stolen, Riley found the bottle. He removed the cap and drank a burning drink and settled down into the writhing oaken roots again with the blood of

Christ and good Scotch mixed together in his belly, thinking, thank God, thank God for something good to drink!

In a little while the church doors opened, and he watched as fuzzy people started coming down the steps. It was too far away, and he was far too richly blessed with whiskey to see the congregation clearly. Might two of them be his wife and child? Might they see him there, in his native element? Had they witnessed his ignoble ejection?

It did not matter.

Riley only knew he had returned to fail them at the first temptation, as always. Beneath the well-known rafters of that church the truth had overwhelmed him, unavoidable. They said some people hit a bottom and then turned and found themselves, but clearly he was bottomless.

He closed his eyes and waited for the pleasant sounds of Christian greetings to disperse. Eventually the silence of a Sunday afternoon in Dublin settled in. Three filthy strangers approached him, hungry eyes upon his bottle. Snarling, he waved them away. An hour or two later some pathetic woman came and meekly asked him for a drink. In reply he curled himself around his golden blessing, shielding it as he took another sip, husbanding the Scotch, tragically aware that it would soon be empty of its beauty.

One did not find such whiskey every day. It was the finest he had known in three long years out on the street. He would not share it with the strangers crowding round him in the park, but oh, how Riley wished to share it! The thought of three more years without Brice and without another bottle like the one God had given him that day began to weigh as heavy on him as the weight of all the years he had stolen from his precious wife and child. Ashes to ashes, dust to dust. *"The wheel is come full circle."* Yet it was not Kent or even Lear who spoke that line; no, it was the liar, Edmund. There was no circle. History was the story of a headlong rush in one direction, straight down to the grave.

Riley rose and stumbled farther up the hill, cradling his answered prayer with both arms like it was the baby Jesus, looking for a place to sleep, perhaps forever. Downtown was nearly empty, most of the shops closed for Sunday or the season. He turned into a narrow dead-end alley, and nearly fell, and leaned against a garbage dumpster to take another drink. His was a simple plan. Half a quart of good Scotch whiskey all at once would grant him sweet oblivion. He would drink as quickly as he could, and sleep, and let the cold come have its way, and greet the morning's sunrise stiff from freezing or from rigor mortis; it did not matter which. It did not even matter if he lived. He only wished to stop the headlong rush into this moment, here and now.

Riley tipped the bottle up and, swallowing, lost his balance and fell down to the bricks. Miraculously, the bottle did not break and not a drop was spilled. The answered prayer made sense to him at last. This was no gift for his trivial enjoyment; it was a final act of mercy, a divine *coup de grâce*. Retrieving the bottle, he crawled across the alley to the wall behind the dumpster, well out of sight of the street and anyone who might come before the cold had settled in. There against that wall he sat up like a man. He stripped off his coat. Upon further reflection he removed his shirt and undershirt as well, determined as he was to hasten the effect. With the bare flesh of his back pressed against the alley wall, he thought of Dylan Thomas, Kerouac, Fitzgerald—all great minds gone from alcohol. He was in good company here in this hallowed hall, prostrate before this altar, this back alley, this dumpster. Again he brought the blessing to his lips.

As the bottle tilted, Riley saw an envelope beside him on the bricks. He paused. He picked it up. On it was the name of the church, preprinted. Apparently it had fallen from his pocket when he pulled off his coat. Apparently he had stolen something from the basket after all. He often did such things without remembering.

Two great gifts in one day seemed impossible, so of course the envelope must contain a check, which would be useless to him. But he noticed it was bulky, not light and slender as one would expect. Carefully, he set the Scotch between his legs and peeled away the flap. Inside was not a check, nor cash, but two folded scraps of paper and a little plastic bag containing pure white powder, enough to fill a bottle cap or two. Cocaine? Heroin? Amphetamines? Riley had never used such things, but his life the last few years had sometimes brought them into contact.

What kind of man put drugs into a church collection envelope? Forgetting how it came to be in his possession, Riley swelled with indignation. This outrage made him want to preach! Then he thought of some befuddled addict taking biblical admonishments literally, tithing ten percent of all the drugs he had, only to have a befuddled drunkard come and steal his profane tithe from the house of God. Rescued from the brink of hypocrisy by that thought, Riley laughed. Who but God could manage such a thing? Who but God could make it work on so many levels? Because of course one could not steal from God, not really, so this was obviously yet another gift from the divine. How merciful of God to grant him laughter in the end.

To prolong the joke, Riley removed the note. Unfolding it he raised the first page close, three inches from his eyes so he could read:

> *May the Lord forgive me, I should have done this long ago. Whoever opens this, please give it to the pastor. He'll know what to do. Tell him it will cure alcoholics, and I want everyone to have it. Tell him if they ever drink again, the urge will return stronger than ever. I used to think there was a way to fix that too, but now I know there isn't. Anyway, this will cure them so long as they never drink another drop.*

Riley read it one more time and then lifted the second page up to his bloodshot eyes. It seemed to be a list of chemical equations and instructions couched in symbols Riley did not comprehend. He let the hand that held the note and bag fall onto his lap. Some of the powder spilled out on his trousers. Ignoring it, propped up against the freezing alley wall much as they had found his old friend Brice against the dryer, Riley stared at nothing.

"This will cure them."

He thought of all his prayers for strength to stand against the urge. He thought of all the silence in response and suddenly remembered God had never cared about his tears. Why should he think God might care about his laughter? Losing Brice and visiting the place where he had married and seen his daughter christened had made Riley lose his focus. The powder was no gift from heaven. Neither was the Scotch, of course. These things were mere coincidence, random substances encountered in his headlong rush to death. He had not dared admit the truth in quite a while, but in the hallowed hall of this back alley, beside the altar of the dumpster, truth must be confessed. Riley had no faith in an unseen god of miracles.

Yet the note said he held a cure, and science was a different matter. Science was the sovereign of cause and effect, a provable kind of god that could not be denied. The teacher in him thought, consider what we know . . . a village hacked to pieces, devastation and despair, despair and drink, drink and drunk, drunk and deadbeat, deadbeat and divorce, divorce and devastation and despair and drink and cause and effect and cause and effect and . . . could this powder be a new kind of cause, come to break the pattern?

With that Riley realized there was just a chance that he and Brice had both been preaching lies. What if the history of life was neither circular nor straight? Neither ceaseless cycle nor headlong rush down to a predetermined end? What if he could take control, change his course, turn away, just by making this one choice? Could redemption rest in his own hands?

In his last stand of consciousness Riley cast his hopes upon a different kind of god, licking a filthy finger and dabbing it in the powder to collect just a bit upon the surface of his skin. He touched it to his tongue and tasted something sweet, impossibly sweet, yet not in the cloying way of saccharine. It reminded Riley of a little shop somewhere down in Brazil, and his wife beside him buying chocolates. How could he have forgotten that day; how happy they had been, how warm it was back then? Riley smiled a little at that memory as the dimming sun declined beyond the western hills of Maine and the cold began to stalk him; then he shivered and he settled in to wait for one end or the other, willing to be cured by his own choice but unwilling to survive one moment longer otherwise.

7

The congregation pressed and flowed around the columns of the portico high above the broad church stairs. In the midst of all the movement, Dublin's mayor paused to look down at her town. She saw the landing at the bottom of the hill to the right, the old gray wharf piled high with traps, the riotous display of multicolored floats on the shingled harbormaster's shed. She noticed a new *For Sale* sign in the window of the McPherson building, and thought about Simmons Marine Chandlery going out of business after nearly eighty years in that location, and wondered who was next. Then she shook her head, denying entry to that train of thought, and whispered words that had become a kind of mantra to her in the past few awful years. "'Sufficient unto the day is the evil thereof.'"

Turning away from the empty building by the landing, Hope stood in that high place and stared at the littered lawn in the park across the street. She made a mental note to mention it to the township's head of maintenance. She saw six or seven dirty strangers sitting by the fountain and a man with shaggy hair and a long beard lying at the base of the old town-meeting oak, sprawled out right there in plain sight, drinking from a bottle in a paper bag. The sight made her think again of Brice, dead on the shelter floor, and the likelihood that Riley Keep was back in town.

The mayor sighed and searched for someplace pleasant to rest her eyes. It wasn't hard to find. In spite of the homeless people's litter, downtown Dublin was still very pretty, or "quaint" as the tourists liked to call it. She admired the antique black and gilded signage above Jefferson's Art Gallery across the way, the golden leaves clinging to the mature birches lining both sides of the street, the lovely verdigris patina on the copper dome of town hall at the top of the hill, and the township's cheerful Thanksgiving banners hanging from cast-iron antique streetlights up and down Main Street. Then, as she had so many times before, Hope considered all the blank windows above the foursquare red brick businesses and wondered if there was a way to make some use of all those vacant second floors. After all, a good mayor thought in terms of possibilities. The only thing was, these days there were many empty first floors too, with some buildings vacated altogether.

As Hope's eyes traveled up the street she spied Dylan on the sidewalk talking to another man. He stood beside her car. She forgot her burden for a moment and wondered if the handsome lobsterman waited there for her.

"Mo*ther*? Will you please come *on?*"

Summoned from her reverie by the frustration in her daughter's voice, the mayor looked down at a swarthy, compact girl standing with her arms crossed at the bottom of the steps. Hope had a fleeting impression of her daughter as if seen through a stranger's eyes: lifeless hair as black as midnight, stainless piercings through her tongue and her right nostril, a dull tattoo along her neck between her left ear and the top of that horrible alpaca sweater. It was like looking down on one of the many homeless people filling Dublin's streets for some mystifying reason, a pierced and tattooed Indian. The mayor forced a smile. "Coming, dear!" she called, with a shrug to Margie Seavey, who stood beside her, and just the tiniest roll of her eyes as if to say, what's a single working mom to do?

Hope began making her way down to where Bree waited so impatiently when someone back behind the mayor called her name. Pausing, she put on her brightest smile and turned. Bill Hightower came through the crowd to reach her, shoving past the people in between like they were weeds out in a field. The colorless man stood head and shoulders above most everyone, with a gray suit and gray military haircut and skin tight upon his bones. Even at six feet four inches, Hightower was probably not much heavier than Hope. She had always been intrigued by the little white ridges of cartilage showing underneath the flesh of his nose and ears, looking for all the world as if they might burst through the surface any minute. A lawyer and a banker both, the son and grandson of lawyers and bankers, Bill Hightower held the paper on Hope's house and most of the others around Dublin. No doubt this explained his position as a councilman. But Hope knew the power of money was not limited to town hall. Hightower also had a lot of influence in the Congregational church.

"Bill," she said, extending her hand as he approached her. "How ya doin'?"

"I've been better." Hightower gave her hand an awkward shake, grasping just her fingertips. "What are you doing about all these bums hanging around?"

"Bums?"

"Panhandlers. Whatever."

She lowered her hand. "Ah. Well, we're workin' on that problem, Steve and me. Went over to see Willa about it just this week."

"She won't do a thing."

"I think she does a lot."

"You know what I mean. If Willa had her way, we'd be building them houses."

"Well, I guess prob'ly. She does have a soft spot for the homeless." Hope smiled.

"You need to get them out of town."

"It's a free country, Bill."

Hightower pointed a long and bony finger toward the park across the street. "Not when they infest our parks and interfere with business and interrupt our church services."

Following his gesture, Hope squinted toward the man on the ground below the meeting oak. His long, unkempt hair draped down, concealing his face like a hood. "Interrupt church services?"

"You didn't see me kick that fella out just now?"

"No. Why'd you do that?"

"He was chugging the Communion wine like shots in a bar!"

She peered closer at the man across the street. "Well now."

"They've got to go, Hope."

"They have rights, Bill. We can't just run 'em out of town for sittin' in the park."

"He chugged the wine! Five or six glasses of it, like it didn't mean a thing!"

"Not sure there's a law against that."

"There oughta be!"

"Ayuh, but I still don't think we have that kinda law."

"What about God's law?"

Hope took a step away from Bill Hightower toward her daughter. "God'll have to handle that himself, Bill. It's not my area anymore."

"You're saying you won't do anything?"

"Not at all. Like I said, we're tryin' to work something out with Willa. Find some way to keep 'em all fed and with someplace warm to sleep."

"You want to *feed* them and keep them *warm*? That'll just encourage them to stay!"

She spoke slowly and distinctly. "Bill. Again. We can't make 'em leave town. And since they're here, I'm sure you agree we can't let 'em starve and freeze."

"Who's going to pay for all this food and shelter?"

It was an excellent question, but Hope refused to let him see her worries. "We'll find the money somewhere."

Hightower drew himself up to his full height, and Hope thought, oh boy, here it comes. Then, as if thinking better of whatever he was poised to say, the man exhaled slowly and seemed to shrink again.

"I'm sorry. Guess I'm still a little upset about what that fella did."

Hope nodded. "Sorry you had to kick him out, Bill. That must of been hard."

"Ayuh." The tall man nodded earnestly. "I hated to do it. And I'd like to help these people too, if we could. But look around, Hope! We're barely hanging on here. We've got to get them *out* of town, not keep them here by making them more comfortable!"

"Well, I guess we'll have to agree to disagree on that."

The usher sighed. "I don't want to go against you. But it seems like you're leaving me no choice."

With that, the tall man turned and stalked off.

Hope did her best to hide her emotions beneath a politician's smile as she walked toward her daughter, yet her annoyance proved too strong to conceal. At the bottom of the stairs she gripped Bree's upper arm with a bit more force than was necessary and, leaning close, whispered, "I told you to stop wearin' that thing in your nose, young lady!"

Bree's broad features revealed no emotion. She shook her arm free, spun on her heel and strode away as fast as her odd bowlegged gait would carry her.

With all the people watching, Hope could only follow.

Up ahead, she saw Dylan, still standing by her car. The man watched Bree approach and said hello to her, but the pigheaded girl went straight to the passenger side without a word. As Hope drew near, her daughter slammed the door. Dylan turned and raised his eyebrows. "Somethin' I said?"

"Naw," said Hope. "She's all spleeny-Jeanie 'cause I won't let her run around like a heathen with a bone in her nose." Dylan chuckled, but she said, "It's not funny. I can't get her to do anything."

Dylan's huge brown eyes softened at the worry in her voice. "She'll be okay."

"Did you get a look at her? It's like she wants to get back to her roots. I wouldn't be surprised if she came home one of these days with earplugs and a spear."

"Ayuh. I'm just glad tattoos weren't cool when we was her age, or we'd be sportin' a few ourselves."

"I never was that wild."

"Oh, I don't know ..." He grinned widely, his straight teeth white against his beard. "I'm rememberin' a graduation party at O'Leary's and a wicked little dance up on the balcony and—"

"Stop your lies, Dylan Delaney! My girl's just right there in the car."

"And she's gonna be just fine, is all I'm sayin'. *You* turned out okay."

"I guess."

"You're the *mayor* for crying out loud."

Hope thought of all the empty buildings around them. "Big deal."

"It is to me."

She looked directly at the handsome man. "Thanks."

Dylan held her eyes with his until she looked away. He said, "Never guess who's been pullin' traps for me, last couple a days."

"Yeah? Who?"

"Jim-Jim."

"I hope you keep a line on him."

"That's the thing. He's sober." He had pronounced the word the Maine way: *sobah.*

"No."

"Ayuh. Sober as a judge for at least a month."

Hope considered his news. James Jameson had been Dublin's town drunk for nearly thirty years. He had been tolerated, even celebrated because of his sunny personality and his penchant for causing creative trouble with the best of good intentions. Far too gone to get a driver's license, he used a John Deere riding lawn mower as basic transportation. The Dublin police had long ago removed the blades after he had cut a three-block swath through dozens of flower beds one morning while courteously repositioning people's copies of the *Bangor Daily News* from their front lawns up onto their porches. Another time he swam out into the harbor and accidentally set a yacht adrift while attempting to tow it to a mooring closer to the landing for its owner's convenience. Most recently Hope had heard he flooded his apartment while trying to install a second bathroom without his landlord's permission. After that, Jim-Jim had been forced to move into Willa's shelter. It had been sad news, but Jim-Jim's stubborn independence in the face of his addiction had inspired a perverse admiration in her, the kind one feels for scrawny boys who won't lie down when schoolyard bullies beat them. Jim-Jim might be a hopeless drunk, but at least he was still here. It was more than she could say for Riley.

Still, the concept of Jim-Jim sober was akin to learning that a moose had typed a letter or Bill Hightower had voted Democrat. Wondering if Dylan was pulling her leg, Hope asked, "How'd he do it?"

Dylan shrugged. "Says he just woke up at the shelter one day and didn't wanna drink."

"That's impossible."

"Just tellin' ya what he said."

"And he's okay pullin' traps? He safe?"

"Ayuh."

"Huh." She considered this latest bizarre news. It was the fourth or fifth such story she had heard in recent months. Then it occurred to her to ask, "What about Willa? Doesn't she need the money?"

"She's the one suggested it. Said she's too old for buggin' now, and besides, she's too busy, what with all these homeless people from away."

Willa had her hands full at the shelter; that was true enough. With so many homeless coming in, maybe the old woman didn't have the time for part-time work as Dylan's deckhand anymore. But all those people left her needing money more than ever. Hope could see it was a real dilemma. Thinking like a mayor again, she wondered how the township could increase support for Willa's shelter. With the tax base shrinking every month they'd have to give up something else. There ought to be some kind of a strategy, some way to convince the council. But as Hope's mind explored the problem it led to thoughts of the shelter and suddenly she remembered Brice, dead on the floor.

Hope tried to turn to pleasant thoughts. "So Jim-Jim's really actin' sober?"

Dylan shook his head. "I don't think he's actin' is the thing. The man's been cured."

"There's no cure. But if he's really not drinkin', that's good." She nodded, looking down the street. "Good on him."

"Ayuh."

They stood together without speaking as only old friends and State of Mainers could, one looking this way, one looking the other. Down in front of the church the last of the crowd broke up at last, splitting off into families and couples and individuals, walking to their cars and trucks. Soon downtown would be vacant, some of the shops closed just for Sunday, some closed for the season, all too many closed forever. Hope felt a little lonely at the thought of winter coming on. Summer visitors could be annoying, but they brought in most of Dublin's money and lent a lively air to the streets. Without them everything looked dead. Shivering, Hope clutched her elbows to herself. Dylan moved imperceptivity closer. She found herself leaning toward him. Suddenly the car horn sounded. Bree, of course, ruining the moment.

"All right, all right," called Hope. "Keep your teeth in." Moving away from Dylan she walked around the front of her car. "Gonna be a little brisk tonight, I guess."

He nodded. "Down ta twenty's what I heard."

"You coming over for supper?"

"Ayuh."

She paused at the door, leaving it unopened. Looking across the car roof at the handsome man, Hope felt a familiar longing. "He's back, you know."

"Ayuh," said Dylan, looking elsewhere. "I expect he is."

8

To Riley Keep's very great surprise, he awoke.

He opened his eyes to a simple world composed only of two great blocks of color, a large green shape above him and a pale blue field beyond. After a minute of concentration he realized he was lying on his back, looking up at the side of a garbage dumpster against the open sky. He rolled his head into an errant ray of sunshine. Squinting, he rolled his head back again and sat up with a grunt. The empty bottle dropped off of his naked chest and shattered. Tiny flakes of frost crackled in the wrinkles of his skin, showering to the alley bricks as he scooted on his bottom toward the dumpster, the bits of ice and broken glass around him sparkling in the morning light. When his bare back touched the freezing metal dumpster Riley flinched and jerked away. Shivering, he leaned forward and drew his shirt and undershirt and coat over to his side. One by one he shook the frost from them and put them on, and then he leaned against the dumpster once again. He blew on his hands and tucked them underneath his armpits. Sitting there that way, he frowned. It was cold, wicked cold, even in the sunshine, so cold his body heat had not stopped the frost from forming on his skin. Why was he not dead?

Slowly, the light shifted until it was full in his face. The slight warmth of it felt good, though his feeble eyes could not abide the brightness. He rose to his feet, grunting again at the effort and the spikes of pain in his joints. He shuffled down the alley to stand where it opened onto Main Street.

Unlike the evening before, he saw people here and there. Not just homeless people from away, but Dublin folks as well. Riley was surprised by this at first, but then he remembered it was Monday morning, a workday. A panel truck slowed and turned down the alley, then abruptly stopped, facing him. Riley looked up at the man behind the windshield, who gestured impatiently, indicating he wanted to drive on. Blowing into cupped hands, Riley got out of the workingman's way and set out along the sidewalk. He was hungry and hoped it was not too late for breakfast at the shelter.

He passed Henry's Drug Store half a block away without a second glance. Farther up the hill someone called behind him.

"Hey! Hang on!"

Barely noticing, Riley kept walking.

"Hey! Hold up a minute, will ya?"

The voice was closer to him now. Riley turned and to his surprise found the man was calling him. A slender fella wearing a plaid jacket and chinos, he stood in front of Henry's store, too far away for Riley's weak eyes to make out any details.

"Weren't you in my church yesterday?"

Riley had some dim recollection of this, and felt a sudden fear. "No," he said.

The man walked toward him. "Sure, I saw you. You're the one Bill kicked out during Communion."

"No, not me."

"Aw, come on. I saw you."

Riley started walking away as fast as he could. The man caught up and fell in beside him. "What's your hurry?"

"I don't want any trouble."

"Trouble? Naw, you got me all wrong. I was gonna offer you a job."

Riley kept on walking.

"Don't ya want a job?" The man made a show of looking Riley

up and down. "You look like you could use the money."

"Why?"

"Well, no offense, but I mean, just look at yourself."

"No, I mean why do you want to give me a job?"

"Oh. Well, I need help, and you obviously need money, so . . ."

Riley slowed, then stopped. "What kind of job?"

"Just this an' that round the drug store there. Sweepin' up. Straightenin' the stock. That kinda thing."

Riley squinted at the man to see him more clearly: a neat, short haircut touched with gray and the shadow of heavy whiskers dark upon his clean-shaven chin and cheeks. "Do I know you?"

"Don't think so." The man reached out and laid a hand on Riley's shoulder. "My name's Henry Reardon. What's yours?"

The light touch of the man's hand and the fact that someone wanted to know his name affected Riley all out of proportion to the situation. To his complete amazement, he began to cry.

"Hey," said the man, giving his shoulder a little squeeze. "Hey now."

Riley kept his eyes down, wiping them with a filthy palm. "I'm sorry."

"No need. No need. You've had a pretty rough time of it lately, I'm guessin'."

Riley nodded, regaining some control. "Ayuh."

"So . . . what *is* your name?"

"I, uh . . ." Riley's natural suspicion kicked in. He knew this man from somewhere, and did not want to give him an advantage until he knew from where exactly. Looking away he said, "Stanley Livingston."

"Nice to meet ya, Stanley. So, how's about it? You wanna job?"

"Ayuh."

"Good. Real good. So, hey . . . let's get to work."

Inside the little drug store Henry said, "No offense, but we gotta get you lookin' a little more presentable, okay?" He gave Riley a small blue plastic basket and led him up and down the aisles, dropping items in. A toothbrush and toothpaste, comb, deodorant, and a pack of elastic ponytail holders. In the restroom, Riley stripped to the waist and washed his hands and face and armpits at the antique porcelain sink. Using tap water and his new comb he tidied up his long hair, pulling it back into a ponytail. He ignored his beard, which hung nearly to his chest and was beyond any form of grooming. Riley was careful not to look into the mirror. Dressed again, he emerged into the stockroom with his coat draped over his arm. Henry grinned when he saw him. "All right," he said. "Now you look like an old hippie, which is good 'cause so do half my customers."

Riley allowed himself to smile, exposing the black empty spaces in his mouth. "What do you want me to do?"

Henry looked around the stockroom. "Well, let's start by makin' some sense a things back here. Needs a good sweepin', then all that stock in the boxes back by the door needs to be carried up front, unpacked an' merchandised."

"Merchandised?"

"Fancy retail talk for 'put it on the shelf.' Just look for wherever we stocked it before an' put it there, with the front label facin' out."

"Okay," said Riley doubtfully.

"Hey, Stanley, don't worry 'bout it. You'll be fine."

"Why are you doing this?"

Henry cocked his head. "You really don't remember me from yesterday?"

"I . . . I'm sorry."

Henry laughed. "No problem. It'll come to ya."

Within the hour Riley had the stockroom floor swept and the restroom scrubbed clean. Without being asked he decided to tidy up the small break area, scrubbing the microwave inside and out and organizing the disposable knives and forks and paper plates. He noticed one of the break area chairs had a wobbly leg, so he found a screwdriver and fixed it. He got out a stepladder and changed a light bulb. When there was nothing left to do in the stockroom area he went outside through the rear receiving door, hoping for some kind of work back in the alley. To his surprise, he was standing exactly where he had met the day. At his feet was the shattered Scotch bottle, and to his right the dark green dumpster. He went back inside for the broom, returned and swept the shattered glass into a pile, then picked it up and threw it in the dumpster. He looked around the alley for more work to do, and decided the whole thing needed sweeping. It was maybe an hour later when Henry came outside. "Hey, Stanley," he said, dressed now in a pharmacist's white lab coat. "What's up?"

"Just cleaning here." Riley swept the bricks furiously.

"The alley?"

"Ayuh."

"Uh, think you've about got it whipped?"

Riley looked around. He had indeed swept the entire alley, from the intersection with Main Street all the way back to the drug store's receiving door. "I guess."

"Okay. Great. So, how's about that stock?"

"Okay."

"Good. Great. You need anything?"

"No."

"All right, then."

After Henry disappeared back into the store Riley stooped to pick up a final little pile of dirt and trash. He pitched it into the dumpster. Inside the stockroom he placed the broom where it belonged and turned to face the stack of boxes by the door. There was no way to avoid it any longer. The time had come to carry something up front. He lifted a box and walked to the swinging door that opened onto the sales floor. He paused, looking through the circular window in the door, out into the world beyond with its clean fluorescent lights and its ordered rows of goods for sale and customers with homes and money and cars and jobs and other people in their lives.

It was one thing to work alone back in the stockroom. He actually kind of enjoyed it. But out there with this box in his hands he could not hide behind his homelessness. With work to do, he would no longer clearly be himself. They might mistake him for one of them. They might have expectations. That lady over there, and the other one across by the checkout counter, would be able to look right at him without turning away. He was not sure he wanted to be seen. It did not feel right, because in fact he was not one of them. He might have clean hands and a job to do, but Riley Keep was still a ghost.

As he stared into the outside world the front door of the drug store opened and a young woman came in from the street. Riley could not focus on her clearly because of the distance, but she walked straight toward the back and turned at the rear aisle just beyond the door where he was standing, and he watched her profile through the glass as she passed, and felt his heart surge up into his throat. Then she was out of sight, back around to the right at the pharmaceutical counter, but he could hear her well, talking to Henry over there.

"Hi ya, Bree," said the pharmacist. "How ya doin'?"

"Got that prescription ready?"

"Ayuh. Just a minute."

A pause, and Riley figured Henry had gone somewhere to find the order. With the box forgotten in his hands, Riley craned to see her through the window, actually pressing his nose up against it, but she was just beyond his field of vision. Then she wandered over to a display at the end of one of the rows where he could see her, and the blood roared in his ears. He could not make out details, but he could see that she was beautiful. She was no longer a young woman in his eyes. She had become a little girl. And she was absolutely beautiful. Seeing her, he thought of dense green canopies and the calls of parrots and the smell of wood fires on the river. He thought of laughter and naked children chasing each other all around his legs and Waytee's wrinkled smile. He forgot himself and dropped the box he was holding. She turned at the sound of it and he ducked below the glass. Picking up the box, he stood slowly, steeling himself against the possibility that she might still be looking, but willing to risk that in order to see more of her. She had moved back out of sight.

He heard Henry ask, "Don't ya have school today?"

"I got a pass."

"Okay," said Henry. "That's thirty-nine fifty." If the girl replied, Riley could not hear her. Henry spoke again. "Uh, Bree? Does your mom know 'bout this?"

"The doctor said you can't tell her."

"I'm not gonna tell her. I'm just kinda worried."

"You better not."

"Okay, but are you real sure you wanna do this?"

"Yeah."

"Because you're kinda young for this."

"All my friends are on the pill."

"Naw, not really. I'm the fella they buy it from, remember? I'd know."

"Well, you just better not tell anyone."

Riley held the box in both his hands and watched through the small round window as she threaded her way back through the store. He thought of going out to talk to her. He truly did consider it for half an instant because Henry was correct: she was too young. He had the best of intentions, but his body would not move. Paralyzed by the enormity of his offense, all Riley Keep could do was think that someone ought to stop her; someone ought to tell her she should slow it down a little, try to wait until the time was right; someone ought to say she could not possibly be ready; she would only ruin it for when she was, and please, please, please won't you stay a little girl a little longer?

But there was no one who could speak that way to her, not a pharmacist, not a middle-aged stock boy—certainly not him—so Riley stood and watched her go while thinking of those things, and of how beautiful she was, how much time he had let pass, how desperately he longed to have that time again, how impossible that was, how hopeless, how vast and unforgivable the nature of his crime. His thoughts reached back into a tranquil village he had gained for God and lost to the devil, and that image glowed with stained-glass radiance on bridal lace and merged into a single drop of water trickling down a christened daughter's forehead. He thought of Bree and of Hope, not in two dimensions tucked back in the corners of his mind but real and out there just beyond his reach. Then all in an instant he remembered Henry, not only as a pharmacist, but also as the pastor of the church right down the street, the man who had married Hope and him, and christened Bree to God; and Riley realized his dear friend Brice had once worked in this very stockroom for Henry's father, long before his old friend had grown up to be a plumber and a drunk; and here he was himself, Riley Keep, once a minister, a missionary, a teacher of young people at Bowditch College, doing the same job Brice had done after school when they had been as young as Bree.

Long after the girl had left the building Riley Keep stared at the fuzzy shapes beyond the stockroom window. Then he remembered where he was and what he should be doing. He took a deep breath and pushed the swinging door and passed into a world where some might think they saw him clearly even though he was but a ghost. With the hesitation of a blind man in an unfamiliar room he went stoop-shouldered down the aisle until he found the proper spot. He knelt to get the box unpacked and merchandised like Henry the pharmacist and part-time pastor told him he should do, but he was not really there, not really doing what it seemed. His glimpse of Bree had unleashed a relentless avalanche, tumbling memories of appalling failures rolling over him all that morning and afternoon, right up until five o'clock had come and gone, crushing Riley down into himself so deeply that he could not notice what had happened, not until that night when he lay down on a musty mattress in the homeless shelter after a meager supper of chicken soup and freeze-dried mashed potatoes and it suddenly occurred to him he did not have the empty caved-in feeling anymore, not even just a little.

Although the landslide of Riley Keep's pathetic history still pressed down upon him, he had not thought about a drink all day. He was in fact completely, inexplicably, astonishingly, cured.

9

Willa Newdale passed a stainless ladle underneath the faucet of the three-compartment sink, scalding her right hand. With a cry of pain she dropped the ladle and jerked her hand back from the water. She crossed to the freezer, shaking her head with frustration, and removed a small chunk of ice to soothe her wound. Willa knew she could not last much longer. She had not slept in forty hours. She had no place to sleep, unless it was out on the streets like those she could not save. She had given her own bed to the man with delirium tremens last night. She had no choice. She could not let him go on screaming in the bunk room while the others listened from their places on the temporary cots and bunks and floor, all of them aware his fate might well be theirs the next night or the next. Four of them had carried him up to her tiny room on the second floor and laid him in her narrow bed and then returned below in blessed peace and quiet, leaving her to sit and hold the man's sweating hand all night with impotent frustration.

When a drunk was that far gone she could do nothing more than keep him warm and sheltered. She could no longer even do that much for most. There were just too many now. And because she had let things come to this, last week one of them had died. Right here in her shelter, right here in the one place where the poor soul should have been safe, she had let him sit down on the laundry floor and die.

Now on top of everything, it was time to go. Every morning and evening she watched the news on television, expecting an announcement. She was surprised it had not come. Probably they did not yet believe, but they soon would, and when they understood the truth she should be far from here. She simply had to go—her life depended on it—but she could not seem to take the final step.

Who would care for all these poor, dear, helpless people?

Leaning on the counter as the pain began to rise beneath the ice, Willa's hard brown eyes shed tears again. They did this against her will. Always resolute in front of witnesses, she could not seem to stop her private weeping. To come so far, endure so much and wait so long, only to see the filthy drunken face of failure as she had last week, to have that man walk in and prove with his degenerate condition that her dream would be forever incomplete, to see the other dead upon the floor . . . what else could she do but weep? She could not make space and food and soap and clothes from out of nothing. She had to sleep sometime. She was not God Almighty, even if she had presumed to act as his right arm. If there had been any strength at all, in the end it had been his. She herself was shamefully weak, unable to wait until the proper moment, unable to postpone deliverance as the Lord so often postponed justice. She had lately learned a new kind of respect for her creator. To hold peace in your hand and yet withhold it for a higher good was a discipline she simply could not match.

The ice had nearly melted into nothing when she heard someone running down the hall outside the kitchen. No one ever ran inside the shelter unless there was a problem. No one had the energy. Willa wiped her eyes with her good hand and went to meet the trouble.

In the hall she heard excited voices from the men's bunk room. She paused outside it, peering through the doorway. Several men stood clustered in a far corner, all of them turned away from her, their attention clearly captured by something or someone Willa could not see. "Take your time, take your time" came a secretive voice from deep within the closeness of their huddle. "I think there's enough for everyone."

Suspecting drugs or booze, Willa Newdale stepped closer to the gang of homeless men. It did not cross her mind to fear them, not when she had lived so long in fear of so much worse.

"Careful!" said the same voice, louder this time. "You'll spill it!"

Willa thought about her options. She could charge right in between them, surprise them in the hope of getting to the bottom of the situation before anyone could pocket whatever they were using. But she knew her chance of laying eyes on it was slim. These were masters of concealment, world-class magicians who could make a mountain of crack cocaine or a sea of booze vanish in a second. Besides, she was too tired. Her heart and mind were willing but her body did not have the strength, so instead of breaking up the party she settled wearily upon a bunk beside the door and watched.

Desire so totally consumed them that they did not even notice. She listened with a heavy heart as their voices echoed from a lost place deep beneath the surface of the world. Willa Newdale believed in hell with the total certainty of a woman who was there.

"Hey, I told you just a little! That's all it takes."

"Yeah, okay."

"Seriously, that's enough. Pass it on."

"You sure this stuff works?"

"Did for me."

"How long does it take to kick in?"

"Don't know exactly. Like I said, I passed out."

She saw one of them—a very small man, almost childlike—lean into the huddle, and heard a sudden snorting intake of breath and then some chuckling. "Ha. What a rush. Ha ha."

"That's not how you do it."

The little man said, "What?"

"Put it in your mouth."

A pause and then the tiny laughing man said, "Ha. Thanks, man. Ha ha."

"Tastes funny. Like candy."

"Hey! Come on, man, gimme some."

They went on like this for maybe five more minutes and then, "I guess that's all."

"Everybody get some?"

"Yeah, man. Thanks."

"Sure."

"So . . . I don't feel nothin'."

"Give it time."

"How long?"

"I keep tellin' you I don't know."

They began to peel away from the huddle in ones and twos until finally one saw Willa sitting in the shadows. To her surprise he did not pretend shame. He simply looked the other way, crossed to a bunk and lay down fully clothed. She waited as the others milled around, wondering who would be revealed as the ringleader when the last of them had moved back from the corner of the room. She thought she remembered who had used that bunk the past few nights, but could not be sure. She waited, hating the thought of sending someone out into the cold, but knowing she would have no other choice. Willa could not have this in her shelter.

Now there were only three of them across the room. When one of those stepped aside and at last she saw him, her heart sank. She knew who he was, all right. He called himself "Livingston" and hid behind that ridiculous long beard and hair, but she knew who he was, and he was the last of them that she would want to send into the cold. He had brought such great disappointment to her when he came; she should have known he would leave it with her when he went.

Standing up, she called the name he had been using. "Stanley." He smiled at her. It was surprising. Surely he could see what had to happen now. "Get your stuff and come with me," she said. He rose from his bunk. With an aching heart she led him down the hallway toward the lobby.

"What's up?" he asked.

"You got to go."

"Huh?"

"You know the rules. You got to go."

"What for?"

Willa shook her head with disappointment. Would he insult her intelligence on top of everything else? "No second chance on bringing dope in here."

"I don't do drugs."

"I was there the whole time. I saw everybody passing it around."

"That wasn't dope."

"Don't disrespect me."

"I'm telling you that wasn't any kind of drugs. Nothing you'd care about, anyway."

In spite of herself, this interested her. "All right. What was it, then?"

He looked away. Up to then he had been looking right down at her, his eyes direct and piercing, but now he looked away. "You wouldn't believe me."

"You can either tell me everything or get out of here right now."

He looked at the front door. She figured it was maybe twenty-five degrees outside and falling. She knew what she was doing; she knew what it meant, and hated it, but it simply must be done. He looked back at her, looked right at her eyes. "It was a cure for drinking."

It took everything she had to stand steady. "There's no such thing."

"There is. I took it, and I don't want a drink anymore."

As the fear rose up she said, "Show me."

He seemed reluctant as he dug his hand into a pocket. "I just gave it all away."

"Get out of here, then."

"Hang on." He was still digging in the pocket of his baggy trousers. He pulled out a plastic bag and gave it to her. "There might be a little left."

She took the bag with a sinking feeling. It was an ordinary plastic bag, the kind you might get at any grocery store for sandwiches. In it was a tiny bit of white powder that could have been anything. There was only one way to be sure. She rubbed a callused finger on the inside of the bag and put the finger in her mouth. She tasted something much like chocolate. So it was not cocaine or speed or heroin or anything like that. It was instead the end of yet another chapter in her life, the final step, come right then and there in spite of all her hesitation.

Willa let him stay the night, of course. It would have done no good to make him go. With the other poor man past hallucinations up in her room but still too weak from his withdrawal, she made a pallet of sheets and blankets on the cold tile floor beside the kitchen sink and lay herself down there. Even though it had been two days since she slept, she remained awake for quite a while. She thought about the hopes that she had brought to Dublin. She thought about her strategy, shot to blazes in more ways than one by this man who lied about his name. She could wait and try again of course, but even as the thought occurred to her she knew she did not have the courage. She thought and thought, searching for a way around it, and when the weakness in her could no longer be denied, at last she fell asleep.

The next day Willa felt the weight of her body in every horizontal joint as she went about her business, and every time she stood or bent or climbed the stairs her muscles complained that a woman of her age had no business sleeping on tile floors. Other than that, everything seemed normal. She had pretty much expected it: the calm before the storm.

She directed several of her charges as they prepared a hot breakfast of oatmeal and coffee. It had been nearly two months since she'd been able to afford to feed them eggs or bacon. There were just too many now, plain and simple. After breakfast she set a couple of the men to cleaning up and then disappeared into her tiny office. It was important to get the paperwork up to date. She made her way through the necessary correspondence and paid what bills she could, waiting all the time. Lunch came and went. She did not feed them all; lunch was just for her and a couple of the ones who had been here the longest. "Trustees," they called themselves, although she did not like the word, a word they used in jail.

At two in the afternoon she put one of them to work on the laundry and went upstairs for the third time that day to check on the man in her bed. He lay awake and calm. He claimed that he could make it fine if she would only help him up. She laughed at that and asked if he was hungry. He allowed it might be so, and she had someone take him up a peanut butter sandwich and a glass of powdered milk.

About five-thirty, while she was getting dinner ready she heard a whoop come down the hall and went to find a shaggy man standing in the lobby with his arms spread out like Jesus on the cross. "I'm free!" he shouted to the half a dozen others who were waiting for their dinner. He spun himself around and around, a lightness in his face, and Willa felt a little leap of joy inside of her, in spite of what was surely coming, what she had been waiting for.

"Settle down," she said.

"I'm free, Willa! I don't need no drink!"

"All right. That's fine. Now just settle down."

He laughed and danced around her and skipped and hopped to the front door and flew outside where he could holler unrestrained.

By the time she started serving franks and baked beans the word was fully out. There were nearly thirty people in the line and five or six had claimed the miracle. Excitement spread through all the others like the Spirit at a camp meeting. Willa tried to keep a lid on things, but it could not be contained. Those who claimed they had been healed were surrounded by the others, fielding questions. Some seemed content to be the objects of the blessing; others were intent on taking credit, telling lies to give themselves the glory. This caused some confusion as to how the miracle had occurred. Willa supposed it might be possible they truly did not know, having been too drunk or stoned the night before to remember. She tried to pin some hope on that, but knew she would not be so fortunate.

The man who pretended that his name was Stanley Livingston came in late for dinner. By that time most of the others were already through the line and seated at the folding tables and eating. The man made it all the way to the serving counter before one of them looked up and said, "Hey! Ain't that the guy?"

Everybody in the room was staring at him now.

The Livingston man said, "What?"

"You healed us, man. It really worked!"

"Hey, that's great." The poor man smiled, and Willa pitied him for his foolishness.

"I wanna get healed!" said a woman sitting near the wall.

"Me too!" said the woman next to her.

The man's smile faded. "I wish I could help you."

"Just give us what you gave them."

"They already took it all."

A big man across the room stood up slowly. "But you can get more, right?"

He shook his head. "I'm sorry."

"Come on, man. You know how bad we need it."

"I wish I could. I really do."

The big man flung a vicious curse across the room ahead of his demand. "You go get some more!"

With many others rising to their feet, the poor man took a step back. From Willa's place behind the counter she called out to them. "You people need to settle down."

"He could heal us if he wanted!"

"Settle down, I said!"

The big guy moved around his table, and those who had been

sitting near him followed. "I come all the way from Houston for this."

"But there's nothing I can do!" said the frightened man beside the serving line.

Willa watched them come, thinking she had seen it happen once before, seen men and women feed on each other's desire and become something less than men and women. She had to stop the momentum of it, yet she felt the old familiar fear returning. For some reason, she pressed one hand against the burned place on the other, causing punishing spikes of pain. She must overcome her fear. She must stand, for once.

Willa spoke quietly to the so-called Stanley Livingston. "Get out of here."

"But—"

"Shut up and get going."

With a strange reluctance Willa did not understand, he put his tray back down upon the counter and turned toward the door. A skinny man with hunger in his eyes rose to bar his way.

"Where did it come from?" asked the big one, moving closer.

"I found it."

"How'd you know what it was?"

"There was a note."

"What did it say?"

"Just that it would cure us, and it had a bunch of symbols and things."

"Symbols? Like a formula?"

"I guess."

"So you could make some more."

"No, I—"

"He could do it! He works at that drug store!" shouted someone from the back. "I seen him over there!"

The big man stepped even closer to the poor fella by the counter. "That true? You work at the drug store?"

"Just the last couple of days. I can't—"

"He probably made it his own self!"

"Let's go," said the big man.

"Go? Where?"

"Drug store."

"It's closed."

"Open it."

"I can't do that! I just work there."

"Then *we'll* open it."

The big man took hold of the smaller one who would not use his real name. The impostor tried to shake free, but the big man was much too strong. Another one grabbed the poor man's other arm and the two of them began to walk him toward the door. As the crowd parted to allow them through, the man's feet went out from under him. The two who had him by the arms did not pause but dragged him with his legs trailed out behind as if he were a corpse.

Willa ran around the counter and beat against the big one's back, but although she hit him over and over as hard as she could with both her fists, although she shouted "Stop! Stop! Stop!" the big man did not seem to notice, preoccupied as he was with hauling the limp man down the hall. Then someone else laid hands on Willa, gripping her from behind and yanking back. She tried to twist away yet she was far too small and old and weak. The strong hands drove her hard against the wall. She heard the hollow sound of her own skull bouncing from the plaster. She saw the lights dim down for just a moment. Still, she tried to resist. She would stand against the violence this time! She reached out to push against the hands that pinned her to the wall. Someone laughed and ripped her precious necklace off. They dragged the poor man to the lobby and pushed him stumbling through the door. He was helpless before their concentrated will. Willa sank to the floor back in the hallway, abandoned now, watching everything as if it were happening elsewhere, knowing that they had fallen far beyond her now; the moment had come at last; she could no longer stay. She found it hard to see and put her hand up to her eyes, and when she removed it Willa saw the audacious scarlet of her own blood, not a little as if from a scratch, but a flood as if to fully baptize her in the savagery again, and then she slipped away.

10

They were a mob. Like all mobs they did not value secrecy. They pushed Riley down the center of the street as if he were the shameful one instead of them, a sinner of some kind to be paraded there in public humiliation. They drove him on before them just as he had seen his charges drive a sacrificial pig through the jungle on a feast day, laughing and making sport and certain of the beneficial outcome for themselves. Who was there to stop them? Because of them, downtown Dublin was deserted at that hour, fully half the businesses completely dead and gone, the others closed much earlier than usual for lack of customers. Because of them, no one would see Riley Keep's ordeal. Because of them, the only witnesses to this outrage were Riley and the other ghosts.

He tried to sit immobile on the frigid bricks. He stubbornly refused to go. In the best of all good humors they lifted him into the air and promised him he must. He floated over them, carried along above their heads by many upraised hands, adrift below the stars upon a rising cloud of their collective steaming breath. There was hopefulness and lightness in the insult they performed, and they swore they meant no harm, but with Riley's sobriety had come renewed powers of imagination, and he clearly saw an ugly moment coming when they learned he could not heal them.

The accuracy of such visions was essential to survival. In another place and time he remembered lying on his back like this, staring at a different set of stars, floating far too high upon his narrow notions, believing he had testified and thereby healed The People. No more drunkenness, no more barbarism, all because of his good work.

His good work.

This imprecision in his dreams had made a ghost of him. He remembered lying underneath the equatorial array of lights, rejoicing in his value to the Lord. Floating now upon the breath of drunkards, he marveled at his monumental failure of imagination.

In front of Henry's Drug Store they paused and set him down. They looked to him expectantly. He remembered giving his professors that same look in seminary, expecting answers. He remembered that same expectant look from his students at Bowditch, and before that from The People. Their look was a temptation to him. He wished to give the answers they desired. He felt a flicker of ambition, an old familiar lust to be the cause of their advancement. But such desires were quickly crushed beneath the weight of Riley's history. He shuddered.

"I told you I can't do this."

Laughing, they crashed right through the glass door.

"What you need?" growled the big one who had started everything. The others went on laughing up and down Henry's unlit aisles, filling their pockets with his inventory, while the big one leaned in very close, unsmiling. "I come all the way from Houston, man. You gonna do it, or I gonna break your neck."

Like a pig before a pit of glowing coals, Riley would try anything to delay the final moment. Looking up he saw the metal bars around Henry's dispensary. A desperate plan occurred to him. He would deal them death if necessary. "What I need's in there."

"Hold him," said the giant drunk from Houston.

Riley stood surrounded by a dozen captors as the big man attacked the bars. Several others joined the man. The security cage had been designed to resist just such an assault, but they were determined. When their combined might did not prevail, the big one said,

"We need something like a crowbar," and they fanned out across the store, looking for the proper tool. A single streetlight cast its yellow glow a few feet through the storefront windows, whereas the sales floor toward the back remained very dark. Riley heard the crashing of Henry's merchandise as they knocked it from the shelves in a vain attempt to search by touch alone for something strong enough to get them to the cure.

"We got to turn on the lights," called one of them.

"Don't do that. Somebody gonna see us."

"At least *we* could see."

"Shut up and keep looking."

In the darkness Riley tried to slip away but many hands were quickly on him. "Relax, friend," said a vague shape at his shoulder. He stood still and listened to them wrecking Henry's store, trying to think of a way to survive the night without doing harm.

"Man, we're not gonna find nothin'."

"Shut up! There gotta be something that'll work!"

Someone close by Riley in the darkness whispered, "Here, man. Heal me first, okay?" The unseen person pressed an object into Riley's palm, which he barely noticed even as he slipped it in his pocket, since the unfamiliar work of making plans required his full attention.

"Hey, how's this?" called someone in the darkness. Moments later the big man was at the bars again, this time with the long metal pole Henry used to crank out the storefront awning. The giant slipped it between the bars beside the cage's lock and stepped back to apply the force of leverage. With his plan now fully formed, Riley waited. The long pole in the big man's hands did not move at first, although he strained against it mightily. Then a pair of smaller men applied themselves beside him and Riley saw the pole begin to dip, the lock gave and the gate moved up with a screeching protest as the mob cheered.

One of the smaller men who had a hand in prying the gate open was the first into the dispensary. He went straight back to the shelves where he began a frantic search. Riley assumed the man desired amphetamines or sedatives, even though the mob had brought him there to free them of all that.

The big one called, "Bring that guy," and Riley felt several hands against his back, pressing him toward the pharmacy counter. The one who had given him the unseen bribe leaned close to his ear and whispered, "Remember, man, I'm first," as Riley went without resistance. He entered the dispensary. Another man squeezed past to join the first one at the shelves. The giant from Houston followed and in one smooth motion clubbed a looter to the floor. Turning to the other he said, "Cut it out."

"What's your problem, man? They got Quaaludes!"

"We not here for that."

"Come on, man. It's the mother lode!"

The big man's arm shot up like a rocket, catching the second looter below his jaw to drop him where he stood. The plastic bottle in the thief's hands rolled across the floor to stop at Riley's feet. The big man said, "Drag them outta here, somebody. This guy need some room to work." When the two limp forms had been removed, he turned to Riley. "Go ahead."

Hoping to attract someone's attention out on the street, Riley said, "I need some light to read the labels."

The big man turned and flipped a switch. A fluorescent tube above them flickered on and off and on and off again before illuminating the small work space with its bluish hue. Riley disappeared between two shelving units, pretending to search for necessary ingredients. He removed a large white plastic jug, made a show of scanning the label, took it to the countertop in front and then went back. He found a smaller plastic container, and another, dragging out his search as long as possible, harvesting the elements of death. He felt as if a great force pressed him down to murder. He felt ghostly underneath its weight. He felt surprise to find the weight familiar, having dared to hope he had been cured of everything that pressed him down that way.

When Riley had assembled ten or twelve ingredients he began to fear the mob would see through his delay, so he sat at Henry's work counter to begin. Before him was a small tray he had seen Henry use to count out pills, and near it was a box with little measuring spoons individually sealed in plastic. With the big man watching closely over his shoulder, Riley opened one of the medicine containers. He shook several capsules out onto the tray. He removed one of the sanitary measuring spoons from its plastic wrap and made a show of opening the capsules one by one and delicately tapping their contents into the spoon.

"Hurry up!" said the man from Houston. "We don't got all night."

"It's gonna take a while," replied Riley, looking up. "Believe me, we don't want to get it wrong."

"Why? What happen if it wrong?"

Riley bent back to his work.

Some of the plastic bottles at his elbow contained powder; some of them held tablets. The powder he simply measured out by the spoonful, being careful to delay even this by opening a new packaged spoon for each new bottle. The tablets he dropped into one of Henry's antique mortars and ground down with a pestle. He made a show of doing this with grave attention, saying it was essential for the powder to be very fine.

"This taking too long," said the big man. "Just wait till you got everything together, then grind it all at once."

"That won't work," replied Riley. "I have to measure everything after it's already ground or I won't get the mixture right."

He moved with infinite care; he delayed in every way he could imagine, but in spite of Riley's inertia the moment came when there was nothing left to add. The giant from Houston drew close. "That it?"

Riley stared down at the little pile of powder on the tray before him. He had no idea what was in the random mixture of narcotics, but it was bound to kill them. He said nothing.

Impatiently the big man said, "Come on, man. You finished or not?"

Thinking that he did not want to do this, thinking they had forced it on him, Riley Keep said, "Yes."

The mob outside the dispensary tried to press through the gate, thirty trying to fit where there was not room for three. Throwing his huge palms against the chests of the ones in front, the giant held them back. In a matter-of-fact way, he said, "I'll break your neck, you come in here."

"I paid him to be first!" shouted someone.

"We got a right to that stuff too!" shouted someone else.

"You gonna get it," said the big man calmly. "Just not all at once. Line up by that window yonder. We gonna pass it out like you was here for something regular."

While the grumbling crowd did as they were told, the big man grabbed the back of Riley's chair and rolled him off to the side. Kneeling in Riley's former place until his face was very near the powder, kneeling right down at desktop level before it, the giant drunk from Houston stared intently at the little mound of poison, saying, "I'll never wanna drink again?" His tone no longer hinted of violence. In his voice was only hope and reverence, as if Riley had become his god, and the cure his saving grace.

Riley closed his eyes. It was all too familiar, this salvific role. He said, "Yes."

"How much should I take?"

"One spoonful ought to do it."

"Ought to?" Something in his voice warned Riley, but it was too late. Before he could open his eyes the giant had already turned. They faced each other. Riley quickly looked away.

"Get over here," said the big man.

"Why? I did what you want."

"Get over here."

Sighing with a pretense of impatience, Riley rose and crossed the narrow distance.

The big man handed him the spoon. "Go ahead."

"What?"

"You first."

"I can't do that."

"Why not?"

"You're not supposed to take it if you're already cured."

"Didn't hurt you none the first time."

"It's different."

"Shut up and take some."

"No, really, I—"

"Shut up!" roared the man, sinking his huge right fist in Riley's belly, driving his diaphragm up into his lungs. Riley dropped to the floor, sucking wide-mouthed at the air like a fresh-caught cod down on the landing. It took nearly a minute for his lungs to fill again.

"Better now?" The big man bent over him. "Ready for your medicine?"

He grasped Riley's upper arm and jerked him to his feet as if he were a feather. He put the spoon in Riley's hand and stood him up at the counter where the pile of powder loomed. He wrapped his massive fingers around the back of Riley's neck, pressing him down over the powder. He said, "Take it or I'll break your neck." He said it the way a man might talk about a cloudy day.

Riley looked down at the poison he had made. He had not wanted to do it; that was the thing; they had made him do it. And as his death drew near he thought about the chain of cause and effect that had brought him to this moment. A village hacked to pieces, devastation and despair, despair and drink, drink and drunk, drunk and deadbeat, deadbeat and divorce, divorce and now a huge hand pressing him into the deadly trap he himself had set. Riley recognized the perfect symmetry of his punishment, the natural result of lives that he had wasted starting with his own, of wife and child abandoned, stained-glass radiance forgotten, golden sunrise diadems ignored. He closed his eyes and saw the last sunrise he remembered, the one he had scorned on the morning of the day he stole the cure from God's own house, the pink and purple of it, the red and blue, red and blue bursting from beyond the horizon, the colors in Riley Keep's mind flashing on the insides of his squeezed-shut eyelids, red and blue, red and blue until the giant's hand relaxed upon his neck to let him rise and see four squad cars pulled nose-in at the curb outside the shattered storefront glass of Henry's Drug Store, their red and blue lights whirling round and round to shine on six policemen pointing weapons at the ghostly mob of those who, like Riley, merely wanted to be cured.

II

Dublin Township's six jail cells were too small to hold all the people arrested in Henry's Drug Store. Riley greeted the morning in a hallway, along with more than a dozen other overflow prisoners, all of them uncomfortable on folding chairs lined up against the walls. His left hand rested in his lap, stained by the ink they had used to take his fingerprints. His right hand hung down at his side where his wrist had been bound to the chair leg by a narrow plastic strap. Throughout the night he had tried to sleep without success, nodding off for maybe fifteen minutes at a time before being awakened by the old-fashioned ringing of a telephone or the slap of shoe soles on terrazzo as policemen passed him by. Riley Keep was not concerned. Incarceration held no stigma for a man in his position, and having gathered some experience while in other jails for vagrancy, he knew it was no worse than the streets.

A policeman with a clipboard called out, "Stanley Livingston."

Riley Keep said, "Here."

The policeman used a pair of scissors to cut the plastic strap around his wrist and walked him to a small room down the hall, where Riley stood beside a metal table as the door behind him closed with a dull click of the lock. He and the table were the only objects in the room. Riley paced the room, stroking his bushy beard in thought. After five minutes of standing, Riley sat on the floor and leaned his back against the wall, stretching his legs straight out in front of him. Almost immediately the lock clicked again, the door swung open, and a tall man entered. He wore a starched khaki shirt and loose dungarees and had broad shoulders and a flat stomach in spite of his age, which Riley guessed to be around sixty. He looked down on Riley and said, "Sorry there's no chairs."

Riley shrugged.

"We had to use them all outside."

"Okay."

The man glanced at a clipboard in his hand. "Stanley Livingston, right?"

"Uh-huh."

"You mind standin' up?"

Riley rolled to his side to get a foot underneath himself and rose, using the wall for support, feeling stiff and sore after his night on the folding chair.

"Okay, Stanley, I'm Chief Steven Novak. Tell me what happened last night."

Riley told him everything. There was no need to lie; anything he had done wrong was forced on him. The man listened carefully until Riley finished, then said, "So that pile of drugs all mixed together on the counter, you did that?"

"They made me."

"'Cause they think ya know a cure for alcoholism."

"Yes, sir."

"Why would they think that?"

Riley's instincts warned him to be careful. What had happened in the alley would sound like it was crazy, or a lie. He had no proof except an empty plastic bag and a note that he himself could have written. He said, "I just came in the shelter for supper and the next thing I know they're hauling me off to the drug store, like I said. I told them I couldn't heal them. You can ask that lady who runs the place; she heard me."

"Uh-huh." The chief pulled a pen from his shirt pocket and wrote something on the clipboard's paperwork. He took his time. Riley began to worry as he listened to the slow, deliberate scratching of the pen. This was not like an arrest for vagrancy; it was more personal, more specific to him. They might try harder to learn his identity, and he did not wish to be known.

"Hang on a minute," said the chief.

The man left the room. The door clicked shut behind him. Riley stood awkwardly beside the table, which did not look as if it would support his weight. He wondered if they had some kind of hidden camera in the little room. There was no two-way mirror, no window, but just four bare walls, a recessed light in the ceiling, and the table. Riley wondered why the police chief had singled him out. A few had escaped, but they must have arrested twenty or thirty others at the drug store. Out of so many, why come for him first? And why the chief, in person? Why not let some detective or policeman conduct the interrogations? Riley waited. He began to wonder if this was supposed to make him nervous, the writing and the waiting. But why would they want to make him nervous? Riley's legs grew tired so he sat back on the floor. Almost immediately the door opened and the chief entered again. This time the tall man held a brown paper bag.

"Sorry to be gone so long," he said. "Got a lot to deal with, what with all you fellas here."

Riley looked up at him, tucking his long hair back behind an ear. "Do I need a lawyer?"

"What ya want a lawyer for?"

"It seems like there's something going on."

"Naw. Just clearin' up the paperwork. Ya know how it is."

"Really?"

"Sure. Fact, I got your stuff right here. Stuff they took out of your pockets when we processed ya." He put the paper bag on the table.

"So I can go?"

"In a minute. First tell me about this." He opened the bag and stuck a hand inside, feeling around as if in search of something.

"Let's see . . . where is that pretty little thing?" He pulled out a plastic bag, small and transparent, and held it up. When Riley squinted, the man came closer to hold the bag right before Riley's eyes. Riley stared at a string of tiny dark brown beads and small beige tubes and a little cross, primitively carved but elevated above the commonplace by a delicate golden inlay. In that barren room, with the light so strong and the policeman playing games the way he was, after a sleepless night on a metal chair and nearly getting killed at Henry's Drug Store, Riley did not recognize the cross at first, but the chief was patient and continued dangling the bag ten inches from his nose until eventually Riley remembered.

Without thinking he asked, "Where did you get that?"

"So ya recognize it?"

Riley thought of sitting under a tin roof as the ceaseless rain beat a loud staccato rhythm overhead. He saw a block of wood and a penknife in his hands, and remembered the peacefulness of that Sabbath day, whittling bit by bit, all alone below the open shed as the rain came down but did not touch him, the wall of jungle at the far side of the airstrip nearly lost beyond the blue-gray downpour. He remembered being filled with love as he fashioned the humble birthday gift for her, many years ago. He remembered cutting a pair of parallel grooves into the face of the small cross and carefully pressing the gold foil into the grooves with the blunt back of the knife, the foil he had saved from a box of chocolates purchased in a Brazilian village. He remembered the taste of chocolate, and now, standing in the jail, Riley remembered the much more recent taste of science on his fingertip and the way the two tasted the same. He felt disoriented, looking at the cross in a hard and empty room in Dublin, Maine, with all the lost time rushing back into the present. He asked again, "Where did you get that?"

"Do ya recognize it or not?"

Riley Keep said nothing. The chief of police waited, staring at him. Riley did not care. He was not there. He was in the jungles of Brazil. Finally the chief said, "Look, we both know ya had it in your pocket, and we both know it's Willa's. I just saw it on her a few days ago. She got it hung up on somethin' in the kitchen at her shelter and I gave her a hand. I touched this thing myself."

Riley's eyes were on the floor. The old woman at the shelter? She had worn the cross, here, in Dublin? How was that possible?

There could only be one explanation.

The chief said, "Why don't ya just tell me how ya took it from her?"

Riley continued to look down, saying nothing. It should not cause him pain to know she gave his gift away. He should not care. His newly resurrected imagination understood her reasons—the multileveled symbolism—and his guilty conscience whispered she had every right.

"Where's Willa, Stanley?"

The question settled down into him slowly as his eyes searched the tiny pebbles of the terrazzo floor between his feet, clean and white and slightly out of focus. If this man asked where the old lady was, it meant she was missing. If this man claimed the necklace had been hers and claimed they found the necklace in his pocket, it meant he thought Riley caused her disappearance. Riley was glad he had been shocked to see the necklace, glad his shock had left him speechless. He decided to say nothing more to anyone.

The chief asked him many questions, eventually turning angry at Riley's silence, then left him alone in the little room. Riley had no way of knowing how much time went by after that. He sat against the wall at first, then lay down on his side and went to sleep. He had slept in harder places.

He awoke when someone tapped the bottom of his shoe. Opening his eyes he saw a uniformed policeman standing over him. "Get up," said the policeman. "You're free to go."

The policeman led him down the hallway, past others still restrained in chairs on either side. The policeman stood him by a tall counter in the front room of the station and poured the contents of a paper sack before him and watched dull-eyed as Riley replaced the meager contents of his pockets: a plastic-wrapped peppermint, a nail clipper, and a thin roll of paper money, the pay he had received so far from Henry. Also, the folded note he had stolen from the church collection envelope. For some reason they had not asked him about that. Maybe they thought the notations on it were pure gibberish. Maybe they were right. The only thing they did not return was the necklace with the cross. Of course he did not ask for it. He would not have asked for it even if there had been no danger in the request. He had long since given it away, and did not want it back.

On the other side of the counter stood Henry in his usual plaid flannel shirt and down-filled vest. With him was a very pale, gray, tall and skinny man in a putty-colored trench coat and a plain gray suit, who reminded Riley of someone he could not quite recall.

Henry said, "Hi ya, Stanley. Doin' all right?"

"Ayuh."

"Glad to hear it. You wanna ride?"

"You're the one who got me out?"

"Ayuh."

"Aren't you mad at me?"

"Way I heard it, this wasn't your fault. Right?"

"No, it wasn't my fault."

"So, you wanna ride?"

Throughout this exchange the tall and skinny man had not looked at Riley. Now he led the way outside the station, through a glass door and into the frigid late November air. Riley followed through the cold along a walkway around the side of the tall brick building. A hillside dressed in deep green spruce rose beyond the level parking lot in back. Riley raised his eyes to see a pair of sea gulls hovering in the onshore winter wind. He wished he had a coat. He had not been wearing one when they dragged him from the shelter. The pale man got behind the wheel of a white Mercedes Benz. Henry got in the front passenger seat. Riley got into the back. A man and woman ran up to the side of the car. The woman tapped on Riley's window. She was wicked good-looking. He touched a button and the glass slid down a few inches.

"Stanley Livingston?" asked the woman breathlessly.

Riley did not answer. The man behind her had a camera on his shoulder with its lens pointed straight at him. Riley looked into the lens and blinked.

The woman asked, "Are you the man who has a cure for alcoholism?"

"I don't have it anymore," said Riley. "I gave it all away."

"So it's true? You did have a cure?"

"Uh, Stanley?" Henry looked back over his shoulder. "Pretty cold out there. Maybe you should roll up the window."

Riley did as he was told. The woman outside kept on speaking to him. She raised her voice. She seemed almost angry.

"Where to, Pastor?" asked the pale man in the putty overcoat.

"The shelter, I guess. Right, Stanley?"

The very thought made Riley's stomach roil, but he said, "Okay."

"Uh, I forgot to make the introductions. Stanley, this here's Bill Hightower. He's a volunteer at our church. A lawyer too. Thought it might be good to have him along. Bill, this is Stanley."

"Hello," said the gray man at the wheel.

The even hum of the car's excellent heater and its faultless suspension blocked all external noise as they glided through the town. Riley saw the homeless everywhere: loitering in recessed doorways, behind O'Malley's convenience store, near gas pumps, and curbside at every stoplight. It was as if all the summer visitors had returned without their cars or kids or money. Riley watched them through the fifty-thousand-dollar window as though he were watching television. Most of them ignored the passing Mercedes the way an actor might ignore the camera, but a few refused to maintain distance, staring back at Riley. Some of their stares were empty; some were greedy. Gazing through the tinted glass, Riley was one of them and he was not. He had been cured, and he had not. He had somehow become someone in between.

How long had he been back in Dublin? A week? Two? In that

short time it seemed to Riley Keep the homeless must have doubled in the streets. It might have been a trick of his unpracticed imagination, but he believed Henry saw the increase too. There was a sadness in the preacher's profile as he stared out his own window. Or maybe the man was only thinking of the damage done to his store. With mournful eyes on the indigent people out beyond the Mercedes Benz, Henry said, "What they're sayin' 'bout you, healing alcoholics . . . anything to that, Stanley?"

Riley felt this man deserved the truth. But as he opened his mouth he remembered his sobriety had been stolen from this man's church, and with that memory came a sudden recognition of the pale one driving, the usher who had seen Riley swill Communion wine as if it were mere alcohol, and with righteous indignation thrown him out onto the street.

"No," said Riley. "I can't heal anybody."

They turned a corner and glided to a stop across the street from the shelter. Several strands of yellow tape barred the front door. A police patrol car sat at the curb and a man in uniform loitered on the nearby sidewalk.

"Huh," said Henry. "Look at that. Hang on a minute, fellas. I'll go see what's goin' on."

Riley watched as the preacher/pharmacist crossed the street and approached the policeman. They shook hands. Henry said something. The policeman said something back. The man behind the wheel of the Mercedes Benz said nothing. Riley said nothing. A pair of ragged men came wandering along the sidewalk. As they approached the Mercedes, one leaned down next to the driver's closed window.

"Hey, mister," called the homeless man, tapping on the glass. "Can you spare some change?"

The pale man at the wheel looked away and Riley heard his answer in the loud click of all four car doors locking at once. Shivering, the homeless man bent to peer in the back window at Riley.

"'Scuse me, sir, can you . . . Hey, ain't you that guy?"

In unconscious imitation of the church usher, Riley turned away, stroking his long beard as he watched Henry and the policeman at the shelter across the street. Outside, he heard the man call to his companion, "Ain't this that guy?" Riley remembered how it was to be lifted from the ground and carried off against his will. His palms began to sweat in the car's dry heat. He refused to acknowledge their existence as the other homeless man said, "Yeah, that's him!" and they both began tapping on the widow. "Hey, mister! We need help! We come all the way from Mobile to get cured! Come on, mister! Won't you help us out?"

Across the street Henry and the cop shook hands again, and the preacher came back toward the car. The homeless men began to beat their palms on the glass. Riley flinched at every blow, thinking of his utter helplessness with all those hands on him, some lifting him up, some pressing him down to murder. Riley wished he was back in the harsh safety of the jail.

The policeman across the street finally noticed the unruly men and strode toward the white Mercedes, a few steps behind Henry. At the sight of his approach the men cursed Riley and hurried away. Hightower unlocked his door, and the preacher slipped into the passenger seat, bringing a gust of icy air along with him. He said, "Man, that's bad."

"What?" asked Bill Hightower.

"Willa's gone."

"Good riddance," said the gray man at the wheel. "Now maybe we can do something about all these bums."

"No, seriously, it's bad." Nodding toward the policeman, Henry said, "Sammy said there's a lot of blood and her stuff is still up in her room." Riley sat in silence on the leather seat, thinking about the woman trying to stop them, standing up for him, and then Henry said, "You mind givin' me and Stanley a lift to my place?"

"How come?" asked Hightower.

"Well, it's a ways to walk."

"I mean how come you want to take him there?"

"The shelter's closed. He's gotta have someplace warm to sleep."

"We don't know him. We don't know a thing about him, except he doesn't mind spoiling Communion."

Watching out the rear window Riley saw the two homeless men accost three others half a block away. The five of them turned as one to stare at the Mercedes. Wiping sweating palms upon his threadbare trousers, Riley would have given anything to avoid walking through the streets of Dublin in broad daylight.

"Come on, Bill," said the pastor. "You gonna give us a ride or not?"

To Riley's great relief, the man started the nearly silent engine of the car.

Five minutes later they rolled to a stop in front of a small Cape Cod style house on the hill above downtown. Henry got out. Riley did not notice they had stopped. With his heartbeat slowed to normal he lingered in the back seat, lost in contemplation of debauched Communions and stolen tithes. He started when Henry tapped on the glass beside him, certain for an instant that the ghosts had come for him again. But he need not have worried. Before Riley could respond the pale man at the wheel stepped on the gas and drove away. In the back seat Riley turned to look through the rear window at Henry, who stood staring after them, his mouth open in surprise. With his eyes still toward the rear, Riley said, "What are you doing?"

"Giving you a ride," replied Bill Hightower.

Riley tried to think of ways to make him stop, but everything would lead to violence and he was sick of that. Perhaps an apology.

"I'm sorry about Communion."

"You should be."

The man followed the winding lane below the ridge of the hill overlooking Dublin and the harbor below, past Bowditch College and up a short half block and onto Route 1, turning right, down east. Three miles along the highway Hightower turned left onto a narrow blacktop road, and the big car ascended through dense woods, gliding effortlessly below the shadowed canopies of pine and spruce and hemlock, past a hulking lichen-covered granite outcropping and into a grove of stark-white naked birches. Now and then they passed the brown and wilted remnants of a fern dell. A little stream appeared along the right and came and went beyond the trees as the car rolled farther inland. Ice had not yet suspended the trickle's merry downhill dance. At a gentle curve they came to a farm, the white clapboard house and barn connected by a long room with a side porch, with smoke curling skyward from its brick chimney, and two silos in the back with metal hoops around their middles like a pair of giant barrels. As the Mercedes rolled past the fallow fields beside the farmhouse Riley suddenly remembered the name of the road, Green's End, named for the family that had lived there since the eighteenth century. He began to look ahead with interest. Soon they would come to a turnout where he and his sweetheart had sometimes sought privacy during their high-school courtship. He smiled to think of foggy windows and passionate kisses and long, earnest conversations about everything beneath the sun. The Mercedes rolled right past it, with Riley looking back now at the spot that held such happy memories, then the turnout was lost behind them as the car went on for what must have been another twenty miles, until finally the gray and tall and skinny man slowed and stopped at an intersection with another road, which was somewhat wider than Green's End and had gravel shoulders.

"Do you have any money?" asked the man. He did not bother looking back at Riley.

"A little."

Hightower shifted in his seat, reaching for his hip pocket. He removed his wallet and counted out five twenty-dollar bills, then turned to pass them back to Riley. "Here's a hundred. You're a good thirty miles from Dublin, but about ten miles that way, there's Liberty. They have a bus stop at the Shamrock station. That's enough money to get you clear to Florida. Now you listen to me. I know some guys who would have taken care of you a different way for half that much. I didn't have to be this nice, understand? Get out of my car."

Riley opened the door and stepped into the shadow of the woods. It was wicked cold without his coat. He shoved his hands into the pockets of his trousers and heard the lonely rushing sound of wind high in the pines. The Mercedes pulled up onto the crossroad, made a U-turn and came back to pause near Riley, who stood just off the asphalt on a soft bed of rust-colored needles. The pale gray man spoke through his open window, saying, "Don't come back," and then he sped away.

The mocking caws of crows pierced Riley's thoughts as he watched the taillights disappear around the first bend in the shadowed wood. He turned to stare up the other road. Ten miles to Liberty. Three hours' walk, maybe two and a half if he hustled. He could be there before dark, buy a little food and a ticket south, stay warm and dry on the bus until he felt like getting off. He thought about the reason he had come home to Maine. He was sober now. Brice was beyond hope. What more could he want?

His fingers wrapped around the money in one pocket and the formula for the cure in the other. There in the north woods with only crows for company Riley thought about his ex-wife and child. He thought about Brice with his own fingers wrapped around an empty plastic bottle of rubbing alcohol. He thought about a little wooden cross with golden insets, carved by another man in another life in another land. He thought of that old woman's blood and all her things still up there in her room and all the questions they had asked in jail and all those ghostly hands lifting him below the stars, and he shivered in the cold and thought again about the reason he had come back to Maine, and then he set out walking.

12

The Massachusetts Bay Transportation Authority bus pulled to the curb with squealing brakes. The door slid open and Willa Newdale stepped down to the sidewalk, picking her way around a stinking heap of plastic garbage sacks. Some kind of animal had been at the litter around the bottom edges of the pile, ripping through the plastic to drag out cans, soiled cardboard containers, and chicken bones. Ignoring this, Willa glanced at a small piece of paper in her hand, checking the Boston address written there against the numbers on the nearby buildings, hoping she had hit upon a strategy they would not expect. Although her hair was shorter and the gray was now coal black, Willa knew a professional could penetrate her pitiful disguise with a glance. Survival lay in unpredictability. As she had so many times before, she had to find a place that would not cross their minds.

She had escaped from Dublin with very little: a simple denim coat, white cotton shirt and blue jeans, and the items in the bulky purse she carried with the strap secure across her chest. She clutched the piece of paper in her left fist. An oblong stain of red marred the bandage on her forehead. She walked with a slight limp, and it caused her pain to breathe, but she refused to let it slow her down. She knew it was unwise for a woman to walk alone in that neighborhood, especially a white woman, with the sun already fallen well below the clapboard buildings on the west side of the road, throwing deeper shadows on a narrow street where buildings stood too close to let the sunlight ever fully reach the ground.

As if in confirmation of the danger, Willa heard someone emerge from an alley and fall into step behind her. She gave a single backward glance and took in a pair of teenaged boys, their baggy trousers low around their hips, their jackets open to reveal the top few inches of their underwear. Both wore Red Sox caps on closely shaven heads, one cap low with the bill cocked sharply to the right, the other high in back with the bill pointed toward the pink and turquoise slice of sky above the street. The dark skin of their necks revealed the uppermost extremities of even darker patterns, etched there permanently with needle and ink. The shorter of the two had one black teardrop tattooed just below each eye. All of this she absorbed with that single glance. She had learned well in the jungle.

Willa did not let them know she realized they were enemies. She did not let them see her fear in any way. She pretended to ignore them, searching the facade of every building, checking the scrap of paper in her hand now and then as if she did not trust her memory.

Ahead, a darkened streetlight flickered and then came fully on to cast a yellow circle on the sidewalk. She passed through this cone of light, then back into the gloaming beyond. She heard the teenaged boys pass through it right behind her. "What you got in that big bag, lady?" called one of the boys. The other one laughed and said, "Big bag lady." She did not turn or pause or move any faster; she simply kept on walking. "Hey, big bag lady," called the boy again, "you got somethin' for us there?"

There really was no need for her constant checking of the number on the piece of paper, no problem with her memory at all. On the contrary, the boys' heckling upon her heels brought back images she longed to forget, the taunts of a little girl's tormentors and the girl herself, dark of skin like these two boys behind her but much younger, and completely innocent. She should be thinking of the boys, preparing herself, but sometimes she could not control these memories, this terror from her past. She could not stop the image of her colleague rising to the little girl's defense, only to be beaten to the ground. She could not help comparing the tears on the little girl's broad cheeks to the tattooed mockeries of grief upon the boy behind her now. She saw the yellow cords that bound the girl and remembered her own shameful ineffectiveness, remembered aching to come to her defense but sitting like a spectator, crippled by the sight of the doctor bleeding on the soil. She remembered all the other blood that came soon after. The memory was strong enough to take her over, even now.

Willa heard the two boys picking up their pace. For the first time it occurred to her they might not be what they appeared; they might have been sent specifically for her. Willa's hand began to tremble. She slipped it in her purse.

They caught up with her, one on either side. One laid a hand upon her purse. Instantly she yanked it away and took one step back. Unprepared for the speed of her reaction, both boys took another step forward. She felt a flood of relief. These were not professionals. They were simply muggers.

By the time they turned to face her, she had removed the little automatic from her purse. The gun shook as she pointed it in their direction, yet she managed to speak steadily. "You fellas see this bandage on my head?"

Neither said a word. Their eyes were wide and focused on the vacillation of her weapon.

"I have a real bad headache and I am not in a mood to put up with your nonsense. Understand?" When both boys remained silent she said, "Do you understand me or do you not?"

"Yes'um," mumbled one of the teenagers.

Willa paused, calming just a little as she realized she could handle this, considering them abstractly. "Just look at the two of ya. Supposed to be a couple of tough guys, I imagine. Chasing after little old ladies' purses with your pants falling down. Can't even wear a ball cap like a proper man. You embarrass yourselves. Straighten up those caps. Go on! Have you no dignity at all?" She covered them with the small gun as the boys rearranged the caps on their heads, shifting the bills to more normal positions. "Pull up your pants while you're at it," she said, the automatic firmer in her grasp as it shifted back and forth from boy to boy. She watched their eyes, wide and white against the darkness of their skin, as they followed the movement of the barrel, each of them forced to keep one hand on the front of his trousers to hold them up. She thought about their mothers, wondering if they had given up, or ever cared. She thought of all the walking dead that she had known in her two years at the shelter, and a jungle clearing filled with dark-skinned bodies, and she knew these boys, like all the others, were most likely doomed. She pitied them. She said, "Oh, go on home before I shoot the both of you just to teach some manners. Go on. Get."

Hands at the waistbands of their trousers, the boys began to edge away. After three backward steps they turned and ran. Willa watched them go and sighed. Yet her actions had restored her flagging courage. Looking for all the world as if nothing unusual had happened, she replaced the weapon in the bulky purse and resumed her walk, searching the facades along the way.

Half a block along she reached a door and stopped. Above the door a hand-painted sign read, *Sisters of Mercy Home for Troubled Women.* Surely they would not think to find a woman who had run one homeless shelter among the homeless population of another. Willa stared up and down the street. Satisfied no one was watching, she reached for the door handle. She paused. Her hand was shaking again. She felt a rush of anger. She should be stronger. But then, that had been the problem all along.

13

The eastern sky blushed with dawn's first glow as Hope emerged from the side door of her house wearing a fur hat, flannel robe, and tall black rubber galoshes. Drawing the robe tighter against the cold, she hurried along the gravel driveway toward the street where her copy of the *Bangor Daily News* lay perilously close to an ice-fringed puddle. She bent to pick it up and, standing, saw a man step from the darkness of the tree line just across the road. Her heartbeat doubled in the time it took to back up two paces toward her house. Clutching the newspaper to her chest, Hope's mind raced to thoughts of Steve's report yesterday: Willa gone missing and the awful riot at poor Henry's store and nearly thirty people in the jail. She remembered Steve's belief that some of these people from away were bound to be hardened criminals, his concern that Willa had been murdered, his prediction that someone else would get hurt sooner or later. She asked for God's protection. Then she remembered her daughter still asleep inside the house and revised her prayer, thinking, better me than her.

The silhouetted man across the street came slowly closer through the darkness.

She backed farther up her driveway, afraid to turn and run.

"Hello, Hope."

She stopped. She processed the voice, and knew it, and felt

release from one kind of dread even as another kind rushed in.

"Hello, Riley."

They stood that way a moment—him in the middle of the street, her in the middle of the driveway, both at a loss for words. Then she turned abruptly, striding toward the house with gravel crunching under her galoshes. Behind her, Riley did not move. After Hope had taken several steps she called, "Come on," but she did not pause to see if he would follow.

Inside, she put the newspaper on the scarred pine kitchen table. She took a mug down from a cupboard. She was pouring him a cup of coffee and trying not to spill it when he finally stepped in, hesitantly, through the mudroom off the driveway. She said, "Still take a lot of sugar?"

"Ayuh."

She stirred it into the coffee and turned to look at him, rage and pity vying for control. Rage died without a whimper at her first clear view of him, a stranger standing in her kitchen's incandescent light, much older than her memories, emaciated, filthy, shivering from the cold. He peered out cautiously from behind his bushy hair and beard, just an upper sliver of his face revealed, as if he wore a mask. If she had not heard his voice, she would not have known him. But she had heard him speak her name, and now there seemed to be two people standing there: this shaggy old drunk come in trembling off the street, and the beautiful young man whom she had married nearly twenty years ago. Hope crossed the kitchen and put the steaming mug into his shaking hands. "Take a seat, Riley. I'll go get a blanket."

Moving with a strange hint of reluctance, he did as he was told.

Hope walked to the linen closet in the hall as if dreaming, removed a fleece blanket, and bunched her fists within it. She shut her eyes and stood motionless.

Through the darkness just behind her eyelids Hope saw the birth pains of that dead man in her kitchen, a clearing filled with bloated, stinking corpses where abundant life had been, and Riley fallen to his knees in supplication to his grief, a young and naïve Riley giving birth to doubt and cynicism then and there, shaking both his fists at heaven in the midst of awful labor, his lamentation's long assault upon her ears as clear as yesterday.

Hope opened her eyes again and wiped them with a corner of the blanket and took it to the kitchen and draped the thing around his shoulders. Riley continued to shiver as she topped off her own cup of coffee and sat down opposite him. They both took a sip. She swallowed. "You look awful."

"I walked all night to get here."

"How come?" Knowing he was here for money, remembering how it had been toward the end, when money was the only mutually acknowledged connection left between them. Knowing she must steel herself to say no.

But of course he was too smart to ask so soon. "Where's Bree?"

"Asleep."

He nodded, his red-rimmed eyes wandering around the room from behind his shaggy mask, taking in everything but Hope. "I saw her a few days ago."

"Where?"

He started to answer, then seemed to think better of it. Instead he said, "She looks beautiful."

"So you've been here a few days?" Catching him in lies already.

"Yes."

"I thought you said you walked all night to get here."

"I . . . uh." He took a sip from the mug. "It's complicated."

Hope watched him. He had yet to look at her directly. She said, "I'm sorry about Brice."

He did not seem surprised she knew. He nodded, looking down.

"Did you go to his funeral?" Setting a trap for him, knowing the answer, knowing because she herself had been there, all alone at the potter's field except for the sparrows and impatient gravedigger.

"I, uh, I was too drunk."

Surprised, she set her coffee down and stared. It was not like the man she remembered to confess to such a thing. Before he left, they had not even been able to agree he was an alcoholic.

He said, "But I'm not drinking anymore."

He spoke these last words in a rush and for the first time looked into her eyes. There was a challenge in his gaze, a strange intensity. With a wisdom born of hard experience, Hope saw he was indeed sober at that moment, and saw he was nonetheless still broken and would therefore drink again as soon as possible. She failed to keep sarcasm from her voice. "Congratulations."

He looked away.

"I don't have any spare cash, Riley. My new job doesn't pay much."

"I heard you're the mayor now."

"Yes."

She saw admiration in his eyes, as he said, "That's really something."

"Thank you. But I still can't spare you anything."

He seemed to shrink beneath her words. "That's okay. I have some money."

"You do?"

"I just ..." He paused, the blanket still around his shoulders, looking gaunt and weak. "I just wanted to see you. And Bree." He rose unsteadily and shrugged off the blanket, draped it over the back of the kitchen chair and stood there swaying slightly. "Maybe ... around town."

"Sure," she said, still sitting.

He turned, took one step toward the mudroom and stopped, his back to her. He wavered, then fainted dead away.

Hope was kneeling at his side when Bree entered the room a minute later, her shiny black hair skewed from her pillow. Rubbing sleep from almond eyes, the girl opened the refrigerator, unaware of Riley and Hope on the floor beyond the table until Hope said, "Honey, I need your help over here."

Bree turned and took one look and dropped the orange juice carton to the floor. "Who is that?"

"Help me get him to the sofa."

"Who *is* that?"

"Come over here and help me, honey."

Together they were barely able to lift the unconscious man and drag him out into the living room and lay him on the sofa. Hope went back to the kitchen to get the blanket. When she returned to the sofa she saw her daughter standing there, short and broad and brown and sturdy, gazing down at Riley's form. Bree said, "Is that Daddy?"

Hope leaned across the back of the sofa and spread the blanket over him.

Bree said, "Is he drunk?"

"I don't think so."

"What's the matter with him?"

"I don't know."

"Why is he here?"

"I don't know."

"I don't want him here."

Hope thought of all the Christian things she ought to say, words of kindness and forgiveness—*"whatever you do to one of the least of these you also do to me"*—yet she would not lie to Bree. She said, "Me either."

They stared down on him together. In the quiet of the little house that she and Riley bought together, Hope heard her grandmother's clock ticking loudly and the refrigerator compressor whirring. Then Riley Keep began to snore, a sound she remembered well, and in it she heard echoes of a different Riley—or this same one in the infancy of his addiction—curled in upon himself on the dirt beneath his hammock, snoring just like this and reeking with the awful stench of vomit and that homemade booze The People concocted. Riley, who had never touched a drop before, a minister of God, a missionary, drunk for fourteen days. The first time.

Distant voices brought her to the present. Hope crossed the living room in her black rubber galoshes and parted the curtains beside the Christmas tree at the front window to peer out. The sun had nearly risen back behind the tree line. She saw a gang of strangers clearly as they passed by her front yard, ten or twelve of them at least, walking down the middle of the street with big sticks in their hands. One of the men turned to meet her eyes. She pulled her robe close around herself and backed away from the window, letting the curtain fall back into place. Should she call the police? What would she tell them? Men were walking past her home? She did not know them but they were too dirty? Too many? Too poor? She turned back toward the wasted man who had surrendered to their cause so long ago.

"You need to get him outta here," said their daughter.

"Let's wait to see what's wrong, honey."

"What's wrong? He's a *drunk.*"

"Yeah, but he's not drunk right now."

"How do you know that?"

Hope sighed. "I know."

"But—"

"Go get ready for school."

"You're just gonna *leave* him there?"

"Let's just get dressed, honey. Then we'll figure out what to do."

Riley's snoring did not pause, even when Hope felt his forehead to satisfy herself that he had no fever. He rumbled in the background as she dressed and prepared breakfast for her daughter. Bree ate sullenly and said little, but that was not unusual. Left to her own thoughts, Hope tried to imagine what it must be like to be so tired you fell asleep while standing and did not awaken when you fell. If she had not seen it happen she would not have believed it possible.

The time came for them to leave for work and school. Hope tried to wake him, shaking his shoulder, calling his name, but he kept snoring. She decided to let him be and left by the side door through the mudroom with Bree. Halfway to her car Hope turned back. She reentered the kitchen and slipped the cooking sherry into her briefcase before walking out the door again.

All morning Hope kept thinking she had made a serious mistake. She endured three meetings in her town-hall office while wondering if he was emptying her house of valuables to pawn. She broke the speed limit driving home over lunch, only to find he had not moved a muscle. Even the rhythm of his snoring on the sofa had not changed.

Hope felt a little better in the afternoon, but still it bothered her to think he was in the house unsupervised. She cut her workday short and left for home at four-thirty, driving up Main below a series of banners dangling from the streetlights—snowflakes, gift-wrapped boxes, Santa, and a manger scene purchased from a company in Chicago after much debate with Jim Rylander, a town councilman and Unitarian who objected to the manger scene on the grounds it was divisive and unconstitutional. Hope sighed at the memory and turned from Main onto the street that climbed up to her house.

Minutes later, entering the living room she saw the blanket neatly folded on the sofa. Hope called Bree's name, and Riley's name, and got no answer. She hurried up the stairs to Bree's room and knocked on the door. Still no answer. Nervously she grasped the doorknob. To open it was a major breach of protocol that could infuriate her daughter, but Hope had to know. She inched the door open just enough to see Bree's broad little back across the room, swaying to the silent rhythm in her headphones as she typed on her computer. Relieved, Hope closed the door again. She stood in the stair hall listening. Was that the sound of water running? She entered her own bedroom. On the far side of it the bathroom door was closed. She called, "Riley, are you in there?"

"Ayuh. Be out in just a minute."

"Okay."

She stepped into her little walk-in closet to change out of her work clothes. Kicking off her shoes she pulled the door closed for privacy and found herself in total darkness. She had forgotten that the light went off automatically. She opened the door enough to turn the light back on, but that made her feel exposed when she got down to bra and panties, so she quickly put on the first things she saw: a pair of blue jeans, an old sweater, and her favorite worn-out moccasin slippers. Riley was still in the bathroom when she came out again. She went downstairs to linger nervously in the kitchen. She wiped the counters with a sponge. She checked the pantry and refrigerator for supper ingredients, though she knew exactly what was there. She had begun to sweep the floor when she finally heard the familiar squeaking of him walking down the stairs. She would have known that sound anywhere, even after all the time gone by.

Riley entered tentatively. Hope had to smile in spite of herself. He had shaved and done his best to cut his hair. His naked face was gaunt, and the dense shadow of his whiskers contrasted darkly with the unnatural paleness of his chin and cheeks, but he did look almost like himself again, like one of those men who didn't bother with their hair or clothes and did not even know that they were handsome.

He said, "There was a package of razors in the cabinet . . ."

"Okay."

"I cleaned up everything. You won't even be able to tell, except for the razor."

"It's okay, Riley."

His eyes searched the kitchen for a place to rest, looking everywhere except at her, just as he had that morning. The awkwardness was contagious. She found herself wiping down the counters again.

"Does my hair look all right?" He turned around to show her the back of his head, asking her opinion, making himself vulnerable. "I couldn't see what I was doing."

"You could use a touch-up by a proper barber, but it's better than it was."

"Really?"

"Sure."

"I'm sorry about . . ." He paused, as if searching for the words. "I don't remember falling asleep."

"It's okay."

"I wasn't drunk, I swear."

e last few years it was that he had
of course, himself. Yet he had not
ld accept charity from his own
the shame involved.

under tires outdoors, followed by
ents later a man entered from the
ed their work side-by-side at the
face the man uncertainly.
)ulder.

He turned toward Riley. "You're
to extend his hand. Riley took it,
, "We played a little pond hockey
on't remember. You were a couple

ylan Delaney?"

y day for twelve straight years."
," said Hope.

look at her is what I meant ta

and turned her attention back to
art constrict. Here was the proof
nunion moment when it occurred
pendent of his fantasies. Here was
an his height, but broader in the
kind eyes (curse him!) and a stal-
ouse without knocking caused no
tions. The fact that he made no
only underscored their intimate
irritating sensitivity to Riley's

wl of pasta on the table. She did

"I know it."

"I hadn't been to sleep in a real long time."

"Why not?" He seemed unwilling to answer. Still needlessly wiping the countertops she said, "It's none of my business."

"That's not it. It's just . . . I'm not sure you'll believe me."

"There's been a lot of lies, Riley."

"Ayuh."

Surprised at the simplicity of his confession as she had been surprised that morning when he admitted his drunkenness the day they buried Brice, Hope paused in her busywork to look at him. Somehow, his clean-shaven face and short hair made his dirty clothes look worse.

He said, "There are a lot of people after me."

"After you? What does that mean?"

"Some of them think I have something, or did something."

His vagueness annoyed her. "If you want to tell me, tell me. If you don't, don't. But please don't waste my time."

"I don't want to get you involved, is all."

"Fine."

"It's for your own good."

"Right. Just like when you left for my own good."

"You kicked me out."

"You left a long time before that!"

"I couldn't help it, Hope. I—"

"Couldn't help it? Oh, *please*. That's what you always say!"

He hung his head, saying only "Ayuh," again.

Suddenly she saw through his surprising confessions and uncharacteristic vulnerability, saw it for the passive aggression that it was. Enraged at her naiveté, Hope felt herself sucked back through time, trapped in the worst moments of her past, doomed to repeat them as she had so many times before. How could this have happened? After all the intervening sanity, how could she be standing here again? How could she be screaming these same things at him again? How many times was she supposed to endure this? Seventy times seven was too much. Hope scrubbed the kitchen counter furiously, teeth clenched tightly against the same old arguments and accusations, the hopeless words she knew would lead to nothing. How many times had she stood here in this very kitchen having this exact conversation? She would not let him drag her back into the powerlessness of all that. Faster and faster the sponge swirled on the counter, until at last she burst out with a cry of rage and threw it at the sink.

"I'm sorry," said the man behind her. "I'll go." It was what he had always said, and she had always let him go, knowing he would return in a few days, knowing he could not do without her, until that last time when he had gone for three long years.

She heard the soft sound of his footsteps as he crossed the kitchen and remembered the next part of this disgusting little drama, the infuriating guilt that she would feel after he left, the acid irony of a senseless shame that would surely hound her days until his return. She felt helpless in the hands of her own history. She had to do something, take control somehow.

Turning, she snapped, "Riley!"

He stopped.

She said, "You wait right there," and she left him standing as she charged back up the stairs to her room. Entering her little walk-in closet she selected a heavy cotton shirt and corduroy trousers from a wide assortment of men's clothing hanging on a rod behind the door. She stooped to pick up a pair of leather shoes and crossed the bedroom to an antique bureau where she found a pair of men's underwear and a tee shirt and a thick pair of men's black nylon socks in the upper drawer. All of this she laid out on the bed. Then she went back down to turn the other cheek right then and there, even if it killed her.

case. If he had learned anything
no right to judge anyone, except
fallen so completely that he c
replacement without awareness

Riley heard gravel crunchin
the slamming of a car door. Mo
mudroom. Hope and Bree conti
kitchen counter while Riley rose

"Hi ya," said Hope over her

"Hi yourself," replied the m
Riley, right?" The man came clo
trying to place him. The man s
way back when, but it's okay if
of years ahead of me in school.'

Riley searched his memory.

"Ayuh. That's me."

"You were in Hope's grade

"Ayuh. Had ta look at her

"You best watch it, mister

Bree stifled an unseemly g

Dylan Delaney smiled. "C
say."

Hope rolled her gorgeous
the work at hand. Riley felt
he had feared ever since that
to him his ex-family might be
the tangible cost of his crime
shoulders and deeply tanned,
wart jaw, whose entrance to
interruption in the supper p
effort to greet Hope with
familiarity. Worse, it show
uncomfortable position.

Bree approached to plac

"I know it."

"I hadn't been to sleep in a real long time."

"Why not?" He seemed unwilling to answer. Still needlessly wiping the countertops she said, "It's none of my business."

"That's not it. It's just . . . I'm not sure you'll believe me."

"There's been a lot of lies, Riley."

"Ayuh."

Surprised at the simplicity of his confession as she had been surprised that morning when he admitted his drunkenness the day they buried Brice, Hope paused in her busywork to look at him. Somehow, his clean-shaven face and short hair made his dirty clothes look worse.

He said, "There are a lot of people after me."

"After you? What does that mean?"

"Some of them think I have something, or did something."

His vagueness annoyed her. "If you want to tell me, tell me. If you don't, don't. But please don't waste my time."

"I don't want to get you involved, is all."

"Fine."

"It's for your own good."

"Right. Just like when you left for my own good."

"You kicked me out."

"You left a long time before that!"

"I couldn't help it, Hope. I—"

"Couldn't help it? Oh, *please*. That's what you always say!"

He hung his head, saying only "Ayuh," again.

Suddenly she saw through his surprising confessions and uncharacteristic vulnerability, saw it for the passive aggression that it was. Enraged at her naiveté, Hope felt herself sucked back through time, trapped in the worst moments of her past, doomed to repeat them as she had so many times before. How could this have happened? After all the intervening sanity, how could she be standing here again? How could she be screaming these same things at him again? How many times was she supposed to endure this? Seventy times seven was too much. Hope scrubbed the kitchen counter furiously, teeth clenched tightly against the same old arguments and accusations, the hopeless words she knew would lead to nothing. How many times had she stood here in this very kitchen having this exact conversation? She would not let him drag her back into the powerlessness of all that. Faster and faster the sponge swirled on the counter, until at last she burst out with a cry of rage and threw it at the sink.

"I'm sorry," said the man behind her. "I'll go." It was what he had always said, and she had always let him go, knowing he would return in a few days, knowing he could not do without her, until that last time when he had gone for three long years.

She heard the soft sound of his footsteps as he crossed the kitchen and remembered the next part of this disgusting little drama, the infuriating guilt that she would feel after he left, the acid irony of a senseless shame that would surely hound her days until his return. She felt helpless in the hands of her own history. She had to do something, take control somehow.

Turning, she snapped, "Riley!"

He stopped.

She said, "You wait right there," and she left him standing as she charged back up the stairs to her room. Entering her little walk-in closet she selected a heavy cotton shirt and corduroy trousers from a wide assortment of men's clothing hanging on a rod behind the door. She stooped to pick up a pair of leather shoes and crossed the bedroom to an antique bureau where she found a pair of men's underwear and a tee shirt and a thick pair of men's black nylon socks in the upper drawer. All of this she laid out on the bed. Then she went back down to turn the other cheek right then and there, even if it killed her.

14

The shower water had been lukewarm, yet it felt good to be clean and well-groomed as Riley Keep sat at the kitchen table watching Hope and Bree prepare supper. The two of them moved around the kitchen with an easy grace, each accomplishing necessary tasks without prompting, each aware of the other's next move and ready to support it or make space for it without comment. Hope, stepping aside from the silverware drawer at the light touch of their daughter's hand upon her back; Bree, opening a cupboard to remove the boiling pot at the sight of the box of pasta in Hope's hand; the two of them a perfect team, the two of them, alone.

Underneath the kitchen table, Riley's hands rested on his knees. He felt the ridges of the corduroy trousers and wondered again whose clothes they were. He should not have been surprised at this, and yet he was. Hope had always been a woman of strong faith, a righteous woman, ready to follow without question when the Lord led them to Brazil, but the presence of an entire man's outfit here at Hope's house could only mean that she had taken a lover. Riley's stomach churned at the thought. He felt the weight of these fine clothes pressing down upon him. He wished to shed them for the humble ones he had received at the shelter, but did not know how to say as much to her. The words that came to mind could easily seem unjust, as if he presumed to sit in judgment, and that was not the case. If he had learned anything the last few years it was that he had no right to judge anyone, except of course, himself. Yet he had not fallen so completely that he could accept charity from his own replacement without awareness of the shame involved.

Riley heard gravel crunching under tires outdoors, followed by the slamming of a car door. Moments later a man entered from the mudroom. Hope and Bree continued their work side-by-side at the kitchen counter while Riley rose to face the man uncertainly.

"Hi ya," said Hope over her shoulder.

"Hi yourself," replied the man. He turned toward Riley. "You're Riley, right?" The man came closer to extend his hand. Riley took it, trying to place him. The man said, "We played a little pond hockey way back when, but it's okay if ya don't remember. You were a couple of years ahead of me in school."

Riley searched his memory. "Dylan Delaney?"

"Ayuh. That's me."

"You were in Hope's grade."

"Ayuh. Had ta look at her every day for twelve straight years."

"You best watch it, mister man," said Hope.

Bree stifled an unseemly giggle.

Dylan Delaney smiled. "*Got* ta look at her is what I meant ta say."

Hope rolled her gorgeous eyes and turned her attention back to the work at hand. Riley felt his heart constrict. Here was the proof he had feared ever since that Communion moment when it occurred to him his ex-family might be independent of his fantasies. Here was the tangible cost of his crime, a man his height, but broader in the shoulders and deeply tanned, with kind eyes (curse him!) and a stalwart jaw, whose entrance to this house without knocking caused no interruption in the supper preparations. The fact that he made no effort to greet Hope with a kiss only underscored their intimate familiarity. Worse, it showed an irritating sensitivity to Riley's uncomfortable position.

Bree approached to place a bowl of pasta on the table. She did not look at Riley. "Hi ya, Vachee," said Dylan. "How was your day?"

Vachee, or "little girl" in the language of The People. Only Hope or Bree could have taught him that. So they had opened up the past to him. The best and worst of everything.

Bree answered, "Awful."

"Yeah? Mine too."

Bree returned to the counter. "How come?" Showing much more interest in the guy than she had shown in Riley.

"Same ol' same ol'."

"Bad catch again?"

"Fifty pounds."

Hope turned to face the man. "I'm sorry," she said.

If they were talking lobstering, Riley knew fifty pounds was a very poor catch indeed. One full trap alone could weigh more than that.

"Well, the day wasn't a total loss," said Dylan. "I got your water heater in the truck."

Bree clapped her hands. "Finally!"

"Maybe Riley could help you bring it in after supper," said Hope.

Dylan looked at Riley. "That'd be great."

Riley said, "Okay."

The meal was total misery. Hope and her lover kept up a steady chatter, with Bree smiling at the man's incessant teasing of her mother even as she studiously avoided any hint of a glance in Riley's direction. Riley tried to concentrate on the food, the best he had eaten in years, but the meal was wasted on him. He watched Bree's profile and remembered the birth-control pills she had bought at Henry's pharmacy. He was helpless before that memory just as he was helpless before the handsome man across the table, knowing what any decent father would do and knowing he was no decent father. Riley was conscious of the lives being lived before him, yet he was not really there. He was a departed spirit feasting at his own wake, back from the brink but still missing from himself. Though Riley had no urge to drink, no physical compulsion, even so he longed for the familiar hiding place he had always found before. But the path to that familiar place had been lost since his awakening in the Dublin alley. Since that resurrection, Riley had been helplessly exposed to everything.

"Some of the fellas down at the landing are saying it's this global warmin' thing." As Riley's attention refocused on the supper conversation, he realized they were discussing lobstering again. "It's changin' the Gulf Stream. Drivin' 'em out farther and down deeper than they ever went before. Some of the others have been sayin' Dublin's under some kinda curse, what with all these street people showin' up at the same time."

Hope said, "That's ridiculous."

"I know it. Pure superstition, is all. But ya hafta admit it's queer the way these street people started comin' in right when lobsters started goin' out. Awful bad luck all around."

Riley was acutely conscious that he was one of the street people this man viewed as a plague upon the town. It occurred to him that here was a chink in this man's armor. Hope was nothing if not kind, and would not abide a man who insulted a guest in her house. But then he remembered that he was clean-shaven and properly dressed now, so this man had no way of knowing he was part of Dublin's strange decline.

"Guess I shoulda stuck with lawyerin'," said Dylan.

Hope said, "Not much difference between lawyerin' and lobsterin' far as I can see. Either way you make your livin' off of bottom-feeders."

Dylan groaned. Bree giggled. Riley swallowed the food in his mouth and dared to speak. "You're a lawyer?"

Hope's lover turned to him with a generous smile. "Used to be. My pop always wanted us kids to get away from buggin'. Said seven generations runnin' traps was enough. Sent me over to Bowditch for a law degree."

Riley wanted to say "I used to teach at Bowditch," but knowing that meant less than nothing he said instead, "And you're a lobster-man now?"

"Ayuh. It's what I always wanted, so when Pop passed on I sold out to my partner and took over the Delaney ground."

"What do you mean, 'ground'?"

"It's our territory, I guess you'd say, where Delaneys have been trappin' lobsters since the seventeen hundreds."

Riley thought about such a heritage, the continuity of it, the steadfastness of it, the unbroken chain of trust passed down through generations. He tried to remember when he had lost the ability to take comfort in such things.

Hope said, "That's a long time."

"Ayuh. And it ends with me."

"Oh, Dylan, surely not."

"I can't keep buyin' diesel and makin' payments on the boat on fifty pounds a day. Gonna have to give it up sooner or later."

Bree stood all of a sudden, her chair's legs scraping loudly on the wide pine floor planks. Riley watched her leave the kitchen and longed to follow. After she was out of the room Hope said, "I think she's weary of bad news." Riley assumed she was talking about his troubles in addition to the poor lobster catch, but that thought was revealed for the twisted conceit it was when Hope continued, "You hear Sam decided to close the printshop?"

Dylan nodded. "Ayuh."

"And there's Simmons Chandlery and now Henry's store, and that's just this month. If it keeps up this way the whole downtown's gonna be shut by summer."

It was Dylan's turn to say, "Surely not."

"There's a critical mass you have to keep for a town to stay alive. We just barely had it; then I took over and we slid on down past the point of no return."

"Ya can't blame yourself for that."

"Who else should I blame? I'm in charge. It's my job to keep this town up and runnin'."

Hope sat staring at her plate. To Riley she suddenly seemed smaller. He could not bear to see her pain. He felt sick to see it, responsible for it, ashamed of it. He blurted out the words without thinking. "I'm sorry."

She looked up at him. An emotion he could not identify flashed in her eyes. Was it anger? Disappointment? She said, "It has nothing to do with you," and Riley knew he had taken too much upon himself again, and he felt ashamed of that as well.

After supper Riley went outside with Dylan to carry in the water heater. The lobsterman took the heavy end where the oil burner was and left Riley with the top end of the empty tank. Even so, Riley feared he would drop his burden as he went backward up the porch steps.

"Ya got it?" asked Dylan.

"Sure," said Riley.

Inside, when they got to the door at the top of the basement stairs, Dylan said, "Lemme go first," and Riley knew what he was doing: taking the steps backward even though his end was much heavier because he could see that Riley probably would not make it otherwise. At the bottom they crossed the basement and set the tank on the stone floor beside the old one.

"Ya ever change out one of these?" asked Dylan.

Riley said, "I replaced the kitchen faucet once." He remembered Hope coming home with the faucet from the hardware store, and the box sitting untouched on the floor for at least a month, and him finally shamed into installing it when he saw her under the sink trying to do it herself, and him forgetting to turn the water off, although the valves were right there in plain sight, and water going everywhere and Hope laughing and him getting mad instead of laughing with her.

"Maybe we can figure this out between the two of us, ya think?" said Dylan.

Riley wondered if the man was talking about plumbing. He thought, if I could figure it out, do you think you'd be standing here?

But he ended up handing tools to the lobsterman and watching silently as Hope's lover worked quickly and efficiently, and in less than fifteen minutes the old tank was drained and ready to move without a word spoken between them about Hope.

Riley could not help but ask, "So, things are bad in town?"

"Guess ya haven't been back long enough to see all the closed-up shops."

Riley had not noticed. "How come they're closing?"

"Lotta reasons. Bowditch shut down their engineerin' school, for one, so that cut back on the students in town. And they opened a new indoor mall over near Rockland. Lotta folks drivin' over there now for their shoppin'. And the last year or so we've had these street people showing up for some reason. Not that many at first, but lately it seems like they're everywhere. Scarin' people off, I'm tellin' ya."

"There must be something you can do."

"We could fix up town real nice like they did in Cambridge. New sidewalks and streetlights and a gazebo in the park, maybe build a pleasure-boat marina in the harbor. Stuff like that brings in the tourists and antique shops and whatnot. But there's no money for it, 'specially with all these businesses closin'."

"They can't blame Hope for that."

"They do anyway. You oughta hear the abuse she has ta take at town-hall meetin's."

As the two of them shifted the old tank out of the way and jockeyed the new one into position, Riley thought about this man here in Hope's house—Riley no longer thought of it as his house—coming in without knocking and installing water heaters and calling his daughter by her pet name. He thought about Hope, so much more beautiful than his intoxicated versions of her, shrinking at the supper table. He imagined her shrinking at the town-hall meetings. In his new sobriety, Riley felt the heavy burden of reality pressing down upon him, driving out illusions. He longed to offer comfort, but he had no right. He had been untrue to Hope and unfaithful to Bree, first with alcohol, then with his own shrunken version of them. His stolen temperance left no inner space to cower with an imitation family, but his drunken past left no place for him in their world of flesh and blood. How Riley longed to comfort them! If only he could do that, surely he could find relief from the relentless weight of shameful memories.

In that instant he heard his daughter scream. Without a thought for Dylan on the other end he dropped the water heater and charged up the stairs two at a time. The kitchen was empty. He ran through it to find Bree and Hope standing in the living room, their eyes on the television set.

"What's wrong?" he asked them, breathless.

They did not look his way. He asked a second time, and Hope waved a hand at him as if demanding silence. She then pointed at the television. Dylan appeared behind him, nursing his left hand. "Man," he said, "ya almost crushed my fingers."

"Sorry."

"Will you two please be quiet?" said Hope.

Riley and Dylan moved closer to the television. On the screen a female reporter faced the camera, saying, "Police are asking anyone with information about her whereabouts to come forward."

Dylan said, "Hey, that's Willa's shelter!"

Hope and Bree both said, "Shhhhh!"

The scene on the television cut to a tight shot of the back window of a white automobile. Someone peered out from the dark interior of the car. The man's face was hidden in the shadows beyond the tinted glass, but his silhouette revealed bushy long hair and a long beard. Suddenly Riley knew who it was.

The reporter's voice-over said, "Police say it's likely the suspect is in the Portland, Maine, area, since Willa Newdale's car was discovered abandoned in a poverty-stricken neighborhood of that city. The chief of Dublin's small police department revealed that they had the man in custody yesterday, but released him for lack of evidence. He gave police the name Stanley Livingston, which they believe is probably an alias. Reliable sources have informed us that the police here in Dublin failed to obtain the usual arrest photographs of the suspect, so this video footage may well be the only image available."

Riley had to will himself not to edge toward the door. He awaited accusations with a pounding heart, but as the footage of him faded, no one seemed to recognize the silhouetted image of the man in the shadowy back seat of Bill Hightower's Mercedes. Then on the screen came a face he knew from the shelter. The female reporter's voice-over continued. "In a bizarre twist, it seems the suspect in Ms. Newdale's disappearance is a local hero, at least to the homeless people of this small New England town."

The camera shifted to a man from the shelter, who said, "Uh, yeah, he healed me. I been a drunk as long as I can remember, but Stanley healed me, and a bunch of other people too."

The screen now showed a montage of homeless people gathered in small groups at various street corners and public places around Dublin. The woman spoke over the footage. "Officials estimate perhaps as many as one hundred homeless people have arrived here in Dublin, drawn by spreading rumors of a cure for alcoholism. Molly Henderson is one such person."

A woman with wild hair, bad teeth, but clear and piercing eyes stared directly into the camera. "I come last August. Heard about it in Oklahoma and hitched all the way up here. Took a couple of weeks after I got here, but one day I just knew I was cured. That's all. Just cured. And that was ... maybe mid-October? You have to understand, I used to drink anything I could get, but now I'm working at the bowling alley and they got a bar but I ain't had a drink since, I guess, more than a month? I lost everything to drinkin' and now I never even think about it, except to count my blessings."

The reporter now faced the camera and said, "We found over a dozen people in Dublin with similar stories. Some attribute their sobriety to Stanley Livingston, some don't seem to have any idea how or why. All of them, however, claim they have been freed from a habit that had driven them, quite literally, to life in the gutter. This is Julia Armstrong, reporting for CNN from Dublin, Maine."

The television screen next showed five well-dressed people behind a large curved desk in a studio, three men and two woman. One of the women said, "Fascinating story. What do you think, Ken?"

One of the men said, "Imagine if it's true. A cure for alcoholism. Imagine what that would be worth."

"And apparently a homeless man has the secret," said another man.

The female moderator said, "Makes you think about panhandlers a little differently, doesn't it?"

Everybody laughed.

The second woman said, "Seriously, what if one of the homeless people we pass on our way home tonight has the cure for alcoholism? What would that be worth?"

"Millions," said one of the men.

"Billions," said another.

The first woman turned toward the camera. "Obviously we'll be following this story very closely, but in other news tonight—"

Hope hit the mute button.

"Wow," said Bree. "We're on CNN."

Dylan said, "Do ya think that stuff about a cure for alcoholics could be true?"

"No," said Hope. "How could it be true?"

Riley, saying nothing, slipped his right hand into the pocket of the corduroy trousers borrowed from his ex-wife's lover. He wrapped his fingers around the folded slip of paper there. He had lost the note somehow, but he still had the paper with the formula. His mind drifted as the others spoke about the story—his story—and he thought about his hope to be a comfort to his ex-wife and daughter. Slowly, a plan began to form. When they were done talking Riley kept the hidden piece of paper firmly in his grasp all the way back down to the basement. Alone again with Dylan he said, "So, you're a lawyer?"

"Ayuh." Dylan stooped to lift the water heater.

"Do you know anything about patents?"

"A little."

They set the tank in its proper place. Hope's lover began working on the connections as Riley passed him tools. Riley had another question. "If someone wants to hire you, and they tell you something, you can't tell it to anybody else, right?"

"Ayuh, 'less there's intention to commit a crime."

"But except for that, lawyers can't talk about their client's secrets, right?"

"Be awful hard to give fair representation if we couldn't keep a confidence."

Five more minutes passed with Riley trying to decide. He had Hightower's hundred dollars in his pocket, and another couple of hundred he had earned working as Henry's stock boy. It might be enough for a start, especially since Dylan wasn't making any money lobstering. But what if things went wrong? Things always went wrong. In one instant he knew he should try, in the next he recognized his plan for the pathetic delusion it must surely be. He wavered between the preposterous and the possible as Hope's kindhearted lover finished the job, packed his tools, and began to climb the stairs. In five more seconds they would be with Riley's ex-wife and daughter again and it would be too late.

Still, Riley wavered. Of course this was nothing but an idiotic fantasy, the usual stuff of drunks and dreamers.

Yet underneath an overpass he had dreamed of miracles in Maine and lifted Brice upon his back and begun a journey that had led him to the cure.

Then again, Brice was dead. Things always went wrong.

Climbing the stairs behind Dylan, longing to save Hope as he had once longed to save Brice, Riley wavered. Terrified of unknown consequences yet terrified of missing this one chance, it was only in the final instant as Hope's lover put his hand upon the basement door that Riley Keep decided what to do.

15

When the reporter on the television said, "The chief of Dublin's small police department revealed that they had the man in custody yesterday, but released him ..." Chief Steven Novak stopped chewing. Staring at the indistinct image of the man in the car, he crushed the sandwich in his fist and listened with a growing sense of futility as the reporter continued. "... the police here in Dublin failed to obtain the usual arrest photographs of the suspect." At that, Chief Novak threw the remains of his Italian at the television with a curse, splattering the screen with dressing, lettuce, and salami. The woman had as good as told the entire country he was nothing but a bumpkin fooled by an alcoholic bum. Good for writing parking tickets, maybe, but not up to serious police work. The chief cursed again, more loudly.

Agnes Miller opened his office door. "You okay?"

He scowled at his assistant. "No, I ain't okay! Tell Dave to get in here!"

Moments later, as the chief picked up a tomato slice from the floor, a lanky man with thinning wheat-colored hair entered the office. Dave Henson's bushy moustache had always annoyed Steve Novak. A serious police officer did not wear a moustache, especially one that hid his lower lip. The chief looked at him. "I just heard 'em say we failed to get a photograph of that fella. Heard 'em say it on the national news! How'd they find that out?"

"I got no idea, Chief."

Steve tried to speak calmly. "It's one thing not to fire Willy for messin' up the memory or whatever he did with the camera. I understand the technology's kinda new and all, and everyone makes mistakes. But I want ya to find out who told the press about it, because I am absolutely gonna fire *that* person over *that*!"

"Okay."

"Okay *what*?"

"Okay, I'll try to find out who spilled the beans so you can fire 'em."

"We can't have people givin' information to the press!"

"I agree."

The chief sat in the chair behind his desk, somewhat mollified. "What're ya doin' right now?"

"Still processing the drug store evidence."

"It's been two days! How long ya gonna drag that out?"

Henson's cheeks turned red. "There's nearly thirty suspects, Steve."

The chief sighed. "I know it. And I don't mean to be so hard on ya. It's just, I really need a hand on this Willa thing. We're lookin' like a bunch of idiots here."

"Well, I should be done by eight. Sally and the kids are doin' somethin' at church tonight anyways, so I could put a couple of hours towards it if you'll approve the overtime."

"Oh, there's no problem with that. Just go give the shelter another look-see, will ya? I keep thinkin' we must of missed somethin' over there."

"What are you gonna do?"

Steve explained, and thirty minutes later he was parking his new Ford Explorer in front of Bill Hightower's house. The lawyer lived in Dublin's largest historic home, built nearly two hundred years before by one of the tycoons who transformed the town from a minor fishing village into a major building center for the three-masted sailing ships of that era. Those days were long gone, of course, and in Steve Novak's opinion it was a sorry situation indeed when lawyers and bankers were the last ones left who could afford the upkeep on a foursquare Federal mansion built with the good old-fashioned sweat of an honest workman's brow, especially when the township couldn't even afford to fix the dent in his Explorer's fender.

The black December sky sent a light snow flurry down upon the chief as he opened the cast iron gate beside the curb and followed the brick walkway to Hightower's front door. The snowflakes were small and icy, nearly like sleet. On the covered portico he wiped the back of his neck and pressed the doorbell and stamped his feet, staring at the Christmas tree alight with primary colors in a nearby window. Hightower answered the door himself, brittle and bloodless in the porch light. The man invited Steve in and escorted him across a tall entry hall and through an ornate cased opening to the front room on the left—a parlor, Steve supposed they used to call it. The two tall men sat on facing settees before a flickering fireplace. Four red stockings dangled from the mantel, the Hightowers' names carefully embroidered on them in golden thread. William, Betty, Sam, and Sarah. Steve had stockings hanging from his mantel too, but the names were crudely applied with glitter stuck in Elmer's glue. Bing Crosby sang carols in another room deeper in the house. Steve refused the offer of a drink. He knew Hightower was a teetotaler, and did not care for virgin eggnog or hot apple cider or whatever poor excuse for a proper highball the man might have in mind.

Hightower said, "Blowing up a little out there, is it?"

"Well, I guess prob'ly. Supposed to get five or six inches, what I heard."

"First real good one this year."

"Ayuh."

"You still have that shelter closed, I guess?"

"It's a crime scene."

"I wish you'd hurry up and clear it. Henry's got them sleeping in the sanctuary."

"Bringin' in the sheaves." Steve smiled.

"It's not funny. All those filthy vagrants on our pews, on the floor, must be thirty or forty of them, stinking up the sanctuary."

"Speaking of vagrants, I'm here about the one ya picked up from the station the other day."

"I see." A lawyer's noncommittal response.

"Henry tells me ya let him off at his place and then drove away with the fella in your back seat."

"That's true."

"Where'd ya drop him?"

"Why do you want to know?"

Steve stared at the stick figure of a man for a full five seconds before answering. "He's a person of interest in an ongoin' investigation."

"The riot at Henry's store?"

"I ain't gonna say, Bill. Just answer the question, will ya?"

Hightower turned toward the dancing fire. He spoke as if to himself. "You already know I'm aware of his arrest with the others at the store, so it can't be that."

"Bill, why don't ya just gimme an answer?"

"It's the Newdale woman's disappearance."

"Where'd ya drop him off, Bill?"

"You think she was kidnapped . . . or murdered."

"Bill."

Hightower rose and used a poker to stir new life into the fire. "We've had a riot, and now maybe a murder. Twenty percent of my clients have gone out of business in the last eighteen months. Are you aware of that? Twenty percent."

"That's a lot."

The thin gray man jabbed the logs, sending sparks swirling up into the chimney. "I don't need the business. That's not what I'm saying. I'm worried about all those poor people out of work, and with winter on us . . . our neighbors are in trouble, Steven. What are you going to do about it?"

"I'm not in charge of that. I'm just a policeman. Now, where'd ya drop that fella off?"

"If someone doesn't do something soon, you'll have nothing left to police."

"What do ya suggest?"

"Run all the indigents out of town, of course."

"How should I do that?"

"Any way you have to."

Steve watched the man's stiff back, noting the vicious way he used the poker on the logs. "What'd ya do to that fella, Bill?"

Hightower turned, surprise apparent in his face. "Do to him? Me?"

"What am I supposed to think when ya won't answer my question?"

"Quid pro quo, Steven. You haven't answered mine."

Steve sighed. "All right. I'm gonna uphold the law, whether that means arrestin' people for vagrancy or for murder—" he paused, staring hard at Hightower—"or for obstruction of justice."

"But that's not enough!"

"It's all I got."

"Then somebody else will have to do it."

"What does that mean?"

"I left him at the intersection of Green's End and Highway 3."

Steve thought a moment. "Nothin' out there."

"That's right."

"Nothin' even close to there."

"True again."

"Why there?"

"It's a long way from here."

"Transportin' a person against his will is kidnappin'."

"I made no threats and he didn't object."

"When I find him, he'll verify that?"

"*If* you find him, and his memory of it differs, it'll be his word against mine, and I'll be taken at my word."

The man was right, and Steve Novak hated it. "I guess the drive out there was your idea."

"What if it was? As I said, he didn't object."

"Why would he object? I told him not to leave town. He's a suspect in an ongoin' investigation, prob'ly a first-degree felony. Way I see it, ya basically drove his getaway car."

For the first time Hightower a seemed a little bit uncomfortable. "Nonsense."

Steve waited a beat, letting it sink in. Then, "Did he mention any plans?"

"I think he said something about the bus station in Liberty."

Steve stood. "I'll let myself out. And Bill?" He waited until the cadaverous man turned his pale gray eyes toward him. "Don't ya be doin' something else about these people like ya said. Don't do that."

Outside, the wind tugged at Steve's coat, propelling thicker snow at a sharper angle as he followed Hightower's straight brick walkway to the iron gate at the street. He swung the Explorer around in a U-turn and headed out of town.

Halfway to Liberty his headlights started blinding him as they bounced back off the swirling wall of solid white. The windshield wipers barely kept up with the slush, even when he slowed to twenty. Snow flowed through the air so fast it seemed to leave a record of its progress, as if each snowflake had been transformed into a tiny frozen comet or crepe paper streamer. Steve began to wonder if it was going to turn into the first blizzard of the winter. He thought about turning back. Then Dave Henson hailed him on the radio.

"Chief, I'm over here at the shelter."

Steve set the radio for hands-free in order to maintain control of the truck. "Real good, Dave."

"I think I got somethin'."

He felt the familiar thrill of the hunt. "Go ahead."

"It's a note, handwritten on a little folded piece of paper. I found it under one of the bunks."

"Read it to me."

"Lemme put on my glasses." After a pause, the detective's voice came back on the speaker. "Uh, it says here, 'May the Lord forgive me, I should have done this long ago. Whoever opens this, please give it to the pastor. He'll know what to do. Tell him it will cure alcoholics, and . . .'"

By the time the detective finished reading, the chief had pulled to a complete stop. He sat staring out through his windshield at the nearly horizontal snow streaking across the Explorer's hood. From the darkness a ten-point buck stepped into his headlight beam. It turned and stood as if paralyzed, with eyes glowing red and majestic antlers spreading up beyond the electric glow to disappear into the firmament. The arctic wind ran icy fingers through the buck's fur and then came to trail them with a hiss along the truck. The chief envisioned his cheek against a rifle stock, his eye unblinking down the barrel. The hunter in him longed to take a shot, but he knew how to wait.

Could those crazy rumors be true after all? Could the man who murdered Willa Newdale really have a cure for alcoholism? An actual cure? The idea excited him, not because it would mean the end of suffering for countless millions, but because it meant sooner or later the bum would try to profit from it, and to do that he would have to step out of the darkness, and when that happened, Chief Steve Novak would be waiting there to take him down.

16

Afloat near the center of Dublin harbor, Dylan Delaney stepped into his battered wooden dinghy and pushed away from the starboard side of the *Mary Lynn*, a thirty-eight-foot Royal Lowell lobster boat. It was late February, and with winter's grip hard upon the coast of Maine, it ought to be the height of lobster season, the period when prices increased and supplies decreased due in part to the casual lobsterman's unwillingness to work traps in such cold. But the lobsters were much farther out to sea than anyone could remember, forcing men to set traps at unheard-of depths, sometimes as much as a hundred fathoms below—twice the usual maximum depth. It meant twice the wait while the pot hauler pulled every string of traps, twice the pot warp, or rope, to mark them, twice the diesel as Dylan idled on the surface, and all of that for a quarter of the usual catch, or less, because even at that depth the lobster population remained mysteriously sparse. Dylan had been forced to lobster in unfamiliar waters never worked by his ancestors. He did not know the bottom there. He was losing traps. He figured he could hold on until the end of the season, but if things did not turn up, and turn up right away, he'd have to sell his boat come spring. He only hoped there would not be a glut of other workboats on the market at that time, with every other lobsterman up and down the coast confronted by the same disaster.

Facing aft in the little dinghy, Dylan rowed toward the landing through the harbor's nasty chop. Now and then he raised his oars and let a wave carry him, ghosting silently toward shore. The world around him watched in shades of gray—the pregnant clouds, the virgin snow, the sparkling ice, the steely water—all painted by a somber god who had misplaced his colors. Yet there was lightness too. Off to port he saw a harbor seal flirting with a mooring buoy, circling it, bumping it, looking for all the world like the marine version of a puppy with a rubber ball. A chunk of ice the size of a shoebox knocked against his dinghy's hull, scraping along the side as he rowed closer to the shoreline where the harbor froze more solidly. The Atlantic wind bit right through Dylan's nylon coat, turtleneck sweater, two undershirts, and long johns. His ears stung like they were on fire. Seawater had somehow found its way into his high rubber boots as usual, numbing his toes with a wicked awful chill. After nine hours on the water working traps, his lower back hurt like crazy. His arms hurt, his neck hurt, and yet he could not think of anything that he would rather do, except of course for anything that he could do with Hope.

As Dylan rowed, thoughts of Hope led to thoughts of Riley Keep, home again these last three months, home again to stay apparently, living in that little garage apartment behind Mrs. Harding's place and waiting tables at the Downtown Diner like he was. The man hardly ever went over to Hope's, mostly just to supper so far as Dylan knew, and then she always made sure he was there as well. Dylan supposed it was a good sign that she invited him whenever Riley came, and after all, Bree was still the man's daughter so of course Hope had to let him come around. But he was still concerned. He could not bear to think of her alone with Riley now, especially not now, when everything else he loved was dying all around him.

At the landing, Dylan tied the dinghy off amongst a dozen others and dragged two plastic crates one at a time up the steeply inclined gangway, having already off-loaded the crates onto the dock from the *Mary Lynn* before he took her out to the mooring. In one of the plastic crates was half the usual hundred pounds of lobsters. In the other was about the same weight of crabs. At the end of a normal day he would have been hauling four or five such crates, completely full.

Up on the landing, he set out for his truck. He scraped ice off of the windshield and the door handle, then sat inside the cab with his gloved hands under his armpits while the engine warmed up and his breath froze on the glass. Eventually he got the heater going and thawed things out enough to clear the windshield. He backed the truck up to the gangway and loaded his pitiful little catch. He drove it over to the buying station and stood by while they weighed it. He took his money—such as it was—and followed a snowplow up Water Street, then onto Main, where he pulled in at the post office.

Inside, he saw four obviously homeless fellas huddled up for warmth by the radiator in the far corner of the lobby, a common sight these days. Since the news reports about Willa's disappearance and the mystery man who supposedly knew how to cure alcoholism, many more indigent people from away had come to town despite the bitter weather. Pastor Henry had taken over at the shelter, running it with the help of volunteers from church—Dylan himself had worked the serving line the last two Thursday nights—but no amount of volunteering could make the shelter big enough to meet the need. Pastor Henry had been forced to reopen the church sanctuary to them, converting pews to bunks with blankets and foam rubber pads. Bill Hightower and a few other influential church members had questioned this decision, fueling speculation among the congregation that Henry was "enabling" the alcoholics. To counter any hint of this, Henry sent his charges out to look for jobs each day, just as Willa used to do. But there were no jobs, of course, so every morning after breakfast the shivering homeless people—over a hundred of them—fanned out across the icy town seeking any warm oasis.

Dylan figured the four men at the radiator were hiding there from Stella Odum, the Dublin postmaster, a chubby little lady in a thick wool scarf and down vest zipped up tight over her uniform. Stella was a stickler for the rules, a lifelong bureaucrat who would probably run the poor men off if she knew they were loitering on government property, even though the temperature outside was only nine or ten degrees. But Stella could not see the men from where she stood behind the service counter in the next room, so when she greeted Dylan with her usual "Cold enough for ya?" he merely smiled as he passed by, saying, "Naw, it's too darn balmy."

The homeless men eyed Dylan warily as he crossed the lobby with Stella around the corner laughing at his old joke. Ignoring them, he opened up his box. Inside were a lot of bills, some of them second or third warnings, and a heap of junk mail that made him think of devastated forests, and a letter from the Hanks Pharmaceutical Corporation. The letter surprised him. It had only been six days.

He put the other mail under his arm and opened the envelope then and there. He scanned the letter quickly and looked up at nothing in particular and said, "Wow." Then he read it again, carefully this time, and he put it back into its envelope and left.

Instead of returning to his truck, Dylan walked to the left down the sidewalk, hunched forward against the bitter wind and watching his footing for patches of black ice. A few doors farther on he ducked into the Downtown Diner, one of only four businesses still open on that block.

The early crowd was there, old folks mostly, who liked to eat by five. Dylan knew them all and greeted them by name. A couple of nervous-looking people from away also sat at a table, yet more indigents seeking warmth from the look of them, nursing cups of coffee. The only tables open were the two up front by the windows where it was coldest. Dylan left his coat on and sat down. In a minute the waiter came over, wearing a white apron.

"Dylan," said the man.

"Riley."

Riley went right to work with an easy confidence about him, now that he'd been at this for a while. "We have a special on two pork chops with mashed potatoes and squash. Six ninety-five. And we have a nice chowder tonight. Sadie bought some real fine scallops over in Cambridge."

Although Dylan could not really afford to eat supper out, he thought, why not? Might as well celebrate a little. "Bowl of chowder sounds good," he said. "And a cup of coffee if it's fresh."

"I'll make up a pot."

Dylan waited as the view through the frosted window beside him faded. The sun was setting later now, a little after five today. Winter going already, and him still with a loss for the season. Well, maybe this letter would change all that. He never dreamed Riley's foolishness would actually amount to something, but there it was in his pocket, sure enough.

Dylan pulled the letter out and read it through a third time.

Riley came with a mug and a pot of coffee. He put the mug in front of Dylan and poured the steaming brew. "Got a letter today," said Dylan.

"Hanks?"

"Ayuh."

"Can I see it?"

"'Course ya can."

Riley put the pot down on the table and wiped his hands on his apron and took the letter Dylan offered. He stood very still as he read the words. Dylan looked up at him, watching his eyes move from side to side, waiting for him to get to the good part, but Riley finished without showing any sign of interest whatsoever, except to say, "So he wants to come here himself."

"Ayuh."

"You have a place where you can meet him?"

"I was thinkin' the harbormaster's shed." Teasing him a little.

"Naw. He'll bring a lot of people. You need a big conference table. Maybe ten or twelve chairs."

"I was kiddin', Riley. I figured we'd use the conference room Hope has next to her office."

"She can't know about this. I already told you."

"Why was that again?"

Riley looked straight at him. "She just can't. Nobody can. You promised me that. If you've changed your mind just let me know and I'll find somebody else. No hard feelings. Like I said before, you might get a little pressure over this."

Dylan thought about BHR Incorporated, the Delaware corporation he had set up for Riley a couple of months ago, because Delaware law protected the anonymity of corporate officers and shareholders. He thought about Riley's strange insistence that the provisional patent be applied for on behalf of the new corporation, with no mention of Riley's name. He said, "Don't worry, I can handle the pressure. And I'll find us someplace to meet. But what makes ya think this fella's gonna bring that many people?"

"He always does."

"Know him pretty well, do ya?"

Riley seemed to stare at something only he could see in the black glass window. "Not really."

"Ya care what day we do it?"

"That's up to you. I won't be there."

"Queer way to do business."

"Can't be helped. Nobody can know it's me."

Dylan knew better than to ask again about Riley's reasons. Everything the man had done so far was enigmatic, and he showed no sign of letting Dylan in on the big secret. In fact, until the letter came, Dylan had not even believed the formulas on the patent application made any kind of sense. He figured Riley for a dreamer, to be humored for the sake of Hope and Bree. But anyone could apply for a provisional patent for anything, be it gibberish or not, so Dylan had dutifully done a little research to refresh his memory on the proper forms and formats, and typed it up, copying the formula from the piece of paper Riley had provided, and submitting the application to the Patents and Trademark Office. The whole thing had cost him a couple of Saturdays, but between the weather and the missing lobsters that had been no big deal. Then Riley had surprised him with another wild request: send a letter to Hanks Pharmaceuticals over in Wisconsin, with a copy of the patent application and an offer to sell the development and marketing rights. Dylan had complied, maintaining Riley's fantasy a little longer in hopes of gaining Hope's appreciation, which was all the pay he had expected in spite of Riley's twenty-percent offer.

But six days ... Figure two days to get there in the mail, a weekend in between, and two days for the reply to return. That meant these people received the letter, read it and the patent application with it, and sent this letter back the same day. In view of that, Dylan wondered if perhaps his twenty-percent commission might be worth a little something after all. He said, "If you're not gonna be there, I guess we'd better talk about the price and terms and whatnot."

"I don't want to drag it out. I want most of it up front, and maybe five percent of sales."

"Five percent of the net?"

"Gross."

It was a lot to ask, but Dylan nodded. Why not start high and settle? "Okay, how 'bout the up-front money?"

Riley stared at the black glass again. "Let's go with twenty and see what they say."

The math was easy: Dylan's cut would be four thousand. Funny, but he felt a little disappointed. An hour ago he had figured Riley for a kook. Now here he was thinking they should hold out for more money. Four thousand would help, but it was a long way from what he needed to make up for his losses. "I don't know ... they seem awful interested, Riley. I was wonderin' if maybe we oughta ask for a hundred."

Riley looked down at him. "A hundred? Really?"

"A hundred thousand isn't all that much money for a big outfit like this."

"Oh. I was thinking millions."

Dylan laughed, but Riley Keep's expression did not change. The man stared at him intensely and said, "It really works. You have to remember that."

"But they can't know it works so quick! It's just a possibility so far. They still hafta figure a way to synthesize it and mass-produce it, and they hafta get FDA approval. That'll take, what? Two or three years. Five? And you don't even have a final patent yet. It's just provisional."

"Dylan, try to get this, okay? They'll test it and find out it works. It really works."

This whole thing seemed so clearly crazy Dylan had not bothered to think it through, but something in the way Riley put it then, so simple and direct, made him suddenly remember the nature of the fantasy: an outright cure for alcoholism, not a treatment method or a way to taper off, but a single dose that completely took away the alcoholic's urge to drink. As Dylan considered that in serious terms for the first time, he began to understand that this could be the epicenter of a seismic shift in mankind's history, like a cure for cancer or a way to end all wars, and then he knew that Riley Keep was right. If it was really true, a hundred million dollars would be nothing to these people.

That night as Dylan lay beneath a cheap comforter and an electric blanket set on high, he did not sleep at all. He rose at four as usual and made a pot of coffee and settled in to wait. He would not take the *Mary Lynn* out lobstering that day, or if he did it would be long after sunrise, because he had to wait until they opened for business in Milwaukee's time zone.

At precisely nine o'clock he dialed the number on the letter, not the one on the letterhead, but the direct line in the body of the letter itself. A woman answered and he told her who he was and why he was calling, and within half a minute he was talking to Lee Hanks, the president and chief executive officer of one of the world's largest pharmaceutical manufacturers. The man greeted him as if they were old friends and told him to name a place and time, happy to meet him, delighted to have a chance to talk about it, anything he could do to help with preparations?

The next two days went by quickly. Dylan had to buy a suit. He had to drive to Cambridge to do it, since the last men's clothing store in Dublin had been closed for nearly a year. While he was there Dylan also bought a black leather briefcase and a legal pad to put inside it. He met with Riley twice more, once at the diner and once at Riley's little apartment. It was important that he get an executed power of attorney and make sure he had a solid understanding of his client's wishes, since he would be making decisions on Riley's behalf at the negotiation table. After two months of working for Riley Keep, Dylan had only just begun to understand he really was a client, and with that understanding came a grudging respect, and with the respect, a deeper fear of losing Hope.

Henry allowed the meeting at the church without asking any questions other than the day and time. Dylan arrived early, feeling uncomfortable and ridiculous with the tie around his neck and his old nylon coat on over the new black suit and his old brown dress shoes. He had forgotten to buy black dress shoes when he bought the suit. He parked half a block away because he did not want them to see his truck, all beat up like it was. He need not have bothered. Hanks was fifteen minutes late. Dylan stood with his cracked and callused hands clasped nervously behind his back, watching through the conference room window as the man's stretch limousine glided to a stop outside, followed by two black Lincoln Town Cars. He counted twelve men and women coming up the freshly shoveled side-walk toward him, almost all of them in black or dark blue woolen overcoats with muted scarves and leather gloves. He felt like David staring out across a frozen battlefield at Goliath and his army.

But they weren't that way at all. On the contrary, after ten minutes in the room with Lee Hanks and his people, Dylan felt as if he had just made a dozen bosom friends. Hanks declined the chair at the far end of the long table and sat down right beside him. He seemed a remarkably energetic man for his age, which Dylan guessed at sixty-five or seventy. The fact that he was completely bald and clean-shaven made the thick black eyebrow that spanned unbroken across his forehead all the more striking. His dark eyes constantly sought Dylan's, the flesh around them crinkling with pleasure as he explored Dylan's interests and background, asking all kinds of slightly personal questions. It was as if the room had narrowed down to just the two of them, as if the others were not listening. Dylan found himself talking freely about his family, their heritage in Dublin going back two centuries, and shipbuilding, and lobstering, and in the midst of the bonhomie when the man asked, "So when did you return to practicing law full time?" Dylan almost answered honestly before he realized what had happened.

The nature of the question meant Lee Hanks already knew the answer, and such a clumsy signal sent on the heels of such skillfully established camaraderie meant this man wanted Dylan to know he already knew the answer. It meant he wanted Dylan to understand he had been thoroughly researched and his weaknesses identified. When Dylan ignored the question and changed the subject Lee Hanks leaned back in his chair and smiled, and Dylan realized he had just lost the first round of negotiations.

It went downhill from there. Without acknowledging in any way that he was toying with a neophyte, Hanks ran the meeting with an iron fist gloved in velvet. He managed to imply sympathy when pointing out the unproven nature of the formula, and shook his head with great regret when Dylan mentioned his client's "research" on a dozen hardened alcoholics, saying, "I'm afraid there must be some mistake, Mr. Delaney. After all, it would be a felony to conduct trials on human subjects at this stage."

"They weren't trials, exactly."

"Oh, of course not. If something like that had been done, why we'd have to back away immediately. After all, you haven't even submitted an IND."

Dylan struggled to compose his face in a way that would imply he knew what an IND was. He put his elbows on the chair's armrests and built a bridge before his face with weathered fingers and nodded at what he hoped were the appropriate moments as Hanks and his immaculately dressed people discussed "our contacts at the CDER" and "PDUFA compliance" and "phase one protocols" and so forth. He smiled and shrugged and did his best to deflect questions he did not understand, saying he would have to get back to them on that, check with his principals on it, et cetera, until Lee Hanks asked him something and would not settle for a vague suggestion of an answer later in the week.

"I'm afraid we'll need a certified letter right away, Mr. Delaney," he said. So Dylan had to say, "What was the question again?" and he tried to write it down, spelling some of the unfamiliar words phonetically, with everybody watching poker-faced as Hanks finally leaned forward and said, "That's 'HPLC chromatograms,' Mr. Delaney," and then he spelled the word.

Dylan sighed and put his number two pencil down on his brand-new legal pad. He looked around at all of them, and focused on a middle-aged man that he had noticed earlier, a guy with a full head of perfectly cut sandy hair, a square jaw, a yachtsman's tan, and the bulbous blue-veined nose and rheumy, gimlet eyes of a person who could not postpone his first cocktail until the sun was past the yard-arm. "Sorry," said Dylan. "I didn't get your name?"

The man smiled, displaying perfect teeth. "That's quite all right, Mr. Delaney. I'm Robert Palmer. I run sales and marketing for Mr. Hanks."

"Ayuh, I thought I remembered that was your line of work from the introductions," said Dylan. "So lemme ask ya something, if I could."

"Certainly," said the man, smiling at a woman across the table who inclined her shoulders slightly as if to say, I suppose we have to humor him.

"I was just wonderin' what ya think a cure like this is worth?"

The man's smile disappeared. He pursed his lips. "I'm afraid asset valuation isn't really my area, Mr. Delaney."

"Oh, I don't mean 'asset valuation.' I was thinking more like, ya know, what would a fella pay for a dose of this stuff? Say like, a fella who had a real nice executive job and a big mortgage and maybe a weekend place to pay for and a wife who's kinda gotten used to jewelry and a couple of German cars and maybe a kid or two he's gonna hafta send to some Ivy League school someplace. Say a fella who used to drink just socially, maybe over lunch or supper just to close a deal, ya know, but can't seem to wait for lunch anymore? How much do ya think a fella like that would pay to take a pill or whatever, and get that monkey off his back?"

Dylan sensed that Lee Hanks's eyes never left his face as he asked his question, but one by one the others had turned to look at Robert Palmer, and Dylan felt a little sorry for the man because of course they all knew Dylan had it just exactly right, and yet he couldn't let this Hanks fella beat him down that way; he had to do something. So he sat and waited with what he hoped was an expression of naïve curiosity upon his face until the vice president of marketing said, "I expect a man like that would pay a great deal."

"Right. A great deal. Okay, we're talkin' about a fella who's pretty well off, so I guess a great deal would be, what, a quarter million dollars? For a guy with a kid at Harvard or wherever? Maybe even half a million. For one dose. That wouldn't be too much to ask, would it?"

Dylan had to admire the poor man; he was still smiling as he said, "I wouldn't know." But the desperate longing in his gimlet eyes made a lie of that.

The woman who had shrugged began to speak rapidly, filling the awkward silence, changing the subject, but Dylan ignored her. Checking his Timex elaborately he said, "Oh, hey, excuse me. I'm sorry everybody, but there's a thing I gotta do. Feel free to stay long as ya like; we've got the room until an elder board meetin' at seven." He stood and slipped his brand-new yellow legal pad into his brand-new empty briefcase. "You folks have reservations somewheres? There's a Budget Inn and an Econo Lodge over on Highway 1, but

I guess ya prob'ly saw that on your way in."

Lee Hanks rose as well, extending his hand. "A pleasure to meet you, Mr. Delaney. I know tomorrow's Saturday, but would you care to continue then?"

Dylan took his hand and looked him in the eye. He did not see respect there, but he did believe there was a reappraisal going on. "Hafta check my schedule, Mr. Hanks. How's about ya call me in the mornin'? I imagine ya have my number."

Lee Hanks said, "Of course," letting Dylan reach the door before asking a final question, "Oh, Mr. Delaney ... I'm curious. Has your client spent much time in Brazil?"

Puzzled, Dylan turned. He thought of Hope's stories about her missionary days, and Bree's shiny black hair and jet black eyes and dark brown skin, and Riley's strange insistence that his name stay out of this, and Dylan thought it was important to be very careful with the words he used. "I have no idea, Mr. Hanks. Couldn't tell ya if I did. Why?"

"It was just a thought." The bald man smiled. "But you might mention that I asked."

17

Even though Teal Pond was way out in the woods at the far edge of Dublin, even though it was still only twenty-two degrees at noon, and even after working the busy Saturday breakfast shift at Sadie's Downtown Diner, in spite of all of that, Riley could have run the whole way. He had put on fifteen pounds over the last couple of months, pure muscle on his chest and arms and legs. He tried to do a twenty-minute workout twice a day—sit-ups, push-ups, and squat thrusts every morning and evening—and he made a point of eating right. Alone in his little garage apartment Riley had constructed his own custom exercise equipment, screwing metal rings into the walls and ceiling to hold large springs and chains and weights, which he pushed and lifted and pulled against in certain ways. In addition to his new eyeglasses, he had a temporary bridge to fill the gaps in his front teeth, generic dentures that would hold him over until the dentist fit the custom ones he had ordered. Sometimes he stood before the full-length mirror, turning this way and that in his underwear, comparing himself to Dylan Delaney, feeling like he was maybe gaining on Hope's handsome lobsterman and feeling all right about the changes to his body at least, even though he still avoided looking at the eyes behind his brand-new glasses and even if he could not bring himself to bare his artificial smile.

Three guys emerged from behind the Wash & Save as Riley cut

across the parking lot, one of them a very large man whom Riley thought he recognized. He knew what they'd been doing—he and Brice had warmed themselves beside laundromat dryer vents a few times in their day—and he knew what they had in mind. Before they got to him, Riley pulled three dollars from his coat pocket. He never left his job or his apartment without a lot of dollar bills. With all the homeless alcoholics coming to Dublin since the news shows started talking about the "mystery man" with a cure, you couldn't walk two blocks in town without getting hit up for a handout. It was a bad idea to show them all your money at once, so he spread the dollars around in different pockets and tried to be ready with one for every homeless guy he passed. The three from behind the Wash & Save came close, pleading hunger. Sure enough, one of them was the giant from Houston. It was the first real test of Riley Keep's disguise: his glasses and his teeth, his clean-shaven face and close-cropped hair, and his new clean clothes. The huge man gave Riley a nearly tooth-less smile and said, "God bless you, mister," as he took his cash, completely oblivious to the fact that Riley was the man from Henry's Drug Store, the man who had the cure. Riley knew their claims of hunger were probably a ruse to garner drinking money, but what of that? What difference would one more bottle make to three men such as these, when Riley had seen to it that they and everybody like them would be healed like him one day?

How he longed to shout it from the rooftops! But he would never get the credit. He would never tell a living soul he was the source of the cure, because that would lead eventually to Stanley Livingston, the man they had arrested with Willa Newdale's wooden cross in his pocket, the man suspected of her murder.

Leaving the giant and the other two beggars behind, Riley hurried on. His lungs burned from the frigid air as he climbed the hill above downtown and followed a narrow gravel road down the other side. It was good that he enjoyed walking. He could not risk a car on minimum wage and tips at Sadie's diner. If people knew he could afford a car, they would wonder how. After the spring thaw maybe he would get a bicycle, and in a year a cheap, used pickup truck, something people would believe a reformed drunk waiting tables could afford, but for now he had to walk.

In the valley on the other side of the hill Riley's healthy strides brought him closer to the pond. A miserly sun loitered in the sky above the coast of Maine, doling out its frigid light upon his progress. The frozen atmosphere felt solid in his nostrils. It was awfully cold for the Easter season, setting record lows every day with the long and bitter winter showing no sign of retreat. He reached the edge of town, where the boundless northern woods snatched at Dublin's fringes, the densely packed spruce and pines standing at attention on either side of the road in spite of mounds of snow weighing down their bristles. Suddenly a pure white snowshoe hare dashed headlong across his path. At first Riley thought the rabbit's panic had been caused by his own crunching footsteps, but then a red fox appeared at the tree line to fix golden eyes on him before slipping back into the shadows. As Riley passed the darkness in the evergreens where the fox had disappeared, he thought of a different forest, a southern place where steam arose from rain-soaked ground instead of from his lungs, where clothing was a liability, nakedness the best protection from the elements, and predators did not bother hiding from a passing human being.

Shaking his head to clear away that mournful place, Riley followed a sharp bend in the road and approached a row of vehicles parked in six inches of fresh powder along the shoulder. He noticed most of them were locked. People had never locked their cars back before Riley and Brice left Dublin, but with the homeless now roaming everywhere, those trusting days were over. Riley glanced at each car door as he passed. Locked. Locked. Locked. It was yet another sadness. But then he came to Hope's brand-new Mercedes and smiled. Riley had selected that particular make and model because it was the top of the line, and would make Bill Hightower's car look common by comparison. He had taken the bus to Portland, paying cash at the dealership and waiting until three in the morning to sneak it into town. Today would be the first time he had seen her since he had rolled into her driveway with the headlights off and parked her gift there with the keys and the title in her name on the front seat. He could hardly wait to see her at the wheel, even if she would never know it came from him.

Riley heard unexpected cheers and shouting in the distance. Snow clung to his boots as he left the road and followed a short trail between the pines. Dozens of footprints marked the way, but Riley could have found Teal Pond blindfolded. He had spent hundreds of hours skating on it growing up. With every step the excited shouts grew louder. Now he heard the old familiar sound of clicking sticks. The pines beside the path thinned enough to grant his first glimpse of the pond in over twenty years. A bunch of kids flew past on the ice beyond the snowy branches, playing eight-on-eight and zipping all around the hockey puck like they were born on skates. The sight and sound of them became a time machine, spinning Riley back through decades to a sheltered world confined to home and school and skating, and just for a second Riley felt he was himself again, living childlike in the moment, clean and pure with nothing to hide, blithely unaware of violence or grief. Drawn forward toward a better past, Riley reached the tree line and the scene before him broadened. His pristine illusions vanished.

He had expected to find Hope alone with Bree and a few other kids. Hockey at Teal Pond had always been something of a secret in his youth—you had to keep it quiet or the cops would come shut down the game—but the trucks and cars along the road should have tipped him off that everything was different now. Here were at least a hundred other people, children and adults strung out around the edges of the ice, dressed in everything from hunter's camouflage to brightly colored snowsuits. He saw real frames with nets set up for goals at either end of the ice instead of just a pair of some kid's boots to shoot between, and boards laid all around to keep stray pucks from getting lost below the snow, and an actual warm-up tent, maybe thirty feet by thirty, at the north end of the pond beside another cleared-off area alive with figure skaters. Over at the embankment, exactly where Riley and Brice and all their pals once built timid little fires and kept them small for fear of being found out, he saw people roasting marshmallows at a great roaring bonfire. Obviously, no one cared about the smoke attracting the police anymore, which had been the sole worry of his childhood on this pond. Against his will came memories of all the other fires that he and Brice had built, in oil drums and in trash cans, and he tried to shut those thoughts away before they ruined everything. Brice was still a gaping wound inside his heart.

It took a minute to spot Hope skating over near the tent. Riley made his way in that direction, moving alongside the hockey game, careful to stay on the snow and not step out beyond the boards onto the cleared ice. Some of the spectators he passed had brought lawn chairs, but hardly anybody used them. It was still too cold to sit around, so everybody stood in close huddles and stamped their feet and drank from steaming thermos cups and laughed while calling out advice and encouragement to the kids.

Drawing closer to the other end of the pond, Riley's eyes found Hope again among the figure skaters. He looked around her but could not find Dylan. Riley kept his hopefulness in check. On the isolated patch of ice across the pond Hope skated among perhaps a dozen others, some of them content to simply circle, while others threw in something fancy now and then. She was all in white, from her figure skates to her one-piece snowsuit to her matching woolen cap and flowing scarf. People skated singly and in couples all around her, children shooting in and out between the adults' legs, old folks moving slow with straight knees and much concentration, younger adults carrying on conversations as if skating took no more thought than walking. Hope seemed oblivious to them all. As Riley watched she suddenly flipped around and gathered speed with a short series of backward crossovers, watching out for others over her right shoulder. He saw the little crowd around her part as if on cue; a section of clear ice appeared and she did a step forward followed by a flawless axel, hanging in the air as if weightless, then moving into a graceful camel after her touchdown, arms extended identically, wrists cocked slightly, fingers composed as elegantly as any ballerina. It was executed so perfectly a nearby woman on the ice cried out in amazement and a couple who had been skating arm in arm behind her stopped dead in their tracks to clap. Hope giggled, hiding her face behind white gloved hands and shaking her head. Wooden now with self-consciousness, she melded back into the swirling flow of skaters as if to disappear among them.

Riley could not breathe.

He watched as Hope restrained her fluid skating to simple laps around the ice, gliding smoothly among her community of friends, exchanging laughing comments, cheeks flushed with rosy health, smile as white as freshly fallen snow. Riley saw in Hope the world as it should be—graceful, effortless, lovely—all the words he knew fell short. The seminarian and professor in him thought of something, probably by Shakespeare. *"As soon go kindle fire with snow, as seek to quench the fire of love with words."* Or maybe it wasn't Shakespeare, but what of that? Riley only knew he longed to mix himself with her, to be in her and draw her into him forever.

The rhythmic pace of every skater near his ex-wife testified that he was not alone in this desire, for he saw their motions subtly shifting to match hers. It was as if Hope's energy had soothed the aimless universe, spreading out to set the tempo of all life. Riley recognized this gathering of unity around her, had seen it often through the years. He remembered it surrounding her in high school, when he first fell in love. He remembered it in church, when he first saw its divine source. And against his will he remembered it in a clearing in the forest, in a wide circle of The People, dancing happily in celebration of Hope's day, holding hands and singing in the smoky sunlight filtered through the soaring canopy, dancing in toward the center together, then backing out again, with Riley between Waytee and a naked man on one side and Hope between two women on the far side, Riley watching from a distance as she laughed in bare feet and a thin cotton shift—laughed, bubbling up and over with her love of life, the entire People moving as one, everybody come together in her honor, matching the rhythm of her steps with theirs, overjoyed because his precious Hope had been born that day and come to live with them. Riley remembered watching from the far side of the circle as the little wooden cross that he had carved for her bounced up and down upon her chest with every barefoot dancing step. Riley remembered thinking, *"This is the day the Lord has made; I will rejoice and be glad in it."* With that memory his eyes began to water—tears freezing on his lashes—because in all good conscience he could not think those words and mean them anymore.

How could he rejoice in memories of such a day? It had been the very day he spoke to The People of other missionaries coming, healing men who would make their teeth feel better and take away their bodies' suffering. He remembered standing in the place of honor at the center of Hope's birthday circle, telling *them* to trust the newcomers, as if the *doctors* were the ones to fear, as if The People were the ones he should protect. Oh, the horrible irony!

If only he had stayed to guide his Christian brothers from the States! He remembered his cowardly resistance to the sabbatical idea, sitting in their tiny cabin in a clearing, the weak satellite telephone signal further eroding his token effort. It was obvious the newcomers would need interpreters, a go-between to warn them of taboos. He was necessary, indispensable. But the missions board had argued well. It was only for two months, they said, a much deserved vacation after all his time away. Allow a month or so to introduce the doctors to The People and then return home to Maine. The doctors will be fine. You deserve a rest. How those words had tempted him. After four straight years at work for the Lord without a break, he had been so very, very tired, so ready for a rest. But in the end it was not weariness that led him to the devil. No, it had been something infinitely worse.

With a worried look from Hope beside him in the darkness of their corrugated cabin, he had listened as the final question came.

Have you not succeeded? What it meant, what he knew they really meant to ask, was had he disciplined their brutishness? And he— almighty Riley, tamer of the savages—could not bear to let them doubt his worth. After all, The People were not killing anymore, or drinking as they once had done. Most were true believers now. They could all be trusted.

Riley Keep had done his work, and it was good.

Wiping frozen tears beside Teal Pond, Riley turned away from the sight of Hope and forced himself to think of other things, less happy things than beauty on the ice. It did not take him long to put his thoughts in order. Returning his attention to the pond he saw her at the shoreline now, with two men by the warm-up tent, neither of them Dylan. The men's backs were to Riley as he approached, but he had a clear view of Hope's face in the instant that she saw him coming. She was smiling and then she saw him and then she was not smiling.

Standing behind the men, Riley said, "You can still skate."

"Oh no. Did you see that?"

"Wow."

"I was so embarrassed."

"Why? Did you do it to show off?"

"I don't think so." She cocked her head, looking at him. "It just came out."

He let her see his eyes, just for a second, without meaning to. "Well then . . ."

The two men with her turned toward Riley, and his heart began to race. One was the chief of police. The other was Bill Hightower. He had done his best to avoid these men, the only ones besides Henry Reardon and the homeless at the shelter who had met him as Stanley Livingston. Riley was in disguise as someone clean-cut now, with his new false teeth, eyeglasses, and store-bought wardrobe. He had regained his former weight and put on muscle. Many people from his former life now recognized him around Dublin—old neighbors and acquaintances greeting him at work and on the streets—

but would these men see past his new disguise and perceive the skinny, toothless, shaggy Stanley Livingston? Would Bill Hightower see him as that person stranded in the woods? Would the chief recognize the prisoner he had accused of murder in his jail? Was this the end of Riley's new life as his old self?

Riley thought of running. Then Hightower smiled warmly and extended a gloved hand. "Reverend Keep, isn't it? Or should I call you Professor?"

Riley let the hand hang in the air a moment longer than he should, loath to pretend civility to this man who had run him out of town, but also celebrating, for clearly Hightower did not see a hint of Stanley Livingston. Finally he took the tall man's hand, saying, "It's been a long time since anybody called me either one."

Hope said, "You remember Bill Hightower, Riley."

"Of course he does," said Hightower. "But it's been a while. I think we last saw each other at some kind of function over at Bowditch. Maybe a fund-raiser?"

Riley did not know what to say. He had been to many fund-raisers in his short time at Bowditch, but remembered very few. Most of them had open bars.

"Any relation to the mayor here?" asked the chief.

"I once had that honor," replied Riley, daring to lift his eyes toward Hope. She had looked away.

"Oh, nicely said!" exclaimed Hightower. "Reverend Keep, this is our chief of police, Steve Novak."

"Nice to meet you, Chief." Riley shook the policeman's hand.

"Call me Steve." The big man searched his face. "Have we met before?"

Riley could not find his voice.

Unknowingly, Hope came to his rescue. "I think Riley left town a little while before you moved here, Steve. He just got back a few months ago."

Still looking straight at Riley's face, the chief said, "Maybe I've seen ya around Dublin?"

"Maybe." Riley cleared his throat. "Uh, I'm working at the Downtown Diner."

"Really? Doin' what?"

"Serving. Cleaning. A little cooking. Whatever Sadie needs."

"But I thought you were a preacher or a professor or something."

"It's a long story."

"I'd sure like to hear it."

"I, uh . . ."

"Steve," said Hope. "Maybe we should change the subject."

"What? Oh, sorry. Always getting too personal with people." But even then his eyes were right on Riley. "Goes with the job."

Hope and the two men kept on talking, kidding each other, gossiping a little, calling to friends and neighbors on the ice, having a good time. Riley said as little as possible. It felt strange, people acting like they were at a party when no one held a drink. Riley had no idea what to say or do. He had been living on another level for too long. He was a child at play among adults; the game was charades and every clue was way above his head. He could not keep from thinking the lawyer or policeman would eventually see through him—especially the policeman, who had a disconcerting way of looking straight at Riley's face. The man was most likely trained to memorize a person's features, to recognize a fugitive—even one so thoroughly disguised as Riley.

His best defense would be to walk away, but how could he explain that when he was there at Hope's invitation? He stole a glance at the beautiful woman who had once been his wife; he watched her as she watched the skaters on the ice, her profile perfect, like a Grecian sculpture of a goddess. In the distance just beyond her, Riley saw a movement. His daughter stepped from the tree line, closely followed by a young man wearing a dark trench coat and a black watch cap. The friendly chatter of Riley's companions became an unintelligible droning in the background as he observed Bree hurry toward them, the young man following, then catching up and reaching out to lay a hand upon her arm. His daughter stopped and

THE CURE

shook the hand off, her posture defiant. She said something to the boy and then set out again, her face an angry mask. When the boy behind her grabbed her arm again, yanking her to a halt, Riley looked at Hope and said, "I'm gonna go say hello to Bree." Hope nodded as he set out toward their daughter.

Bree stood facing Riley's direction, her arms crossed in defiance. The young man's back was turned. She looked past the boy, seeing Riley come. He rejoiced at the relief in her eyes. Removing his gloves as he drew near, Riley called, "Bree? You okay?"

The young man turned. Up close Riley saw a silver ring in each of his ears, another through his nose, and a fringe of hair below his cap in alternating shades of blond and green and purple. The young man's eyes flashed with annoyance at the interruption. Twin puffs of steamy breath shot from his nostrils like smoke from an angry cartoon bull. He was maybe twenty pounds heavier than Riley, three inches taller, and twenty-five years younger. He said, "Who are you, man?"

Riley ignored the boy, looking past him. "Bree?"

"I'm okay."

"You sure?"

The young man looked back at Bree. "Who *is* this guy, baby?"

Bree set her jaw stubbornly, saying nothing.

Riley asked, "You wanna come warm up in the tent with me a while?"

"Yeah," said Bree, pushing past the boy.

"Wait a minute!" The young man reached out to grab her arm again.

Riley said, "You need to let her go."

"Hey, man, this ain't your business."

"Just let her go, okay?"

Bree could not break the young man's grip this time. She winced at the pressure of his fingers on her arm. At the sight of that, although Riley knew nothing about fighting, although it never crossed his mind to even move, his fist shot out and connected

165

solidly with the young man's jaw. The sudden attack seemed to surprise both the boy and Bree. It certainly surprised Riley. Releasing her, the young man swung around to face him squarely, one hand rubbing his jaw, the other hanging loosely at his side.

Bree touched the young man's arm. "You okay?"

"Sure."

She gave his arm a pat and set out toward the warm-up tent without a backward glance at either of them. Riley remained facing the young man near the ice. Suddenly he remembered taking off his gloves while he was walking over. He realized he had intended for this to happen. He had prepared for it. He felt ashamed. Watching the young man's hands he said, "You okay?"

The boy spat into the snow. Riley saw no blood in it. Looking down on him, the boy said, "You hit like a girl."

"I know. Just . . . leave her alone."

"Hey, man, I *love* her!"

Me too, thought Riley, turning away from the boy.

He followed his daughter's slightly bowlegged gait toward the warm-up tent. To his left he saw Hightower on the ice, a towering scarecrow plodding along on his skates. He saw Hope and the police chief still in conversation beside the tent. Riley felt relieved. It seemed no one had witnessed his pathetic demonstration.

Up ahead, Bree slipped between the flaps of the tent's entrance. Riley followed. Inside were a lot of unoccupied folding chairs and ten or twelve people standing next to a folding table. Several hissing propane heaters struggled in vain against the freezing temperature. On the table was a steaming pot of cider, its fruity aroma rich in Riley's nostrils. He helped himself to two foam cups and filled them and carried them toward Bree, who stood at a heater near the back, smoking a cigarette.

"Here you go," said Riley.

Wordlessly, she took the cup.

He said, "I didn't know you smoked."

Looking away, she did not reply.

He said, "Why would you do that?"

"You oughta know. I'm *addicted*."

He let that settle in. Then, "How's your arm? Did that boy hurt you?"

"You didn't have to hit him."

"I'm sorry, Vachee."

She glanced at him, and then away again. Was that disappointment in her eyes? She took a long, deep drag and then ground out her cigarette on the earth beneath her boot. They stood silently, sipping the hot cider. Riley heard voices through the fabric of the tent: Hope and the police chief, standing just there, three feet away but out of sight. He tried to ignore them. He tried to remember the last time he had been alone with his daughter. He could not recall.

"Sometimes I say things to him," said Bree. "I can be kinda mean. I don't know why."

The confession made his hand tremble as he took a sip. It was the first time she had said anything important to him. He tried to think of a wise reply. He heard the policeman's voice beyond the fabric of the tent, telling Hope she had to take something more seriously. His mind wandered back and forth between the conversations as Bree kept talking.

"He's not a bad person. I know you think he is, but he's really not."

Riley thought a moment. "He's a lot bigger than I am but he didn't try to hit me back. That's something."

When Bree did not reply, he wondered if he had made a mistake, saying something positive about the boy. Should he have disagreed with her? Told her there was never any excuse for a man to lay his hands upon someone the way her boyfriend had? But how could he say that when he himself had walked into her life from out of nowhere, out of nothing, and punched her young man in the jaw?

Outside the tent the police chief's voice warned Hope about the Mercedes. People wanted to know how she could afford such a car on a mayor's salary. People were talking. A councilman had asked the chief to investigate officially. He did not want to do it, but maybe Hope should go ahead and let him know where the car had come from.

Hope replied, her voice almost too weak to hear, saying she was sure the car had come from Dylan. He had a new client, some company in Delaware, and he was making lots of money as a lawyer, and he wanted her to marry him.

"I don't know what to do," said Bree.

Marry him. What to do. With a wooden heart Riley forced himself to focus on his daughter. What did she mean? Was she talking about the way the young man grabbed her arm? Was she talking about whatever caused the confrontation in the first place, whatever happened between the boy and Bree back in the woods? Or was she talking about something completely different? Should he ask these questions, gather more details? What if she then wanted his advice? What if she listened to him and took some course of action and it did not end well? Riley sipped his cider and thought about his other foolish plans for Hope and Bree, already set in motion. The hundred-thousand-dollar car was nothing—a mere hint of the destruction he could cause with good intentions.

Outside, the police chief spoke again, saying yes, of course he believed Hope's story, yes, he did have better things to do, and yes, of course he was still working on Willa's disappearance. He would find that man; Hope could count on that. He was working several leads right now. He was getting close. But people were still asking him about this expensive car, and the best thing he could do for Hope was prove her innocent of taking bribes. So he would make Dylan admit to giving her the car, and if it turned out she was wrong, he would find out where the car had come from. It would not be difficult. She could count on him to defend her reputation, just like she could count on him to find the man who murdered Willa.

"How come men don't talk about things?" asked Bree. "How come they just wanna have sex all the time, and never wanna talk?"

Was she trying to shock him? Did she really think that possible?

Riley remembered the birth-control pills in Henry's store and knew he had to tell her something, even if she did not really want an answer. She was asking him this question, and he had to respond as if she meant it, and after all, he did have thoughts on the subject. But look at who he was and what he had become. How could he be trusted? Who was he to give advice on anything to anyone?

Riley glanced at his daughter's profile, her sloped forehead, glistening black hair, curved nose, copper skin—so like a sculptural relief on a Mayan temple, so perfect in his eyes—and he remembered telling the missionary team that they could trust The People; they would be safe. How certain of his facts he had been that day. How self-assured he had been, the almighty Riley, rolling into Hope's driveway with the lights turned off. Bribery and murder and his little Bree, crying in amongst the bodies.

He had done all that. He and no one else.

Who was he to tell her anything about men and women?

"You should ask your mother," Riley said.

"Sure," she said, walking away. "Or maybe I'll ask Dylan."

18

Near the back corner of the little grocery store, the old woman applied a price tag to another can of Del Monte kernel corn. Her hair was auburn now and had grown nearly to her shoulders. She had acquired a pair of eyeglasses in Omaha, the lenses clear and undistorted because there was nothing wrong with her eyes, the frames square to underscore that same quality in her face, and thick and heavy on her nose, pressing painfully into the flesh but worth it for the distraction they provided. She had toned down the makeup quite a bit because nearly half the people living in Trask, Kansas, were Mennonites and she desired above all things to go unnoticed, to fit in, to survive.

Trask was not so different from Dublin. Folks in both places lived a simple life, centered on family and work. Life from the ocean, life from the fields, a sea in either case, flowing from horizon to horizon, bountiful or barren as the good Lord willed. The men and women at the controls of hulking combines and rolling lobster boats were hewn from the same rock as far as she could tell, wresting sustenance from the elements on behalf of their less hearty brethren, worn down to the fundamentals by the fundamentals, certain of their standing in the scheme of things.

She too had lived a practical life the last two years in Maine, driven hard from waking to sleeping by the mundane tasks required to serve her charges, much as any farmer or fisherman was moved along by seasons. But they produced a bounty from their fields and fishing, while she had withheld hers. How she envied the secure boundaries of farmers and fishermen, so well established by heritage and law. How she coveted their family ground, their indisputable station among those who went before them, and beside them, and behind. How weary she was of the solitude of exile, of impermanence and dread. How she longed to throw aside the yoke of insignificance and live a life that mattered, as theirs did. Yet in her shameful weakness, still she dared not take the risk.

Willa had drifted into these envious daydreams about her neighbors without a conscious departure from the task at hand—sticking price labels on cans of corn—and so was taken by surprise when someone touched her elbow. With a startled cry she spun to find a boy there at her side, about six years old and three feet tall, the shortness of his stature very common for his people. Staring up at her with solemn features, he said, "*¿Donde esta mi mama?*"

In her surprise Willa's heart threatened to come bounding from her chest, but she forced herself to smile, doing her best to convert a reply from English to Portuguese to Spanish, saying, "*No sé, pero vamos a encontrar ella. ¿Esta bien?*" She set out with the child in search of his lost mother, who was soon found on the next aisle over, picking out a loaf of bread.

The woman seemed surprised to hear her language spoken in that northern place. Obviously a migrant worker with much Mayan blood, possibly illegal, she paused suspiciously before offering hesitant thanks for this kindness. She then took the boy by his hand and led him away, sternly promising that he would suffer a terrible fate if he did such a thing again, perhaps even including the prohibition of candy.

Watching them go, the mother and child so short and broad and sturdy and brown, Willa Newdale had a sudden, awful memory. She thought of The People, and their own source of sustenance, their sea-like verdant jungle flowing from horizon to horizon, bountiful or barren as the good Lord willed. She remembered her last contact with them, her own terrible fate, walking through the undergrowth with two others from the States, and sudden thuds, gentle moans, the others down and bleeding by the path, impaled on sharpened sticks. She remembered watching as the light went from their eyes, forgetting to flee, standing over them as if alone, and turning to find Waytee, old Waytee, there from out of nowhere less than half a spear away. She remembered looking at his eyes, twin holes of perfect black in a wrinkled fleshly frame, an enigma, and she with empty hands and without words to beg for life.

Willa watched the Indian woman lead her small son to the cash register, and she looked away and did her best to turn her thoughts to work.

Soon enough, the time came to leave. She took a loaf of bread from the shelves for herself, and a box of cereal and a quart of milk, and stood behind a customer in line at the single cash register, examining the small array of sundries on the impulse purchase rack— batteries and rubber bands and nail clippers and the *National Enquirer* and *Better Homes and Gardens*. She did not see many of the other magazines one so often found in grocery stores, the ones with covers showing women in low-cut dresses or bikinis. She assumed this was because of the Mennonites. She found it comforting. It implied a distance from the outside world, a distance that did not truly exist, of course, but it was nice to pretend.

After paying cash (credit cards were so easily traced) she donned her coat and packed her purchases into her large purse and slipped the strap over her shoulder and emerged from the small store onto the sidewalk. The late April air was brisk but not uncomfortable compared to Maine. She set out along the one commercial street in Trask, heading west. A pair of teenaged girls passed by on Rollerblades, gliding down the center of the empty street, holding hands, wearing down vests over loose-fitting cotton dresses with long sleeves and hems down to their ankles, the fabric flowing back behind, their hair drawn up in severe buns and covered by little white doily-looking things. Willa smiled at the contrast between the girls' old-fashioned apparel and their modern in-line skates.

Two blocks later the one-story brick businesses gave way to wooden houses. After three more blocks the sidewalk petered out and she was forced to walk along the ragged edge of a gravel road. She soon reached the outer limits of the tiny town, and her apartment in one of three buildings clustered around a treeless asphalt parking lot. Knee-high winter wheat stretched away from the apartments for as far as she could see, countless lush green rows beneath a feverish pink and violet sky.

Willa checked the parking lot and saw no unfamiliar vehicles, having memorized all of her neighbors' cars and trucks within the first two days. Approaching her apartment she noted the position of the window blinds, exactly as she left them. She paused at her door to reach into her purse. She felt around the small handgun and found her key and entered. With her fingers on the weapon in her purse, she traversed the single room that served for cooking, dining, and living and went through the door to the one small bedroom. It was clear. Then she checked the bathroom and slid the rolling closet door aside. When she knew that it was safe she took off her coat and hung it up and pulled the groceries from her purse and carried them back into the front room where she put the milk in the refrigerator, and the bread and cereal in a cabinet. She removed a packaged dinner from the freezer and peeled back the cellophane cover and placed it in the oven. She set the oven to four-hundred degrees, checked the time on her wristwatch, and went to the bathroom to take a shower. Fifteen minutes later, wrapped in a plaid flannel robe with her newly colored hair toweled off but moist, she sat down to eat.

The apartment had come furnished with a threadbare sofa, a plastic laminate dining table with tubular steel legs, four mismatched chairs, and a low table beside the sofa bearing a ceramic light fixture with a battered avocado-colored shade. Several weeks ago, after cashing her first paycheck at the grocery store where she worked, she had purchased a tiny black-and-white television set and a pair of folding metal tables: one for the television and the other for her dinner. Now she sat on the sofa watching the evening news, the wrinkles of her face sketched in shadow by the television's pale blue glow.

Everything around the world was normal—bombs in the Middle East, unemployment down, stocks up, motion-picture actors pregnant out of wedlock, politicians at each other's throats—and then the handsome anchorman said, "We move to our ongoing coverage of a remarkable story out of Milwaukee, where Julia Summers reports on what may well be the medical breakthrough of the century. Julia?"

The image on the television changed. A woman wearing a conservative blouse and dark suit coat spoke directly to the camera. "Connor, the building behind me is the global headquarters for Hanks Pharmaceuticals Corporation, one of the world's largest drug manufacturers. Yesterday, a high-level source within the Hanks organization revealed that they intend to develop, manufacture, and distribute what he claims is an outright cure for alcoholism."

Alone in the empty apartment, the old woman let her fork drop to the folding tray. She slumped back against the sofa as the television showed an interview with a well-dressed man with a perfect haircut, tanned complexion, and the varicose nose of a longtime drinker. The man said he had come forward because he could not remain silent while his employer "planned to profit from the misery of millions." An internal memo flashed onto the screen, bearing the Hanks Pharmaceuticals letterhead with the title *Confidential.* One highlighted line on the memo read, *A price per unit of $5,000 will be both necessary and viable, given the single-dosage product application and the level of demand.*

The television reporter said the actual release of the medicine was several years away, but Willa barely noticed. She thought about the men and women she had left behind, paupers every one of them. She thought about the cots and bunk beds filled with them, the empty stomachs and the empty eyes of them, the utter hopelessness of them. Five thousand dollars might as well have been a billion to them.

Willa thought about the months down in the jungle, the violence, gore, the shouted threats she knew were based in fact—*"there is no place to hide; we won't stop looking; no matter where you go, we'll find you"*—and her blind flight and desperate furtiveness, five years of hiding here and there around two continents, and two more years in Dublin, waiting, hoping for the missionary's return.

She thought about the moment when he came at last, the moment when she saw his hopeless look in the mirror and knew her wait had been in vain, for how could he possess the secret she required when he himself remained in desperate need of it? She thought about those next few days and nights, going through the motions even though she could no longer avoid her self-delusion, pretending there had been good reason for delay, withholding on a noble pretense when the truth was more mundane.

She had always been a coward.

It had taken a dead look in a mirror and a dead man on the laundry floor to finally make her face that fact, and even then she had equivocated, putting everything into a passing basket, trusting far too freely in the hands of fate. She should have gone to the authorities. Every day of the last seven years had been another opportunity, and every day another failure of her faith. Then had come the final chance, when all the other hopeless ones had come to force it out of him and she had thought to say, "It's me you want." But still she had held back, let him go, fleeing yet again, saving herself . . . for what?

She looked around her hiding place, saw the cast-off furniture, the empty walls, the rectangular eye of her shallow electric companion glowing on the dinner tray, and Willa knew her fundamental problem had not changed: her enemy would still kill to keep his secret and he would not stop looking, no matter where she went. Indeed, it was all the more so now. The only change was in the vanished pretext for her silence. Those who could afford the price would be set free; all the others would go down to death so that she could keep her life. Until now there had always been another possibility, a justification for delay—waiting for the missionary, the second portion of the secret, and as she waited, a hope some other means might come. But five thousand dollars had brought the end of all excuses. It was to be her life or a million others; the choice was unavoidable. She could perhaps survive for ten or even twenty years, hiding in slums and backwater towns before dying of old age in the company of strangers. But she could no longer pretend the cost was hers alone.

19

Riley dropped an anonymous cashier's check for one hundred thousand dollars in the collection basket. It was the fifth time he had done so in the ten weeks since Dylan closed the deal. They said it was better to give than to receive, but he felt no joy in the experience, having stolen it in the first place. To get around that scruple Riley sometimes told himself that every offering was originally a gift from God anyway, and if all anybody ever did was give back what the Lord had given, was he any different? Unfortunately, that logic wasn't doing any good. According to his banker in New York, Henry had not cashed a single check so far—more than half a million dollars' worth of paper in the preacher's drawer or somewhere, unaccepted—so apparently not all offerings were the same. Maybe after he had given God an even million they would be square. Maybe it would take ten. Or maybe there wasn't enough money in the world.

Pushing his new eyeglasses higher on his nose, Riley decided not to think about it anymore. He settled in to listen to the sermon as Pastor Henry approached the podium. Thirty minutes later, the lady to his left passed him the Communion tray. It felt strangely heavy in his hands. He stared down at the concentric circles of plastic thimbles, red wine in the center, grape juice around the outside. At least that was the usual way they arranged the blood of Christ. But what if someone made a mistake? What if the wine was on the outside this time? Riley thought about the note he had stolen from the offering basket.

... if they ever drink again, the urge will return stronger than ever.

Staring at the juice and wine, Riley remembered the chief of police outside the tent at Teal Pond, asking Hope to explain the Mercedes. He remembered Bree walking away when he could not bring himself to give advice about her boyfriend. He remembered the powder he had piled upon a plastic tray at Henry's Drug Store, the surprising weight remaining, pressing him to poison those who needed healing most. He thought of Dylan Delaney entering Hope's kitchen without knocking. He thought of his old friend Brice's last sensation, the caustic taste of rubbing alcohol granting sweet oblivion. Riley saw the start of everything, the equatorial sunlight slanting through pollen-laden air to illuminate a clearing filled with corpses, and in his hands he saw the multicolored stained-glass radiance reflected in a dozen little circles on the tray, every color in the universe absorbed into monotonous blood red, everything the same no matter what he did, and suddenly he did not care which one he drank.

Riley closed his eyes, picked a random thimble, and tossed the liquid down.

He set the tray onto the pew beside him and stood and walked out of the church alone, descending the tall steps and crossing town on foot to his garage apartment, where he lay down to take a Sunday nap with the unrelenting taste of grape juice in his mouth.

The next morning he showered and shaved and dressed himself and went to work the lunch shift at Sadie's Downtown Diner, where he overheard a couple of the local fellas talking. The men weren't making any secret of their conversation in the little dining room, so Riley couldn't help but overhear their comments about Hope. The fella doing most of the talking was named Jim something. He wore a plaid wool cap with earflaps, even though the temperature outside was finally up into the sixties now that it was May. Jim had recognized Riley when he first started working at the diner a few months ago, said he knew him from his days before in Dublin, remembered he had left for Brazil as a missionary and then came back to teach at Bowditch for a little while. The man had asked a few embarrassing questions about the time since then—"where ya been, what ya been doin'"—but Riley had grown used to lying about that.

The other one was named Billy or maybe Bobby, someone Riley kind of remembered from back in high school. The guy used to be a troublemaker hippie-type if Riley remembered right, but now he saw this Billy-Bobby fella over at the church sometimes. At least maybe he did. Riley couldn't be sure, because he tried not to look at people's faces when he went to church. He usually sat in a pew near the back, alone, hoping his short hair and clean-shaven face and new clothes would do the trick as they had with Bill Hightower and Henry and the chief, hoping even God would not recognize him for a thief as he waited for the offering basket to come around, in disguise as his old self.

"I hear the mayor's talkin' 'bout puttin' these bums up in town somewheres," said Jim, the one with the hayseed-looking earflaps. "Plum foolish in the head, ya ask me."

"Ayuh," said Billy or Bobby, slurping his vegetable soup and getting a splatter on his greasy tie. "Don't make no sense at all ta treat 'em like they's tourists."

"Don't I know it!"

"Ya know what?"

"Huh?"

"She got a million-dollar car parked in her backyard!"

"Go on ya!"

"Saw it with my own eyes."

Earflaps chewed his food a moment, then said, "Ya think that's got somethin' ta do with all them bums?"

"It's got somethin' ta do with *somethin'*—ya can bet on that."

"She's on somebody's payroll, an it ain't ours."

"Ayuh. Oughta put her in the pokey and get a whole 'nother mayor's what we oughta do."

Billy-Bobby and Mr. Jim Earflaps fell silent after that, chewing their food methodically like a pair of cows. Riley wondered why they had spoken about Hope right in front of him that way. Maybe they did not remember he was her ex-husband. Or maybe they assumed the divorce meant he did not care about her anymore. Whatever the explanation, as Riley cleared the table next to them, he had the strongest urge to knock their ignorant heads together. He had piled all the dirty dishes into the gray plastic tub and nearly finished wiping off the tabletop when Jim said, "I'm thinkin' maybe Mr. Hightower's got the moxie ta handle things." More silent chewing, then, "Hey, ya goin' ta that town-hall meetin' he called tonight?"

"Well I guess prob'ly!"

"You gonna stand up?"

"Naw. Ain't much on talkin' in front a people. You?"

"Maybe. Time somebody gave that woman a piece a their mind."

The two men griped another ten minutes before finishing their meals and leaving. Riley thought about their words as he worked through the lunch rush. He felt the familiar weight descending and resisted it. There was no time for that. He had to *do* something!

Riley made a phone call to find out what time the meeting was to start. He got Sadie's permission to leave an hour early, and when the time came he removed his apron and stepped out the front door into a beautiful spring afternoon. The azure sky was cloudless. The air felt clean and cool and comfortable against his face. The stately birches touching branches along Main Street were finally in leaf, their virginal green crowns as soft and pale and delicate as low-lying fog. It would have been a picture postcard view of a small New England town except for the shabby men and women loitering everywhere, most of them filthy, wearing far more clothing than the weather called for, sitting on the curb and leaning against the birches or the facades of business storefronts. Riley knew exactly why they were there. They were there for him, waiting for the man who healed a few of them last winter, hoping he would reappear. Riley felt the weight of their desire added to the weight of all that he had done to Hope. Yet he still felt a frantic need to fix things.

In the distance Riley heard voices shouting something over and over. As he scanned the street to find the source of the commotion he saw two well-dressed women emerge from a boutique across the way and hurry toward a fancy car with Massachusetts plates, neither woman looking right or left as they passed a huddle of vagrants. When their car backed out of the parking spot Riley saw the woman on the passenger side turn to lock her door. With a sigh he set out up the hill, heading for Bill Hightower's meeting.

Dublin's town hall straddled the top of Main Street, high above him. With the foot of the street at the town landing and the businesses and churches set well back from the curbs along the street, there was a clear line of sight from down at the harbor through the overarching birches all the way up to the brick and granite building. When approaching the landing from the water, the town hall's position made it the natural focus of attention, and the old copper clipper ship atop the weather vane on the building's cupola the most prominent man-made object in all of Dublin. This was the founding fathers' intention, Riley supposed, since their town was built on shipbuilding.

As he neared the high end of Main Street, Riley saw about a hundred people on the sidewalk below the town-hall steps. The crowd was the source of the repeated shouts he had heard down by the diner. He paused to listen to their words.

"One, two, three, four, we won't let you kill the poor!"

"Five, six, seven, eight, cut the cost and end the wait!"

Pushing his eyeglasses higher on his nose, Riley saw a few homemade signs waving above the heads of the people: *Cure Us Now!* and *Heal the Homeless!* and *Murder for Hire!* He felt as if every word they shouted, everything written, was focused right on him. He wished there was a way to explain.

He saw television news crews at the fringes of the demonstration with camera and sound operators and reporters looking out of place in their suits. Eyeing the cameras around the crowd, he thought about his darkly silhouetted shaggy image in the back of Bill

Hightower's car, broadcast onto millions of television screens on the nightly news. He did not want to repeat that experience. He wanted to remain unnoticed, as unconnected as possible from the "mystery man" of Dublin and the events of the previous autumn. He almost turned back down the hill.

Then he remembered the ugly conversation in the diner, the way those men had spoken about Hope as if she was not a person with feelings, but rather a symbol or an object, a scapegoat. Riley wiped his sweating palms upon his shirt. If there was going to be a scape-goat, it ought to be him. He wove his way through the crowd and began to climb the steps.

Memories of the glory days of shipbuilding were built into every brick and board of Dublin's center of government. To reinforce the imposing sense of power already well established by the building's situation above downtown, the sixteen granite steps tapered as they ascended, providing an illusion of deep perspective, as if Riley's climb would take him to the heavens. At the top of the steps stood four imposing white Corinthian columns with ornate capitals hand-carved with images of ships in every stage of construction instead of the usual clusters of Grecian grape leaves. The columns rose from a broad landing. Behind them were two front doors, twelve feet tall and built of African mahogany by a long forgotten master ship-wright. On the panels of each door were bas-relief carvings of more shipbuilding scenes. To Riley's dismay, in front of the doors stood Chief Steven Novak and two uniformed policemen wearing helmets.

One of the policemen moved to bar Riley's way, but the chief said something to him and the cop stepped back. When Riley reached the landing at the top of the stairs, the chief spoke loudly so he would be heard above the chanting demonstrators. "Hi ya, Riley. Here for the meeting?"

"Is that okay?"

"Ayuh. Open to all residents. Most of 'em used the side door, though."

Riley had forgotten that option. He turned to look back down at the crowd. "What are they doing here?"

"Mad about the price of that new cure for alkies, best I can tell. Wanna get it for free."

"But why are they here at town hall?"

"Wantin' a photo opportunity, I imagine. Prob'ly figure Bill Hightower called the meetin' to talk about getting rid of the alkies, and this is the town where that so-called cure got invented, so—"

"Invented? Why would they think that?"

"Don't ya watch the news? They've been talkin' 'bout a connection between this new cure and the troubles we had last fall. The 'mystery man' and the riot at Henry's store. Ya know about all that, right?"

Riley did not trust himself to speak.

The chief turned to look at him. "I'm kinda hopin' they're right. Mebbe they can find that fella for me. Sure do wanna talk to him 'bout Willa Newdale." The chief bent closer to speak into his ear. "Did ya know Willa?"

"I don't think so," lied Riley.

The chief continued to lean close to Riley, searching his face. "We never had a chance to finish talkin' 'bout how come a professor is workin' over at the diner, did we? Sure like to hear your life's story one of these days."

Riley felt his heartbeat rising. "Okay."

"Maybe I'll drop by for lunch or somethin' after we get a handle on all this." The chief waved toward the crowd and Riley followed the gesture, relieved to look away from his searching eyes.

Down below, Riley saw people he recognized from the shelter. He saw the giant from Houston, standing head and shoulders above everyone else. He thought of that night—was it really six months past already?—being manhandled down the street against his will to Henry's Drug Store, and the helpless fear of knowing he was out of miracles when they had placed so much naked hope in him. He thought of the night before that, giving out the little bit of powder he had found—all of the cure he ever had—and the joy on the faces of those few he had cured. The weight had lifted then, for just a little while. He thought of his excitement when he figured out a way to fix everything, a way to make things easier for Hope and Bree, and to help Dylan, the good man who had come to take Riley's place. He thought of all these homeless alcoholics, who like him had heard that miracles were happening in Maine and staked their lives against the ravenous winter on the hope that it was true. Riley thought of his brief weeks of satisfaction when he foolishly believed he had found a life worth living, and then he thought about five thousand dollars and the fact that his grand scheme to help the world was yet another blessing that had been forbidden him. He should have known such good fortune would not be granted to a ghost.

Five thousand dollars. He remembered first hearing that figure and not understanding what it meant, alone that night in his garage apartment. He remembered people coming on the television to explain the implications. The rich would never suffer alcoholism again, but of course the poor would have no hope. A new class distinction would be born, a brave new world where the wealthy could purchase sobriety with its attendant virtues, while the poor remained addicted and exposed to all the sins that drunkenness inspired.

Five thousand dollars was the difference between salvation and slavery. The price of willpower. The cost of freedom. The value of a human life. Riley remembered hearing the people on the television say these things, and the weight coming down again as he began to realize what he had done. In his simpleminded eagerness to help Hope and Bree, and Dylan, and a world of broken people, he had failed to consider one simple, obvious detail—all the millions they were paying him had to come from somewhere.

At first Riley had assumed it must be a mistake. He knew Lee Hanks would make it right. Mr. Hanks was the fine Christian man who had sent him off to save the pagans of Brazil. So Riley had asked Dylan to make a call, to explain the problem, and the solution. Riley would cut his own price, cut it down to nearly nothing. Then Mr.

Hanks's company could sell the cure for much less, perhaps even give it freely to those too poor to pay.

But although Dylan had left many messages, Mr. Hanks had not replied.

As if the thought had conjured up the lawyer from below, Riley saw Hope's lover come uphill along the sidewalk, approaching the crowd at the foot of the steps. Dylan did not pause but tucked his head and pressed right into the mass of them. Riley watched him nearly make it to the bottom step, then a man stubbornly refused to get out of his way. There was a little flurry of movement, and several other demonstrators moved to block his progress. He seemed to stumble, but then he straightened up and turned to go back through the crowd the way he came. A couple of men stepped up to block his retreat in that direction too.

"Uh, Chief . . ." said Riley.

"I see him." The chief pointed at Dylan and said, "Hey, Dave, you and Ronny wanna go get that fool and bring him up here?"

With their black batons drawn, the two policemen hurried down the steps and muscled their way into the crowd, arriving at Dylan's side and hustling him toward the steps. The protesters parted reluctantly before the three men, but they made it back to the stairs without the use of force. Soon a pale and nervous Dylan joined Riley and the chief in front of the town-hall doors.

"Seems like them fellas don't like ya very much, counselor," said Chief Novak.

"Ayuh. Been gettin' that a lot," said Dylan.

Riley glanced at his profile and saw his swollen black and purple left eye and felt a rush of sympathy. The man had been a target ever since CNN broke the story and the whole world learned Dylan was the legal representative of BHR Incorporated, the Delaware corporation that held the provisional patent on the cure. People had vandalized his truck, thrown rocks at his house, and a homeless man had walked up to him in the street and socked him in the eye without warning. But in spite of everything, Dylan had not broached the subject of going public with Riley's identity.

The chief said, "Bet they'd back off if ya told us who your client is."

"We've been all through that," said Dylan, carefully looking away from Riley.

"Ayuh," said the chief. "But I still think your man mighta killed our Willa. Be a good thing if ya gave him up."

"I just can't, Steve. I can tell ya he's no murderer, if that makes ya feel any better."

"Naw. Won't feel no better till I have that fella in my jail."

Riley stared at the angry faces in the crowd below, the ones who had slept with him in the shelter, who had remained in Dublin through the bitter cold winter, who had come here seeking a miracle and would not leave without it. If they would treat Dylan this way, what would they do to him? He remembered the giant's rage in Henry's pharmacy, and felt a new fear supersede his concerns about the police chief's investigation of Willa Newdale's disappearance. It was an awful thing to be the focus of such fury. If Dylan ever wavered under the pressure to reveal his client's name, Chief Novak's jail might be the safest place in town.

As if reading Riley's mind, Dylan said, "Shouldn't ya get more men up here?"

The chief nodded, his eyes also wary on the crowd. "Would if I could."

"What else could they be doin' that's more important than this?"

The chief faced Dylan. "Well, counselor, let's see. Five a my fellas are on riot alert down at the park already, and another couple of 'em are handlin' some of these people at the landin', and for some reason these alkies keep wantin' to break into Henry's Drug Store again so I had to send some fellas over there. Like I keep sayin', if you'd just gimme a name maybe we could settle a lot of these people down."

Dylan sighed and said nothing, as Riley eyed the other two policemen. Three men at the top of the stairs, and a hundred at the bottom. He asked, "Are we safe?"

"I tried to get Bill Hightower to call this off, but the pig-headed ..." The chief's voice trailed off as Riley saw him make a deliberate effort at self-control. After a moment, staring down at the protesters, the chief continued, "I told 'em a while ago not to set foot on the steps, and so far they're stayin' back. You fellas stop your worryin' and go on in. We can handle this out here."

Riley watched the giant from Houston chanting angry slogans with a massive raised fist beating time above his head. Riley thought about leaving Dublin. Probably with all his money there was a way to go someplace where people could not find him. But he did not know how to use money in that way. What if he did it wrong and made things even worse? Everything he did made things worse. It might even be better to vanish without the money, go back to what he was before. Riley knew exactly how to disappear into the midst of those he had betrayed. He could head south to the overpasses of Florida where no one could ever find him. He could be Stanley Livingston again. Given all his failures here in Dublin, the prospect had appeal—a simple life, beholden to no one and responsible for nothing.

Then Riley thought of the naïve girl who had shared his dream to save the world. She had followed him so willingly into danger, followed in a dugout canoe, and after four long years she had dragged him home insensate. He remembered going through the motions here at home, and Hope's apparently unending patience until that final night, was it four years after they came home from Brazil? Yes, at least that long. One did not go from holy man to homeless alcoholic overnight. Four years of steady decline from failed mission-ary to failed professor, failed husband, failed father. And the final form of danger he inflicted on her that last evening in their kitchen when he had raised his hand to Bree and Hope had charged between them, suddenly a tigress, furiously driving him out into the street, into his native element once and for all, back into the jungle where she should have left him in the first place.

He had spent three years in that jungle, homeless on the streets, thinking all the time of alcohol. What a surprise to learn he could not go home now that he was sober. He would always love her, but look at what he had accomplished with sobriety. As it had been with The People, so it was again. In trying to provide for Hope, Riley might well have ruined everything. He should leave as soon as possible. He should have stayed away completely. He saw that now—too late, of course—but before he went he had to find a way to lift this weight from Hope, a way to make it right for her forever.

"Riley?"

He turned to find Hope's lover standing there, battered and bruised on his behalf, a fine, good man, the kind of man Hope and Bree deserved, holding the imposing hand-carved door open and staring at him curiously.

"I was just thinking," said Riley.

"Sure."

With Dylan following, Riley entered.

20

With her car window down in honor of the beautiful spring afternoon, Hope cruised aimlessly, counting desperate people, passing numbers thirty-eight and thirty-nine, two men combing through a trash can. She was in the old Pontiac because the opulent Mercedes made her nervous. She had driven it only once or twice since learning that it caused so much suspicion. Other than that, she left the expensive car in her backyard out of sight. Hope understood why it bothered people. No one gave a gift like that for nothing; someone somewhere wanted something in return. It had just about given her a conniption fit trying to figure out who it was. At first she lived in daily expectation of some fella from away dropping by her office, asking for a special-use permit to build a slaughterhouse or a paper mill or some such blight on the community. She fantasized herself saying "No sir, mister man, you just take these keys and get on back to whatever rock you crawled out from under." But when weeks went by and nothing like that happened, she began to think the gift had most likely come from Dylan.

At least Dylan was the only one who had the motive and the opportunity. Three years ago, soon after Riley left town, Dylan had begun to come around. He was helpful and handsome, and he went to her church, and in her loneliness she might have encouraged his attentions. He had asked her to marry him last year, and she was pretty sure the thought was still never far from his mind even now, so yes, the car had probably come from Dylan, who had lots of motivation.

As for opportunity, incredibly, that had come along as well. Soon after the luxurious Mercedes so mysteriously appeared in her driveway, Dylan had purchased a new pickup truck for himself, an expensive one, with a big diesel engine and double tires on the back axle and a crew cab. He also put the *Mary Lynn* on the hard at Mc-Sweeny's Yard for a complete refit, including a paint job. Meanwhile, every lobsterman in town continued to bemoan the unexplained migration of their livelihood to other waters, which only added to Hope's worries. She had wondered where on earth Dylan's money could have come from if not the sea, and why he did not speak of his sudden wealth. She wondered if he was hiding something. He had mentioned going back to practicing law, working for some company from away, but although she knew Dylan was as sharp as a tack she still questioned how a small-town lobsterman who hadn't practiced law in years could attract such a client. Hope feared to ask her question because of the implied mistrust. She had opted instead to do her best to keep suspicion from her thoughts. But that had not been possible. She lost a lot of sleep over that Mercedes.

Then Bill Hightower had called to say her mortgage was paid off. Even after finding a hundred thousand dollars' worth of car parked in her driveway, Hope had been shocked, but not too shocked to think of asking where the mortgage money came from. It seemed a private bank in New York City had wired the outstanding balance on behalf of an anonymous client. So, with nearly twenty years to go on her payments, suddenly Hope Keep owned her whole house, free and clear, and she had become . . . what?

Angry?

Frightened?

It was hard to put a name to the emotion. Frustration entered into it, certainly, because Bill Hightower of all people had handled the transaction, and of course it would give him just the leverage he had been looking for to force her hand about their homeless problem, more than a quarter million between the house and car, and her not knowing who it came from.

Then this news about a cure for alcoholism, and the astonishing announcement that Dylan was involved—was representing one of the companies, just as he had said—and while it certainly explained the money, it left her even more confused about her feelings. She had asked Dylan to take the car and money back in some public way that would clear her name, yet he refused to admit the gifts had come from him. He did assure her there was no law against accepting them, as if that would be a comfort. So long as she did not compromise her political integrity, and so long as the car had not been stolen, in Dylan's professional opinion as the world's most successful part-time lawyer and lobsterman she could keep the Mercedes and the money, although she would have to pay income taxes on their value.

Until then she had not even thought of income taxes. Now she contemplated the injustice of that on top of all the rest as she counted homeless person number sixty-three, an old woman sitting on the curb. The old woman had as much chance of paying taxes on a quarter million dollars' worth of gifts as Hope did, what with living check to check on a meager mayor's salary in a shrinking town of four thousand hard-hit souls. Hope had a daughter on the verge of college, Lord willing, and payments to make on her new boiler. She had considered selling the Mercedes and using the proceeds to pay the taxes on the mortgage money, but what if the car really had been stolen? Wouldn't someone want it back?

Homeless person number eighty-eight stepped in front of her, stepped right out as if the Pontiac wasn't coming, and staggered to the far side of the street all jerky knees and arms akimbo like some bit actor doing a zombie from *Night of the Living Dead*. As Hope braked to a halt, all her worries chased around and round her head. Why were these people still here? Why stay through the winter? Why did more show up every day? She had asked these questions of a homeless man that very morning and learned they hoped the "mystery man" would reappear, or some clue would be found in Dublin of his whereabouts. They all knew it would be years before the government approved the cure for sale, and even then no homeless drunk would have a prayer of paying what Hanks Pharmaceuticals said they planned to charge. Yet hopes of getting healed were all these people had, and those hopes were centered here, in Dublin, where a mystery man had healed a few of them last fall for free.

Still counting, still driving slowly around town, Hope remembered when the newspapers and television first announced the whole thing was connected to a lawyer in the little town of Dublin, Maine—Dylan, of course. She was so surprised by this she had barely noticed that Hanks Pharmaceuticals was also mentioned. It took her almost a day to associate the company with another man she knew, Lee Hanks, the billionaire whom they said would sell the cure when it was ready. Of course she did not really know him. She had only met Lee Hanks the one time, during an interview with the missions board that sent her and Riley to Brazil. But when Hope remembered that interview, and thought about the fact that she and Dylan were ... whatever they were, and she had a top-of-the-line Mercedes in her backyard and the title to her house all free and clear, she sensed some kind of disaster coming, especially when it finally occurred to her that Riley had apparently not had a drink in half a year.

How was all this possible?

She remembered heady days of long ago, leaving that missions-board interview with everyone's best wishes, Mr. Hanks among them. She had pictures in her head of Riley a few weeks later, pausing in his headlong rush along the jetway to smile back at her, and she herself a little later sleeping with his shoulder for a pillow on the TAM flight direct from Miami, Florida, to Manaus, Brazil, and waking beside him to look down from ten thousand feet upon the mighty river, a golden ribbon in the sunrise, draped haphazardly across the black forbidding wilderness below.

Hope remembered another thing, the memories tripping over each other now, a riot of multicolored rope hammocks hanging everywhere on the riverboat—the *Tartaruga*, or "Turtle" as she later learned, which was a poor name indeed, for any turtle Hope had ever seen could easily outpace that rusted hulk—and the diesel fumes, and the smoke of cooking fires upon the deck, and Riley swaying in his hammock right beside her, tickling her through the webbing, and a dozen deep bronze third-class passengers laughing at her helpless giggles. Now as she drove past the blazing cherry branches on the Bowditch College campus, Hope remembered a glorious *ipe* tree aflame with pink in Mãe do Deus, that stilted village of roughhewn boards and woven thatch and corrugated metal roofs far beyond the remarkable confluence of the black-and-white waters of the Rio Negro and Rio Solimões—kilometers and kilometers beyond container ships and riverboats, where Riley had transferred their meager possessions to motorized dugout canoes so they could venture upstream into the shallows, always upstream, beyond the last vestiges of everything they knew and understood except for Jesus and each other, and the whine and rattle of the ancient outboard motor, and the unsmiling man who sat behind her steering, and the river streaming past, and Riley sitting up in front of her, twisting to reach back and hold her hand, smiling wide and unafraid, and she, therefore, also unafraid.

As Hope drove through the campus counting heathens—counting number one hundred seventeen, a man on hands and knees without a shirt, vomiting in a doorway as she passed—she thought of weaving slowly through a massive flooded forest, the *igapó*, and leaning back against her bundles to trail her fingers through the jet black waters, home to the *tambaqui*, a fish that lived on fruit, and the water in the air so thick, the air so hot, she sometimes felt a pot of tea could be brewed without a fire or kettle, just drink the pollen-infested air, the sullen, sodden, smoldering air. Although it had now been eleven years, she could still see herself and Riley just like it was yesterday, drifting among silent giants three times taller than the tallest building back in Dublin, the canopy above so thick and dark it felt like blue instead of green, the ancient trunks mottled with lichen and moss, the limbs exploding with scarlet bromeliads and purple orchids and interwoven strangler figs as thick as her sun-burned thigh, passing by those towering columns, passing by like ants upon a floating leaf, and Riley's sweat-drenched back before her. Riley, her dear husband, always going first, eager to be the first among The People, eager to be about his Father's business.

She would have followed Riley anywhere, or so she thought back then, back before she knew where they were really going, the price of failure after four years in the jungle, four long years and then a mass grave in the clearing where the village used to stand, and Riley certain everything was all his fault.

Hope remembered arguing with him from behind her own thick veil of grief, the understanding growing in her that the horror was not finished; it had simply moved to him, the boy she married who had never touched a drink before, now dead drunk to the world. Two weeks drunk that first time if her memory served, two weeks of rav-ing, of "doing penance" as he called it, taking their affliction deep inside himself.

How she had argued! How she tried to make him see no man could bear so much responsibility. But the thing in Riley that had led them to the deepest Amazon had then led him deeper still. Two weeks drunk after a lifetime without drink was further up into the shallows than even she could follow. She had radioed for help, and help had come, a pair of missionaries in a bright yellow Cessna, from another village down the river.

Hope's heart had soared to hear their airplane's engine. Two weeks there alone with Riley had been a harder trial than all the years before, harder than the language, harder than the loneliness and apparent lack of progress in the early days, harder than all the Western things she had learned to do without. Riley drunk and weeping for the dead had nearly broken Hope before the brothers came.

She remembered standing by the clearing as they landed, waving and trying to smile. She remembered the hugs, smelling soap on one of them when they walked up close. She remembered how the compassion in their faces changed when they laid eyes on Riley, snoring in the dirt. The abruptness of their choices, telling her to pack no more than fifty pounds and be prepared to take off in two hours. Carrying Riley to the Cessna, looking at each other but not at him, not at her. Sending them away. After four years in the jungle with The People, sending them away.

She remembered looking down from high above as the little airplane banked, seeing fresh-turned soil at one end of the clearing, a common grave for everyone, and the river like a golden ribbon in the sunset, draped haphazardly across the black forbidding wilderness below as the engine rumbled up ahead and Riley snored beside her.

That had been, what? Seven years ago? Maybe seven and a half. Then had come four more years with him slowly sinking here in Dublin, and three more after that with Riley gone in body as he had already gone in spirit.

Hope drove past the gorgeous cherry trees of Bowditch College, feeling the burden of all those years, Riley in his full retreat, running back to Dublin and a teaching job, the gradual disintegration, late nights, hung-over mornings, unremembered rides in township squad cars, regurgitation on the front lawn, a month before he told her he had lost the college job, a year before he stopped pretending he would find another, ridiculous attempts to hide it from their neighbors, another year of solitary drinking in the garage, losing dignity and dreams, losing home, losing them. In spite of everything that had happened down among The People, Hope sometimes thought the mighty Amazon had been kinder than these dark jungles of Maine, where she had writhed for years in the quicksand of despair as Riley floundered and sank below the surface, and was gone.

Returning downtown now, still counting on the left and right, Hope turned onto Main Street and looked up the hill and felt as if she had been punched in the stomach. A small army of vagrants in tattered clothing milled aimlessly around the park above her like survivors at a bomb site, sprawling on the grass, standing, running, shouting, sleeping, young and old, calm and rowdy, strewing garbage indiscriminately and waiting for something she did not believe existed.

Hope rolled slowly past the park in her old Pontiac and tried not to hate them. She tried not to dream of better days with Riley as he once had been. She had to focus on this, right here and now. She had to think the problem through. She was the mayor. The responsibility was hers, and there were so many problems to be solved.

For instance, what were all these people going to eat?

And where were they going to the bathroom? (She winced at the thought.)

And where would they take shelter if there was a bad spring storm?

And most of all, how could they be controlled, so many of them, when they began to realize they could simply take the things they wanted?

Hope had covered only half of Dublin and already she was up to 137 obvious indigents out on the streets. There was no reason to assume she would find any fewer if she drove the other side of town as well. Add all of them to these people at the park and Hope believed there might be five or even six hundred homeless men and women now. Last autumn had been bad enough, with maybe fifty of them roaming through her little town, but they had kept trickling in all winter, and spring had brought the promise of survivable temperatures for the next six or seven months, and then came the news story about this alleged cure of Mr. Hanks's with its Dublin connection, and they had swarmed up the coast like locusts. So on top of everything else—half the downtown businesses closing, population shrinking, lobsters vanishing, costly gifts from who knows whom for who knows what reason and all the painful memories Riley's return had thrust upon her—on top of all of that had come this plague of biblical proportions.

Hope had called to ask the governor to send the Maine National Guard. Someone at his office said he would get back to her as soon as possible. That had been three days ago. She figured at least fifty more homeless men and women had come walking into Dublin in that time. According to Steve Novak, in the last twenty-four hours alone the police department had received two reports of stolen vehicles, eight burglaries, and three separate assaults, which was more than the number of criminal offenses Dublin might see in half a normal year. There were nearly constant complaints of graffiti everywhere, garbage everywhere, vandalism everywhere, elderly folks afraid to sleep with their windows open, women frightened to walk outside in broad daylight. Landry's Sporting Goods over on Highway 1 had sold out of handguns, shotguns and rifles, then restocked, and then sold out again. And it was not just her townsfolk getting armed; in two of last night's burglaries, firearms and ammunition had been stolen.

The shelter had been overtaxed all winter, so that was nothing new, but Reverend Reardon was now turning them away from the sanctuary of the First Congregational Church. Imagine all the pews full every night, and the floor too! Hope would not have believed it had she not stopped by last Friday evening to see for herself. The stench of unwashed bodies in the church had been horrible, far worse than the smell of passengers sweating in their hammocks on the third-class deck of the riverboat *Tartaruga*.

Hope passed the swarm of homeless people at the park, climbing Main Street toward town hall, where Bill Hightower had called an emergency meeting. She dared not be late, not if she wished to keep her job. And in spite of everything, Hope did want to keep her job. The pay was lousy, the pressure sometimes nearly overwhelming, but she had important work to do. She had to save this town from surviving at the cost of hatred. She had to save herself from that same mistake. So she would not run away and she would not hide. Riley Keep might be that weak, but she was not. She would drive on toward the top of the hill, toward the trouble that surely lay in wait, and leave her memories at the bottom.

21

Inside Dublin's town hall, Riley crossed a vestibule with dark wood paneling and a marble floor to enter a large meeting room with a two-story-high ceiling. The walls were rounded at the far end and square at the entrance where he and Dylan Delaney stood. The floor sloped down from their position toward seven people who sat behind a richly varnished desk or counter that followed the curvature of the rounded wall. Hope sat in the middle of the counter, with three town councilors to her left and three more to her right, including Bill Hightower. At the center of this semicircle below Riley and Dylan was an ornate podium. Rising up from there, about a dozen rows of fixed wooden seats had been arranged along the sloping floor. Riley remembered eager hours listening to lectures on soteriology and ecclesiology in a hall arranged like this during his seminary years. But the walls at seminary had been painted sheetrock and the seats were made of plastic and aluminum. This hall, with its elegant wood furnishings and soaring multi-paned windows, was an unusually fine council chamber for such a small town, a testimony to the days two hundred years ago when the builders of mighty clipper ships and whalers had created wealth far in excess of any other time in Dublin.

The seats were almost completely packed with locals. Riley and Dylan slipped along the back row past a couple of people and settled in to listen as Hope spoke to Bill Hightower, her amplified voice reverberating in the lofty space, easily heard above the muffled chanting of the protesting crowd outside. She said, "It just seems to me we have to face the fact they're here and make the best of it. Technically you're right: we could arrest 'em all for vagrancy, but what's the point of that, when the jail will only hold a fraction of 'em?"

From the far seat on her right, Bill Hightower said, "So your solution is to commandeer the private property of business owners? Force them to give up their businesses to shelter these freeloaders?"

"They wouldn't give up their businesses, Bill. Like I just explained, they'd only make the upper floors of their buildings available, which as we all know haven't been used for much of anything in a long time. And the space wouldn't be commandeered. They'd be reimbursed at a fair rate."

"Reimbursed with what? Where's the money coming from?"

"I'm open to suggestions on that."

Hightower shook his head. "All right, let's ignore the fact that the tax base is shrinking and these indigents who have descended on us only make that problem worse, let's pretend we can print our own money, or one of the council members or one of these good citizens can work a miracle and figure out a way to pay for your plan. Even if we could afford it, do you really think it's a good idea to have hundreds of vagrants living downtown? I fail to see how that would improve our situation."

Riley heard the muted voices of the demonstrators outside as Hope replied, "They'd have a place to sleep. They'd have bathrooms. We could set up some simple cookin' facilities—"

"You're talking about turning downtown into a ghetto!"

Hope said, "I can't think of anyplace else with enough space to—"

"Hundreds of drunks, camped out above our downtown businesses, partying on the township's tab? Come *on*, Hope! Do you really want to do that to your neighbors?"

The hall erupted in applause, drowning out the distant voices, with some in the audience rising from their seats.

Hope beat a gavel and called for order, but it took several minutes to get the people to calm down. When she finally had control again she said, "If these people choose to live here, the township attorney tells me we have no legal basis to run 'em out of town. This is not the Wild West. And let's remember these are human beings we're talkin' about. We can't let them go on livin' on our streets and in our parks. It's not right. So since there are way too many to arrest, and we can't force 'em to rent or purchase dwellings, I can't think of anything else to do except provide shelter for them. And I—"

"What about the state? What about the federal government? Why haven't you reached out for help from them?"

Again, there was a spontaneous round of applause from the audience, but this time Hope managed to get control more quickly. She said, "I've been callin' the governor's office. Apparently he's too busy to call back."

Hightower spread his hands and shrugged. "Maybe you're not calling the right number, Mayor Keep. I phoned the governor this morning. He's ready to send us all the help we need."

Hope frowned. "You spoke to him? He took your call?"

"Of course. He's an old friend."

"I . . . uh, what kind of help, exactly?"

"Tents, Porta-Pottys, National Guard troops, whatever we need."

"You could have mentioned this before."

The pale man turned toward the audience and shrugged again. "I thought we ought to hear your ideas, Mayor. Besides, I assumed it was *your* job to network with the governor."

Several people in the audience laughed. Hope sat staring down at her hands, which were clasped tightly together on the counter before her. To Riley she looked small and defenseless. His heart ached. He had to do something or he would explode.

Hightower said, "Mayor, I'd like to touch on another matter."

Hope seemed relieved, yet cautious. "All right."

"I'm sorry to have to bring this up, I really am, but I understand you now own a new Mercedes Benz, model—" he lifted a paper from the counter and read—"S600, which it says here is priced at one hundred forty thousand dollars. Could you explain how that's possible on your salary?"

Hope mumbled something.

"I'm sorry, Mayor. I didn't hear that."

She leaned closer to the microphone. "I said it's a gift."

"My, that's quite a present." He shuffled through the papers and lifted another. "I also understand you paid off your mortgage recently. That must be a relief. Not many of us can say we own our house free and clear." The audience rumbled its assent. "I believe your final payment was . . ." Hightower pretended to read from the paper, which Riley knew was just a ruse. The man was Hope's banker, to whom Riley's New York bank had wired the funds. Hightower said, "One hundred twenty-three thousand dollars. Do you mind if I ask where you got that money, Mayor?"

"I . . . I don't know."

"You don't know? Well, was that money a gift as well?"

Hope's whisper was only audible because of the microphone. "I don't know."

In his seat high up at the rear of the hall, Riley watched his ex-wife shrink before the questions. How could he have been so foolish? How could he have failed to consider what it would look like, a woman in her position, suddenly driving around in that car, suddenly free of debt? First he had sown salt into the wounds of millions by failing to set a reasonable price for the cure before he sold it for a fortune; now he had sown ruin in Hope's life by the way he spent the fortune. Everything he touched became corrupted. As Hope squirmed under Hightower's examination like a gorgeous butterfly pinned alive by a sadistic boy, Riley's every instinct was to get away. Whatever he did now, it would only make things worse. Overpasses in Florida came to mind again. He must run, retreat from everyone and everything that he might harm, forget his failures. But could he do that without drinking? He had no model for a life like that, no example of the possibility, no system to avoid the awful truth about himself. How did one gain the necessary ambivalence about dishonor with a sober mind? It was the ugly irony of his so-called cure—his stolen freedom would not let him rest.

Of course he could always do the right thing. He could rise up here and now, and say out loud for everyone to hear: It was me! I gave the car and money to her! I sold the cure to that big company! I forgot to set the price! But the chief of police stood just outside this building at the top of the front steps, ready to arrest the "mystery man of Dublin" for the death of Willa Newdale. And a hundred angry alcoholics marched at the bottom of those same steps, ready to tear that mystery man to pieces for the price he let them set upon the cure. It would be suicide to confess the car and mortgage were from him. He faced a devil's alternative. He could let Hope suffer, or he could accept death, or prison.

Suddenly Riley felt a strong sense of déjà vu. He remembered going to sleep on the bricks of a back alley last November, a prisoner of alcohol shamed at last to the point of seeking the escape of hypothermia, and waking up alive and free. But that awakening had led directly here, to a choice between a different kind of shame, or death or prison. Sober or not, nothing really changed, and if honor, life, and freedom could not coexist on either side of his addiction, then they must not really exist at all.

Riley Keep kept silent.

"Mayor," said Bill Hightower. "Again, I'm sincerely sorry to have to ask the obvious question, but here in front of the people that we serve, it must be done. Has the person or persons who provided these *gifts* benefited from the powers of your office in any way?"

Oh, he was crucifying her! Riley moaned aloud. Dylan turned to him, a question in his battered eye. Riley shook his head. Then he thought of a way out, a fourth way, beyond shame, captivity, or death. He stood and bent to whisper in Dylan Delaney's ear. "Come with me."

Hope's lover rose and followed him. When the meeting room

door had closed behind them and they were alone, out in the vestibule, Riley paced back and forth while Dylan remained motionless.

Riley said, "I want you to write a note and get it passed to Hope. I want you to tell her she has two million dollars available to fix this. No, three! Tell her to make the announcement, to tell them she's found an anonymous donor for a shelter to be built at the edge of town somewhere, and . . . I don't know, maybe incentives for new business? An industrial park or . . . something. A convention center! Whatever she wants!"

Watching Riley pace, Dylan said, "I'm not gonna do that."

"But Hightower's *killing* her in there!"

"I know it."

"You have a better idea?"

"I was prayin' as hard as I could for her till ya brought me out here. Does that count?"

Riley stopped his manic pacing. "This is serious! We have to *do* something!"

"I'm not gonna help ya buy her affections, Riley."

"*What?*"

"I've respected your wishes. I haven't said a word to anyone about the deal with Hanks, but we both know where the car and mortgage payments came from. It's not right to hide the money from her and dole it out this way. I'm a little outta practice, but this is prob'ly some kinda crime, and I can't be a party to it anymore. You gotta tell her about the money, Riley, or I will."

"You said you couldn't tell anyone about my business. You're my lawyer!"

"I also told ya attorney privilege is not a license to break the law."

"What law?"

Dylan sighed. "Come on, Riley. Let's not play that game. Ya know this isn't right. I guess ya have some kinda plan to get her back, but so far all it's done is cause her grief. If ya want her, the right thing to do is be honest about it. Come right out and tell her everything."

Riley balled his fists. "I thought you were a better man than this."

"What's that supposed to mean?"

"You're willing to let them strip away her job and ruin her reputation, just to keep me from helping. Just to keep her to yourself."

Dylan creased his brow. "Keep her to my*self*?"

Riley spoke with urgent sincerity. "Listen, you don't have to worry about that. I know I don't have a chance with her. I just want to make things easier for her and Bree ... and for you. It's why I chose you for my lawyer. To get some money into your hands, so you can support them."

Dylan stared at him, and Riley thought he saw a sense of wonder beneath the bruises on the man's face. "Ya really have no idea."

It was Riley's turn to frown. "No idea about what?"

Hope's lover walked away, crossing the lobby toward the coatroom. There, he stopped and stood with his back turned. Riley saw his shoulders rise and fall as he took a deep breath. "I can't believe she hasn't told ya."

"What are you talking about?"

Lifting his face toward the ceiling, keeping his back to Riley, Dylan sighed. "You're right about one thing. I do love her. I've loved her for a long time. So last year I asked her to marry me."

In a flash of inspiration Riley understood and felt his heart sink just a little lower. "You did it, didn't you? You and Hope are married, but you're keeping it a secret for some reason."

Dylan laughed. "You're pretty close."

"Don't laugh at me!"

"Believe me, it's not you I'm laughin' at."

With haunted eyes, Dylan turned to stare across the lobby at Riley. "I assumed you knew this, or I woulda told ya sooner. A lot of this money belongs to Hope already, Riley. Maybe half of it. Maybe more. In Maine, most property acquired during marriage is subject to division between the spouses, and the thing is, Hope won't marry me because she's already married, Riley. To you."

22

There. It was done at last.

When the old woman finally stopped talking, the young man pushed back from his desk and stood. Wiping her eyes with a tissue, Willa watched him closely as he walked around to the tripod and pressed a button, shutting off the camera. She had given him bits and pieces earlier, of course; it had been necessary to interest him in her case, but this was the first time he had heard her story through from start to finish, the first time anyone had heard her story, for that matter. She wondered what it meant to him. Having kept it to herself for all these years, knowing it was death to speak aloud, she had dreaded the revelation of her secret even as she longed for it, but she had not expected this cathartic sense of connection, intimacy, and gratitude. She wondered if he understood.

The young man leaned across his desk to twist the gooseneck light back to its usual position, shining it on the photos of his wife and children instead of on her wrinkled face. Willa searched him for some sign that he also felt a bond between them, forged by their shared secret. But he seemed unchanged by the information. Sadly, he did not seem to recognize the risk she had just taken.

"You'll type the complaint yourself," she said. "After hours, when your staff is gone?"

"Yes."

"And you'll file it yourself? In person?"

"Yes. Don't worry."

Don't worry. She looked around his office wearily, saw his golfing trophies, his undergraduate and law school diplomas, a series of framed nature photographs with little motivational words printed underneath. Big ideas whittled down to bromides. *Integrity: Never be ashamed of doing what is right. Perseverance: Do not stop, do not give up. Teamwork: Find strength in the gifts of others.* She turned back toward him, his perfectly trimmed hair, glowing complexion, ready smile, sincere eyes. He had no idea how terrified she was. How could she explain? How could she draw him from his normal little world and make him see the horror she had lived with all these years? Pitying the young man for what she must now do, Willa waved her right hand toward the photos on his desk. "Is that your family, dear?"

He smiled very slightly, modest, even in his pride. "Emma and our daughters. Jillian is twelve and Hailey's ten."

"He would slit their throats and bleed them out like pigs in front of you."

His smile vanished. "You don't have to say a thing like that."

"But I do. You have to understand. If anyone learns about this before you get it filed, and the word reaches him, he'll do that and more to stop us."

"I *know*. I just heard you describe what he did."

"Hearing it is not the same as believing it—knowing it, in your gut." She thought of the girl, screaming for her mother, and the wooden stares of all the others standing powerless, and that animal at the vortex of the swirling screams, making his demands with the indifference of a butcher carving meat. She stared at the young man. How could she convey the terror? She had come into the open finally, but it shamed her to have taken all these years, and if she was driven by her shame, he must not think her choice courageous.

"You have to try to internalize this," she said. "For the sake of your family, you have to be *afraid*."

The young attorney seemed embarrassed by the word. He

dropped his eyes. He picked up his Mont Blanc fountain pen and then he put it down. He said, "I'll be careful."

"But are you afraid?"

"I . . ." He picked up the pen again. "You've been very clear, and I will follow your instructions."

"We're the only ones who know it now. Before it was just me, but now you're in it too."

"I know."

"I have no evidence except for that." She pointed at the video camera. "That deposition is everything. If we're killed before you get it someplace safe, all these years I've hidden will have been for nothing."

"I *know!*"

She sat still for a moment, eyes on him, praying for him, and when she had called on God's protection for him she rose. "You know how to contact me."

"Yes."

"Please don't write it down."

"No. I have it memorized as we discussed."

"Thank you."

The young man led her to the office door and out into his little lobby, where he held the hallway door open for her. He cleared his throat. "I, uh, I wanna say how much I appreciate you letting me handle this. It'll probably put my girls through college and pay off my house, this one case by itself."

She paused, halfway in, halfway out, forcing him to remain there holding the door open. It was the weekend. They were alone. She could speak freely. "Forget about the money, sweetheart; that's a distraction. Focus on what I said about the pigs."

His face hardened. "I'm just trying to thank you for this opportunity."

He had no idea what kind of opportunity this was. Might she rise up like a phoenix because of it? She was so terribly, terribly afraid. After all this time it did not matter if she was resurrected, allowed to be herself again; it was the standing up that counted, doing the right thing regardless of the consequences . . . finally.

But this young man, with his lovely wife and darling daughters—they were different. They had no sins to purge, at least not in this way, and so did not deserve the risk. The old woman said, "I used to know a lawyer a long time ago. He said it didn't matter if he believed his clients or not. He said all that mattered was how well he did his job for them."

"It's one of the first things they teach you in law school."

She laid a hand upon his forearm. "This time, you need to believe."

"I do. I really do."

"Good, dear," she said, patting his arm. "In that case maybe you'll survive."

23

The first two days after Dylan told him he was still Hope's husband, Riley Keep continued his routine as if the information made no difference, working at the diner, walking back and forth from here to there in the fine spring weather, giving dollar bills to ever-present beggars who accosted him along the way. Another man might have gone straight to her, but not Riley Keep. True, she had not divorced him, but he could think of many disappointing explanations. Why rush out to meet them? As long as Riley did not know for sure, anything was possible. Therefore, just as he had delayed his first transcendental sip of golden Scotch among the oak tree's roots, so now he postponed words with Hope, savoring a long-shot fantasy of reconciliation and trying to ignore the odds against it.

On the third day at about lunchtime Dylan came into the diner. The man who was quite possibly *not* Hope's lover took a seat up by the window and ordered coffee. He never touched the cup but remained sitting there an hour later. Riley knew exactly what he wanted, only it seemed too soon. Riley Keep had drifted off to sleep the last two nights with unresisted visions of his sweetheart in his head. For the first time in three and a half years, he had not shut his mind to her or compressed her down into a size he could more easily ignore. For the first time in three and a half years, Riley Keep indulged the hope that fantasies do come true sometimes, forgiveness does exist, and notwithstanding Mr. Wolfe's lament, every now and then a fella could go home again. He had counted 1,308 nights since the night she turned him out. Just two nights of sweet delusion out of all those others did not seem enough. A mere two nights to savor the possibility she might accept him back before he had to go and hear that she would not. But Dylan had no pity. He remained there as Riley worked the tables, saying nothing, watching with the patience of a fisherman.

Finally, Riley stopped beside him, the leavings of a turkey and dressing supper on a plastic plate in one hand and a soggy dish towel in the other. He said, "You don't have to come and sit around like this."

"Half of it's hers, Riley."

"I know it. I'm gonna tell her."

"When?"

"I guess maybe tomorrow."

"How's about tonight when ya get off?"

"I can't."

"How come?"

"I have something planned already."

Dylan stared at him, and Riley knew he wasn't fooling anybody. Then Dylan said, "She's gonna find out anyway. I got a letter today. Bad news, I guess. Says ya stole this cure of yours. Says they want it back. Want the patent for it, and everythin' ya've made off of it so far. Says they're gonna sue ya for it in a week unless ya sign it over. Gonna sue Hope too."

Riley stood facing Dylan's table, dirty plate in one hand, dirty towel in the other, dirty apron covering his thighs and chest and belly, wondering how it could take so little time to ruin everything. He had inhaled, savoring the ripe fantasy of telling Hope she was a multimillionaire, and then exhaled into the stench of Hope without her car, her house, her job, her liberty.

Dylan said, "I don't know who this Dale Williams is, but I guess he did his homework pretty good. Can't figure how he knows you're behind BHR Incorporated, or how he knows you guys are married. Must of hired some real good lawyers."

Riley put the plate and towel on Dylan's table and dropped into a chair. Dylan cocked his head and stared at him. "Did ya steal it from this fella, Riley?"

A thought occurred to Riley. It made him feel tired. "If there's a lawsuit, will people know it's me?"

Dylan continued to stare, his head tilted toward one shoulder.

Riley said, "I didn't steal it. Not from him. I never even heard of him."

"'Not from him'? Ya make it sound like there's somebody else ya stole it from."

Riley looked away. Across the room, the thin red second hand of Sadie's giant wall clock swept round and round. Riley watched its steady progress, thinking. You breathe, good goes in, bad goes out, time passes, and there's nothing you can do about it but stop breathing. Again he remembered twilight by the dumpster behind Henry's store. He could not escape the memory, the sunset somewhere back beyond the western hills of Maine, and cold creeping down, ravenous. He remembered waking up the next day, waking from one nightmare into another, this one precisely here, although at the time it had seemed like something better. He realized he was wrong to wake up. He should have kept on sleeping there forever, because now look what he had done.

Dylan said, "I notice ya aren't askin' about me, or Hope. Ya just wanna know if people will find out it's you." Dylan leaned forward, closer to him, the one and only time Riley had seen the man get angry. "Well, they will. If this goes ta court, it'll be in the public record, and everybody's gonna know exactly who ya are."

Riley put his elbows on the table and his face into his hands. He thought of the police chief holding up the cross he had carved for Hope almost a decade ago, the chief claiming it belonged to Willa Newdale, asking what he had done with that old lady's body. Riley looked out through his fingers like they were prison bars. Mumbling past his palms he said, "I thought about Hope first. I just didn't say anything."

Dylan sat back. "You gonna go over there an' tell her tonight, or am I?"

Riley rubbed his face all out of proportion, then pulled his hands away, wiped them on his dirty apron, and stood, saying, "You do it. I have other plans."

With his back to the wall, Riley pressed against the springs and pulleys of his homemade exercise machine. He had stripped to his underwear so the sweat wouldn't soil his last clean shirt and trousers. He was eleven minutes into a twenty-minute set. It was his third set that day. He might do two sets more, or even three. What else was there? Eating, sleeping, exercise, and television—a prisoner's life, what he deserved. He had not left his upstairs garage apartment in eight days, except to purchase groceries. He could feel his muscles growing every minute, but that was not the point. He never looked into the mirror anymore. He only hoped to find that empty place a hard workout might get him to—"the zone," some people called it, a place to hide from thinking.

As the threatening letter's week of grace had passed, Riley strained against his pulleys and his springs, seeking a clear mind. Decisions must be made. Time was short. So as he worked on biceps, triceps, latissimus dorsi, and deltoids, of course he thought again of leaving. Once the word got out, he knew the chief would pounce upon the weakling, Stanley Livingston. He ought to run while there was time. But the pulleys and springs and car and cash and wooden cross had pressed him down right where he was, no matter how he strained. He had a wife and child to think about—a *wife*, although she might deny it—and a strange sense he must stay to lift his own weight here in Dublin.

In the background as he exercised, a newscaster on the television spoke of Maine National Guard troops in the streets of Dublin, sent by the governor to control at least a thousand homeless people gathered there. Then the anchorperson got around to Riley again. They had been flocking to the lawsuit story since it broke last night. How they loved to talk about the giant corporation buying the medical miracle of the century from a small-town waiter! For increased resistance to his actions, Riley hooked another spring to his contraption. There was just one problem with the contrivance he had built. It gave him no way of measuring the force applied against him, no way to know if he could lift his own weight now. He only knew he had to keep on trying. He began to push again. As the pulleys whined, the news continued.

They showed that same video clip from last night, the one of Hope, or "Mayor Keep" as the reporters called her in their effort to connect the lawsuit to her job, hinting at political corruption as if things weren't bad enough. Riley did not need to watch the clip again to see it in his mind—Hope at her front door, blinking against their camera lights, saying she had just found out herself about the lawsuit, saying she knew nothing about anybody stealing any formula, really, nothing whatsoever, and then falling in their trap, saying yes, that new Mercedes in her driveway was hers, and yes, her mortgage had been paid off, but that had nothing to do with any formula or lawsuit, her face going blank in the instant that she said it, Riley and the whole world watching as she realized live before the cameras how it looked, and then she had no comment, looking small and helpless in the glare, obviously confused as she backed away and closed her door.

Riley groaned with effort, doing his dead-level best to pull the hooks right out from the wall. No one could have built a better exercise machine, one more suited to his needs. He had been up all night, thinking of that video clip and of carving Hope a little wooden cross, and golden chocolate foil, and buying her a car for cash, paying off her house, curing hopeless men in shelters, curing himself.

Would he never learn?

Someone knocked on Riley's door. He had been expecting it, of course, waiting since the news broke on the television, wondering why he was still free. He figured maybe the chief did not watch the news. Or maybe it had taken them this long to find out where he lived. Dublin was a small town, but he was just a waiter, after all, not the town's mayor. Before yesterday, probably the only people in town who knew both his name and his address were Dylan Delaney and Mrs. Harding, his ancient landlady. Still, it had been twelve hours since the news broke, so he was ready when they knocked. He took his time, toweling off the sweat and slipping into his last clean pair of trousers and his last clean shirt—the outfit he had kept unsoiled for Hope—and he went downstairs to the door, wondering who had found him first, the police or the reporters.

It was neither.

At first Riley did not recognize the bald man standing in the dewy grass outside his weathered door, not until the man said, "It's been a long time, Reverend Keep."

Riley knew him then. "Mr. Hanks."

"How have you been?"

"Good." An automatic lie.

"Glad to hear it. Mind if I come in?"

Riley looked past the man. A fog had settled in during the night, but he could still see a gleaming black Cadillac parked in the gravel driveway that ran around Mrs. Harding's house from the street to the garage below his apartment. A pair of young men in dark suits leaned against the Cadillac. Riley stepped back from the door, holding it open, saying, "Sure."

The bald man gave the two beside the car a little wave and stepped onto the concrete stoop, where he paused to wipe his flawless shoes on the threadbare mat Mrs. Harding had provided for that purpose. He entered past Riley, paused, and went up the narrow stairs since there was no place else for him to go. As the treads and risers creaked beneath his visitor's ascending weight, Riley cast a last look at the men outside, closed the door and followed.

Up in the little room where Riley cooked his meals and exercised and watched TV, the most powerful man in the pharmaceuticals industry stood waiting. Riley said, "Would you like something to drink?"

"A cup of coffee would be nice."

"I only have instant."

"That's just fine."

Riley put some water in a scorched pan and set it on the two-burner stove as Lee Hanks glanced around at the sagging sofa with its stained chenille bedspread cover, the small dinette set, the raw boards on concrete blocks below the small television, and the oblong braided rug on the battered pine floor. The man took a step closer to Riley's homemade exercise machine, the cables, springs, and pulleys hanging from hooks on the plaster wall. Riley did not want to talk about that. He said, "You can sit there on the sofa."

"Thank you, sir."

Hanks settled onto a cushion on one end, next to a little table where Riley kept his reading material—a cheap Bible and a copy of *Alcoholics Anonymous* or The Big Book, both of which he had received at Willa Newdale's shelter, plus a few paperbacks from the used-book store downtown. Riley went to the cupboard beside the window and took down a mug and a small jar of freeze-dried coffee. On the side of the mug were the words *World's Greatest Dad.* Like the furniture, the mug had come with the apartment. It was thick and held heat well, otherwise Riley would have thrown it out.

"Haven't we paid you something like twelve million dollars so far?" asked the totally bald man on Mrs. Harding's sofa.

"That sounds about right."

"Why are you living like this?"

The water in the pan began to rumble. Riley poured it into the mug too fast, sloshing a little bit of coffee out onto the counter. "It's a long story."

"I'd sure like to hear it."

The very words the police chief had used when speaking to him at Teal Pond, asking why a minister and professor worked a job at Sadie's diner, except this time Hope was not around to change the subject. Riley stirred the coffee with a plastic spoon and then dropped the spoon in the sink. He brought the mug to Mr. Hanks, who reached up with both hands to receive it. Riley noticed a drop of coffee quivering on the bottom of the mug. He watched it apathetically, his mind on other things. He said, "The money's not for me."

"No? Who's it for, then?"

"My wife. My daughter. A friend of theirs. You."

"*Me?*"

Riley walked to the window at the top of the stairs. Through the fog he saw the men in coats and ties down by the Cadillac. One paced back and forth, talking on a cell phone and using a lot of hand gestures. The other leaned calmly against the hood, whittling on a stick with a pocketknife. The one with the knife was pretty large, his shoulders even broader than Dylan Delaney's. He had a short, military-looking haircut and a way about his movements with the knife that made Riley think he was something other than a driver or a businessman.

"Is that big guy a bodyguard or something?"

Lee Hanks said, "I've been getting death threats."

Riley turned. "Since that fella leaked the news about the formula? About the price you plan to charge?"

"Yes."

"I'm sorry."

"I don't understand, Reverend. You said the money is for your family and *me?*"

"Don't you think five thousand dollars is too much?"

"I know a lot of people feel that way, but we have very high expenses."

Out on the misty street beyond the Cadillac, Riley saw ten or twelve ragged figures pass by Mrs. Harding's gravel driveway, walking toward downtown. Two uniformed National Guardsmen with ugly black rifles emerged from the fog behind them, keeping pace on the far side of the road. The homeless fellas reminded Riley of his own days on the streets with Brice. That led to thoughts of his old friend dead upon the floor with a plastic bottle of rubbing alcohol cradled in his hands. Riley bit his lip to stop the pain, then said, "What about the poor?"

Lee Hanks sipped his coffee. Turning toward him Riley saw the way his eyebrows came together above his nose, one bushy black line across the man's face. He noticed the man's clothes, casual but expensive, a raw silk sweater and linen slacks, the kind of thing a billionaire might wear to a country club. He saw the drop of coffee clinging gamely to the bottom of the mug. He thought of mentioning it again, but did not want to distract the man from answering his question.

Lee Hanks swallowed. "That's not half bad."

"Do you remember what you said to my wife and me? That day when you and the others on the board approved us for the mission to Brazil?"

"Not exactly, no."

"You said you envied us because you don't usually get to see the fruits of your own labor for the Lord. You said you had nothing to offer but money. You said most of us must be content with one isolated part of the harvest. You said your role was to pay the workers and purchase the tools, but Hope and I were going out to virgin soil, to clear it, plow it, plant it and reap the harvest, all ourselves."

Lee Hanks nodded. "It's a blessing to be involved in everything the way you were."

"But the money. You said your role was to help with the money."

"That's the gift I've been given."

"So how can you talk about charging homeless alcoholics five thousand dollars?"

"Look, I understand what you're saying. I really do. I wish there was a better solution. But how do you think I got all that money to spend on missions work? I live in the real world, Reverend. I make compromises. Sometimes it seems as though people think we lie about expenses, but they really are extremely high. We have to maintain enough cash flow to pay for research and development of new medicines, for clinical trials, marketing, production, distribution. Not to mention legal defenses against everyone who sues us. Do you have any idea how many lawsuits were filed against our company in the last twelve months alone?"

"But—"

"Now along you come, refusing to reveal the source of your discovery, trying to hide your identity. I look around this little place of yours and I don't see so much as a high school chemistry set, and I feel like a fool. You send us this formula from out of nowhere in the mail, and our chemists and medical researchers think it's going to work, and I just go along with everything, hook, line, and sinker, and here we are, getting sued again in a very high profile way, thanks to you."

Riley noticed a small round stain on Lee Hanks's perfect linen slacks. The drop of coffee had fallen. He should have mentioned it before, or wiped the mug more carefully. He should not have offered coffee in the first place, if he could not do it properly. He said, "I'm sorry."

"Well, thanks, but 'sorry' and a dollar will get you a cup of coffee, as they used to say. Except it costs more like two-fifty these days, doesn't it? And you think five thousand dollars is too much to cure an alcoholic!" The bald man shook his head and set the mug of instant coffee on the table next to The Big Book.

Looking at the book, Riley thought about the fourth step. *We made a searching and fearless moral inventory of ourselves.* He remembered his delight in the apparent symmetry of selling the development and marketing rights to this man—believing with that one act he would cure all alcoholics everywhere, and help Hope and Bree get past the chaos he had caused, and offer something back to this stranger who had also suffered at his hands. But here the stranger sat, offering yet more evidence that Riley's good intentions left a stain on everything he touched. Riley said, "Why are you here?"

"Would you mind sitting down someplace? It hurts my neck to look up at you."

Riley dropped into one of the plastic chairs beside his dinette table.

"I'm here," said Mr. Hanks, "to ask you where you got that formula."

"I . . . I found it."

The bald man looked away and sighed. "All right. Let's say you 'found' it. Would that have been in Dr. Williams's pocket?"

"Dr. Williams? Who's that?"

"I haven't insulted your intelligence. Please don't insult mine."

"But I don't know who you're talking about."

"Oh, come on, Reverend. We knew you were the one behind your little BHR Incorporated almost from the start, obviously. I mean, you must have *wanted* us to know, using an attorney from here, where you and your wife grew up, where she is the mayor, but you clearly had some reason for staying out of things personally, so I respected your wishes. But—"

"Thank you," said Riley.

The man ignored his interruption. "—since your skills are not in pharmaceuticals, we also assumed you had a partner. Now Dr. Williams comes along with the lawsuit—"

"Oh, you mean *Dale* Williams, right? The fella suing us?"

"Are you seriously going to sit there and try to make me think you don't know her?"

"Her? I thought he was a man."

"Dale Williams is a *female* research chemist I sent to Brazil with the medical party, as you know very well."

Riley felt the little room begin to tilt. He wanted the man to believe in his goodwill, but something didn't fit. He said, "I didn't know you sent a chemist. I thought they were all doctors. Why would you do that?"

"To help us discover how that tribe of Indians got sober all of a sudden, of course."

Riley thought of old Waytee, a notorious drunk ever since a Brazilian prospector had shown The People how to get a wicked kick from fermenting fruit. He thought of venereal disease and tuberculosis and the other plagues that walked into the village with the miner and his greedy friends from down the river. He remembered the day Waytee came to say The People would drink no more. Riley remembered his joy that day, his certainty that God had used him to produce a miracle. Riley said, "I led them all to Jesus. That's why they quit drinking."

"It's one theory. I sent Dr. Williams and the others to explore different possibilities."

"But the missions board said the team was there to heal The People."

"That too."

Riley tried to get his thoughts in order, to receive this information in some way that made sense. "You're saying they had another mission? Something I wasn't told about?"

"I don't recall what you were told, Reverend. All I know for certain is that I spent quite a bit of money and many of my employees gave their lives to find a cure for alcoholism, and now you and Dr. Williams both claim to own it."

"I don't know this Dr. Williams. I don't even remember meeting any women in the medical party."

"She went down after you began your sabbatical, as I think you know."

"But I *don't* know! I've never even heard of her!"

"Oh, Reverend, please. Obviously we both know where you got the formula. It would be a kindness if you put me in touch with her. It's been many years. I thought she was dead all this time. I've carried her on my conscience."

The man's black eyes were fierce beneath his single bushy eyebrow. Riley felt the weight of them, felt them adding to all the other downward pressure of the lives he had damaged. Fighting to bear up he said, "It wasn't your fault. It's all me."

"No. She worked for me. I sent her down with all the others. That's all there is to it. Now, I want to see her. I want to apologize to her. I want to touch her, so I can know she's really alive. I want to know how she survived. I want you to tell me where she is."

Riley shook his head. "I don't—"

The man sprang to his feet. "Do *not* sit there and try to tell me you don't know!"

The explosion rocked Riley back against his seat. For a moment Lee Hanks loomed above him with clenched fists, projecting a ferocious energy out of all proportion to his size and age. Then the man seemed to call upon some inner source of self-control, relaxing his fingers, adjusting his posture to let his shoulders slump. He turned away from Riley and lifted the coffee mug from the table. "I apologize," he said, crossing the little room to pour the remaining coffee from the mug into the sink.

"You don't have to do that," said Riley, uncertain himself if he meant the mug or the apology.

"I've carried this with me for so long," said Lee Hanks, squeezing soap into the mug, rubbing it around with his finger, rinsing it out, and putting the clean mug on the counter. "Then your letter came, and my people researched your lawyer and this town and told me your wife was the mayor out here, and for the first time I thought there might have been some benefit to someone after all, something positive from all that misery, you know. I had such high hopes, and . . . I'm sorry I lost my temper."

"It's okay," said Riley. "I wish I could help you."

The older man turned to look at him, standing at the kitchen counter with his hands wet. "You really don't know where she is?"

"I never heard of her until this lawsuit came along."

"But how did you get that formula?"

There was a loud knock on the door downstairs. From where he sat, Riley could look out through the beads of condensation on the window to see both of Lee Hanks's men just below. Apparently they had heard their employer's outburst. The larger man with the military haircut held a handgun. He leaned forward and hit the door again, pounding with his left fist. Riley said, "You'd better tell them you're okay."

Wiping his hands on his slacks, Mr. Hanks stepped up to the window. He tapped on it, waved at his men below, then turned back toward Riley. "The formula, Reverend Keep?"

"I found it. That's all I can tell you."

Hanks crossed to the top of the stairs. "Have it your way."

"It's the truth."

"Reverend Keep, you haven't told the truth since the day your lawyer mailed that letter to me."

"I found it! I'm telling you I just found it!"

"You stole it. You know it and I know it. The only question is who you stole it from. I funded that expedition down to Brazil and all those people were on my payroll. Any decent attorney could make a solid case that the formula is mine from that alone. But now I have this woman coming from out of nowhere after all these years, suing me, someone I thought was dead because of me, and after paying you twelve million dollars and investing far more than that in research and development, it looks like I'll just have to cut my losses or face a public relations nightmare given everything she's suffered."

"I still don't understand what Brazil has to do with any of this. I found that formula written on a piece of paper right here in Dublin."

The bald man stared at Riley. "I think you're serious."

"I am!"

"All right. Who wrote the formula?"

"I don't know."

"You expect me to believe that?"

Riley stood up. "I don't know *anything*!"

Lee Hanks started down the stairs. Riley remained standing at the top, watching him descend. At the bottom Hanks opened the door and paused. "You mentioned that you live this way because the money's not for you. You said you wanted it for your family, and for me. I'll ask one more time, what did you mean by that?"

"I got your people killed down there," said Riley. "I should have stayed with them. I should have known what The People would do to them after I left. So I thought maybe if I gave you a chance to sell the medicine . . . I knew you had a heart for missions work, and I thought it might help you feel better about everything if you could be part of getting the cure out to people. I thought maybe you could make some money too."

"*Some* money?" Lee Hanks looked up at him and gave one short bark of a laugh. Then, shaking his head, he stepped outside.

Riley watched through the upper window as the two young men in suits escorted their powerful employer across the dewy grass to the gravel driveway where the Cadillac awaited. The smaller man opened the rear door for him, but Mr. Hanks paused to speak to the man with the broad shoulders and the military haircut. The bodyguard turned to stare up at Riley's window, then looked back at his employer, and nodded. Mr. Hanks got in the back seat, the smaller man got in behind the wheel, and the Cadillac reversed out of the driveway, leaving the broad-shouldered man behind.

For thirty minutes Riley stood at the window, watching the man. Lee Hanks's bodyguard paced in the mist below Mrs. Harding's elms a little while, examining the ground. Then he stooped to pick up a short fallen branch. He snapped it in two, dropped the longer piece, and carried the shorter piece in his left hand to the concrete bench beside the untended rose arbor in Mrs. Harding's side yard. Riley thought about the man's suit slacks getting wet from sitting on the concrete. The bodyguard did not seem to care. He began to whittle. Riley noticed how quickly he opened his knife, the way he did it with one hand, the way he did not even look down at the knife to open it. Riley noticed how seldom the man looked down at the short stick in his hand as the blade shaved bits and pieces from it, the way he kept his eyes up, looking back and forth between Riley's garage apartment and the street.

Another group of homeless people happened by, this time without a military escort. The man whittled for a few more moments, then rose to his feet. Both his hands were empty. Although Riley's eyes had never left him, Riley did not see him put the knife away. The knife was simply there in his hand, and then it was not.

The man walked through the fog toward the homeless fellas. They turned toward him warily. The man spoke with them for at least five minutes and then he walked away, strolling casually toward downtown as if it were the most natural thing in the world to be on foot in a dark business suit. When the man had passed out of sight, Riley focused his attention on the homeless fellas. All of them were still standing on the street in front of Mrs. Harding's house; all were staring up at his apartment.

Riley Keep decided it was time to leave.

He would use the door in back.

H ope opened her front door to Riley just as a drab olive Humvee rolled past her yard, complete with four soldiers and a machine gun mounted in the back. The governor had responded quickly to Bill Hightower after ignoring her requests. She shifted her attention from the passing troops to Riley and snapped, "What do you want?"

Riley took half a step backward. "Don't you think we ought to talk?"

"It's a little late for that."

She turned and strode back to her kitchen without a word, but behind her the door remained wide open.

At the counter she resumed her work, mashing boiled potatoes. Woman's work. The only kind of work Riley had left to her. She heard his footsteps coming in, the familiar sound of them, the rhythm that was his alone, ingrained within her psyche like a muscular memory. How she wished she could forget it, be surprised that it was him. How she wished she did not know him as she did. But just as she knew his footsteps, she knew he wanted her to turn, to acknowledge his presence. She would do no such thing.

He said, "I guess Dylan explained about the lawsuit."

"So we're gonna start there, are we?"

"What does that mean?"

"I was just wonderin' how you'd break the ice, with so many interestin' things to talk about."

"Hope—"

"I was thinkin' we should start with the way you got me fired before we get to how you got me sued."

"They haven't fired you, have they?"

She drove the potato masher into the pot, bearing down on it with all her strength. "There's a recall election scheduled for next week, 'cause of that car and the mortgage money. They'll do it then."

"But with this lawsuit, people will know there's been no bribery. You got the car and all from me."

"You think that's a *help*?" She twisted at the waist, looking at him finally, showing as much of her back as she could manage while still laying angry eyes upon him. "Everybody knows how you got that money, Riley, just like everybody knows we've got a thousand homeless people and the National Guard and a military curfew all because of you."

"Not all those homeless guys are here because of me. There's always been those old guys who hang out by the docks."

"Oh, excuse me. That's right; we'd still have Jim-Jim and John Donnelly to worry about, and let's see ... Nehemiah Shore and Marty what's-his-name." She turned and began chopping onions for the potatoes, putting her entire upper body into it. "Yeah, we'd really have our hands full either way."

"I didn't start this! The word was already out about a cure before I got here. It's the whole reason Brice and I came home."

"So you didn't come for me and Bree. What a surprise."

That got him pretty good. He didn't reply for almost a minute, when finally he said, "I didn't know."

She lifted the chopping block to scrape the onions into the potatoes. "Didn't know what, Riley?"

"You have his clothes up there in your closet. I ... I just assumed you got a divorce."

She stopped. She spoke to the bowl of potatoes. She would not

THE CURE

let him see her eyes well up. She would not let him think that she
was crying about him when it was just the onions. "Have you ever
slept with another woman?"

"No."

"Then what did you expect?"

"So that's the only reason?"

Laughing bitterly, she wiped her eyes. "Did you come over here
with romantic notions, Riley?"

"Well, I was kind of thinking maybe—"

"Don't flatter yourself. When we got married, I made a commit-
ment. Not just to you, either. I believe in Jesus, Riley. I *really* believe.
So I'm gonna try to do what Jesus wants me to do, even if it kills
me. There's been a lot of people told me I should divorce you, but
I'm not gonna weasel out by pretending alcoholism is adultery. It
isn't. And neither is abandonment. Jesus meant what he said, plain
and simple, and I'm not done believin' just because life stinks. Com-
mitments matter to *me.*"

He said nothing as she moved her attention to the garlic. Riley's
silence gave Hope a small sense of satisfaction. She had waited more
than seven long years to pierce him with those words, the first four
watching helplessly as he dissolved himself in alcohol, the last three
wondering if he was out there dead somewhere, and now that she
had finally spoken her mind on the matter, her words had clearly
driven deep beneath his skin just as she had always hoped.

Why not wound him just a little? Every word was true. Why
should she avoid the obvious? Had they not made the same promises,
invested the same emotions, endured the same hardships? Had they
not suffered the same horrors? Yet he had run away while she had
stayed. It was something to be remembered, something to remind
him of whether he liked it or not, whether he was sober or not.

He broke into her thoughts. "Would you like to be divorced?"

"What I'd like and what I've got are not the same. I can't change
that, so it makes no sense to wish for any different."

"I could always find a woman, give you the reason you need. If you want."

She dropped a clove into the press. He was right. He had put on a lot of muscle, built up his shoulders, made himself look pretty good again. Any women would find him attractive. But if he thought he was going to trap her that easily he had another thing coming. "Adultery is more than sex, Riley. You have to put your heart into it. Can you do that?"

When he did not answer right away she despised herself for pausing in her work, for waiting without breathing, and when he finally said, "No," she hated the relief she felt.

She crushed the garlic. A siren screamed in the distance. She tried to ignore it. His familiar footsteps behind her back moved to the window. He said nothing as she finished with the garlic, stirred the potatoes, put them in the refrigerator, and removed a package of chicken breasts. Finally he spoke. "You could win that recall vote if you wanted to. You could announce plans for a new convention center or something. Whatever you think would work."

"You just don't get it, do you? I won't take your money."

"You're the only reason I have it. You and Bree."

"I won't take a penny from you."

"Mom! He's only trying to help."

Hope turned to find Bree standing in the kitchen door. She looked from her daughter to Riley. "Did you know she was standing there?"

"No!"

She saw that he meant it, but that did not matter. This was all his fault. Everything. "Honey, your father and I need to have a private talk. Would you mind goin' to your room for a while?"

Her little girl said, "I'm not sayin' you should take his money. I'm just sayin' he's tryin' to help us."

"There's things going on here you don't understand."

Bree said, "I understand more than you think. I know why you don't want his money. But I also know he's tryin'. That's really hard for him. You should cut him a little slack." Bree's eyes were on her father, her face softer than Hope had seen it in a very long time, almost as if Bree were a parent looking at her child, instead of the other way around.

Hope watched Bree and Riley looking at each other and saw the two of them as they had been in Riley's last few moments living in that house, a marauding memory of three years back, when in a drunken rage Riley raised his hand to Bree, and Hope had stepped between them. She remembered that eternal instant underneath his upraised fist. She remembered wondering if he would bring it down on her and finish them forever. She remembered begging him to leave, just leave, and the drunken dawn of understanding as he saw the way she looked at him. She remembered terror in his eyes as he escaped into the cold November night—the last time she would see him for three years—and as Hope saw him looking at their daughter now, a sudden rush of fear returned. She saw a reckless hope in him. She saw that hope reflected in her daughter. She had to stop it before he gave her any ideas, before he hurt her little girl again. She said, "Bree, you need to go upstairs right now. This is a private conversation."

"Did you tell him about the baby?"

"Bree! Get upstairs!"

The softness vanished from her daughter's face. With a clipped "Yes, *Mother*," she spun on her heel and stormed away.

Riley said, "What was that about a baby?"

Hope turned back to her work. Barefoot in the kitchen, doing women's work. The future gaped before her, black and bottomless. How could she have failed her daughter so completely? "We were talkin' 'bout your money, and the fact that I won't take it."

"But what baby is she talking about?"

She had to head this off. She went on the offensive. "You shoulda told me she was standin' there! What's the matter with you?"

He took the bait. "I didn't know!"

"She's too young to hear about this stuff between us, Riley."

"I agree."

"All right, then, just so's you know." Then, in case he wasn't totally distracted, she added, "And I will *not* take your money."

"You don't need my money. Dylan said half of it is yours already."

Hope paused, her hands cold upon the chicken. She had not thought of that. She understood they had named her in the lawsuit because she was Riley's wife, but in the madness that her husband and her daughter had inflicted on her life she had not thought it through.

She heard more sirens, at least three altogether. There was a time when she would have phoned to find out what was going on, but her town was in other hands now. Whatever the problem, let Bill Hightower and the governor and his army sort it out.

She said, "How much money is there, exactly?"

"I don't know. It changes with the stock market. Some days we get another hundred thousand, some days we lose a hundred."

"On average, then."

"It's grown to around seven million, last time I checked."

"Altogether?"

"Your half."

Seven million dollars to her name. If the number had been smaller, she might have been more tempted. But this was something she could never hold inside her mind. It was purely theoretical, a number like that, and therefore easier to deny. She shook seasoning on the chicken breasts and said, "You keep it."

"All right."

"Well, don't knock yourself out tryin' to change my mind or anything, Riley."

"I don't care one way or the other, so long as you're happy."

"Happy?" She laughed. Then, "Don't you wanna ask me why I won't take it?"

"I know why."

"You don't know a thing."

"I do. It's the five thousand dollars."

It surprised her that he understood. She kept her back to him and flipped the chicken breasts to sprinkle on more seasoning. She did not want him to see the confusion he had planted in her. Yet upon reflection, it should be obvious why she would not take the money, even to Riley. She thought about the two homeless alcoholics in New Jersey who had walked into a newspaper office and set themselves on fire to protest the price Lee Hanks planned to set upon the cure. Dead, both of them, and on front pages all around the world. She thought of the massive wave of outrage rolling through the country, the picketing and sit-ins, the rallies and marches, good people throughout the nation rising up against the injustice of it. She said, "You also need to take back that car and mortgage money."

"All right."

"All right. Now tell me 'bout this lawsuit."

"I don't know a lot about it yet. Dylan just got a copy himself. He said it's about the patent rights. Some woman named Dale Williams says she invented the formula and I stole it from her."

"Did you?"

A pause. "No."

She noted both the pause and the lack of indignation. Not "Of course not!" but simply "No." She felt a sudden rush of pity. He was such a simple man, naïve in so many ways. It was why he had fallen so completely to the bottom in the face of undiluted evil. Like a little boy, he would be surprised when the judge or jury saw through his lies. He would be putty in their hands. She asked, "We both know you didn't figure out that formula yourself, so where'd you get it, Riley?"

"I . . . I sort of found it."

The poor fool. "Where?"

"I can't tell you that."

"Why not? If you didn't steal it from this woman, why can't you tell me where it came from?"

"I just can't."

"Okay, how'd she know it was you behind the patent if you didn't get it from her?"

"I don't know."

"Dylan told me you set up some kind of company to hide behind, right?" It was all over the news about BHR Incorporated. She had already figured that one out—Bree, Hope, Riley. But BHR and Riley weren't the only defendants named in the lawsuit. Her name was in the complaint, so she had a right to ask these questions. She said, "I think it's important to find out how she knows who you are. You guys worked really hard to keep it secret. You didn't even tell me. But this Williams person knew anyway. She even knew about me."

Riley said nothing.

Hope said, "Maybe she found out from Dylan."

"Dylan wouldn't do that."

"You trust him."

"He's a good man, Hope. You and him . . . I see why you like him so much."

Hope thought of Dylan, of how she had suspected the worst of him when the car and mortgage payments came, wondering if he had done something illegal to get his money, wondering if he was some kind of criminal in spite of all the ways he had shown himself her friend, in spite of all the times she had watched his lips while he looked elsewhere, longing to kiss them, to tell him everything there was inside of her, to press herself full length up against him. She thought of all the lonely nights wrestling with her demons, desperately resisting the apparent equation of abandonment and adultery. Weren't they much the same? Her husband had chosen alcohol over her. Was that not infidelity? Oh, how often she had longed to release herself to the common sense of that. But in her weakest moments, when Dylan's handsome kindness nearly overwhelmed her, she had been unable to elude the plain sense of her Savior's words, so she had whispered, "Rescue me," and although she did not understand the reason for her torture, Hope had tried to accept it as a necessary part of something greater than herself, and by so doing, somehow, she had survived.

"Yeah," she said. "He's a good friend."

"Is that all he is?"

She did not know the answer to that question so instead she said, "I understand why Dylan couldn't tell me 'bout all this. He said you wouldn't let him. But I still wanna know why you didn't say anything. Why'd you make me find out this way?"

"Do you remember your last birthday in Brazil?"

"What does that have to do with anything?"

"We went shopping in Mãe do Deus a few days before, remember? I bought you that box of chocolates, and you gave them all away to the kids?"

She said, "Yes," and without the excuse of onions her eyes began to well up again. Many of those children might have had children of their own by now. Oh, Bree, what have you done?

"I carved a little wooden cross for you. I took some of that gold foil from the chocolates and used it as an inlay."

"Why are you talkin' about this? I don't like to think about it."

"I'm answering your question, Hope."

She saw their faces, their perfect, angelic laughing faces, all of them, and Bree. "I don't wanna talk about it."

"I remember seeing that cross around your neck, when we were all dancing at the party, but I can't remember seeing it again after that."

She stopped her work and turned toward him, to implore him. "Can we please just change the subject?" He still stood at the window, staring out. And beyond him, through the glass she saw a rising column of black smoke in the distance. So the sirens had been fire trucks in the streets of Dublin, down at the bottom of the hill.

He said, "You wanted to know why I didn't tell you about the cure. I'm trying to explain. I gave you that cross, and you wore it at the party, and the next time I saw it was here in Dublin, in the police station, when they pulled it out of my pocket and said it belonged to Willa Newdale."

"What?"

"I kind of remember someone giving it to me, putting it in my hand and asking for the cure, but everything that night got all balled up and my head wasn't working right yet—I mean, I was still pretty messed up, I'm telling you, even though I was sober—so I can't remember for sure how it got in my pocket, Hope. I swear I can't. But I keep thinking if I knew how it got there, where it came from, I'd understand everything."

"I don't . . ." She had been staring at the distant smoke above her town. She had missed what he was saying. "What was that about the police station? You had something that belonged to Willa?"

"I had something that belonged to *you*, unless you gave away that cross."

Riley at the police station? Riley with something of Willa's? Suddenly it all came together. She thought of the bruised and shaggy man who had reappeared with the dawn at the end of her driveway as if rising from the curvature of the frozen earth. She thought of the televised image of a silhouetted form in the back of Bill Hightower's car, the "mystery man of Dublin," the one who had broken into Henry's store with all those homeless people the night a kind old woman disappeared. Hope said, "You're the one Steve's been looking for! He thinks you hurt Willa!"

"I didn't do anything to that woman."

There was a pleading in his eyes—he clearly did not think she would believe him—and in spite of her defenses, she crossed the kitchen to stand behind him by the window and placed her hand upon his shoulder. "Oh, Riley. I know that." He turned, and his eyes contained the same pathetic hopefulness she had just seen him give to Bree. She removed her hand. She did not want to lead him on.

He said, "Did you give that cross to Willa?"

The telephone began to ring. She did not move. Now that she understood the reason for it, Hope let the memories come. The phone rang on unanswered as she remembered Riley, shyly offering the crude little trinket, the finest kind of gift he could manage under the circumstances, and more than enough to swell her heart with adoration. She remembered The People, coming to their camp to lead them back, a grand procession to the meeting place in honor of her special day, a great party with slaughtered pigs and the juice of *araca-boi*, that bright yellow kind of guava they so loved, and memories of dancing, and endlessly exaggerated fireside stories about her four years among them told by all the old ones, and laughter at their magnificent lies, and children running everywhere and the thought occurring to her that surely there was something of Eden in that place. And memories of later, when the old man came alone to offer her the finest birthday gift of all, reaching up to touch the little wooden cross around her neck and saying, "I see Jesus very very much." Her thirty-second birthday. She was forty years old now, which seemed almost as impossible as the cross somehow in Riley's pocket in spite of so much time and distance between then and there and here and now. Standing close beside her husband at the window in the kitchen, with smoke rising from the bed of fog that lay over Dublin down below, and the telephone still ringing, ringing, ringing, Hope asked, "Are you sure it's the same cross?"

"Absolutely."

"I don't see how that's possible. I gave it to Waytee."

He shook his head, looking through the glass. "Did you . . . did you find it later?"

She knew exactly what he meant. She too looked out the window and saw the column of smoke getting thicker, rising from a hidden source beneath the settled mist down in the valley, and she knew the fire was bad, and she saw the clearing, the charred and blackened village, the long and shallow pit that she and Riley dug, and filled, and covered as their final act of ministry, and little Bree, last of all The People, bathed in blood and crying in the bushes, and "I never saw that cross again" was all that Hope could say.

26

From the National Guard's command and control position, Chief Steven Novak struggled to see through the wicked thick fog blinding Dublin as nearly a full block of houses burned, some at least two hundred years old. The invisible flames roared beyond the mist, which glowed an eerie orange and yellow. Even with all three of Dublin's fire trucks on the scene it seemed pretty obvious the fire was out of control. And in spite of all the troops hanging around with rifles, the chief saw people running in and out through the gauzy mix of fog and smoke with televisions, stereos, computers—anything light enough to carry. Sometimes the soldiers caught them, but most of the looters seemed to vanish into the ether. Steve Novak seethed with impotent rage.

Colonel Peterson stood on the far side of a row of haphazardly parked Humvees, surrounded by a bunch of do-nothing weekend warriors who did not have enough moxie between them to stand up to a domesticated kitten, much less this army of homeless predators that had descended on his town. Steve had just wasted five valuable minutes trying to get the colonel to authorize deadly force, but the man insisted it was not necessary. Homes that had been in families for eight generations were being burned to the ground, and it was not necessary. Innocent people were making frantic choices about whether to save photo albums or the family Bible as they fled the fire, only to have their belongings ripped right from their hands by phantoms who emerged from out of nowhere, then disappeared into the fog again as this so-called soldier insisted it was not necessary to fire their weapons. Steve had asked the coward if someone must get murdered right out there in the middle of the street before he started shooting. The colonel—a dentist under normal circumstances—had suggested he should be more professional and remain calm.

The fog parted across from his position, and Steve caught a glimpse of old man Summerset standing on his front steps holding a shotgun at something like port arms while cinders fell all around him and his two grown boys doused the shingles on his roof with water from a pair of garden hoses. The chief crossed the street.

Yelling above the roar of the nearby inferno he said, "Mr. Summerset, did ya see how this got started?"

"Ayuh," called the old man, his clear blue eyes on the mayhem down the way. "Was a bunch a them bums from away. Them drunks."

"Did ya see 'em set the fire?"

"Naw, but I seen 'em just before they did it."

"Where were they?"

With the shotgun the old man pointed toward the far side of the street. Steve followed his gesture, but all he saw was an iridescent flickering in the mist. "Over at that apartment behind ol' lady Harding's place where that new fella lives. Mad as hornets, they was. Standin' all 'round his garage. Yellin'. Wanted that fella ta come out pretty bad so's they could clean his clock, seemed ta me."

"Did they get their hands on him?"

"Dunno. Mebbe. I went in ta get my gun."

"Who's this fella you're talkin' 'bout?"

"Dunno his name. New fella, like I said. Works over at Sadie's."

One of the old man's sons overheard the conversation and called out, "It's Mr. Keep, Chief. Mayor's ex lives over there."

Steve frowned. "What would they want with him?"

"Ain't you seen the news this mornin'? He's the one invented that medicine for drunks, got everyone so riled up 'bout the price an' all."

"Riley Keep?"

"Ayuh. Somebody suin' him, I guess. Say he stole the medicine from 'em. Say his wife did too from what I hear."

Riley Keep. The chief visualized the man, who had always seemed like a pretty good egg to him. Kind of quiet. Maybe a little nervous. Steve was used to that. For some reason a lot of solid citizens got nervous around the police. But now that he thought about it, there *was* something a little different about the man. Steve always had the feeling they had met before. And if it was true what old man Summerset's boy said about Riley and the cure . . . Steve thought about the homeless fella he had interrogated the night Willa Newdale disappeared, and in his mind he compared the eyes and nose and upper cheeks, and suddenly he felt like an idiot.

Then he thought about the rest of it—a news report that named Riley *and* Hope. If there was a mob after Riley because of that news story and if the story also mentioned Hope Keep, chances were they'd go after her next. He turned without a word to hustle back toward his Explorer, which was parked almost a block away. He considered calling for backup, but that fool of a colonel needed all the help he could get, so Steve didn't want to pull his guys away from the area, especially not when he could be at Mayor Keep's house in under five minutes. Remembering the way that fella had stonewalled him in his own interrogation room, then hidden in plain sight right here in Dublin all this time, Steve decided he would see to this himself.

He almost had his truck in sight when a high-pitched scream drew his attention to the side yard of a house on his left. Squinting through the fog he saw a cluster of gray shapes. He heard the scream again and changed direction, heading off that way. Drawing closer, he could just make out a woman struggling with a pair of men. He unsnapped his holster, drew his side arm, and ran straight at them, calling, "Stop! Police!"

Before he could reach them, a ghostly figure came around the far corner of the house and charged into the attackers. The men released the woman, who dropped like a rag doll to the grass. They turned on her rescuer, punching him and kicking him, but the man landed a few good hits himself, and when Steve shouted again, much closer this time, the two assailants turned and ran.

When Steve finally reached the woman, the men were nearly to the back corner of one of the nearby houses. He knelt beside her.

"Are you all right?"

She cursed and said, "What are you waitin' here for? Go get 'em!"

Steve turned to the man who had tried to rescue her. He was a stranger, obviously one of the homeless, with a grizzled beard and filthy clothes and blood running from his nose. Steve said, "You all right?"

The homeless man looked him in the eye and said, "Yessir," as the woman pulled her torn shirt together over her chest with both hands, screaming, "Don't you let 'em get away!"

Steve took off running. As he rounded the corner and entered the backyard of the house on the right, through the drifting smoke and fog he saw one of the men attempting to scale a six-foot wooden fence on the far side of a swing set, with the other right behind him. He called, "Police! Stop or I'll shoot!"

Neither of them paused. Steve fired a warning shot into the soft ground a few feet away from his own position. Still, the men kept going. He took aim through the mist at the one on the fence and squeezed off a round. The suspect fell back to the ground, where he gripped his upper thigh and writhed in pain. The other man froze in place, throwing up his hands. Shouting commands as he ran to them, Steve had both men frisked for weapons and handcuffed to each other within three minutes. He removed the wounded man's belt and wrapped it around his thigh, cinching it as tightly as he could. Only then did he bother with his handheld radio. "Dave. Dave."

"Ayuh" came the answer.

"What's your twenty?"

"Over here on the north side of the fire."

"Good. I need ya ta get up ta the mayor's place. I think the arson suspects might be headin' that way."

"Why would they do that?"

"Just get up there, Dave. I'll be right behind ya."

"Ten four."

"And Dave? I need someone to pick up a pair of two sixty-one suspects over here behind the green house on the, uh, the south side of Maxwell. Jen Whittaker's place, I think. Eleven forty-one on one of the suspects and the victim."

"Ten four." There was a short pause. Steve knew Dave was ordering a couple of officers to his location to pick up the prisoners and calling for a pair of ambulances, one for the man with a bullet in his leg and one for the woman back between the houses. Dave came back on and said, "Roberts and Brown will be at your twenty in three or four. What's your situation?"

"Had to fire my weapon but I'm okay. Get goin' on the other thing."

"Ten four."

True to Dave's word, Roberts and Brown came running around the corner of the closest house with their weapons drawn. Steve quickly apprised the uniformed patrolmen of the situation, sending Brown to look after the victim and leaving Roberts with the suspects. Then he sprinted toward his truck.

The massive fire crackled and howled around him as he ran. Human screams echoed from he knew not where. He passed a family gathered into a tight little cluster in the middle of the street, hugging each other tightly as they stared at their burning home. Soldiers chased wraith-like men and women in and out of sight through the misty air. Hot cinders rained down everywhere. Steve thanked God for the firefighters standing foursquare in the midst of the chaos, their hoses snaked across lawns and pavement as they calmly sent water arcing up through the fog to fall onto the raging flames on every side. It was as if Dublin bore the curse of Sodom and Gomorrah. In nearly forty years as a peace officer, it was the worst thing he had ever seen. It was the first time he had ever shot anyone, the first time he had even fired his weapon in the line of duty, and as he ran through the living hell of Dublin, Maine, Chief Steve Novak decided he should take time to reload.

27

Staring down the hill at Dublin, Hope ignored the ringing tele-phone. The air was perfectly still, which allowed the fog to blanket the town below, obscuring everything except a fearsome iridescent flickering within it, and a plume of smoke that seemed to collect the fog into itself and swirl straight up many thousands of feet before the uppermost wind currents sent it streaming inland. It was as if the clouds had fallen from on high and an upside-down tornado had arisen to do damage to the empty heavens instead of dropping down to devastate the earth in the usual way.

Bree shouted from upstairs, *"Mother,* will you *please* answer the phone!" Hope sighed and tore herself away from the spectacle outside her kitchen window. With Riley still standing there looking down the hill, she crossed the room and lifted the portable phone from its cradle.

"Hope, are ya all right?" Steve Novak sounded frantic.

"Sure, Steve. What's goin' on?"

"We got arsonists settin' fire to houses on the north side a town."

Hope closed her eyes. "Anybody hurt?"

Steve paused a moment before saying, "There's a chance Riley was in one a the buildings, Hope. I'm sorry."

"No. He's okay. He's right here."

Another pause. "Everything all right up there?"

"How come you keep askin' that?"

"I, uh . . . I got a report the fires were started by some fellas who are after Riley. They could be comin' up there next."

"I see."

"Ya don't seem surprised."

She glanced across the kitchen at Riley's back and the roiling tower of destruction he was watching in the sky beyond the window. "No."

"I'm on my way to your place now. Dave Henson's also comin' in another car. He might get there first."

"Okay."

"Till we get there ya need to lock up the house and close your window blinds. If someone comes, just pretend nobody's home. Don't open the door to anyone but me or Dave."

"All right."

She hung up the telephone and said, "Is anybody out there?"

Riley said, "Ayuh. A few people coming up the street."

"Get away from the window."

"How come?"

"Just get away, Riley!" She rushed across the kitchen and reached for the cord to drop the window blind.

Riley said, "Hey, they're coming up the driveway!"

In spite of herself, Hope paused to look out through the glass. The column of smoke looked solid as it stood over her town, a living creature with undulating skin, a repulsively obese serpent uncoiling high above its prey. But close by was the greater danger, at least twenty strangers marching toward the house. She saw others coming far behind them. Everyone held big sticks and rocks, their filthy, bearded faces set in masks of fury. Then she saw one man who seemed oddly out of place. He had a powerful body underneath a clean black suit. His hair was neatly cropped close to his skull. As Hope stared at him in fascination, he raised his hand. In it was a handgun.

The glass before her face exploded. A wave of darkness strewn with stars draped itself across her consciousness. She sensed her body falling and heard a snap and felt a spike of pain drive up her spine, and she was on the floor, her vision clearing, staring up at the ceiling. A brick crashed through the window just above, soaring safely past but leaving a comet's tail of jagged glass to shower down upon her. She threw an arm across her eyes, burying her face in the crook of her elbow. Then Riley was there, moving her hair to look at the side of her head, asking if she was all right. More stones and bricks flew through the shattered window. She saw him shield her with his body, saw the stones and bricks go bouncing off his back. She heard the endless stream of dull thuds, like a gorilla pounding on its chest. She watched Riley wince, and wince, and wince again, and heard him grunt with pain, but he did not move from over her. If anything, he moved closer.

"Get Bree . . ." she said.

Stones and bricks continued crashing in, and he did not move. There was no more gunfire near as she could tell, but she saw a large rock hit the back of Riley's head. He cried out at that, and she thought she saw his eyes losing their focus, but still he sheltered her. Finally, when it seemed the cursing mob outside had directed their attention to another window, he gripped her arms and began to pull her toward the middle of the house. Burning pain shot through Hope's hip as he dragged her across the kitchen floor. She tried to help him, but the pain was just too much. She heard other windows crashing. She was assailed by ugly curses from just outside her home. Riley left her in the hallway, and she heard her husband's familiar footsteps charging up the stairs, and then she heard her daughter's voice nearby. She opened her eyes (had she been asleep?) and Bree was there above her, her daughter's beautiful face above her, filled with fear and worry just for her, and she thought, oh, she does love me, she really does.

"Where are the car keys?" shouted Riley.

Bree's voice was very calm. "I'll get 'em."

A moment later they were lifting her, Riley on the left and Bree on the right, and when they raised her upright, a carnivore sank its fangs into her flesh from somewhere on the inside, savaging her body to get out. She screamed, but Bree and Riley did not stop. She begged, yet they kept moving. In the mudroom Bree peered through the shattered glass in the upper half of the door.

"I think they've gone around to the front," she said. "Come on!"

Hope's legs were completely useless, trailing behind them as they carried her down the steps and along the driveway.

"Not the Pontiac," said Bree, the burden of her mother's weight heavy in her voice. "Dead battery."

So they dragged her to the Mercedes. She heard the jeers and curses getting louder. She heard more glass breaking.

"How do I work this?" asked Riley.

"It unlocks itself when you get this close with the key," said Bree. "Just open the door."

The predator inside Hope's body kept gnawing on her bones as they laid her in the back seat. Through the waves of pain she smelled the leather. She tasted her own blood. She heard someone shouting closer than the others. She heard him shouting, "Back here! Back here!" and she thought, please hurry, and Bree got in the back seat beside her, Bree cursing, and she thought, watch your mouth, young lady. She heard Riley say, "How do I start this thing?" but Bree must have leaned over the seat to push the button on the shifter instead of answering, because the next thing she heard was all twelve cylinders roaring, then came another spike of vicious pain, another swipe of the creature's claws within her as the impossibly expensive car Riley thought she needed charged down the driveway.

Hope screamed again as Riley took a right turn out of the driveway, throwing her against the door in spite of Bree's hands on her shoulders. "Please!" she screamed, but the only answer was the engine's roar. "Oh, please, please, please," she pleaded, but by then she was whispering, begging God to make it stop.

Incredibly, Riley stood on the brakes. Only Bree's firm grip kept her from rolling off the back seat and onto the car's floor. She heard her daughter shout, "Run 'em over! Run 'em over!" but Riley did not run them over; instead he twisted in his seat, throwing his arm across the back and staring out the rear window, staring through the air above her, ignoring her as he reversed the car at top speed, the transmission whining as they backed up the street.

This time, she could see his face. This time, she saw it coming and she braced herself as best she could, and the pain was only terrible when he hit the brakes. Then she lay staring at the ceiling of the car, trying to breathe, hearing the engine idling, hearing Bree say, "You got to go right through 'em!"

"I can't do that," said Riley.

"You got to!"

"I can't!"

"They'll kill us!"

"What's happening?" asked Hope.

"What's the matter with you?" screamed Bree.

"What's *happening*?" screamed Hope.

"They're coming up both ends of the street," said Riley, calmly. "We're boxed in."

"They're gonna kill us, Mom!" said Bree. "Make him drive through them!"

"No," said Riley. "It'll be okay. They won't hurt us."

Hope knew he was wrong, of course. She heard the first blow on the trunk of the car, and a face appeared in the side window above her, leering down at her, teeth bared like the animal within her, an outer extension of that inner slashing beast within her bones. Then another savage face at the opposite window, the same rage in it, the same barbaric bloodlust in it, and another, and another, and she thought this must have been what it was like for those poor doctors when The People came for them, except the doctors had guns and could fight back. The glass around the car completely filled now with the heads and upper bodies of them, even on the hood and trunk, the metal sides of the car resonating with the terrifying pagan drumbeat of their sticks and stones, the top of the car reverberating with The People's pounding feet as they danced the death dance over her, the tempered glass crinkling in a dozen spider webs of cracks as they pounded to get at her, the car shaking, provoking the carnivore within her, which bit down on her bones again as the car shook side to side with screams within and curses without, and the certain knowledge that her husband had been wrong again to trust them.

Then she heard a gunshot, very close.

And another.

And she thought, now they'll kill us.

Then they were all gone.

The sudden silence was enormous, a tangible thing, like the smoke towering above her town. She stared up at the bowed-down ceiling of the car and said, "What's happening?"

"It's hard to see out through this glass," said Riley. "But I think it's over."

She lay still, knowing it was Steve, of course, or Dave, or both, and knowing this was far from over, knowing Riley Keep was not yet done with being wrong.

28

Riley slammed his shoulder into the car door until it opened. Outside, the mob had fallen back, at least a hundred of them in a ragged circle, glowering under the threat of handguns wielded by Chief Novak and another policeman. Riley felt the weight of every angry eye upon him and knew he had to bear it as his own. He saw Brice in all their faces . . . Brice dead on the laundry floor for want of medicine beyond his means. The prospect of five thousand dollars left Riley with no place to hide from the sullen accusations in their stares. He had no defense. How could he deny his guilt when his fellow ghosts saw him so very very well?

"Everybody okay?" called the chief as he approached the Mercedes with his eyes and weapon on the crowd.

"No," said Riley, tugging on the rear door, which opened more easily.

Chief Novak backed up to the Mercedes and took a quick glance at Hope where she lay in the rear seat. He looked back toward the gang of angry alcoholics and said, "Hi ya, kid."

"Hi," said Hope.

"Where does it hurt?"

"My head and hip."

Riley saw a bright red bloody sheen slowly coursing across her forehead and face, but that seemed the least of Hope's own concerns as she pressed against her right hip with both hands and squeezed her eyes shut tightly.

The chief called out, "Radio for an ambulance."

Over between a Ford Explorer and a Crown Victoria patrol car Riley saw the other man lift a radio to his lips, then the man walked in their direction, his weapon panning the crowd behind the chief. When he got close enough to avoid being overheard by them he spoke softly. "They're all en route to the fires, Steve. It'll be at least an hour."

Riley glanced at the mob, a besieging wall of anger. He would not wait if he were them. He would want satisfaction. They deserved that from him, at the very least.

The chief's words mirrored Riley's thoughts. "They'll rush us way before then. We gotta get out a here."

"You drive me," said Hope. Riley saw her eyes open, staring up at him.

Steve said, "We'll put her in my truck and go together."

Hope groaned. "Don't let them move me, Riley."

The chief spoke to him. "Even if this car still rolls, ya can't see out the windshield."

Riley wished for orders or instructions, but the chief faced the mob without a word and Hope lay mute within her solitary world of pain. This was somehow up to him. He glanced at the intricate network of cracks on the windshield. After so many vicious blows, the way ahead would not be clear. He leaned close inside the car and said, "Don't worry." Then, turning to Bree in the back seat he said, "Cover your mom." It might have been the first time he had ever told his daughter what to do. She leaned across Hope, turning her back to Riley as he slid into the front seat and lifted both feet up to the glass. Drawing back, he kicked against the inside of the windshield again and again until it broke free and fell away.

Minutes later they were rolling in a convoy with Chief Novak up front in the Explorer, the other policeman behind in the squad car, and Riley in the middle at the wheel of the Mercedes, the air blowing fresh against his face through the hole where the windshield used to be. Ahead he saw the chief holding his drawn weapon high in his right hand while steering with his other. Riley kept his front bumper less than a yard behind the Explorer. As the Mercedes passed, his accusers pounded it with palms and fists. He wanted to beg them for forgiveness, but it was too late for that.

Soon they were free and moving more quickly down the road. Riley backed away from the chief's truck as their speed increased. They turned at the first cross street, descending toward the center of town into the fog. The lower they went, the deeper into the mist, the more people Riley saw out on the streets. Dark silhouettes of citizens standing in front yards, almost all of them holding weapons of some kind—everything from rifles and handguns to shovels and baseball bats. He saw others, citizens of another world, drifting in and out of obscurity, large groups of indigents along the sidewalks and standing together in parking lots. Some dashed furtively here and there between commercial buildings, all of which were closed for business. Riley saw three homeless men standing at the entrance to a restaurant, refusing to allow their friends to break in. Ahead, the chief slowed and stopped as five military vehicles rolled slowly out of the murkiness to cross the intersection, the helmeted troops inside the transports holding rifles upright, index fingers straight and at the ready beside trigger guards, eyes hidden behind goggles. Alarms sounded everywhere in the background—car alarms, burglar alarms, sirens from ambulances and fire trucks and squad cars. The chief rolled on, with Riley close behind, smelling smoke.

A wall of white drifted across the street as they came to Riley's neighborhood, or a few blocks from it, which appeared to be as close as anyone could get. The streets they passed were cordoned off with metal barricades and soldiers standing guard to turn away all traffic. Riley saw flames a few blocks over, leaping higher than the rooftops. Then the fog flowed across his line of sight and he could only see a glowing hint of the destruction, as if a murderer had drawn a translucent cloak around himself even as he did his grisly work.

"Riley" came Hope's voice from the back seat.

"Uh-huh."

"I smell smoke." Her words were strangely slurred, as if she had been drinking.

"Don't worry, we're almost there."

"Is everything okay?"

"Ayuh."

"Don't I smell smoke?"

"It's comin' from the houses."

"How many?"

"Hard to say."

"Well, would ya guess at least?"

"Maybe twenty."

"Lord protect us."

Riley glanced back to see Bree sitting stiffly with her hands upon her mother, and Hope lying very still.

At least a dozen cars and pickup trucks sat unoccupied in the no-parking zone outside the hospital emergency portico. Ahead of Riley, the chief rolled up as close as he could get and parked and ran through the fog toward the entrance. Riley parked behind his truck, got out and opened the rear car door. He knelt on the pavement, reaching in to lay a hand on Hope's shoulder. The bleeding at her forehead had stopped, but although her eyes were open she did not seem to notice he was there. Bree stroked her mother's hair. She did not speak. They were a long way from the emergency room doors, and a lot of people stood outside those doors. Riley wondered if there was room inside for Hope. After a few minutes, the chief emerged from the mist with a woman in hospital scrubs, who pushed a gurney. Between them, Riley, Bree, the chief, and the nurse managed to get Hope out of the back seat without causing her too much pain, though she did cry out once.

Riley would have followed as the nurse pushed Hope's gurney back across the pavement, but the chief laid a hand on his arm and said, "Bree, honey, go on with your mom, will ya? Your dad and I gotta talk a minute." Bree's attention was so focused on her mother, she barely seemed to notice.

When they were alone the chief said, "Those fellas figure out where ya are, they'll try to kill ya again. Hope too, prob'ly."

"She didn't do anything!"

"I'm sendin' an officer to stand guard, just the same."

"Thanks."

"You need to keep a low profile." The chief's hand was still wrapped around Riley's arm, giving his words the weight of a command.

"All right," said Riley.

"But don't leave town."

"What?"

The chief's grip tightened. "I know who ya are, Riley. Gettin' rid of the beard and hair and cleanin' up like ya did, that sure fooled me, but I know now."

Riley watched his daughter enter the hospital behind Hope's gurney. He said, "I don't know what you're talking about."

The chief shook his head. "My town's burnin', so I got no time for ya right now. But don't leave Dublin. If ya do, I'll come for ya. Wherever you go, I'll come, an' I won't be too awful worried 'bout the fine points of the law." The chief released Riley's arm. "Gimme the keys to this car."

"What for?"

"I'm impoundin' it. It's a crime scene."

Riley dropped the little black box into his hand.

"What's this?" asked the chief.

"It doesn't have keys, exactly. You just get in with that thing and push a button."

An ambulance rolled into the parking lot, its siren screaming. The chief glanced at the battered Mercedes, then back at Riley. He had to shout above the siren. "It'll have your fingerprints in it. We'll match 'em to the ones we took before. We'll prove you're the fella had her necklace."

"I never did a thing to Willa."

The chief's eyes lit up with triumph. "Well, ain't that queer, Riley? If ya don't know what I'm talkin' about, how come ya went and mentioned Willa?"

29

Every seat was taken in the emergency waiting room. Except for the main path from the entrance to the receiving desk, the aisles of the waiting areas were crammed with victims sitting up and lying on the floor. Some were blackened by smoke, others pressed bloody cloths to wounds. A nurse held an elderly man's liver-spotted wrist between the thumb and first two fingers of her right hand, taking his pulse. Able-bodied friends and relatives crowded around the desk, vying for attention from the administrative staff. Everybody's eyes contained the same strange mix of detached shock and panic.

Near a pair of scratched, brown metal doors, Riley saw Hope lying motionless on her gurney, with Bree standing alongside, pressing a large piece of gauze to her mother's forehead. He went to them.

"Where's the nurse who brought you in?"

"She was just an aide or somethin'," said Bree. "We have to wait here for a real nurse."

He touched Hope's hand. "How are you feeling?" Her eyes did not even flicker underneath the lids. Her face was ashen. He bent closer. "Hope? Can you hear me?" Still no response.

Riley went for help, with Bree behind him saying, "Mom? Mom?"

Across the room the nurse in green hospital scrubs had moved on from the old man and now stood speaking to a younger woman, who replied while cradling one arm with the other. As Riley hurried toward her, stepping over other victims on the floor, he called, "My wife's in trouble over here!"

"She'll hafta wait, mister." The nurse did not bother looking away from the young lady's arm. "I'll be with you as soon as I can."

"But I think she might be dying!"

The nurse turned. Riley saw deep weariness in her eyes. "What makes you think that?"

"She got shot in the head."

"Where is she?"

Riley pointed to the gurney.

After saying "I'll be back" to the woman with the injured arm, the nurse hurried straight to Hope. She spoke to her and got no response. She touched her cheek. She lifted an eyelid and stared at her pupil. She asked Riley a few questions. When he mentioned Hope's slurred speech on the ride to the hospital, she pushed Hope's gurney through the brown metal doors without another word.

As Riley watched the doors swing to and fro behind Hope and the nurse, Bree covered her face with both hands, put her back against the stark white concrete blocks of the emergency room wall and slid down to the floor. Pulling her knees up to her chin, she curled in upon herself at Riley's feet. He wondered if he should sit down beside her, maybe put his arm around her shoulders. But why would Bree want his company when this too was a misery he had caused? He remained standing up above her.

"Hope Keep? Hope Keep?"

Riley saw there was a woman at the receiving desk calling Hope's name. Relieved at the excuse to take some action, Riley went to her, leaving Bree alone down on the floor. Someone moaned very loudly on the far side of the waiting room as he reached the desk. He said, "You called for Hope Keep?"

Behind the desk a woman said, "You her next of kin?"

Riley turned to point toward Bree and said, "No, she—" But then he stopped, and thought, and said, "Ayuh. I guess I am."

"Fill out this form." A long strand of hair had escaped the woman's ponytail. She did not seem to notice.

Riley asked, "Is she going to be okay?"

The woman did not look at him. "Doctor'll see you soon."

"I just wanted to know how she's doing."

Still the woman did not look up. Instead, she wrote something on another piece of paper and shouted, "Samuel Eisen? Samuel Eisen?"

Riley took the clipboard and walked back through a sea of moans to stand beside his daughter. He filled in the blanks, surprised that he remembered Hope's birthday and social security number and the fact that she was allergic to penicillin. The questions on the form engrossed him. The answers that he knew promised something to him. The ones he did not know became a measurement of the distance he had fallen. He was disappointed to have to ask Bree about Hope's health insurance. At his feet she mumbled, "I don't know."

Riley felt his broken heart constrict. How strange, that Bree's answer rose up with the sound of mourning. Given all the misery in that room, why was "I don't know" the thing that drove most deeply into him? He thought of Hope signing insurance papers, and wondered what other important choices she had made alone. He wrote *contact Dublin Township* on the form and moved on, filling in the blanks of the solitary life he had so selfishly imposed upon his wife.

"What're *you* doin' here?"

Riley looked up to find a man standing directly in front of him. The man's freckled forearms lay folded across his chest like a pair of two-pound hams. A conical head rose from his shoulders without much intervention by a neck. He was shorter, but looked to outweigh Riley by at least fifty pounds of muscle. His tiny bloodshot eyes stared with an utter lack of empathy, as if examining an insect. Riley said, "I'm sorry?"

"I asked what you're doin' here." He had the kind of deep voice that carried. Riley saw other people turning their way.

"I came with my . . . with someone who got shot."

"Shoulda shot you."

"What?"

"I said they shoulda shot *you*." The man moved half a step closer to Riley, bringing him within arm's length. Riley became acutely conscious of the solid wall at his back, which offered no escape.

"Why would you say that?" asked Riley, trying to smile. "I don't even know you."

"I know *you*. You're that medicine fella on the news."

From a seat nearby, a fat little woman with a swollen nose stood and said, "Hey, he's right. It's that guy!" Her red hair was very thin and stuck straight out as if she had been struck by lightning. Riley saw reflections of the fluorescent lights shining on her scalp.

Bree rose up at Riley's elbow. "Maybe we should go."

Transfixed by the muscle man in front of him, Riley did not move. He was guilty, and he wanted to be judged. The man said, "I gotta little brother, been on the sauce for twenty years. He ain't got no money. I ain't got no money. How's my little brother supposed to get sober, what with you guys plannin' to charge five thousand dollars for that stuff?"

"I'm not going to charge that. It's the company's decision. I just—"

"You gonna stand there and tell me this ain't your fault? I heard how much they paid you." The man inched forward as he spoke. Now only about a foot away, he thrust his pugnacious chin toward Riley, daring him to make a move. "You got stinkin' rich 'cause of charging all that money." Riley realized he was holding the clipboard with Hope's information between them like a shield. He lowered it.

The fat little woman waddled closer. With her came a disheveled old man and a haggard young woman not much older than Bree, who said, "My grandpa says he'd take that stuff if he had the money."

"'Course he would, sweetheart," said the fat little woman. "He'd take it in a heartbeat." Riley smelled the booze upon her. "But we ain't seen that much money since he got his severance from the power company." The small old man beside her belched quietly, spots of blood upon his filthy shirt, woolen trousers hitched high up over his potbelly and cinched tight by a worn leather belt. Though he swayed where he stood, his rheumy eyes remained on Riley.

The young woman said, "How come ya got to charge so much for that medicine, mister?"

"How come?" said the muscular man in Riley's face. "I'll tell ya how come. He don't care 'bout nothin' but the almighty buck is how come."

The girl ignored the man. "Hey, mister? I got nearly a thousand in my savings already, and I bet my grandpa could raise another five or six hundred. Could we give ya that and pay the rest later?"

"I don't . . . I'm not the one you pay," replied Riley. "And they're not actually selling it yet. There's still some government stuff they have to work through, and—"

The girl interrupted Riley as if she had heard nothing. "'Cause the thing is, Grandpa used to make a lotta money." She had a broad streak of soot across her forehead, and the whites of her bulging eyes showed all around her irises. "He's an electrician, you know. But he can't work 'cause of his drinkin' problem. That's why he can't make enough ta pay ya now. But he could pay you easy if ya make him sober, mister. He could get some work then, and pay the rest."

"I wish I could help."

"Ya can!" She pushed at the muscle man to get closer. "It's all twisted up is what it is, mister. See, he's still got his drinkin' problem 'cause he can't afford to pay ya for the medicine. And he can't afford to pay ya 'cause he's got the drinkin' problem. See? He's gotta get sober before he can pay for gettin' sober, but he can't pay till he's sober, is what I mean to say. See how twisted up it is?"

Several other people had approached them as the young woman spoke. Riley saw the outrage in their eyes. He shook his head. "I wish . . ." He wished to tell them of his plans, how he was going to fix everything for Hope and Bree and Dylan, and all of them too, how it was supposed to be a win-win situation, except he had forgotten to name the price, he left that up to Mr. Hanks, and now it was too late. He wanted to tell them how he knew nothing about business, how it was an honest mistake. Anyone could have made it. But it was not true. He was anything but honest. In his heart of hearts, he had always known the price would be beyond the reach of everyone. Was he not a minister, a missionary? Who better understood the unregenerate poverty of man?

He said again, "I wish . . ."

Bree touched his sleeve. "Come on," she said, tugging on him.

This time Riley went with her, and as he did the people wandered after him like sheep behind a shepherd, all the way over to the emergency room doors, all of them completely silent except for the muscular little man who cursed Riley calmly and without ceasing in his deep voice that carried. As the electric doors slid shut behind him, Riley glanced back at the people on the inside of the glass. Inside they had mistaken him for one of them, presenting him with expectations. But though the air outside was thick with smoke and fog, Riley figured they could see him better now, see him for the ghost he was.

Beside him underneath the portico Bree lit a cigarette. Riley watched the embers on the tip of the cigarette glow brighter as she sucked the poison in. He visualized someone taking the cigarette out of her mouth and grinding it beneath their heel. Someone else. Someone who had earned the right to do such things.

She seemed to read his mind. "Maybe I oughta stop doin' this."

"Ayuh."

She glanced at him. "You know what I'm talkin' about?"

"It's a bad habit." His personal area of expertise.

"I'm hooked all right." She took another drag and dropped the cigarette. "Maybe I should take your medicine."

Her words scared him for some reason. Why? He did not understand himself. He only knew he had to say, "No. Don't do that."

Every kind of alarm and siren wailed in the background of their conversation. The fog might have cleared a little, but the surreal column of smoke remained above Dublin as straight and thick as ever.

Riley and Bree watched it side-by-side from the shade of the portico. She said, "They say smoke is bad for babies."

Riley did not reply.

"I have to decide what to do. Ronny says I oughta get an abortion. Mom wants me to put it up for adoption."

Riley was glad to have the clipboard to hold on to, the personal details of Hope's life written down in tiny boxes on the form. The clipboard shook in his hand. Again he clutched it to his chest, just as he had when the muscular man confronted him inside the hospital.

"I been thinking about keepin' it, but if I got the abortion I could keep smokin'."

Dear God, thought Riley, do something.

She said, "I'm kiddin' ya about the smoking."

He said, "Good."

"So . . . do ya think I oughta keep it?"

No, thought Riley.

Yes.

I don't know.

She waited silently beside him, someone else with expectations.

He said, "You should do what you think is right, Vachee."

"I'm askin' *you* what's right."

"I don't know." He said it while looking away from her, looking at the inferno he had unleashed upon the town. "I'm sorry."

"It's okay. I understand."

He turned back toward her, the last of all The People, now pregnant at the age of sixteen, by a boy with green and purple hair, in a burning town in Maine. "You understand?"

"You're afraid you'll say the wrong thing."

He drew a deep breath and slowly let it out. Afraid. Yes.

She said, "You don't have to worry. I'll do what I want anyway."

He tried to form the words, but in the end what came was, "Be careful."

She laughed, and took his hand, prying it away from Hope's information. Her skin felt completely correct against his. He wanted to close his fingers around hers, to hold on tight. Yet he did not dare. Yet he feared she would withdraw her hand if he did not react somehow, so he compromised, giving her hand a squeeze and then releasing the pressure, allowing her to hold on until she decided to let go.

She did not let go.

A siren detached itself from the cacophony in the distance, growing stronger than the others. Through the mist, Riley saw an ambulance careen around the turn into the parking lot. It stopped at the edge of the illegally parked cars at the emergency entrance, and the driver emerged, running back to throw open the rear ambulance doors and pull a gurney down along with his partner, who had been riding in the back. A clearly pregnant woman lay on the gurney with her eyes closed. Riley held his daughter's hand as they watched the men rush the woman across the parking lot and in through the emergency room doors. Bree's fingers felt impossibly small in his hand.

"If you decide to keep the baby," said Riley, "I'll take care of everything. I'll buy you a house and a car and pay all your expenses, and pay for a baby-sitter so you can finish high school and I'll set up a college fund for you and the baby both, and . . . everything."

"I knew you'd say that." She squeezed his hand and let go.

"So?"

"No thanks."

"But, if you decide . . . you can't earn much money, Bree. Trust me, it's not good to be poor. If you have a baby, it's gonna need things. I'm just tryin' to do right—to help you do what's right. Don't you think?"

"No," she said again. "I think sometimes the right thing is the wrong thing. I made a bad mistake. I need to live with this, you know? Not take the easy way out this time. I think that's how God shows you the way to be a person."

A new kind of sound joined the chaos in the background, a distant popping.

"What is that?" asked his daughter.

Riley knew but did not want to frighten her. "Maybe we should take these forms inside and ask if they have any news about your mom."

"You'll get hassled by those people," she said, taking the clipboard from him. "I'll go."

She took three steps away from him and paused beside a trash can. Reaching into her hip pocket she removed a pack of cigarettes. She crushed them in her fist and threw them away.

Riley thought, if only it were that easy, and suddenly a moment came to mind, a terrible memory of a morning five or six years ago when he awoke beside Bree's mother and realized he was already thinking about a drink before any other waking thought, the first thing on his mind, a drink, and the fog inside his mind had parted just for one brief moment and he had clearly seen his situation, known beyond all doubt that he was gripped by something inescapable. He remembered feeling utterly alone while lying there beside a sleeping woman who would not divorce him even after three long years abandoned, utterly alone with a daughter sleeping down the hall who would stand with him against an angry mob in spite of his abandonment of her. A thought occurred to him, the least that he could do for Bree and Hope. He said, "Hey, Vachee. Maybe you should call Dylan. Let him know about your mom."

Bree stopped and turned, searching his face, her coal-black almond eyes a mystery. She said, "Okay," and Riley watched her back until the electric doors whispered shut behind her. Then he gazed up at the top of the pillar of fire and smoke, at the high place where the jet stream lopped the top off of it. He thought about people's expectations, including his own, and wondered if the right thing could ever be the wrong thing, and he did his best to ignore the popping sound of gunfire in the distance.

30

It could only be the lawyer. In spite of her dire warnings he had obviously been careless somehow. Maybe it had been a note in a desk drawer, or a file on the computer in his office, or maybe they had tapped his phone line or bribed his secretary. It did not really matter. After seven years of hiding very well, she was in the back seat of a black Cadillac on Maine State Highway 1A, heading south across the short steel bridge in Frankfort, and all that really mattered was the duct tape on her wrists and mouth.

One of them had held her down on her hotel bed at the Bangor Keystone Suites while the other applied the tape, already inside her room and covering her mouth before she even knew she wasn't dreaming. Apparently they had left her ankles free so she could walk out to their car. She tried to tell herself that was a hopeful sign, since they could have killed her then and there if that was their intention. But the tape across her mouth was something else again. Her allergies had been acting up—the spring pollen season in the northeast always had caused havoc in her sinuses—and she found it extremely difficult to draw in enough air through her nose alone. It was okay if she stayed very still, but any movement that increased her respiration made her dizzy. Once, as she bent down to get into their car out in the hotel parking lot, she had nearly slipped into unconsciousness.

Now they were a mile below Frankfort, the full moon's reflection dancing on the ripples in Marsh River on their left as the Cadillac continued south. Glowing numbers on the dashboard clock read *3:15 a.m.* The young man in the back seat beside her and the driver up front talked baseball as if she were not there. The driver—who was also young—claimed someone named Garcia should be fired, while the man beside her disagreed, quoting batting averages and RBIs and listing other players' percentages of this and that as if he were a statistician instead of what he was. She watched the moon out on the river and focused on her breathing. She hoped they would not hurt her, reminding herself again that they could have killed her much more easily back in her room, but of course she was sitting here in a cotton shift, they hadn't even let her put shoes on, and she was bound and gagged, so she supposed realistically it was best to assume the worst.

The old woman began to think of certain things. Her mother and father, who had both been dead for nearly half a century. Her brother, Jimmy, lost to alcohol. That boy she knew in college, that beautiful boy, whom she thought might last forever. A swan she saw some-where, was it the Adirondacks? Yes. When she was seven or eight, when her parents sent her to that summer camp. Her first wild swan, the most graceful thing, gliding across the pond with the strangest sense of permanence, as if it were possible to move and yet not move, with all time here and now and the fallen world a lie.

She remembered the beautiful boy in college saying no.

The moon leapt along the river, keeping pace with her. She strove to forget swans and focus on her predicament. She started off thinking about how to get away but ended up remembering how this had begun—with Mr. Hanks talking that night around a campfire, promising big bonuses for everyone, stock options, he and a couple of the others speculating about what an alcoholic would pay to get the cure, like it was a game for them, like a funny bidding war. Mr. Hanks saying, "A thousand dollars for a dose," and someone else, "I'll raise you two hundred." Keeping it up until

Mr. Hanks got to five thousand dollars, and everybody laughing as if it was absurd, but she remembered seeing calculation in his face and knowing he was serious.

They said your whole life flashed before your eyes. For her it was just bits and pieces. She remembered lying on her cot beneath a hot Brazilian moon, thinking of her brother, Jimmy, and Mr. Hanks planning to charge so much more than poor Jimmy could afford, and all the poor people in the world who suffered like her brother, and rising in the middle of the night and taking the dried tubers that Waytee had given her and walking terrified into the jungle to hide them.

Would she do that again, knowing it would lead to this?

She tried to breathe past the tape across her mouth, feeling her heartbeat rise, and the panicked, dizzying sensation of too little oxygen. She should turn her mind to peaceful things, yet the memories persisted independent of her will, visions of rage and violence, of Mr. Hanks the next morning, storming into the village with eight men at his back, demanding the plants that he called "his," and The People's elders telling him there were many plants—so much lost in the translation—Mr. Hanks making threats, the elders' faces passive as one of Mr. Hanks's hard men spoke the words in Portuguese, a language lost on most of them. She remembered the way The People's non-reaction angered Mr. Hanks, and his "translators" coming back a second time, eight of them with rifles.

Her thoughts knew no chronology, dashing forward, up to Dublin, to the last two years and a tattooed girl with metal in her nose. Then back again, Lee Hanks's men returning to their camp with the little one, maybe nine or ten back then, her wrists conjoined with yellow nylon rope, a savage on a leash. Staring through the window of the Cadillac she saw them out there on the river, leading her around the tent and barking at her like she was a dog, laughing, mocking, terrifying in their utter lack of empathy. She looked to the stars above the river Marsh and saw a fellow doctor there, a man of conscience rising up to aid the little girl, and Lee Hanks speaking to his translators, then the doctor in the dirt, jaw collapsed and bleeding. She heard Mr. Hanks in all his confidence insist the Indians would trade to save the girl, assuring everyone he would not mean it when he went to tell The People he would kill the child at sunset if his plants were not returned.

Back inside the car she turned her head and stared at the young baseball fan beside her. How troubled he must be to break into an old woman's room and bind her, to drag her out against her will, sixty-three years old and looking much, much older. She stared at this problem solver on the payroll and remembered understanding Mr. Hanks was crazy, knowing she would get the same treatment as the doctor with the broken jaw, but knowing he had given her no choice but to make her full confession—it was not The People; it was she who hid the cure inside the jungle—and she remembered being marched toward the dreadful tree line at the edge of the camp, sensing hidden savage eyes upon her, prodded by the threat of rifles in the hands of problem solvers much like these young men in the Cadillac, the latent violence of their muzzles at her back most likely saving her because the rifles made it obvious she wasn't on their side. Oh, she would not wish it on these youngsters with her in the car, to take ten steps into a jungle far from home and be speared without a sound. She remembered Mr. Hanks's men falling, and she herself with eyes closed waiting for the pain of penetration, wondering if she would quickly fade or linger underneath the broad leaves of the canopy, and Waytee's breath upon her eyelids, there before her somehow without one single sound, slipping his necklace over her head, a sign to all the others.

Well. She had no necklace for protection here. Just silver tape across her mouth, a bleached white moon above the valley of the shadow, and an old pair of strong eyes to watch the treetops on the far side of the passing river, their jagged crowns in silhouette against the infinite beyond, the stars and planets merely whispered hints of what the cosmos really was. She closed her eyes and tried to think of heaven instead of watching from the jungle as The People crept up to the camp, the silence just before the end, every one of them attacking in one moment, even the women and the children, and most of her colleagues going down beneath The People's spears and clubs before Mr. Hanks's young problem solvers started shooting and every single Indian was slaughtered in mere seconds. She squeezed her old eyes shut much tighter, shaking just a little, hating the image of herself there in the brush, hiding like the coward she had been as Mr. Hanks's young men walked among the fallen People in the clearing, firing down into their bodies, and her two surviving colleagues tried to stop them, murdered for their trouble before her very eyes, leaving her the last one living somehow.

The hot Brazilian moon that night had risen red and angry. She remembered backing into the underbrush, and eventually, some sleep. What woke her the next morning had been the sound of Lee Hanks shouting in the distance, promising not to hurt her, promising they would both get rich together. Just bring out the tubers.

She had remained in hiding of course, even as he shouted to her off and on all day while walking back and forth between the carnage at the clearing and The People's empty village. His men searched for her around the camp and village, but she had learned a thing or two about moving through the jungle in her weeklong walk with Waytee. She eluded them, as she had ever since. Until this night.

It had taken seven years, but they had found her now.

She saw the peculiar flickering on the underbelly of the looming cloud bank long before they reached the edge of Dublin. She understood it fifteen minutes later when they slowed to turn onto a residential street and she smelled the acrid smoke. Twisting in her seat, she saw gigantic flames leap high beyond the rooflines of a residential area. The young man sitting there misunderstood her movements and gripped her by the forearm.

"Sit still," he said.

She turned her eyes forward again. She found to her surprise that she was thinking of these two young men in something like the way she had so often thought of homeless alcoholics. As with all those others, these were two more cases of *"there but for the grace of God go I."* She knew a lot of people thought themselves beyond this kind of barbarism, and she knew that for an ignorant conceit. She remembered listening to Lee Hanks shouting in the clearing, remembered the thoughts passing through her mind, what she would have done to him, if possible. Anyone could murder, given enough cause.

A military truck pulled onto the street ahead of them. The Cadillac's headlights lit up the soldiers riding in its canvas-covered bed. The men sat on a pair of benches facing inward toward each other, the color of their uniforms and helmets unidentifiable in the starkness of the Cadillac's headlight beams, their weapons standing upright between their knees, ugly and lethal. The first soldier on the right turned to look back at the Cadillac, then leaned forward, saying something to the man across from him.

"Think they got a curfew?" asked the driver.

"Absolutely," said the baseball fan beside her.

"What if they wanna stop us?"

"Don't worry about it."

"Yeah, but—"

"Hey. I'll handle it, all right?"

"Okay."

The transport slowed ahead of them, with all the soldiers in the back now turned in their direction.

The driver started cursing.

"Settle down," said the one beside her. "I was in the Rangers, ya know? I know how to talk to these guys."

Her heart began to soar. She thought of rolling to her side and kicking at the door, making all the noise she could as soon as one of those beautiful young soldiers came up close. She knew the man beside her would not hesitate to strike her, but it was worth the risk.

The truck slowed nearly to a stop, and she became convinced her nightmare would be over soon, even though the man beside her had removed a gun from underneath his jacket and now pressed it hard into her ribs. She did not believe he would really shoot her there in front of ten or fifteen witnesses holding automatic weapons. She felt her plan would surely work; her delivery was almost certain.

The truck stopped in the middle of the street. One of the men in it waved to the Cadillac, clearly indicating his desire for them to stop as well. The men in the truck began dismounting. She was seconds from salvation. Then popping sounds came from the direction of the burning homes. One of the soldiers shouted something to the others, and all of them went running off into the darkness, leaving her and her two captors sitting in the Cadillac, alone.

"Must be doin' somethin' right," said the driver as he rolled two wheels up on the curb to inch beside the truck.

"Absolutely," said the one who held the gun against her ribs.

The Cadillac slipped quietly across the little town. Everything seemed strangely dark until she realized most of the streetlights were not working. She saw a pair of shadows step out through the shattered glass of a business storefront with full hands and then quickly disappear into an alley. She heard sirens wailing all around. She saw small groups of soldiers standing here and there along the road. As they drove through one intersection, she looked up the cross street and saw two fire engines parked at angles nearly half a block away. Firemen lit in pulsing shades of orange and red and yellow aimed streams of water high into an entire row of houses lost in flames. The bitter scent of burning wood and plastic swelled the linings of her nostrils. Already short of breath, she had to focus hard on breathing. The worst thing she could do was panic, get her heart rate up, her body needing more oxygen. Whatever was about to happen, she wanted to be conscious.

They rolled on, and once a soldier tried to wave them over. "Yeah, right," said the driver without pausing.

Another few blocks passed and then, "It's the next left," said the one in back with her. To her surprise they turned into the parking lot of Dublin's small hospital. She knew her surroundings well, having spent many hours there attending to her charges when they overdosed or hurt themselves in all the foolish ways that alcoholics will. She had expected her captors to take her someplace private and secluded, someplace they could question her, or do whatever it was they had in mind. Although she felt exposed beneath her cotton nightgown she never considered rape, being far past the age when she believed young men like these might think of her that way. But she did know certain things, and expected their employer would want to know them too.

The parking lot was just as dark as all the streets had been. She supposed marauding bands of rioters had amused themselves by smashing out the pole lights. The Cadillac pulled into a parking stall quite near the street, on the far end of the lot from the hospital building. The driver killed the engine, saying, "We must be early."

The man beside her checked his wristwatch in the moonlight through the window. "Maybe a few minutes."

The two men sat in silence. She prayed, and did her best to breathe.

Another car pulled into the parking lot. It stopped a short distance away, its headlights aimed at them the way theirs had lit the military transport just a little while before.

"All right, lady," said the young man beside her. "You're on."

He opened the door on his side and made her slide across. He pulled her out, the strong fingers of his left hand tight around her bicep. He stood her up beside the Cadillac. She lowered her face against the glare, but he put his hand below her chin and lifted it, forcing her to face into the headlights. She heard a car door open and close beyond the lights. She heard a voice say, "Yes, it's her. Please remove the tape from her mouth."

"She might scream."

"Listen. Can't you hear that? Everybody's screaming."

It was true. The air was pregnant with the shrieks of citizens and sirens. The man released her arm and ripped the tape away in one quick motion. Then he gripped her arm again. From behind the light she heard, "You don't have to be afraid, Dr. Williams. I just need the answers to a few questions, and then we'll let you go. Okay?"

She did not reply.

"Do you understand, or not?"

"Yes," she said.

"There's too much noise. I need you to speak up."

"Yes!" she shouted.

"Very good. Now, the first question. How much do the Keeps know?"

"The Keeps?"

"Help her understand me, will you?"

The man twisted her arm behind her back and lifted. The pain was excruciating.

"How much do the Keeps know?"

"About Brazil?"

"Of course."

"I haven't told them *anything!*" The pain in her arm was awful. She screamed just a little.

"Take it easy" came the voice, and the man relaxed the pressure. She heard the voice continue, "Whom have you told?"

"Nobody."

"Why should I believe you?"

"Why should I lie?"

"Help her think of a better reason."

The man twisted her arm and raised it up again. She rose to her tiptoes, trying to reduce the excruciating pressure. She cried out again. She heard the voice behind the headlights say, "Whom have you told?"

"Nobody! I swear!"

"Let's give her a breather."

The man relaxed the upward pressure on her arm. She began to weep. "I've never told anyone. You have to believe me! It's how I stayed hidden all this time. Why would I risk telling anyone?"

The voice behind the headlights remained silent for a time. Then she heard, "I believe her. We're done here."

After a few more seconds, the headlights shifted away from her as the other car began to roll. She watched the lights until the car had left the parking lot, then the young man pushed her forward, walking her across the pavement and into the surrounding darkness. Still temporarily blinded by the headlights, she did not see where he was taking her until he stopped behind another car, a different one, a Mercedes Benz. It was in terrible condition, dented and scraped all over, the safety glass of the rear window battered with a dozen blows at least. Then the driver was there with them. He bent over the lock on the trunk of the Mercedes for a few seconds, and the lid rose up.

"No key no problem," said the smiling driver.

"Get in," said the one who held her by the arm.

She had been passive all along, lulling them in preparation for this moment. With no warning whatsoever she twisted violently to her left. It worked. He lost his grip. She set out running toward the lights of the hospital, her bound hands swaying back and forth in front of her stomach, her bare feet slapping loudly on the pavement as she called for help as loudly as she could, her cries lost among so many others, and the sirens, and the roar of the inferno, and she felt a massive weight crash into her back, one of them upon her, then she was down on the asphalt.

Looking up she saw smoke parting in the night sky above Dublin, saw the full moon up there beaming down, and the poor lost young men looking down at her beside it, and now that this was finally going to happen after all her years of dread she realized it was not as she imagined, not as she had always feared, and she wished she had not wasted so much time on faithless worries. But no, no, that was wrong. There was no reason for regrets, no condemnation now, for after all those years of dealing with her worries all alone she was in the here and now at last; she had given up her fears to God and sealed the bargain with a lawsuit.

"Don't be so afraid," she said, looking up at the young men and the full moon just behind them. "You don't have to be."

"What was that?" asked the driver. "What'd she say?"

And the young man who had ridden there beside her said, "Who cares?"

31

Steve Novak did not sleep for two days straight, then he lay down on the shiny vinyl floor in his office for a couple of hours and dreamed of pulling tuna through the transom gate of his cousin's yacht. When he awoke he had a bad crick in his neck. He washed his face in the station's public toilet room and went back out into the mayhem.

He discharged his weapon sixteen times before it was over, firing warning shots mostly, but returning fire twice. He hit his assailant both times. During calmer moments he worried they might die. He hoped to find the time to check on them at the hospital.

The total stillness of the fog-laden air that first day had been Dublin's only blessing. It had allowed the city's three fire trucks to contain the blaze somewhat until more trucks arrived from nearby Cambridge and Pennyton. In the end, with thirteen fire crews working they were able to limit the destruction to a five-block area. By the third day Steve still did not have a final count, although he thought maybe a hundred homes had been destroyed. It would have been much worse with the usual onshore breeze. Still, Steve did not feel grateful.

Colonel Peterson never did formally authorize the use of force or issue rules of engagement or whatever it was they called it when the National Guard gave soldiers permission to shoot civilians. But when

looters started firing at his men, the soldiers just defended themselves, and that got to be the way things were. For about twelve
hours during the worst of things, it was pretty much shoot on sight
without bothering to determine if the target was a hostile or a citizen
protecting his own property. After the worst was over, Steve decided
to file a formal complaint about the colonel at some point, but the
paperwork and lawyering about this mess would probably go on for
years, so there was plenty of time for that. Besides, the media was all
over it, and Steve figured they would have the colonel's command at
the very least. Probably have Steve's job too, but that was a worry
for another time.

Four days into it, volunteers were still sifting through the smoldering ruins, searching for casualties. So far they were up to seven
Dublin citizens dead of one thing or another. Smoke inhalation, gunshot wounds, heart attacks. Steve did not know any of the victims
personally, but he knew people who did, and he understood the wide-
spread desire for vengeance. A military truck with a loudspeaker had
been weaving through the streets for the last forty-eight hours,
warning people not to step outside their homes or businesses with
weapons. Steve knew a few of the diehard Mainers would have no
patience with that. He had seen a lot of homeless people doing their
best to control the rioters, helping with evacuations, putting out
small fires, but that wouldn't matter either. A stranger took his life
into his own hands walking through Steve's town unless he wore a
uniform or carried a news camera.

Driving through Dublin, Steve saw very few remaining homeless
people anywhere, rioters or not. At last report nine of them had been
shot dead by persons unknown, on top of the seven Dubliners who
were dead from one thing or another. So that was sixteen dead so
far. As crews dug through the ashes, he fully expected that number
to increase.

Steve cruised past the lot where Just Right Liquor used to be.
All three liquor stores at the edge of town had been targets, of
course. Two got away with just broken windows, but Just Right had

been burned to the ground, probably by a few students from over at Bowditch who had joined the mayhem in sympathy with the protesters. They had pitched furniture through library and administrative building windows, and used it to build a bonfire on the mall. Downtown, Henry's Drug Store had been ransacked again, just like last winter. This time they tried to burn it too, but four National Guardsmen ran them off before the fire got out of hand. Most of the storefront glass downtown had been shattered, and although the Guardsmen managed to keep looting to a minimum down there, a lot of stolen inventory still lay where the thieves had dropped it along Main Street. Even the town hall had suffered damage. Only Willa's shelter and the Congregational church stood untouched.

Thinking of Willa reminded Steve of Hope's husband or whatever the man was, and that reminded him of Hope's Mercedes. He lifted his radio's handset. "Dave, Dave."

After a short pause he heard, "Ten four."

"What's your twenty?"

"Still over here at the hospital."

That was what he thought. "While you're over there, would ya get that Mercedes towed for me like we talked about?"

"You bet."

Steve replaced the microphone in its cradle. To his surprise, he felt a little weepy. In the last seventy-two hours, Dave had been unstoppable. Steve doubted the man had slept at all. He had been all over town, a calming influence wherever he went. Steve thought about his whole department, the way they had risen to this challenge, days without sleep, lives on the line, no hint of slowing down, every single one of them a hero or a heroine as far as he was concerned. He wiped his eyes with the back of his hand. Normally he was not emotional. Probably it was the exhaustion setting in.

He got a little more sleep that night, and a full four hours straight the next. A couple of times he thought about finding Hope's ex-husband or whatever he was and grilling him about Willa's whereabouts, but Steve had nineteen dead for certain now, and that many actual deaths to investigate left little time for looking into something that was just a possibility. Still, Willa was a very special person, and whether she was dead or not, something wasn't right. He would get to Riley Keep.

Colonel Peterson had been replaced by a General John Sanders, who seemed to be a master of logistics. During the general's first two days temporary trailers arrived and were set up in a field near Teal Pond for those who lost their homes and had no friends or family to put them up. They were delighted to move out of the high school gymnasium.

Another day went by before Steve Novak got the call about the car.

Things were a bit less hectic by then, yet after seven days the body count was up to twenty-three, including so-called natural causes brought about by stress. The news media had long ago descended on Dublin like flies on a swollen carcass. Steve had to detail a patrolman just to keep them off his back whenever he went outside the station. Everything he did was observed with telephoto lenses, which was why he appreciated the wall of corrugated steel around Nehemiah Shore's junkyard.

After Steve drove in through the gate, Nehemiah's sole employee pulled it shut behind him, and the reporters who had tailed him from the station were forced to wait on the gravel road, out of sight. Dave waved to Steve from over beside the Mercedes, which was parked along with a group of cars that looked relatively clean compared to the dozens of cannibalized wrecks Nehemiah had stacked haphazardly around the yard. Steve rolled to a stop near Dave and got out of his Explorer. "Just get here?" he asked.

"Ayuh."

Nehemiah walked up, wiping filthy hands on filthy overalls. Steve said, "Thanks for callin'."

"You bet. Uh-huh. You bet."

Steve cocked his head to consider the skinny man. He looked pretty much as usual—greasy hair, stringy beard, Adam's apple busy as a squirrel in autumn. The sour smell of whiskey on his breath was hard to take, even in the open air. "When'd ya first notice it?" asked Steve.

"Ha'd to say. Ha'd to say. Yestidy, mebbe. Mebbe, ayuh."

"All right, Nehemiah. Give us a little room to work here, will ya?"

The man started nodding, and did not seem capable of stopping. "Ayuh, ayuh. I'll be ovah there." He waved toward the corrugated metal shack that was his office and his home.

"That's fine, Nehemiah. We'll call ya if we need ya."

Still nodding, the junkyard owner walked away. After a few steps he stopped and looked back. "Wasn't me what noticed first. Not first. Was the dogs, ya know." He kept nodding. "Dogs first, ayuh."

Steve sighed as he walked up to the Mercedes. He knelt beside the rear bumper and examined it carefully. His heart sank at the sight of dried blood. He'd seen enough of the stuff the last few days to know what he was looking at. He stood. "Go ahead an' pop the trunk, will ya?"

Dave walked around to the driver's door.

"Use a pen or somethin'," called Steve, thinking about finger-prints.

Dave grunted and pulled a pen from his shirt pocket. He leaned in through the open window and a second later the car's rear lid rose up with a pneumatic hiss. The stench was nearly overwhelming. Steve stood looking down into the trunk as Dave came back to stand beside him. For some reason, out of all the tragedy Steve had seen over the last week, this hit him the hardest. He wanted to throw up. He wanted to sit down in the dirt and wail at the top of his lungs. But he was Dublin's chief of police, the man responsible for standing between good citizens and things like this, so he just looked into the trunk, pretending to be strong.

After a minute, Dave said, "Well, that about cinches it."

"Ayuh," said Steve, thinking about Riley Keep. "It surely does."

32

Riley sat in the corner of the hospital room, watching the rising and falling of Hope's chest as the ventilator fed her lungs. Beside her bed, Bree and Dylan played a game of checkers. The two of them were very easy with each other, communicating almost without words as good friends often do. When Riley could no longer stand the sight of it he rose and went out to the hall.

"Hi ya, Riley," said the uniformed policeman from his chair outside the door. He had been assigned to guard Hope's room full time, since it seemed the riots had been started by a mob intent on harming her and Riley. The cop said, "How's she doin'?"

Hope had been unconscious since that first day a week ago. The bullet had only grazed the side of her skull. Far worse damage had been done when she fell. Her hip was broken, and her head had apparently hit the kitchen floor very hard. The emergency room nurse's quick diagnosis of a subdural hematoma and Hope's subsequent surgery were initially a cause for hope, but as the days of her coma continued to add up, the doctors seemed more pessimistic. It was impossible to tell how permanent her brain injury might be until she regained consciousness.

Riley looked at the cop and shrugged. "She's about the same. You want a soda pop or something?"

"Naw. I already gotta go pretty bad as it is, and my shift ain't done for another thirty minutes."

"Go on to the john. I'll sit here for you."

The cop smiled and shook his head. "Chief'd have my job."

"Oh well," said Riley. He walked to the end of the hall where he pressed the button for the elevator. When it arrived, a pair of nurses stepped out. Riley said, "Hi, Helen. Becky."

Becky said, "Hi ya, Riley," but Helen walked right past as if he were not standing there. Becky had explained her co-worker's attitude to Riley a couple of days before. Helen had a son with a drinking problem.

Riley ignored her snub. "Any news people down there?"

Becky said, "Didn't see any," then followed Helen toward the nurses' station.

Down in the lobby, Riley exited the elevator and glanced left and right to make sure the coast was clear before heading toward the cafeteria. Being at the hospital full time made him an easy target for reporters, who somehow always found a way to get past the tightened security. He had eaten all his meals here since the day they admitted Hope, sleeping in the hospital every night, leaving the building only long enough to shower and change clothes at Dylan's house, which stood in a neighborhood that had not been burned and still had working plumbing and electricity.

Riley dropped a few coins in a vending machine and pressed a button. He worked his shoulders up and down as he waited for the soda to drop into the little hatch. The stones and bricks he had taken on his back for Hope had left a maze of bruises, and a doctor had put nine stitches in his scalp where something had laid it open. Also, he had not been able to keep up with his exercises, so after sleeping in a waiting room chair last night, he felt stiff all over. Walking back toward the elevator, Riley opened the can and took a sip, hoping the caffeine would compensate for another nearly sleepless night.

Upstairs again, he turned the corner and saw Dylan and Bree standing out in the hallway along with Jerry the policeman, all three of them staring in through Hope's door. Riley's heart sank. Something was wrong. If it was just a matter of making room for the orderly to change Hope's sheets, they'd be standing around talking to each other, not focused on her room that way. He hurried down the hall. Drawing close, he asked, "What is it?"

Bree turned to him, her face shining. "She's awake!"

Riley had to lean against the wall to keep from falling.

At first they kept Hope on some kind of sedative to make the plastic tube that still stuck down her throat a little easier to take, but in spite of her sedation, she was clearly with them once again, blinking her eyes and making guttural noises in response to Bree's and Dylan's excited words. Riley did not say much. Mostly he stood back and watched.

Each time the nurses came to check on Hope, Bree pled with them to pull the ventilator tube out of her mother's throat. Twelve hours after Hope emerged from her coma, they called the doctor in, and he agreed. Everyone had to leave her room. Ten minutes was all the time it took and the doctor and nurses were finished. They let Bree go in while Dylan and Riley stayed in the hall. They said Hope wanted it that way.

Sipping coffee from a paper cup, Riley watched Dylan closely as they waited for their turn to be with Hope. Dylan had been there almost since the start. He too had slept in chairs most nights. He too had taken most of his meals in the hospital cafeteria. And as the three of them had lingered day and night in Hope's room, he had often suggested that they pray. Watching Dylan now as he stood waiting outside Hope's room with such obvious joy, Riley could not stop the recurring memory of Hope's words: *"He's a good friend."* He remembered asking if that was all Dylan was to her. He remembered that she did not answer. He wished he had not asked, because now the question felt like doubting something pure and true. Hope deserved a man like Dylan, and Riley deserved . . . nothing.

Bree emerged from the room. Dylan said, "How is she?"

"She's all balled up," said Bree. "I don't think she remembers a thing that happened."

"They warned us about that," said Dylan. "Remember?"

"But she's talking?" asked Riley.

Bree nodded. "She's pretty hoarse from that breathing thing."

The doctor had explained that talking would be an excellent sign. Riley thanked a God he no longer knew and then he said, "Can I go in and see her now?"

Bree fixed her cryptic eyes upon him. "She asked for Dylan next."

Riley let a moment pass, more time than he would have hoped, because he knew it made his feelings clear to everyone. "Uh, sure. Dylan, you go ahead."

Dylan frowned. "She's just confused, man. I think you should go."

"No."

"I really think—"

Riley threw his half-full cup of coffee at the wall. "I'm not gonna stand out here and argue about this! Go!"

As the coffee flowed across the floor Dylan looked away, but Bree's unblinking eyes remained upon him. Riley returned his daughter's stare defiantly. How he hated her! How he hated Dylan, and Hope, and everything—himself most of all. Naked and ashamed at the center of his daughter's pitiless examination, Riley spun on his heels and strode down the corridor. Around the corner he collided with a man holding a camera, nearly knocking him down. A nearby woman said, "Riley Keep! I'm Julia Armstrong, with CNN. Can we please have a moment of your time?"

Riley roared in frustration, shoving the cameraman away and breaking into a run. Bypassing the elevators he entered the emergency stairwell, his footsteps echoing hollowly in his headlong descent to the lobby, where he burst through the doors, looked left and right to get his bearings, and then charged to the exit.

Out in the parking lot, Riley Keep kept running. He had no idea where he was going; he only knew he had to get away. Weaving through the cars he made good time. This was what he had been training for all winter. A marathon away from Dublin. Soon he was across the parking lot and loping with an easy stride across a recently mown field. He was not even breathing heavily. He was in the best shape of his life. He could have run all day and night, and might have had he not heard his daughter's voice calling from far behind.

"Daddy! Daddy!"

It stopped him in his tracks.

He had not heard that word in ... in a long time, longer than a lifetime. He stood motionless in the middle of the field, not turning around. He heard the buzz of insects and saw a cloud of gnats rise up around him. The sun felt hot upon his shoulders. The ripe smell of cut green grass brought vague memories of childhood, of laughter, of rolling on the surface of the earth. Some of this was real, but Riley knew he was imagining the best of it. Still he did not turn. He did not want to turn and find he was alone. He stood in the field, breathing in and out, trying to maintain the illusion of that word on his daughter's lips, but knowing better, knowing those could not possibly be her footsteps in the grass behind him, knowing he could not possibly have heard her breathless voice.

The cloud of gnats hovered golden in the sunshine, burning like the cherubim of Eden. He closed his eyes and lifted his face toward heaven and saw the glowing through his eyelids. To maintain the illusion, he said, "Did you just call me Daddy?"

A pause and then, "Well, yeah, I guess."

Reluctantly, he turned. Bree did indeed seem to be standing there. Still uncertain of reality he opened his arms. She walked into them stiffly. Her broad little body stood rigid against him, distant, and yet possibly right there. He said, "I love you," which was so deeply true even if nothing else in his life was, and she said, "Oh, Daddy," and the muscles of her back began to soften underneath his hands, and both of them began to weep, and through his tears he saw Chief Novak and a uniformed policeman coming for him on the fresh-mown field.

33

Many of the other prisoners had sworn to kill Riley Keep, so although every other cell in Dublin's small jail was packed to overflowing with looters and arsonists arrested during the riots, he had been confined alone. The walls between the cells were solid concrete, but only open rails separated him from the men just across the corridor. They cursed him unmercifully. One raving lunatic threw feces at him. Riley pulled the thin mattress down from the top bunk and propped it up on the end of the lower bunk, creating a barrier to hide behind. Since the men across the way could no longer see him, they lost interest after a few hours. Riley passed the time by staring at the tan paint on the wall beyond his feet, trying to decide if what had happened in the field with Bree had been real, or if it had been just another of his pitiful delusions.

They interrogated him five times in the first two days, putting manacles and shackles on him every time as if he were a homicidal maniac, short-stepping him along between the six little cells as cursing men spat and flung toilet paper from the left and right. The chief always interviewed him personally, asking the same endless questions. After denying everything again and again, Riley just quit talking.

On the third day they put a man in his cell. He was three sheets to the wind and very small—maybe five feet tall and a hundred pounds at most—so probably they assumed Riley could handle himself if the guy caused any trouble. But there was no trouble. The little man was a friendly drunk, laughing to himself and talking cheerful nonsense without ceasing. Riley knew from long experience the fruitlessness of answering his drunken questions. So Riley lay on his bunk silently while his talkative cell-mate paced their tiny cell. Eventually the man sat on the floor with his back against the wall and started snoring. An hour after that they turned the lights off in the cells and Riley fell asleep.

Early the next morning he found the small man curled up on the bare concrete floor. Feeling guilty, he put the mattress back on the upper bunk and climbed up there to make room should the newcomer desire to drag himself to bed when he awoke. Riley lay staring at the paint as usual, hoping the prisoners across the corridor would not notice he was exposed to them again. Finally he started to drift back to sleep.

"Hey, man. Don't I know you?"

Shifting to his side, Riley opened his eyes to see his cell-mate standing by the bunks, staring up at him. Their faces were about a foot apart. When the man's rancid breath hit his nostrils Riley rolled away to face the wall.

"Yeah, I know you. Ha. You're the guy what cured me that time."

Still half asleep, the significance of this remark did not occur to Riley for a moment. Then he rolled back to face the man. "What?"

"Don't ya remember me?"

Mainly to get the man to move away so he wouldn't have to smell his breath, Riley said, "Hand me my glasses, will you?"

"Huh? Oh, yeah. Ha ha."

The little man took a step away, lifted Riley's eyeglasses from the single steel shelf beside the sink and gave them to him. Riley sat up on the bunk, put on the glasses, and looked down. "Were you at the shelter last winter?"

"Yep. Timmy Frank, that's me. Man with two first names. Ha ha." He held a grimy hand up to Riley, who reached down to shake it. The man asked, "What're you in for?" and Riley started to reply, but heard the answer in his head before his lips could form the word. *Murder.* Unable to say it, he kept quiet. His cell-mate did not seem to notice. He continued, "Me, I'm just drunk and disorderly. Ha. Least I think that's all this time. Mighta had some stuff I borrowed on me, some kinda misunderstandin' 'bout that maybe, them thinkin' I borrowed it without permission, so to speak. Ha ha. Yeah, I think I remember somethin' about that. Ha. Oh well." Timmy Frank crawled onto the bunk below. "Oh, my aching head. Ha ha."

Riley watched a housefly as it furiously circled the ceiling light above him. "You said something about me curing you?"

"What? Oh yeah. Ha."

"You're one of those guys? The ones I gave it to?"

"Yep. Taste like chocolate. Whole different kinda kick to it, though. Ha ha."

"Didn't it take away your urge?"

"Oh, sure. Absolutely."

"But . . . you were drunk last night."

"Ha ha. Was I ever."

The fly kept slamming itself against the glowing light, again and again and again. Riley kept his eyes on it, the most interesting thing in sight. "How come you started drinking again? Did the urge come back or something?"

"Naw. Least not till after I started up to drinkin' again. But after that first drink it sure came back—tell ya that for sure. I mean, with a vengeance. Gotta drink? Ha."

"But, if you didn't have the urge, how come you started drinking?"

"Hey, who wants to be sober, ya know? I mean, like they say, it ain't the drinkin' that's the problem, ya know? It's the *not* drinkin'. Ha ha."

Riley thought about that, and remembered closing his eyes and picking a clear plastic thimble from the Communion tray, not caring if it contained grape juice or wine. Still watching the fly he said, "You sure laugh a lot."

"Ha ha. Yessir. Yes, I do. Like my dear ol' momma used to say, it's either that or cry. Ha."

Timmy's forced cheerfulness grated on Riley's nerves at first, but after a while he realized it was just a habit, the way some of his young students back at Bowditch used to say "like" at the start of every sentence, or threw in "actually" all the time. That too had annoyed him at first, but he had learned to ignore it. Soon he didn't notice Timmy's constant chuckling either. Days went by, with Dublin's little jailhouse slowly emptying around Riley as the other prisoners were freed, released for time served, or transferred to other jurisdictions. When they came to free his cell-mate, Riley was sorry to see the little fella go, but Timmy couldn't wait to get outside and bum a drink and left without a backward glance.

One day Chief Novak appeared at Riley's cell with a suit of clothes and a guard. "Here ya go," he said, passing the clothes through the narrow opening in the door. "Get dressed for the court-house."

Riley had been issued white cotton socks, a pair of terry-cloth slippers, and white cotton overalls with a broad orange stripe down the outside of each leg and sleeve. His beard had grown out half an inch. When the chief arrived he was reading the Bible and thinking of his old friend Brice and his new friend Timmy, and the impossibility of getting five thousand dollars one handout at a time while the devil in your belly demanded constant payment. The Good Book said, *"Blessed are the meek, for they will inherit the earth,"* but Riley Keep's experience indicated otherwise.

He closed the book and rose and took the two steps necessary to reach the cell door. Accepting the clothing he said, "Did I forget a hearing?"

"Naw," said the chief. "Spur of the moment deal."

Riley stripped out of the coveralls and donned the shirt and suit and tie and put his hands through the opening in the door, waiting for the guard to cuff him as usual before letting him out. It was a familiar routine, although it was different for the chief to come to get him personally. Because Riley's wealth would have made travel to another country very easy, he had been denied bail during his first courthouse visit. Dylan had found him a whole team of the best criminal defense attorneys available, and they had filed a lot of motions, but the judge would not be swayed. According to Dylan, the best he could hope for was an early trial date, maybe within six months. The worst-case scenario was life without the possibility of parole.

"Guess I must of lost track of the days," said Riley. "I thought this was Saturday."

"Ayuh," said the chief as the guard closed the handcuffs on Riley's wrists. "That's right enough."

The door swung open. Riley moved out and then two steps to the left, as usual. The guard closed the door as the chief backed to the far side of the corridor. They did not put shackles on his ankles this time, which was strange. Instead, the guard gripped his upper arm and steered him toward the cell block entrance. The chief fell in behind.

"What's going on?" asked Riley without looking back at the chief.

"Hard tellin' not knowin'."

"But Saturday?"

"Ayuh. It's a puzzler."

Beyond the steel door at the entrance, Riley turned right and entered the sally port. The gate shut behind him. Then the door in front of him opened, and he was led directly into the back of a police car. He settled back on the gray vinyl seat as an officer closed the rear door and the vehicle pulled away from the Dublin Township jail.

Swaying with the squad car's motion, Riley raised his manacled hands and scratched his beard. The lawyers wanted him to shave and trim his hair, but he wished to abandon his disguise since it was no longer needed. There was no point in hiding as his old self now that the whole world knew who he really was.

The squad car passed the homeless shelter, which had been shut down. Riley stared at the empty black glass storefront and thought of meetings with his lawyers, of sitting mutely as they warned of the persuasive power of the cross in his pocket that had been tied to him with his fingerprints, along with Willa Newdale's murdered body that was found in the trunk of Hope's ruined Mercedes. In the smoldering debris of Riley's garage apartment an arson investigator had discovered his homemade exercise system. The prosecuting attorney claimed the metal rings and chains had been used to restrain Willa during the months between Riley's alleged bloody assault on her in the homeless shelter and the discovery of her body in the car. Riley knew his lawyers had been trying to get Lee Hanks to agree to testify in his defense. Mr. Hanks was the one person other than Riley himself who had been inside the garage apartment during that time. He could verify that Willa was not there, but so far Riley's lawyers had not gotten through to Hanks in spite of many calls and letters. Riley did not understand this. Mr. Hanks had spent a fortune paying men and women to go throughout the world to spread the Gospel. How could he fail to come and tell the truth when a brother Christian's life depended on it?

Now the squad car passed by Henry's Drug Store, and Riley thought of the giant from Houston who had terrorized him on that night so long ago. Riley's lawyers said the man had been arrested in the riots, then he had obtained a reduced charge by agreeing to testify that he saw Riley beating Willa in the shelter. It was a lie of course, but unlike Mr. Hanks, Riley understood it.

The hardest part had come when Riley's lawyers told him that Hope could not remember who had fired the shot that struck her—short-term amnesia was a common side effect of head injuries like hers—and the prosecutor had accused him of trying to murder her as well as Willa. The police compared the bullet that nearly killed Hope with the ones they found in Willa's body. They were a perfect match. When a nurse had come forward to say she saw Riley fly into a rage, throw a cup of coffee in the hospital hallway, and run away after Hope awoke from her coma, the prosecutor claimed Riley was afraid Hope would identify him as her assailant.

Every bit of the evidence against him was circumstantial, but according to the defense team, many people had been jailed for life on less.

Dublin Township had rules against outgoing telephone calls or written messages from inmates to their alleged victims for obvious reasons, and they allowed no incoming calls to inmates whatsoever, except from lawyers. As far as the outside world was concerned, Riley might have been a corpse in a tomb. The only news he received came through his lawyers, or Bree, who had visited him as often as she was allowed.

Bree often relayed verbal messages from Hope, expressing her mother's concern. Riley was not sure what to make of that. He had not been allowed to visit Hope, of course, and her condition kept her at the hospital, so she had not come to the jail or attended the hearings. Riley suspected Bree's messages might be a childish ploy to resurrect her parents' marriage by telling each of them sweet lies. Fearing this, he had asked no questions of his daughter. It was often better not to know the truth. It was like the exhilaration he felt when he first got sober, which quickly disappeared. You dream of something that will make your life complete, and then against all odds it comes, and ... nothing. As the days and weeks went by, Riley had begun to wonder for the first time if his chronic discontent was based on something independent of his character or circumstances. He might be free of alcohol, might be free to love again, might even find some goodness in his heart, yet he was still a ghost.

The squad car rolled to a stop. He sat patiently, handcuffed wrists at rest atop his thighs. The guards opened the door, sending a slice of early morning sunshine in across his face. Squinting, he climbed out and stood beside the car, awaiting orders.

They led him to the corridor outside the courtrooms as usual, only this time they surprised him by passing the courtroom doors and turning into a smaller hallway farther down. Moments later, he was shown into a large office, richly paneled with dark wood, a desk topped with green leather at one end of the room and a long mahogany conference table surrounded by bookcases at the other. On the far end of the table sat a television set, looking strangely out of place. Around the table were the judge, who wore chinos and a plaid shirt open at the neck instead of his usual black robe, and the prosecuting attorney, and a woman with an open stenographer's pad, and Dylan, and a woman from Riley's team of lawyers, and another man whom Riley had not seen before—a young man with an earnest, freshly scrubbed appearance who, except for Riley, was the only person in the room dressed formally. All of them rose and turned to face him, which was yet another surprise on top of all the others of the morning.

"Remove his handcuffs, Deputy," said the judge. Riley lifted his hands toward the guard, and when it was done, the judge said, "Please be seated, Mr. Keep," indicating a chair at the end of the long table, beside his lawyers.

Riley did as he was told, sitting down next to Dylan. Across from him sat the judge, a man with consistently disheveled bright red hair who seemed to always have a razor nick on his pallid chin. The judge cleared his throat as the others settled into their seats. "Mr. Keep, I believe you know everyone here except for Mr. Keller."

The young man in the suit nodded at Riley.

Riley said, "Hello."

"Mr. Keller approached the prosecuting attorney yesterday afternoon with new evidence in your case," said the judge. "The prosecuting attorney made me aware of it at my home, and I decided it was important enough to call us all together first thing this morning. I apologize for interfering with everyone's weekend plans, but given the nature of this evidence, it seemed best not to wait.

"Mr. Keller is an attorney. The new evidence comes to us in the form of a videotaped deposition he took in connection with another matter that concerns you, Mr. Keep. We have all seen the video, and rather than explain the details I think we should just let you watch it yourself."

Turning to one of the guards who had remained by the door, the judge said, "Deputy Harris, would you please turn off the lights?"

With the room dark, the judge said, "Mr. Keller, if you would," and the freshly scrubbed young man leaned forward and pressed a button on the television. There was a brief pause, then the screen filled with a close-up image of an old woman's face. It was Willa Newdale.

34

A bright light cast shadows deep into the furrows on her brow. Beside her nose and around her eyes and lips were wrinkles like the hairline fractures earthquakes cause in granite. As she stared away from the camera, Riley heard a man's voice say, "My name is Robert Keller, plaintiff's attorney in the matter of Willams versus Hanks Pharmaceutical Corporation, BHR Incorporated, Mr. Lee Wallace Hanks Jr., Mr. Riley Preston Keep, and Mrs. Hope Leigh Keep. It is 3:00 P.M. on the fifth of May. Our location is my offices at 1979 Westwood Drive in Wichita, Kansas. Umm ... Would you please state your name and address?"

Riley saw her blink in the light. She let a couple of seconds go by without responding, her hesitation reminding him of the way he felt the day he led his wife into a dugout canoe to ride beyond all roads and wires and help. No turning back from here. No help left where we are going.

She licked her lips. "I really have to say where I'm living?"

The man off-screen said, "If you're having second thoughts . . ."

"No." She blinked again into the bright light. "But you'll keep this in a safe-deposit box at your bank, like we said?"

"Absolutely. You have my word. On camera, even."

Willa Newdale smiled a little. She drew a deep breath slowly in and let it out all in a rush. "All right, then. I live at 131 Pine Street, number three, Trask, Kansas, and my name is Dr. Dale Williams."

Riley tried to process this information. Willa Newdale was Dale Williams? The one suing him? A doctor, not a social worker? As the voices on the television continued talking, he considered what it meant. The lawsuit was not coming from some stranger with a name he had never heard before, but from the old lady who had taken him and Brice into her shelter on that cold November night. So Willa Newdale knew he was the one behind the cure, and she must have known he stole the cure even when he was passing it out around her shelter. And if she knew that way back then, it meant . . . what? Riley tried to think, but the wrinkled woman with the strong jaw on the television kept on talking, distracting him.

"I was—I *am* a research chemist. My job involved finding ways to synthesize naturally occurring compounds that showed medicinal promise."

The off-camera voice said, "Could you describe your work in layman's terms?"

"Well, I specialize in creating methodologies for the replication of chemicals normally found in plants, developing laboratory protocols for synthesis in lieu of extraction to facilitate economical mass production."

Mr. Keller's voice chuckled. "You think those are layman's terms? Okay, Doctor, to put it into words even I can understand, is it accurate to say you looked for ways to make chemicals artificially that would normally be found in nature?"

"Well, it's more complicated than that, but okay. Essentially that's right. Yes."

"Great. Now, could you explain why you've filed this lawsuit?"

"Okay. It started more than seven years ago, when I was assigned to a field research effort in Brazil. I, uh, I flew into a remote camp in the upper Amazonian river basin run by a pair of missionaries."

Keller said, "What were their names?"

"Riley Keep, uh, Reverend Keep, and Hope Keep."

Riley blinked at the screen. Who *was* this woman? What was

going on here? He felt exposed, vulnerable, like he was being stalked. He thought of his soft footfalls on the snowy road to Teal Pond, when he had been so certain of his solitude only to find a fox had been watching him with golden eyes all along from the shadows of the evergreens. He had to forget his preconceptions. He had to pay attention now. He must not miss a thing. He had to focus on this woman's words.

". . . because Mr. Hanks, my boss, sat on a lot of missions boards. Back then I thought it was for religious reasons, but now I think he did it to keep his ear close to the ground on native remedies. And to have a cover story. He needed the missionary agency so he could send his own people in to find new product opportunities without tipping off competitors or local governments. A huge percentage of the medicines we produce began as native remedies, you know. So it shouldn't have surprised me that—"

The voice off-camera interrupted. "Could you stick with what happened, Doctor?"

"Oh, I'm sorry. Uh, so one of the boards Mr. Hanks sat on was getting reports from the Reverend and Mrs. Keep that their tribe— the indigenous people they were sent to work with—were being miraculously healed of alcoholism. Mr. Hanks arranged for a team to visit the tribe to find the source of their recovery."

"He believed it was caused by a plant?"

"Yes."

"How do you know he believed this?"

"He told me so, in a meeting at Hanks Pharmaceuticals' home office on . . ." She looked down and there was a rustling of papers, then she provided a date.

"You said the missionaries reported that the Indians were being miraculously healed. Did you mean that literally? Did the Keeps think it was a, uh, a miracle?"

"I guess so."

"But Mr. Hanks suspected these Indians had a plant that cured alcoholism? That must have caused some tension when you showed up with all your testing equipment and whatnot."

"It probably would have, but Mr. Hanks knew what he was doing. He only sent a small advance team at first. Three medical doctors. He told them to present themselves as part of the missions effort. And he got the missions board to tell the Keeps to help with the team's insertion into the indigenous population."

"So the Keeps introduced these doctors to the Indians as fellow missionaries?"

"That's right. The search for the cure would have been impossible otherwise. The Keeps had been there about four years, and had the Indians' complete trust. They told the Indians the doctors were Christian missionaries and . . ."

Riley put his head in his hands and covered his eyes.

"Please pause the video, Mr. Keller," said the judge, leaning forward.

Riley did not trust himself to speak. He sat in the darkened room, seeing horrible things, gruesome things.

The judge said, "Mr. Keep? Are you all right?"

He looked up. On the television, the old woman's face was frozen, her eyes aimed someplace back behind the camera, her forehead, cheeks and chin a complex web of creases folded in upon themselves. He looked at her and saw these things, and other things besides. Himself, telling those three doctors they could trust The People. He saw Sam, Melinda, and Rory. Those were their names. They were not "three doctors," but the sons and daughter of grieving parents, the friends of people who probably still missed them, three human beings who had trusted him with their lives. Riley saw their faces as clearly as he saw this woman's on the television screen, saw them overflowing with excitement as he left them for his sabbatical, and saw them as they had been on his return, mostly eaten by the living jungle.

The judge said, "Would you like a glass of water?"

Riley cleared his throat and forced the horrific images back into the deep place where they lived. "I'm okay."

"You're sure?"

"Ayuh."

"All right. Mr. Keller, press Play again, if you would."

"... got the team accepted pretty quickly," spoke the woman on the screen. "The doctors examined The People—that's what they called themselves—and provided some medical care. But while they were doing that, they also went about their real mission, looking for anything that might explain the Indians' sudden sobriety."

"Just to be clear, did these doctors find a plant that cured alcoholism? The plant Mr. Hanks believed was there?"

"No. It took them about a month to decide through blood tests and so forth that there was probably some substance being used, but they couldn't identify it, and The People wouldn't talk about it."

"How did Mr. Hanks react to this news?"

"Well, this is where I came in. He sent a second team, which included me, another research chemist, three medical technicians, and eight men who were supposed to help us with logistical support and translation."

"Translation? These men spoke the Indians' language?"

"As it turned out, no."

"No? Okay, we'll come back to that, but first would you tell us what the defendants, Reverend and Mrs. Keep, were doing during this time?"

"Oh, they weren't there by the time we arrived. Mr. Hanks had the missions board recall them to the States for a vacation and debriefing. I was told . . ."

She continued speaking as Riley remembered his joy at hearing they would have a chance to get away for a few weeks, their first trip back in four years, in the whole time since they had made contact with The People. He remembered wondering if it might be a mistake to leave the three newcomers there to minister to The People without their help. But he had been so deeply weary. He had suppressed the whispered warnings, convinced himself all would be well, placed his own desires above the leading of the Spirit. He had been tired, just tired. And because he wasn't strong enough to stay the course, all that blood was on his hands. So much blood . . .

". . . was worried we might have trouble without them, but the first team had established some relationships among the tribal leadership by then, so we were able to conduct our research pretty well."

"Dr. Williams, in the interest of time, let's move on to the central question. Did the team ever discover a cure for alcoholism among those Indians?"

"No, but I did."

"Please explain how that happened."

The woman on the screen looked down again. Riley could see the gray at the roots of her auburn hair. When she looked back up, her steady eyes were moist. "We ate every meal with The People in order to track the full range of their diet. We ran a full analysis on everything. We tested their water sources. We even analyzed the logs and branches they used to build fires in case the substance was ingested as an inhalant."

"Why didn't you just ask them?"

"Well, of course we tried. But only a few Indians knew any Portuguese, and their vocabulary was limited. None of us spoke their language. And the main reason, you have to remember the Keeps and the Indians all thought we were missionaries, so it was really hard to move the interviews from talking about 'miracles' to talking about plants or medicines without coming across like we were skeptical about their faith."

"You worried they would guess you weren't really missionaries if you pressed too hard for other reasons they were sober?"

"Sure. I mean, we couldn't go in there and say, 'Hi, we're Christians and praise God and all that, but what do you *really* think cured you?' So we just weren't making any headway. I started to worry that Mr. Hanks might pull us out of there. I couldn't stand the thought of it."

"Why did it matter so much to you?"

"My father died of cirrhosis of the liver and I had a younger brother who hadn't been sober for thirty years. I felt like if I could find whatever made The People sober all of a sudden, it would do so much good for so many people. I knew my brother . . . couldn't last much longer, and I thought a little deception wouldn't matter. I . . . I . . . uh, could you shut it off a minute?"

"Is something wrong?"

The old woman wiped her eyes. "Just shut it off, will you?"

The television screen went black for about two seconds, then her face returned. Robert Keller's voice off-screen said, "All right, Doctor, your last words were 'I thought a little deception wouldn't matter.'"

Riley saw the old woman's face on the screen, nodding. "Okay. I . . . I started spending time with two men who were habitual drunks. The People called them 'ghosts.' Some strip miners had shown them how to make their own alcohol from a kind of guava. Terrible stuff. Tasted like a cross between sour milk and bile, but they loved it, and like all the other Indians, they were always willing to share everything they had. So I started drinking with the 'ghosts' every day. I did my best to limit my intake and exaggerate the effects. Soon The People started calling me Falls Down Woman, or something like that. I let my personal hygiene deteriorate. I picked fights. I was a mess, and generally made a spectacle of myself every way I could.

"One day, an old Indian asked if I was happy. At least I think that's what he asked. My Portuguese was bad and so was his. But I was lying on a sandbank by a stream near their village—it was a place the others went to drink—and this old man, his name was Waytee, he came out of the jungle and asked if I was happy. I told him . . ."

Riley closed his eyes as she continued on. To hear the woman speak of Waytee, to hear that he had asked if she was happy . . . it was all he could do to keep from leaping up and running from the room. He sensed something dreadful stalking him here, those pitiless golden eyes within the shadows of this story she was weaving. He thought of swallowing the same foul brew of river water and rotting guava this old woman now described, of lying drunk for days on soil that had been sanctified by the blood of those he had thought were saints, of joining the lost missionaries' suffering as best he could this side of suicide, embarking on a life of ceaseless penance, surrendering his essence to become a drunken shell like the brutal savages who had martyred them.

If there had been any comfort in his life since then, it was only in the fact that all his suffering was just as it should be, justice rolling down upon him like a mighty river; he had seen to that at least. He had always been so certain of his failure, so sure he was the cause of everything. But if those people were not really missionaries at all—if it had been as this old woman said—then who were the savages, and who the saints? And which of these was he?

"... so Waytee asked if I wanted to stop drinking. I said sure, but it was impossible. The Indian said he could help, if I was willing to go for a walk with him.

"That night I told the others on the team. It was our first hint of success. The team leader got so excited he called Mr. Hanks with the good news on a mobile satellite phone. The next morning, Waytee came for me. I thought we'd be gone just a few hours, but we walked for three days, sleeping wherever we were when the sunlight faded. Waytee gathered fruit and berries along the path and started hunting an hour or two before the sunset every evening. He built fires at night and roasted whatever he had killed. It rained hard almost every afternoon. He taught me how to use the largest leaves to form a funnel and send the rainwater into my mouth. He taught me a lot of things about surviving.

"We reached a shallow valley where he found an unremarkable tuber, about seven inches long, reddish brown on the outside like a common yam and white on the inside, supporting a broad-leafed vine. Waytee dug a pit and built a fire in it and allowed the fire to burn for several hours. When the lower half of the pit was filled with glowing embers, he put three of the tubers in it and covered them with soil.

"That night we slept near the pit he dug. In the morning, Waytee uncovered the tubers. He handed one to me and made eating motions, so I took a bite.

"The taste surprised me. It was sweet and rich, a lot like chocolate. I never felt anything and had no clue if it really was a cure, but Waytee kept patting me and saying something like, 'You no drinking hurt,' in Portuguese. I remember using pantomime and my little bit of Portuguese to ask him if I was cured of drinking. He made me understand the urge was gone. But he warned me very sternly that the 'drinking hurt' would come back if I ever had any more alcohol at all. I remember he kept saying, 'No more. No little, no big. No! Or you be more drinking hurt.' He made that pretty clear, so I . . ."

Riley heard the rhythm of The People's voices in the woman's quote of Waytee. How he missed their simple way of speaking. So direct. So guileless. He let himself dwell among The People in his memory, hearing lyrical laughter, seeing bars of slanting sunlight slip across the lazy smoke of cooking fires aloft below the verdant canopy as this woman spoke from beyond the grave of Mr. Hanks arriving in a Cessna, and celebrations and mock bidding wars and five thousand dollars, a price it seemed the man had not set just lately, but over seven years ago. He thought of Waytee's words as the woman in the video described her efforts to conceal the cure for fear that Mr. Hanks would price it out of the reach of people like her brother, and a little girl held captive, a pair of tiny hands bound up in yellow rope. Mr. Hanks, the one he had hoped to pay back with the cure, a wolf among his flock and not a victim after all. And now that Riley knew the right-side-up truth of things, again he wondered, what did that make him?

He remembered digging the pit beside the bodies, Hope using their one and only shovel, him on hands and knees with a metal dinner plate, violently refusing help from everyone else in the search party, both of them beyond all words, beyond humanity itself, and then a glimpse of something moving at the edge of the clearing, a flitting sense of color, and dropping the plate to run toward it, hearing it just beyond that tree, just around those bushes, following for five, ten, fifteen minutes until at last he saw her, the sole survivor of her people, a little girl, bleeding wrists still wrapped up like a gift in yellow rope, Waytee's grandchild, the last living daughter of those savage murderers—or so he had thought them then—the only innocent, who would become his perfect Bree, standing in a fresh-mown field, amidst a halcyon swarm of gnats or angels.

The frowning judge had turned to look at him. Riley forced himself to listen as the off-camera lawyer spoke again. "Mr. Lee Hanks said they would kill the girl? You heard this personally?"

"Yes."

"What did you do then?"

Riley heard the woman speak of rifles at her back, and white men speared like rodents, and Waytee, giving her the cross that Riley himself had carved for Hope on the occasion of her birthday, the cross Hope gave to Waytee on the day the old man told her he saw Jesus very very much, the cross someone had thrust into his hand in the darkness at Henry's store, given to him as a payment for the cure. Riley thought of that cross somehow stolen from the old woman by a savage from another tribe in a different jungle, the cross trimmed with golden foil from a box containing chocolates that Hope had given to the murdered children of The People, that cross protecting the old woman, so she said, as every member of his little flock was slaughtered in the clearing, and Riley remembered the flavor of sobriety in the alley by the dumpster, the surprising chocolate flavor, and he thought about the cross that had traveled this full circle and returned into his hand, the cross that put him in a cell for murder, just as he had been imprisoned by his conscience all these years for that very crime, a crime of which it now seemed he was innocent, and Riley Keep began to wonder if there might be weights that you must lift and lift and lift again until they crushed you, or until you understood.

"Mr. Keep, are you all right?"

He nodded at the judge, saying, "Yes, sir," forcing himself to stare at the woman on the screen, who said, "For the first few years I moved every three months or so, changing my name and appearance every time. I lived in South America, then Mexico, then Arizona, Texas, Utah, and Nebraska. I spent all my spare time and money on synthesizing the chemicals in the plants. It was really hard under those conditions, but after almost five years, I learned how to do it. I figured out how to make the cure.

"Then I took a chance. I went to see my brother. I knew Mr. Hanks probably had someone watching, but I had to give the cure to my brother. It worked, of course. Everybody knows it works, now. But after a few weeks my brother started drinking again. He didn't have the urge anymore, but he started drinking anyway. And when he took that first drink the urge returned, just as Waytee said it would. I couldn't stop it. My brother died six months later.

"That's when I knew I had to find the last piece of the puzzle, the way to make it really last. So I tracked down the reverend, or at least I got as far as finding his wife and their adopted child. I—"

"Excuse me, but are you talking about Reverend Keep?"

"Oh, sorry. Yes, Reverend Keep."

"Why him?"

"Waytee told me he had the secret of making the cure last."

"Are you saying Reverend Keep had part of the formula and you had the other? Because if that's the case, then we need to rethink this lawsuit."

"No, I'm not saying that at all. I'll get to it. I just want to tell this next part first, okay?"

"Of course."

"Okay, so I moved to the Keeps' hometown of Dublin, Maine, and changed my name and appearance again, and I waited. See, the reverend had disappeared. Nobody could tell me where he was. I was afraid to show too much interest, because then someone might wonder why I cared. I was afraid of way too many things back then. I was always afraid, always thinking Mr. Hanks would find me. I was even afraid Mr. Hanks had killed the reverend, but Mrs. Keep seemed to think her husband was still alive, so I waited.

"The worst part of that stupid fear was having the secret to the cure and not being able to share it. I knew Mr. Hanks would come for me if I made it public, but I wanted to help as many alcoholics as I could, so I went to work at this little homeless shelter they had in Dublin. It was horrible, getting to know those guys but not being brave enough to give them the cure. I couldn't stand it after a while, and started healing some of them. I didn't give it to everyone. That would have attracted too much attention, and besides, I had already seen it was useless for people like my brother. But many of them really seemed to want to stop. I did my best to sort them out from the others and I slipped it into their meals at the shelter. That way they wouldn't know it was me, or anything else about how it happened. They just realized all of a sudden that they didn't feel the urge to drink anymore.

"So, anyway, I did that for a year or so without any problems. Then the man who ran the shelter retired, and I took over on my own, and I guess I got impatient. I started curing too many of them. Word got out and more and more homeless alcoholics came. One of them was Reverend Keep.

"Well, I was devastated. I mean, I had no idea he was an alcoholic. I sure didn't know he was living on the streets. As soon as I saw what he was, it was obvious he didn't have a clue about the cure, much less any way to make it permanent. So I gave up on that. I decided it was time to figure out a way to get the formula into the hands of the public just the way it was.

The man off-camera said, "You say 'get the formula into the hands of the public.' Does that mean sell it to a pharmaceutical company? Make a lot of money for yourself?"

"Oh, no! I just wanted everyone to have it. Everyone who needs it."

"Then why not just call a press conference? Make an announcement?"

"I should have. But I was so afraid of Mr. Hanks. It was like a disease, my fear. It clouded my thinking. I thought I had to find a way to get the word out without attracting attention to myself. But everything seemed too risky. I kept thinking of scenarios and then shooting holes in them. I just knew Mr. Hanks would figure out I was behind the cure, no matter how I made it public. Some days it seemed safer to just keep it to myself. Other days I knew I couldn't keep it secret anymore. I went back and forth like that for a couple of weeks.

"Then a man died in my shelter. He sat down on the floor and drank a bottle of rubbing alcohol and died then and there. I knew it was my fault. I killed that man! If only I had enough courage to give the cure to the world back when I first discovered it, he would have lived. I felt sick. I mean I literally threw up, okay? I remember sitting by the toilet thinking about how afraid I'd been for so long, and realizing my fears were going to kill me too, if I didn't find some way out from under them. That's when I knew I had to get the word out, right away."

The lawyer's voice asked, "How did you finally do it?"

"Well, I already had a plan, so I just went with it. The part-time pastor of one of the churches that supported the shelter was a pharmacist during the week, so that next Sunday I wrote down the formula for the cure and the instructions for its synthesis. I also wrote a brief explanation of the purpose of it, and Waytee's warning that anyone who drinks after taking it will get the alcoholic urge again. I put all that in a little envelope and gave it to that pastor's church anonymously, along with a small sample of the compound. I put it in an offering collection basket in the middle of the Sunday service. That way, I figured there was no way anyone could tie it back to me, and since the minister is a good man and understands the pharmaceutical world, I knew he'd get the cure out to the people."

The lawyer interrupted again. "Just to be clear, it was your intention to donate the formula for the cure to alcoholism to the First Congregational Church of Dublin, Maine, where the minister is Henry Reardon. Right?"

"Right."

"Okay. What happened then?"

"I'm not sure. Somehow, Riley Keep ended up with the formula and the sample. He apparently took some himself, and then gave the rest to a few of the men in my shelter."

"He healed them?"

"The formula did, yes. But there was only enough for about a dozen doses. When Reverend Keep ran out, there was a riot. I thought they were going to kill him. I tried to stop them. They attacked me too, and then they carried him away. I knew the word would spread. I had to disappear or Mr. Hanks would find me. So I did what I always do—I ran away and hid."

The lawyer off-screen said, "I think we're almost done, Dr. Williams. There's just a couple of other things."

"Okay."

"Uh, a few minutes ago you said you went to Reverend Keep's hometown to find a missing ingredient for the cure, a way to make it permanent?"

"That's right."

"You still haven't mentioned what made you think Reverend Keep knew how to do that?"

"Oh, yeah. Okay, well, when I was in the jungle with that Indian, Waytee, before we got back to the village, I asked if there was a way to make the cure last, even if I took another drink, and Waytee said there was. He mentioned Reverend Keep and he used some words I didn't understand. When he saw I didn't know what he was talking about, he left me for a minute and went into the jungle. He came back with a short branch from some kind of bush. The branch was covered with thorns. I asked if I was supposed to eat it, but he just frowned and kept pointing to it, saying 'Riley.' I remember he pricked himself with one of the thorns and held his finger up so I could see the blood. I still didn't understand, but I figured I could get it straightened out back in camp. I started to put the branch in my backpack, but Waytee took it away from me and threw it into the jungle. He seemed really frustrated. I was a little scared, I guess, so

THE CURE

I never went to look for it. I sure wish I had. I wish . . ."

Riley was not listening anymore. He was in the jungle with his knife in his hand, working on his translation of the Bible into The People's language. He had found a prickly vine and cut a section free to carry to the clearing in the village. He had found old Waytee sitting naked on a log, charring wooden spear points in a fire to harden them.

Riley spoke in their language, dangling the vine before him. "Waytee, say how this?"

At first the old man gave him the word for *vine*, but Riley cleared up the confusion and Waytee told him what he needed to know, about the thorns. Then the old Indian said, "Why sound want you?"

"Is in God's carvings."

"True? How in?"

"I say story?"

Riley remembered the old man setting his spear aside and composing himself to listen. Riley remembered speaking of a thorn in the flesh, a messenger of Satan, sent to torment. He remembered finishing with the words *"when I am weak, then I am strong,"* and Waytee taking his spear into his hands again and slowly rotating the tip in the fire's embers. Riley Keep said nothing more. He had learned to wait on Waytee, to expect some form of wisdom when the old man shut him out to think like this. It took perhaps ten minutes, and when it came, the Indian spoke it without pausing in his work.

He said, "Is same when I not ghost."

Riley had often wondered what the old man meant by that. Waytee never did explain. Now, hearing what the Indian said to Willa in the jungle all those years ago, he thought of healing a very small man, Timothy Frank, and that same man dead drunk again, passed out on the concrete. *"It ain't the drinkin' that's the problem. It's the not drinkin'. Ha."* He thought of Willa—he would always think of her as Willa—and her brother who had been healed, but drank again and died of liquor anyway. He thought of carrying Brice to Dublin, of

317

making millions, giving cars, paying mortgages. He thought of hanging in the background, waiting tables, healing strangers, setting Dylan up to care for Hope and Bree, being very, very strong although his heart was breaking. He thought of Waytee's finger, bleeding from a thorn, and missionaries murdering and savages who healed. Everything Riley thought he knew was upside down and backward and he himself was inside out. He thought about the weight that never lifted no matter what he did. Sober, drunk, broke or flush, in love or alone, it did not matter. And suddenly he realized what it was he had forgotten in a clearing choked with carnage seven years ago, the reason for his incapacitating weakness. When I am weak, then I am strong.

The man's voice off-camera said, "You're not hiding anymore. Why is that?"

For the first time, the old woman looked directly at the camera. Sitting at the conference table, surrounded by lawyers and guards and the judge, Riley felt as if it had become just him and the old woman. He felt as if she somehow knew he would be watching this. He felt as if she spoke directly to him, as if she was a prophetess, a mentor, an oracle sent for him. She said, "Reverend Keep sold the formula to Mr. Hanks. I should have known he'd do it. In a way, I guess that's my fault. They know each other from the reverend's missionary days, and the story Mr. Hanks circulated about the massacre in Brazil made the whole thing out to be the Indians' fault. Mr. Hanks told the world the Indians got drunk and attacked the team without provocation. I never came forward with the truth, so the reverend has no reason to think Mr. Hanks is anything but a good man who owns a huge drug company. Now Mr. Hanks has the cure and he's doing what he said he would—he's pricing it out of reach for those who need it most. And my brother's dead. And that poor man in the shelter is dead. And I can't hide anymore.

"I should have done the right thing seven years ago, but it seemed too hard. I was too afraid. I thought it was unfair. Why should I be the one to take the risk? But the thing about being afraid is you have to embrace it, you know? You have to just let it come, whatever makes you frightened, because it's not the thing you're worried about that will kill you so much as it is the worrying. Now I know I have to do this, just because it has fallen to me, and no one else. Seven years have gone by. Who knows how many people alcohol has killed in those seven years? A million? Two? All those deaths are on my hands because I was afraid, and Mr. Hanks is about to see to it that they keep on dying, just so he can make another billion off of those who can afford to pay. It has to stop.

"So I'm gonna file this lawsuit, and you say I have to use my real name. That means Mr. Hanks will know it's me, and he'll probably find me. If he does—if I'm killed—I want you to make sure the cure gets into the hands of *all* the people who need it, not just the rich ones. And I want the world to know what kind of man Mr. Hanks is. He murdered The People, and if I'm killed, I want everyone to know he murdered me. He'll make it look different, he'll lie about it, but no matter how it looks, he's the one who killed me." Still staring straight at the camera, the old woman said, "You'll make sure he doesn't get away with it, won't you?"

35

The decision had apparently been made before they called him to the courthouse, the prosecuting attorney and the judge showing him the video just so he would understand why they were dropping the murder charge. It also seemed the young lawyer from Kansas had engaged in a telephone conversation with Willa—Dr. Williams— just a few hours before the coroner's estimated time of death, and she was already in her Bangor hotel bed while half a dozen witnesses had seen Riley at the hospital down in Dublin, watching over Hope. The prosecution's theory had been that Riley slipped away from the hospital and went to his apartment where he had kept Willa New-dale confined for months before he killed her and hid her body in the Mercedes, which was out in the parking lot. Obviously if Dr. Wil-liams was alive and well and working with a lawyer during that time, Riley Keep was innocent of her kidnapping. And if Dr. Williams had been in a hotel bed in Bangor while the witnesses placed Riley at the hospital, he obviously had not had time to slip away and bring her back to Dublin. Since all the evidence against Riley had been circum-stantial, and this new information seemed to cast reasonable doubt upon the situation, he became a so-called free man that Saturday afternoon.

Dylan offered Riley a ride to the hospital, assuming he would want to see Hope, but Riley was not ready. He did not think he could face her from a proper distance. It was time to face the facts instead. He might be reconciled with his daughter, but his wife had offered no such possibility, and he still felt the heartbreak that had driven him to flee when she awoke from her coma and asked for Dylan. No, Riley knew how it would be. He had been through a difficult time, and she was a fine Christian woman. She would politely say she was glad he was out of jail *again*, and ask about his future plans, with Dylan there beside her. So Riley thanked Hope's good friend or whatever Dylan was to her, and he walked out of the judge's office into the midsummer sunshine, alone.

He had a lot of thinking to get done. He strolled the streets of Dublin for hours, through the sunset and deep into the night. He reached the edge of town, the road out to Teal Pond, and turned around and walked back down the hill, slapping at mosquitoes. He passed the church at least three times—the scene of the crime, where he had chugged Communion wine in his misery, desiring gallons and gallons of it above all things, and where he had later closed his eyes to pick between a thimbleful of that same wine or perhaps only grape juice.

He reached the campus on the other side of town, Bowditch, where he had hidden poorly for a year during his long fall from grace. He turned and walked back down again. He paused outside the empty homeless shelter and pressed his nose against the store-front glass, making out a plastic chair in the streetlight's overflowing glow and a dead housefly on the windowsill. He thought about returning home in the back of a pickup truck with Brice, and sermons about meekness around oil-drum fires, and *Dublin* carved on rest-stop tables, and Willa with the cross around her neck, Willa knowing what he was but coming round that kitchen serving counter anyway, coming round to save him, one old woman standing up for him against the savages in the jungles of Maine.

Perhaps she had thought she failed that night. But he saw her clear eyes staring at the camera, speaking from the grave to save him after all. How humiliating to discover that even his contrition had been foolish . . . and yet how liberating.

He had not believed Lee Hanks's story until the moment when he stepped into the clearing littered with their swollen corpses. He had invested too much of himself to believe The People—*his* people—would return to drunkenness, much less the savagery required to murder servants of the Lord. Then, faced with so much apparent proof, he had become a savage too, and in following them to drunkenness, Riley had begun the long, slow murder of the last victim in that place, the final man of God to die, himself.

There had always been escape in his addiction, of course, but he had also taken it upon himself as penance. If his work among The People had led to nothing but drunkenness and murder, then let him also die from drink; then at least the scales could hang in balance. This sense of contrition had been a comfort when he lay in gutters. Although he had been a failure in the eyes of others, it had let him think his failure was a humble choice. But if Willa's story was the truth, if The People had not killed in drunken bloodlust, then contrition had not been required and he had simply failed.

Riley thought he understood the problem now, where he had gone wrong. The only question left was what to do? What did you do when the utter failure of all doing was the problem? You did nothing, of course. Yet how did one do that?

He thought about going back to the jungle clearing to start over from the place where he went wrong, but that was impossible. There was another place, however, where he could start again, and by sometime around midnight Riley had his plan. He walked to Dylan Delaney's house, to ask that excellent man for one more service. Then at last the walking wearied him. Because the other jungle was too far to go, because he had decided on the one at hand, Riley passed into the shadows behind Henry's Drug Store.

The next morning he awoke upon the alley bricks behind the garbage dumpster, still dressed in his courthouse suit. He lay still, staring up at the deep purple sky as darkness fled before the inescapable advance of light. Purple turned to ultraviolet and violet to lavender. Riley watched it happen and thought about his own methodical illumination, the inescapable rising of madness in him, given so he could be cured. Lying in the alley, he saw the death of Reverend Keep, that brave missionary, that bold evangelist. In the growing light he saw that dying man very very well—his confidence, his strength, his wisdom, his need for resurrection. The corpses in a clearing called out for him to lie down with them in the grave.

Church bells started ringing. Riley Keep rose up.

He tried to make something out of his wrinkled suit, dusting himself off, straightening his tie and tucking in his shirttail. He thought of Hope, who had seen what he had seen and yet remained right where he left her to this day. Riley thought he finally understood how she had done that, and why. She knew how to do nothing, just as all the dead must know. She had been already dead long before they reached that clearing. Dead and born again.

He thought of a little girl among the bodies of The People, her wrists bound by a dozen twists of yellow rope, a little girl who always seemed to be alive, and yet had put out her final cigarette and refused a fortune in favor of the way to be a Person.

He thought of an old woman hiding for exactly as long as he himself had hidden, only to stare straight at him from death and say, "You have to embrace it."

He checked the inside pocket of his suit coat. Dylan's paperwork was there. He was ready. He set out toward the bells.

Along the way he passed the havoc he had caused with all his good intentions. Plywood over shattered glass, filthy, hateful words painted for good reason on the bricks, piles of garbage still there after all these weeks because the citizens of Dublin had to first rebuild a place to live, had to rebuild homes burned by the homeless, homes that had survived 250 years of hurricanes and blizzards, survived everything that time and nature could throw up against them, everything except the righteous indignation of those who had been cursed by Riley's cure.

Here and there a campaign poster had been stapled to the plywood. He saw Bill Hightower's name. The citizens of Dublin could not wait to replace Hope. Riley did not believe she could remain in her hometown, and he knew the fault for this was also his.

They glared at him as he climbed the steps and entered the sanctuary. Accepting their enmity as his due, Riley kept his head down and took a seat in the very back. He knew not everybody felt the same. Henry Reardon was a merciful man. In the courthouse hallway, after the judge had dismissed the criminal case against him, the young attorney from away had explained that the civil suit would also be dropped. It had died with Willa, because the people who by rights should own the formula—Henry Reardon and his church—had decided to let Riley keep the cure. With yet more righteous indignation, the fresh-faced young attorney had said this was a tragedy, for it meant evil men like Riley and Lee Hanks would continue to make fortunes on the backs of the poor. But hearing what Henry had done, Riley understood he had been offered something far more valuable than any formula. Now he had come to collect.

Riley rose with the others and sang an old familiar hymn. He thought of a toothless old Indian, smiling anyway as he told an old woman that Riley knew the secret, the way to make it last. He thought of thorns plucked prematurely. Well, Waytee, he thought. Here I am, come to make it last. Can you see me very very much from way up there?

They sat down, and Henry made announcements. Then they sang another hymn and passed the collection basket. When it came to Riley, he held the basket for a moment before dropping in a small white envelope. On the envelope was the name of the church, preprinted. Inside was a single piece of paper, which after midnight Dylan Delaney had written and Riley Keep had signed. He passed the basket on and felt the weight begin to lift. He did not worry about Henry's reaction, or how well he would handle the responsibility of a billion-dollar cure. He thought instead about the Bible in his jail cell. *"Blessed are the meek, for they will inherit the earth."* He had been taught what it meant, had received the theology of it from learned men in robes, but never understood the common sense of it till now, never understood that only those who deemed themselves too weak yet took no pride in weakness could hope to bear the awful weight.

Henry preached a good sermon. Riley tried to pay attention, but his mind kept wandering. He had begun to remember certain other things he had read while lying in his cell. He had begun to remember crosses to be lifted up and carried, and follow me, and follow me.

Then it was time at last. Time to make it last. They passed the silver-plated tray. He took it from his neighbor. He stared at the little plastic thimbles. Grape juice around the outside, red wine in the middle. He thought about an old woman's tithe, which he had stolen from the house of God Almighty, and the answer to his illness in her handwriting . . . *"the urge will return stronger than ever. I used to think there was a way to fix that too, but now I know there isn't."* Riley thought of all the things that he had tried to fix. He did not want to fix things anymore. He did not want the earth anymore. He merely wanted to be meek.

Taking red wine from the middle with a steady hand, Riley raised it to his lips.

36

H ope," said the nurse, "I got bad news."

She had been expecting this. Ever since they let Riley go and he had not come to see her, she had been expecting something awful, as usual.

"Your husband was just admitted," said the nurse. "I'm so sorry, but he's in critical condition with some kinda poisonin' or overdose."

"Overdose?" She stared straight at the nurse, thinking, have faith, there's a reason for this too. She would not look away. She asked, "Was he drinkin'?"

"Ya got me, sweetheart. I'm just here ta get you ta sign these forms. You're the next a kin, right?"

"Take me to him, will you?"

"He's in intensive care. They're not gonna let ya see him."

"I don't care. Please just take me down there."

"But there's nothing ya can do."

"Becky, I'm not gonna argue with you. Either get a wheelchair and help me down there, or I'll start crawlin'."

Ten minutes later the nurse parked her beside a window where she could look into Riley's room. Hope saw Riley lying on a gurney with lots of wires attached to his chest. His face was strangely blue. Dylan came from somewhere to stand by her.

"He was at church," said the good man who loved her. "I saw

him come in. I looked over at him a few times. He stood up and sang the hymns like he was sober, and paid attention during the sermon, then in the middle of Communion he just fell into the aisle."

She kept her eyes on Riley. "They didn't find a flask on him or anything?"

"I don't think so."

As a doctor and a nurse worked over him, Hope saw something fall from the gurney to the floor. She put her hands on the wheel-chair tires and tried to roll herself into the room. Dylan held her back.

"Let go of me," she said.

"Ya can't go in there while they're workin'."

"I have to!"

"It's better for him if ya don't."

She strained at the wheels, even as the good man held the handles in the back, unmovable. "Let me go!"

"Hope, do ya wanna help him or just make things worse?"

She leaned back in the wheelchair. "See that thing that fell off the bed?"

"What?"

She pointed with her right hand. "That little plastic thing right there on the floor!"

"What about it?"

"Would you please get it for me?"

"Hope—"

"Come on, Dylan! Just go in real quick and pick it up!"

He brought it to her after that, confusion on his face. It was a plastic thimble, something both of them knew well. She took it, put it to her nose, and realized what it had contained, and remembered what she'd heard about the cure, what happened if you drank again.

In the first weeks after waking from her coma, Hope had not remembered much about the months before, but the memories rose up in time—of Riley's return, his sobriety, his extravagant gifts and self-induced poverty, his apparent acceptance of Dylan in spite of

Riley's obvious ongoing feelings for her, and those last few moments before the end of her memories, when the rocks and bricks had come and he had offered up his body as her shield. Hope's near-death experience had put some things in perspective. She wasn't angry anymore about the end results of Riley's recent actions; she saw them for the sacrificial offerings they were. But she also remembered the infuriating, unending burden Riley Keep refused to set aside, and knew his sacrifices weren't enough for him.

Hope looked from the Communion cup to the man on the gurney. She sniffed the cup again, just to be sure. She frowned. Would Riley throw sobriety away so easily? Could the guilt that so intoxicated him blur his judgment this completely? She stared through the glass at Riley, and for perhaps the ten thousandth time she begged her maker for some kind of mercy for this foolish man.

They kept Riley in the intensive care unit for hours and made Hope wait outside. They tried to send her back to her room, just as they were trying to make her abandon Dublin, but she was unmovable. She would watch the man for days from the hall if necessary, and pray for him, and wait for an explanation for the wine.

It came at last when he awoke for one brief moment. She called to the nurses and they rushed back to his bedside, eager to learn about the poison in his system. They asked him what he took, what he drank, but he did not understand the questions. They asked again and again, and finally Hope heard him moan and say, "The blood of Christ."

With those words she knew for sure what he had done, and in the midst of whispered prayer she understood the reason, and although in her weaker moments she had sometimes dreamed of something easier, she had kept his clothing in her closet all these years in hopes of just this day.

Although Hope did her best to make Dylan go, he waited with her through the night, and when they rolled Riley down the hall to a regular room, Dylan pushed her right behind him. As they moved Riley from the gurney to a bed, Dylan stood watching over her. It was a double room. The other bed was empty. When they left, Hope said, "Please put me in that one," and Dylan bent down and easily lifted her, gently carrying her to the empty bed. She asked him to do one more thing; she asked him to push her bed up close to Riley's. He did that for her too.

Hope touched the good man who loved her and said, "Thank you," then she turned away from him and reached out for her sleeping husband's hand.

37

With one thimbleful of red wine, it was as if every drop of alcohol that Riley Keep had ever drunk returned to him. His stomach was a lathered, rabid dog howling for escape, his head a raging storm of whirling razor blades, his pasty skin a fetid, loathsome shroud. Every other hangover Riley Keep had ever suffered was a mother's loving touch compared to this. It was two days before he knew Hope lay beside him in the hospital, and three before he cared. But it passed; by the grace of God it passed and in its place the urge returned.

How it could be possible he did not know, but even as the torture finally began to ease he felt a masochistic lust for alcohol. Even as they lay together for the balance of the week, talking, healing, rediscovering each other, even then he warned Hope he might fall again, probably would fall again from time to time, because the temptation to put faith in discipline was strong. She accepted this, of course. When had she been unwilling to accept his weakness? It was his maddening imitation of strength she could not bear. And if he sensed a subtle sadness in Hope at the thought of his falling now and then, even so he felt a sorrow in himself at the thought of life without just one more drink. But this sadness was no weight to press him down. On the contrary, Riley Keep now took solace in his suffering, for he knew it offered holiness.

Many ripples rolled across the world from Dublin, Maine. At the judge's order, Dr. Dale Williams's video was made available to the public. Within a day it had been seen by nearly a third of the nation. The price of stock in Hanks Pharmaceuticals plunged as investors rushed to sell their shares before a federal court could issue an order reverting ownership of the cure's development and marketing rights to the First Congregational Church of Dublin, Maine. In many cases, shares were sold out of pure disgust. While the video was not enough to get Lee Hanks arrested on its own, both the United States Department of Justice and the Brazilian authorities announced new investigations into the events it described. With the story of the murders in Brazil now common knowledge and the investigation under way, Riley Keep believed he need not fear Lee Hanks. And although Riley did not know if he and Hope would be allowed to keep their fortune, they decided if they did it would be spent on Dublin Township and the homeless, every penny. No matter what was done about their millions, Riley hoped to convince Henry Reardon to go ahead and cash the checks that he had given to the church anonymously, and he had the satisfaction of knowing that the rights to his part of the deal with Hanks Pharmaceuticals had already been conveyed by Dylan's paperwork in the offering basket, much as Willa had originally desired.

International investigations, miracle cures, and massive wealth were nothing next to Riley's newfound place among the living. Bree came to the hospital every day, the pregnancy showing unmistakably now, her expanding belly awkwardly displayed by hip-hugging jeans and short tops. Riley hesitantly suggested that she try some of her mother's looser, larger blouses, and to his surprise she did. Throughout that first week as he watched Bree speaking with her mother about babies, Riley thought of many things he wished to say. In time he found the courage to offer his opinions as a father, and once, when Bree asked why she ought to do as he suggested, he replied, "Because I'm right." At that, Bree had fixed her solemn almond eyes upon him, and he had shrugged and said, "Well, I *am*," and she had laughed and squeezed his hand.

By Thursday Riley's weakness passed. They discharged him from the hospital on Friday. Hope insisted upon going too, with Bree and Riley helping her to the Pontiac. Riley drove them through the wounded town and up the driveway at Hope's house. When they entered through the mudroom and saw the rock-strewn kitchen, Riley surveyed the damage and said, "It wasn't their fault. They never fell away like I did."

Hope seemed to know he did not mean the savages who had done the damage at their feet. She seemed to know he was thinking of the damage in a different jungle, years ago and far away. She said, "No, they never fell at all."

Riley's weak eyes lost their focus for a moment, looking past the stones and broken glass upon the kitchen floor, seeing himself in another shattered world, assuming the worst about Waytee and the others. How he wished he could apologize. He said, "I miss them all so much."

"No need. They're waiting for us, and we'll be there soon enough."

Riley smiled.

Hope and Riley Keep slept in the same bed that night, holding hands. On Saturday, with Bree still helping, Riley began replacing windows at Hope's house—their house. He was strong enough, but more than once he had to pause until a fit of shaking passed, and no food he ate could fill the constant emptiness within. Each time the urge began to spread beyond his boundaries, Riley thought of thorns and crosses and confessed it with a whispered, "Heal me." He was empty, and it made him weightless, and he prayed with all his heart to be like that until the day he died.

Sunday came, his first full week of true sobriety complete. The Keeps arrived at church together, the alcoholic with his crippled wife and pregnant daughter, and they did not stop in back but helped each other to a pew up near the front, where a beaming Henry Reardon watched as Riley sat with Hope and Bree, who were not just inside Riley's head anymore but lived real lives out beyond him now, seeing real things and breathing true air, on his left and on his right, singing ancient hymns. Nothing pressed him down. He thought of sunrises on the Atlantic and the harbor at the center of his hometown and bridal gowns and belated christenings in that very place where he was sitting. He savored the familiar lofty space above him, the firmness of the pew beneath him, the smells and sounds and dimly recognized people and a loving wife and child who lived in total independence of his fantasies. Nothing of consequence outside of Riley Keep had changed. He was still addicted to his sins. He could still go from mourning for his friend and longing for his wife and child to lusting for good whiskey in the time it took to sing a hymn. But Riley was no longer dead; his ghostly days were over, and as Hope passed the silver tray, as he took the grape juice in a shaking hand and passed the tray to Bree, Riley praised his maker for an answered prayer, because here at last was something truly good to drink.

ATHOL DICKSON studied painting, sculpture, and architecture at university, followed by a long career as an architect and then the decision to devote himself to writing full time. He is the author of five novels, including *River Rising*, winner of the 2006 Christy Award for suspense. Dickson has also written the bestselling memoir *The Gospel According to Moses*. He and his wife, Sue, live in Southern California.

www.atholdickson.com

Looking for More Good Books to Read?

You can find out what is new and exciting with previews, descriptions, and reviews by signing up for Bethany House newsletters at

www.bethanynewsletters.com

We will send you updates for as many authors or categories as you desire so you get only the information you really want.

Sign up today!